THE

OCCULTISTS

To my dear friend Philip!
you're a constant inspiration.
Please never STOP!

POLLY SCHATTEL

JOURNALSTONE
YOUR LINK TO ARTIST TALENT

This is a work of fiction. All of the characters, names, incidents, organizations, and dialogue in this novel are either the products of the author's imagination or are used fictitiously.

The views expressed in this work are solely those of the authors and do not necessarily reflect the views of the publisher, and the publisher hereby disclaims any responsibility for them.

ISBN: 978-1-950305-44-5 (sc)
ISBN: 978-1-950305-45-2 (ebook)
Library of Congress Control Number: 2020937687

First printing edition: July 17, 2020
Published by JournalStone Publishing in the United States of America.
Cover Design and Layout: Mikio Murakami
Edited by Sean Leonard
Proofreading and Interior Layout by Scarlett R. Algee

JournalStone Publishing
3205 Sassafras Trail
Carbondale, Illinois 62901

JournalStone books may be ordered through booksellers or by contacting:
JournalStone | www.journalstone.com

To Christine. For saving me, and letting me save you.

"The lips of wisdom are closed, except to the ears of Understanding."
— The Kybalion

"Three may keep a secret, if two of them are dead."
— Benjamin Franklin

ONE FIRST THING: 1937

WHEN HE HAD RETURNED from his roaming and was hired as a cook in one of Atlanta's biggest hotels, he would sit in the lobby and try to read the newspapers without seeing signs that the world was coming apart. It never worked. In New Jersey, the Hindenburg had recently imploded into flames; for most of the previous decade, the Nazis had been gathering power, terrorizing and silencing the Jews, and were now preparing to occupy Poland; in the East, both sides of the Chinese Civil War had paused in their fighting to join forces in a nervous united front against a looming Japanese invasion. Lines everywhere were being drawn, allies and uneasy confederates assembling on one front or another, and it was clear to him that another Great War was on its way.

His hair receding now, his body still mostly shoulders, knees, and elbows, he would take off his glasses and rub at his eyes. It would never end, he knew. Never.

Sometimes the Chef, as he was called in the kitchens, would sneak a piece of key lime pie or coconut cake to the young lady who had recently started working nights at the front desk. Employees at the hotel were forbidden to eat from the kitchens; the new owners had been cracking down on "worker pilfering," as they called it. But the new girl was wide-eyed and underfed, so he would bring the treat out hidden behind his back under a folded cloth napkin, tented just so as to not spoil the meringue. With a magician's flourish he would uncover it, and the girl would clap a hand over her mouth and laugh at his wickedness. He would hide the treat with a fork under the front desk and put a finger to his lips and say, "Sssshhhhhhhh..."

In another violation of hotel policy, he had taken to spending much of his off time on the roof of the building, mainly since the magpies were bringing him trinkets again and hadn't yet stopped. The shiny baubles—a marble, a polished creekstone, a woman's gaudy earring—had begun to pile up, but he couldn't bring himself to throw them away. He didn't want to seem ungrateful to the generosity of the birds, even if they would never find out. And besides, how could he be sure they wouldn't?

Later he would retire to his room in the upper floors of the hotel, to wash up and lie in the bed and try to ignore the auguries in the cracks in the ceiling. Maybe some song would be playing faintly through the walls—Fats Waller, or Teddy Wilson—and reluctantly his mind would return to the fires. As the hours ticked on and the hotel went to sleep, his thoughts would shuffle along hallways of loss, down corridors of grief, to his unpaid debt. Sometimes the debt felt like a guillotine above him waiting to fall; sometimes it felt less sinister, like the arrival of one of those clammy-fisted kitchen equipment salesmen who came slumping through the lobby's front doors, briefcase in hand, silhouetted with the sun at their backs. Always in silhouette. Always with the sun at their backs. You couldn't see their faces, even when they'd come to sell something rather than take it from you.

Lately he'd begun thinking of writing it all down. He thought it might help shut the door on all those shadowy hallways and lonely corridors. And also he wanted others to know what had happened, to bear witness. Which presented the problem: there were those who wanted to keep things quiet. This wouldn't stop him from doing it, of course. Their need for obscurity and his need for peace was just the way it was.

It would always be this way. Always.

BOOK ONE

DEAD LETTER OFFICE

ONE: THE PURLOINED BOOK

MAX GRAHAME FIRST LEARNED about the unsettling library on the second floor of the post office in the unseasonably wet midsummer of 1904. He was fifteen years old, and had started working there less than a week before, but hadn't been able to do much because it had rained for four days straight and his deliveries had all been put off. During the time indoors—sweeping, sorting, listening to the showers pelting and popping on the old house's tin roof—he'd settled into an easy rhythm with the Postmaster and his wife. This was unexpected, because he'd been dead positive the job would be miserable. It was his first reluctant wading into the Great American Workforce and all the wretchedness that came with it. But instead he found the soggy-slick Georgia sweat of it oddly agreeable, and the warmth of the Postmaster and his wife, a pair of older Scots who shared the same high giggle and an annoying satisfaction with small things, made the bad parts a little better. Because of this, and because he was distracted with trouble at home, the weird books, and the weird second floor room that contained them, came upon him with the startled thrill of a first forbidden kiss.

The day was busy because the sun had finally come out. Customers stamped in with muddy feet, packages and letters were traded, sorted, and sacked. For most of the morning, Max swept and mopped, and later, with a *Back in Ten Minutes* sign on the front door, he and the Postmaster took lunch at the counter. They perched on stools opposite each other as the old man studied from some kind of book—*Apollo and His Sons and Daughters*, the spine said—and took huge, distracted bites from his two sandwiches, eating from one and then the other. Occasionally he slid the book away to mark in a ledger.

The Postmaster was unlike anyone the boy had ever met in steep little Selleford. His crooked old man's nose hung like a promontory from the face of a cliff; his features were mostly hidden under a salt and pepper beard which meandered up almost to his eyes, two fierce dark pebbles stamped into heavy brows, and all of it topped by a dashing flip of silver hair that whooshed straight back. He looked more like an epic hero from an adventure tale—a Civil War general, maybe, or a mad hot air balloonist—than a career-minded civil servant. But that was part of the unexpected appeal: Max was learning that these people, and this place, held surprises.

The old man stood suddenly and slid around the counter and headed across the room, leaving the boy free to take a sideways peek at the ledger. In his bare-twig scrawl the Postmaster had written, "*assembly? retaliation? censure?*" Below that was a series of six or seven Latin phrases the boy had never seen before—he recognized the contours of the language from his *Global Cyclopedia* at home—and the words, "*visions and visitations. mere intention* can and does *kill—*

claude bernard, paul bart, louis pasteur..." Then the old man was coming back and Max glanced away, dry-swallowing the rest of his own sandwich.

Addie Sylvester, the Postmaster's wife, stepped in from the kitchen. "Time for you to head home, young man," she said. She was a stout, short-haired woman, thick about the waist and loose in the bosom, who with her lilting Scottish brogue sounded more like a bonnie lass from the windy highlands than a small town postal clerk in the faraway hills of the southern United States, all of which Max found deeply charming. "You'll be workin' plenty when you get older, trust me."

"But first," the Postmaster said, "with all this weather, we haven't had a chance to move those up into dead letter. Could you do that for us?" He nodded toward a stack of unmarked boxes over by the window.

The Selleford, Georgia post office was an old house that had been converted from a private home to a place of business. To create the large bottom chamber, the walls had been removed and the load-bearing columns left standing, and now there were shelves and countertops sprouting with papers, maps, train schedules, advertisements, civic notices, ripped-out Farmer's Almanac pages tacked to the walls, most-wanted posters with pictures of dead-eyed men staring back, and in the far corner of the room, a lonely staircase slumping up into shadow. The first day he'd started working there, Max had asked Peter Sylvester what was upstairs. "Oh, we use it for a thing or two—storage, meetings, dead letter," the old man told him. "I'll show you sometime." That had been the last of it.

Now Max went over and hefted one of the boxes. It wasn't big but it was heavy, one of the flaps hanging open to show a stack of pamphlets as stark and miserably solemn as church hymnals. There were six boxes in all, and as he started up the stairs, the Postmaster said, "Upstairs bathroom, in with the papers. You'll find it."

Max came up to the second floor. A dim corridor, bare walls, half-drawn windows leaking rhomboids of hot sun inside. Down the hall was an indoor lavatory, still rare in a mountain town, beyond the open door of which were stacks and piles of letters, old faded tracts, water-damaged pamphlets and periodicals pillared up almost to the ceiling. A toilet crouched in the corner, closed and weighed down by a load of tattered booklets on top. Yellowed newspapers gone brittle and dry in the clawfoot tub.

So this was the fabled dead letter office: an unused bathroom. One of the tracts was called *"The Seer and Celestial Reformer,"* written in whimsical lettering above a stylized drawing of a pyramid in the desert. It reminded Max a little of his worn-out copy of *One Thousand and One Nights,* with its sketches of tawny palaces and camels cresting long, sandy hills. He was a sucker for anything Moorish or Arabic, for anything suggesting deserts and minarets and scimitar swords.

He put the box in the bathtub and was headed out to get the others when he paused: Down the hall was another lonely door, another open doorway. On a different day he might have let it go, but just now he'd sat across from the Postmaster as he wrote about things like *visions and visitations*, and other things that *can and do kill*. Peculiarities like this practically begged Max, who was always curious and prying, to learn more. So he edged down the corridor and peeked inside. A bigger room, also dim, with bars of bleached sunlight slanting across a deep red rug. A dozen or so chairs huddling in a semi-circle around a scarred communion table. In the far corner two bookcases leaned against the wall, struggling under sloping stacks of books. This snagged Max's eye. His own overstuffed library in his room at home was the best part of that big, bleak house. He had read and reread his favorite books with the moony desperation of a prisoner in solitary, and whenever he found himself at someone else's home, he made a point to explore their bookshelf; it told vastly more about a person than they knew.

He slipped inside and went straight to the books. The haphazard stacks on top seemed ready to collapse, and on his touch several did come down in a sudden bird-flap of pages. He caught one of them, and turned it over: *The Moon in Her Sleep*. He opened it randomly to find a diagram of the human eye, with hand-drawn charts and knotty glyphs he couldn't identify. The language was something different, not Latin, with curvy, spindly, crookbacked characters he'd never seen before. He flipped through more pages and toward the end found a blurry photograph of people gathered around a circular mirror placed flat on a table. *The male is not so easily developed into seership as the female,* someone had scribbled in slanted English off to the side, *but becomes exceedingly powerful when they are so. Virgins see best. Next to them are widows.*

He slipped the book back into the shelf. Most of the others were slender and faded and old, and had odd titles written in antique script—*The Book of Memory and Fear. Der Ablehnung. The Worm at the Heart: A Methodology of Arabic Summoning.* He removed this last one. There was something curious and unusual in it—in this book, in all these books. They weren't the kind you found at the public library, the listless, insufferable guides on histories and statutes and statistics and all that. These had a gravity to them—a darkly adult energy, a secret hidden life all their own. Max had heard about this sort of thing, of course; spiritualism seemed always popular, if kept somewhat hush-hush, among the jaded parlor set. But he had never wasted much time thinking about such claptrap silliness; he liked biology and botany and other areas of inquiry you could touch and hold, things as firm and real as the leaves and the bark on a tree. These books were something else—they seemed elaborate, weirdly vast, unconcerned with silly indignities like whether you believed them or not.

He glanced around the room. A dusty melancholy had settled into the place, or maybe had been there the whole time: stale air, curtained windows, empty doorway. Footstep prints tracing a path in the fabric of the rug. It was the same feeling in the rooms in his own big house—a failed cheer, a lonely promise, too much space for too few people. Nobody home.

He opened the first few pages—

—and just then there were footsteps coming down the hall. He shut the book and stuffed it in the back of his pants. He crouched to gather the others, and in a moment Addie Sylvester's thick frame filled the doorway.

"You okay, honey?" she said, peering at him through her spectacles. "Peter asked me to come up and see if you needed help."

"No, ma'am, I'm sorry. I heard these fall over."

Addie went to the window and heaved the curtains back, and the chamber brightened; some of the gloom went away, but not all of it. "They never do a good job of putting these things back, do they? Use 'em and forget about 'em, that's how men operate." She came over, and Max saw there was a wariness hovering behind her eyes; maybe it was about whether he had gotten a good look at the bookshelf. "Why don't you let me take care of these while you get the rest of the boxes? In the bathroom down the hall, if you please."

"Yes, ma'am." The book was sharp and cold against the small of his back. He had never stolen a thing in his life; this rash move was not like him at all, but he certainly wasn't going to put it back now. Desperately hoping it didn't show, he left the room.

Max hadn't wanted a job at the post office, but he had to take it, because it was the only way he could think of to get out of working for Sig.

Sig was his mother's second husband, a radium tonic salesman who jounced around town in a converted ice wagon with a crudely painted logo on the side that said, "Jonathan 'Sig' Sigfried and Associates—Tonic's the Ticket!" Max's real father had killed himself years ago—strychnine, sawdust floor, workers pounding at the door of a locked storeroom—and after Sig and Max's mother had married, the big man took them grandly into his house. The place wasn't exactly glowing with good will. It was cold and oppressive, even in May, and Max claimed the empty room at the top of the stairs mostly because it offered the quickest egress out from under the fickle weather of Sig's moods.

All through the spring and summer, Sig had ominously and persistently been circling around the notion of the boy working for him delivering the radium tonic. It was a terrible idea. For some reason the big man's temper was flaring more than ever; maybe some bills were due, maybe a business arrangement collapsed, no one could say. But the previous week, when he and Max were riding together in the ice wagon, the big man had suddenly slammed the boy several times in the head with his river rock of an elbow, once so hard in the temple that zephyrs and daystars bloomed like flowers in the air. A roaring headache had ricocheted around in Max's skull for the rest of the night.

He still didn't know why it had happened. But he did know one thing: he had to fix it. Running away wasn't the answer. He was too nervous, too shy; he would be eaten alive alone out there in the big bad world. He had to find another way to get out of the house and away from Sig.

And so, by midnight, the skeletal outlines of a plan were already in place, and by 10 a.m. the next morning he was in his only suit, a wrinkled sack coat he'd inherited from one of his mother's friends, and down the tree-raftered lane into town, fussing with his collar and practicing a speech he'd come up with that morning over breakfast.

It was a miserable day. Clerk after clerk, shopkeeper after shopkeeper turned him down, even after long and well-reasoned—at least in Max's mind—appeals. The Breakaway Plan, as he had started thinking of it, wasn't going so well. But toward the long slope of the afternoon, when the cicadas were ratcheting up their evening song and his worry was cresting like a wave, he found himself on the far side of town, at the post office. He knew nothing about mail, or parcel post, but the older Scottish couple who ran the place seemed oddly pleased when he happened upon them in their yard. Almost ready for him. The woman's smile was vague, but the Postmaster stared for a long time at the boy—unblinking, stubbornly oblivious of his surroundings, like an entomologist considering a rare insect.

"A job," the old man said, tasting the word after Max had given his spiel. The two Scots had been leaving to go somewhere, and were loading up their mudwagon in the post office's bare patch of lawn. "Come here, sonny."

Max stepped closer. "Yessir?"

"Young man like you. How old are you?"

Max met his gaze and pushed his chin out and his shoulders back. "Old enough to work, sir."

The Postmaster gave a grunt of disapproval. "You don't need a job, boy, you need to be out in the fields and rivers. Studying the similarities of trees to capillaries. Fluid dynamics, phyllotaxis spiral patterns, flowers and shells. You need to learn how the trout swim near the waterfall but not into it. Which way the ivy grows in the morning and which way it grows in the afternoon. Why the lady fern spreads in such curious little echoes of herself, down down down into infinity. That's what a kid with your talents needs to be doing, not trying to make a dollar in some windowless room somewhere."

"Yessir." Max wiped his palms on his pants. *A kid with his talents?* He wasn't sure what that meant. "And I have been. But I—" He stopped, reluctant to tell them about his stepfather, about the dark temper and the violent elbows and the threat of working side by side with him every day. The whole dreadful situation rolled out in front of him like a nightmare cyclorama. "I need to find work. I don't think I can go home until I find some today."

The Postmaster glanced up at the darkening sky. The clouds, their pregnant bottoms heavy and bulbous, were beginning to turn violet. It would rain that night, and the rest of the week, too. "What kinda world do we have where a boy your age needs work?" the old man said to no one in particular.

But Max was just getting started. "I need to find a place—any place; if I don't, I'll be—my, my stepfather—"

Just then a motorcar, one of the newer models, sped by, bleating its horn at a mud-splattered brougham that had paused in the middle of the road. The Postmaster's draft horses stamped nervously as the drivers of the car and the carriage cursed each other's mothers.

"We live in a strange time, sonny," the old man said when the commotion had died down. "An in-between time. Electric lights and gas lamps fending off the darkness. Horse-drawn carriages and petrol-powered autocars colliding in the middle of the street. Modern medicine and ancient legends studied side by side. Makes no sense at all. And here we are, lost and in between ourselves, so I may have a situation for you. The pay's not what it should be, but there's work to be done, if you're up to doing it." Max didn't answer, or even move; a tiny beautiful fluttering of hope had woken up inside of him, and he didn't want to mess it up. "We're startin' one of the state's first rural free delivery routes, and that's taken one of us out of the office for at least half a day, every day. We're in need of someone to help with local correspondence."

"A delivery boy."

"A desk boy. A janny. Light deliveries. Right now, my wife here clerks in the afternoons. She's moving to rural free delivery, and I have no one to help me in the office."

Rural free delivery. The term sounded odd—utilitarian and idyllic at the same time, like what the old man had said, straddling two different worlds. The woman, Addie, stood grinning on the far side of the wagon, her eyes bright somehow despite the coming storm. Maybe Max wouldn't be going back home to face another clap on the head after all.

"But it's not just wiping the lavvy. Sometimes the wife steps in and helps me, which is how one usually comes to understand the operation. It's a training, if you will, for the post office itself."

"I—I don't know much about all that."

"It's not what you know, young sir, it's how hard you work. I suspect even you can accomplish quite a bit when you put your mind to things." The street was a good ways off, but the Postmaster leaned down to whisper anyway: "And never tell an employer what you can't do, sonny. Always tell them what you *can*. Always time to learn later." He winked at his wife.

"Now, I believe you know how to ride a bicycle," the old man went on. "You have your own?" Max nodded. He didn't have a bike but he could get one. Sig wouldn't like it, but Max and his mother could handle it on the quiet from her own small private cache of money. "Not one of those dreadful penny farthings, mind you. Those enormous front wheels cause more problems than they solve. Lord knows we've seen many a smashed skull and a broken wrist from those things. I'm talking about a standard two-wheeled, pneumatic safety bicycle."

"Not a problem," Max assured him. There was a wad of bills Sig didn't know about, hidden in a special place in her knickers drawer. His mother had told her son where it was stashed—*in the case of my rapid decline*, she'd said.

The Postmaster straightened up. "Well, let's call it settled." He turned to his wife and laughed: it was the sound of delight, of new beginnings and cool relief. A mysterious, complicated machinery seemed to work behind their gaze, behind every word they said; to some people it might have been off-putting, but to Max it was the only truly interesting thing about them. "Thanks to the four corners of the globe—earth, air, fire, and water! Thanks to the courage of Thoth and Hermes! I am pleased, Mrs. Addie. Are you pleased?"

Addie's hair fluttered in the wind. She wasn't like the other older women Max had met, half-broken and wasted by time; there was something lively about her—spirited and odd, but still kind. "He's a good kid," she agreed. "A good good good kid."

Lora and Sig were happy Max had found a job, particularly with such a—in his mother's estimation—*respectable* line of business. "Good inside work," Sig agreed, before he speculated about the prospect of postal discounts for his radium tonic shipments. They were sitting at the dinner table in the dark dining room, all polished oak and cedar paneling; to Max it felt as claustrophobic as a cave. "We spend almost six dollars a month on freight alone, but if we could get that down to two or three, there's something in it for you, bucko." Sig was a big man with the round head and square shoulders of a wooden nutcracker, but his features were soft and limp, as if he had been left too long out in the rain. A glistening bite of rib roast quivered on his fork; he brayed a laugh in Lora's direction and chewed the fatty bite with relish.

The boy and his mother traded nervous glances. Another tantrum, another outburst averted. Max felt his heart thrumming and realized he'd been almost as worried to tell Sig about the job as he was in looking for it in the first place.

No one knew much about Peter and Addie Sylvester. They were from some place in the south of Scotland, Sig had heard somewhere or other, and for the last several years they'd run a small mercantile on the western edge of town, with their postal duties being only a side effort until it began to take up more of their time. This was common, Sig said; store owners operating as postmen could count on a good amount of customers stopping by just to get their mail. His mighty forearms were perched on the table and his fists clenched a knife and a fork like weapons; he needed only a gladiator's shield to finish the picture. "I gotta figure a way to do that with the tonic!" But that was where Sig's knowledge of the Scots ended. The old man was respected and had done a decent job as Postmaster, but no one Sig knew had spent any time with them, not even to invite them over for dinner. Around town the Sylvesters were familiar, but unusually private.

Max was about to excuse himself to go upstairs to his room and examine that weird *Arabic Summoning* book when Lora said, "But we haven't heard about what you did. How did it go?"

Max felt Sig's gaze crawling all over him. When Sig looked at you, you felt the weight of it. "Um. All right. I got to deliver, uh...lots of things."

"*Things*," Sig said. "What kinda things?"

"Just...stuff. I don't know. We haven't done much with all the rain."

"That postal's a big place. What do they got up top in there?"

Before Max could answer, Lora broke into a phlegmy, chesty cough. The mucous in her lungs splattered audibly into smaller pellets, like wet sand. This was a depressingly common affair in their house; Lora was sick, and had been so for some time. In half a decade Max had watched her dissolve from a graceful, relatively attractive woman to a ragged castaway, a bone-rack of hollow clavicles and haunted eyes. The stress of her condition had been a constant presence for so long it had become part of the hiss and hum of their daily lives. The big man put a plump fist on her back and waited for her to finish; he reached for a medicinal green bottle there on the table—he kept one within arm's length for her, almost all the time—and he poured a slug of it into her glass. "Wash it down," he ordered.

"I don't want it." Lora's voice was a croak.

"We do what's right whether we want it or not. Take it."

The tonic was Uranithor—uranium water, a commercial variety Sig had acquired the sole rights to distribute in their little mountain town. Sig had built a sprightly if somewhat limited business selling it locally, though he was having trouble matching the bulk prices available down in the bigger towns like Gainesville and Augusta. Despite his enthusiasm for the stuff, whatever had afflicted Lora showed no signs of backing down: physicians in several surrounding cities had considered and rejected various conditions and diseases—consumption, pleurisy, bad blood, biliousness, anemia, dropsy, wasting, phthisis, puerperal fever, domestic illness, milk fever, hectic fever, trench fever, ship fever, winter fever, putrid fever—all of these and more. Nobody could fix her, and as the months and years went on, she sank deeper and deeper down in a hole.

"Here," Sig said, "show her how to do it," and handed the bottle to Max. The boy had tasted it before, of course, but to appease Sig he looked at it again. *Uranithor, Tonic for Perpetual Health!* the label said. Below that were the words, *Just a tiny bottle of apparently lifeless, colorless and tasteless water is all that the eye can see or the tongue can detect! Yet in this bottle there reposes the greatest therapeutic force known to man! Radioactivity!* At the bottom was a stylized drawing of a snake wrapped around a Tesla coil with lightning bolts shooting off from either side.

"Drink it," Sig said. Max uncapped the top and sniffed. It had no scent, but he didn't want to anyway. "*Drink it*," Sig hissed, and when Max hesitated he snatched it away. "Taste the goddamn stuff, this is how you do it!" He upended the bottle and downed a gurgle or two. He passed the bottle back to Max, who put it to his lips and made himself take a tentative sip. Plain distilled liquid, with a slightly metallic tinge, like water from bad pipes. There was also a vaguely familiar sulfuric taste, which made Max wonder darkly if Sig had been putting it into their maid's cooking broth without telling them.

"Uranium! Good for you, good for the lymph, good for the blood!" Sig barked. In the absence of any hobbies or pursuits of passion, pushing the tonic had become his only real concern. "Got people all over going crazy for this stuff!" As Max and Sig watched, Lora took her glass in her bony fingers and raised it to her lips and slowly drank, grimacing as if she had swallowed a bug. When she finished, she set it down and, hands loose in her lap, sat staring expressionless at the table. She looked terrible, maybe worse than ever.

Sig broke the silence. "So, Max. Post office. What's up there?"

"What?"

"You can tell me, Max. I'm not as dumb as you think." He licked a pink bit of roast juice from the side of his thumb. "You know that. So one more time, one smart guy to another, what do they got up on the upper floor?"

Sig was right, Max did know that; the big man had made sure of it many times. For a brief time in his life it looked like Sig would be the first in his family to attend college and get a degree from the university down in Athens. But something had gone wrong, his father had gotten himself killed in some kind of accident, a grinding or a crushing or some industrial workplace mishap or other, and Sig was forced to quit and go to work for the family. He'd kept a hot grudge about it ever since. In response to this lack of education, he'd done his best to seem schooled, to lose the small town cadences of his speech, the hayseed vowels and dropped "g's" of farm talk, but when he got angry—which was often, practically every day—his natural mountain dialect edged itself back in.

"Oh, God," Lora said in a tired voice.

"Just let him answer the question, Lora. What's up top?"

Max swirled the water in his glass. "Uh. Nothing much, I guess. I don't know."

"There's gotta be somethin' up there."

Honestly, Max didn't know what was up there. Dead letter. A crowded bathroom. A lonely chamber with chairs and some very odd books. A chapel or a meeting room of some sort. Whatever it was, it was dim and spooky and he knew he didn't want to share it with anyone, not yet, least of all Sig. He felt like a dog guarding its bone; for now, the weird room upstairs at the post office was his own and no one else's, and it would stay that way.

The big man was taking another fatty bite. His temples and his jaw pulsed in and out as he chewed. "What's up there?" Max said. He lifted his eyes, forced himself to meet Sig's sour gaze. "Nothing. Nothing at all."

TWO: THE DOWAGER

IN THE BIG HOUSE.
IN THE DARK HOUSE.
IN THE BIG DARK HOUSE.

For some reason, Sig's house was always dark. Funeral parlors were cheerier. In the first few months of living there, Max would wander the place—the weird, filled-in fountain around back, the spooky cellar, the ostentatious staircase which hugged three walls on its way up to the second floor. Above the stairs an octagonal stained glass window let in a little sun: *For there is nothing covered that shall not be revealed; neither hid, that shall not be known—Luke 12:2*, the glass said, and showed a garishly colorful scene of someone on a hillside—presumably Jesus, but the face had been scored too crudely to really be sure—speaking to a crowd of people. The green of the grass, the red of the men's robes, the smear of golden sky were the only bursts of color in the whole house. When Max sat on the top stair and looked at the window, occasionally his finger would trace a scar there in the wood on the step, a gash that started small and narrow but widened out, like a pyramid. It comforted him in a weird way he couldn't explain; it was hidden in plain sight, a secret friend in a bitter place, a co-conspirator no one else knew about. Every time he went up or down those stairs, he took care to step right on the pyramid, the small, private totem from which he alone drew courage.

Just off the stairs was Max's room, where he spent much of his time with the door closed. Tonight he sat on his bed and thumbed through *The Worm at the Heart: A Methodology of Arabic Summoning*, which was written in old, outmoded English, with a spattering of graphs and symbols here and there; pyramids, domes, parabolas, algebraic geometry, elaborate Middle Eastern mosaics, snakes on a caduceus, stylized hieroglyphs of a more-than-slightly creepy baboon-headed deity named Thoth.

At the front of the book was a faded photo of a brown-skinned man with a high, bulbous turban perched on his head. According to the inscription, his name was *Abu Yūsuf Ya'qūb ibn 'Ishāq as-Sabbāh al-Kindī*. Behind him, books and folios were scattered across a rough table in a sunlit room with intricate tile work on the walls. The book—the cryptic contents, the quiet rasp of the pages, the texture and weight of it in his hands—felt somehow different, inscrutable, like a missing link between his beloved *Cyclopedia* and *The One Thousand and One Nights*. The obscurity and longing of it caused a wistful flutter in his heart, a hunger he could only satisfy by venturing further.

This was not a new thing. On the sagging bookshelf across the room were mostly adventure novels: Jules Verne, Mark Twain, Mary Shelley, *Lord Jim*, *The Grey Fairy Book*, *Bulfinch's Mythology*, *Aesop's Fables*. Recently Max had taken to reading tales set upon the seven seas—sea battles and sea monsters, scurvy and mutiny and lone sailors surviving half-alive on partially-sunken galleons, navigating groves of listing booms and mizzenmasts and thirsting to death in an endless barren of undrinkable salt water. Ghost stories were fun, too: his friend Charles Tully had recently introduced him to a writer named Poe, whom he found neat and scary, and then there was Stoker and his vampire, and Wells and his time machines and Martian invasions. But Max always had to be careful when he read: if the cover was too fantastical or too unrealistic, Sig would sometimes snatch the book from his hands and toss it across the room, bellowing, "Real life, my boy—real goddamn life!"

Tired from his new job, Max wicked the lamp down and stretched himself out for sleep. This book was something new. It had a call, a kind of intrinsic, upwardly-spiraling grandeur that Max had never encountered before. If he believed in magic, he would say it was casting a charm over him, but it was a good charm, a happy charm. As the night train of his awareness chuffed away into the misty dark, his last thoughts were of the man in the turban. Who was he? And what did he know that other people didn't?

The next morning Max was getting dressed when a knock rapped on his door. It opened suddenly, and Ethie stepped in with bed linens and folded laundry piled high in her arms. Ethie was Sig's maid who cleaned and cooked twice a week; she looked smart this morning in her dress and starched apron.

"You're just now getting up?" she scoffed. She liked to carry a constant sense of cool disapproval for Max, but it was more from a sarcastic and playful affection than anything else, like an older sister, or a younger-than-usual aunt. She was the best thing about this oppressive house. "I thought I heard something about a job."

It was early. The light from the window was still timid and brittle, and the room, Max noticed with embarrassment, smelled like sleep—a musky quality hanging in the air, cloying and sweet. "Do you know where my work shirt is?"

"*Work?*" Ethie mocked a gasp. "*Max Grahame?* I'm appalled."

Max didn't laugh. His dreams were still fresh in his mind, vague, shadowy impressions: reedy yards and pale hallways, followings and chasings and last-second evasions, the ever-present violence of something terrible about to come around the corner at any moment.

Ethie opened the bureau and started arranging the folded things inside. With her brown hair pulled back and her pleasingly sharp features, she practically radiated competency and hard work. Even at his young age, Max knew that if she had been born into other circumstances, she would have been an elegant lady, the kind of woman his mother had been before she got sick. A nurse or teacher, if that was what she wanted. Or a wife. Oddly, Max had never seen her look at men at all, not even once; she seemed to live in a world entirely separate from anyone else. She turned to him, and he grinned sheepishly, caught in his observing.

"Well, I was hoping to enjoy a little freedom," he said, "before life comes crashing down around me."

"I don't know about you, but at your age I was working full time as a parlor maid at the boarding house on Wright Street. Fourteen hours a day." She held a couple of socks up to the light and started matching them. "You're one of the lucky ones, you know. I never got a proper childhood. Talked to my mother about it one time. She told me, *Life's funny, Ethie—easy to learn, but tough to know.*" Ethie was full of sayings like this, half-cryptic proclamations that Max would find himself puzzling over for days or even months afterward, and he wasn't sure what she meant by this one, either. They were quiet for a moment. The room went suddenly dim as the sun slipped behind a cloud.

"It's gonna rain again," Ethie said. She pulled one of the shirts from the pile and threw it at him. "Take this one. I'll fix a sandwich to go with you."

Max rode his new bike to work, and as he got closer to town the landscape gradually rearranged itself, like those mosaics from the *Arabic* book that almost imperceptibly replaced one pattern with another; the private homes set back from the road and hidden behind stately oaks slowly disappearing, the hedges thinning out and making room for sidewalks, yards flattening into lots, buildings trading wood for brick, the road swelling into a dirt street that ran two lanes and occasionally even three.

Selleford, Georgia, was settled into the foothills of the Appalachian Mountains like a toy lost in rumpled bedclothes. The town was small but did its best to appear dignified: four tight blocks of proud mortar, brick and oak, with a single brave building reaching as high as three stories. As Max rode there were more carriages and more people now: children playing in weedy alleys, women wearing hourglass dresses and leg-o-mutton sleeves, men in business breeches and vests and bowlers. Chimneys and sidewalks, awnings and telephone poles and windows; the stink of horse dung and sizzling meat and bitter auto exhaust. More than once Max had rolled his fingers into a tube and squinted through it, blocking out most everything but a few busy corners, pretending he was in a big city: look at it just right, and he could be in Manhattan itself.

The post office stood tall under the skeleton reach of an old dead oak, and when he coasted up to it, he could hear a strange melody seeping from the building, sounding roomy and vibrant even out in the yard. He went up and inside to find the Postmaster perched on the counter and sawing at a fiddle tucked under his chin. The music, a jaunty cross between a classical sonata and a Scottish reel, echoed off every available hardwood surface until it seemed there were four or five players in the room. The old man's face was lost in concentration as his fingers roamed up and down the neck with uncanny precision.

Near the window, several people sat listening at a table. One of them was a lady who seemed to be in her 70's, maybe older, with an extravagant fox stole wrapped over her afternoon dress. The dead fox, still sharp-faced and smart, appraised Max with shrewd black eyes. The woman's hair was matted by flamboyant fur-muffs that seemed punishingly unsuitable for the late summer heat, and an ornate, expensive-looking necklace glimmered from her age-spotted breastbone. The other person was a blandly handsome younger man, timid and deferential and sitting oddly far away, as if he'd been scolded by the woman all morning and was hoping to put an end to it by simply being out of reach.

The woman, noticing Max sheepish and hesitant near the door, said, "Why, who is this handsome new creature?"

The Postmaster broke off his playing, and the room fell silent. "C'mere, sonny," he said to Max, "I have somebody I want you to meet." Max went over to the counter and the old man threw a pleased arm around him. "This is Max," the old man said with more than a touch of pride. "We like to think of him as our secret weapon."

The woman pushed herself up and came over to get a better look. Her feet were hidden under long skirts, and she seemed to glide across the room. "You're *new*," she said, leaning a little too close. There was a low fire in her eyes, like coals, and she grinned so widely Max could see her gums.

"Yes, ma'am," he said, keeping himself from recoiling.

"What magnificent celestial concurrence brought you to us, *hmm?*"

Celestial occurrence? Max was too embarrassed to answer. Without taking her eyes off him, the woman said, "How long's he been here, Peter?"

"Um, just about a week? Am I right, Max?"

"Ten days," the boy offered weakly.

The woman's scrutiny was like a sunburn. Inside her eyes was that dusty glow, and she was tall and clearly had once been beautiful, maybe strikingly so. "Just because he's your secret weapon," she said, "doesn't mean he should be kept a *secret!*"

"Max is often out on delivery, or up in dead letter. We keep him pretty busy."

The old woman drew in a theatrical gasp of air. "*Dead letter!* All those useless monthlies! Read only by old men with too much free time and not enough sense!" She turned to the Postmaster. "Is he...?"

Another odd silence; Max waited politely, feeling ill at ease, abandoned to the elements. But Peter Sylvester must have understood, because he nodded slightly. The old woman's smile grew wider. Even more gums now. "Well, there shouldn't be any *worry* about showing you this." She went back to the table, where the young man sat gnawing a thumbnail. She dug in her purse and produced a letter.

Peter Sylvester frowned. "What is that?"

The old woman marched the letter over. She held it in front of the Postmaster like a summons. "From Mme. Z—," she said. She pushed it closer for the old man to read.

Peter Sylvester's face became hard, even under his beard; to Max it felt as if the air in the room had changed, grown colder, as though a sudden hailstorm had blown down from the mountains. The old man took the letter and went back to his stool behind the counter to study it more closely.

After a time, the woman said, "What do you think?" She shot Max another gummy smile.

"What do I think?" The Postmaster put the letter down. "I think she can choose between the struggle of life and the peace of death, that's what I think."

"What will you do?"

"I'll call a meeting." The old man leaned over and with the sleeve of his forearm he swept dust from the counter. "They've been pushing since Czolgosz and McKinley, of course. Buddhism and Hinduism and going public and all that nonsense. Nothing left to do now, but..." He didn't finish his thought, but instead seemed to be struggling with another sudden burst of anger.

That name: *Czolgosz*. Max remembered it—if it *was* a name; it sounded like *Tchowgosh*—but he couldn't quite place where he'd heard it before.

The Postmaster stood and went around the counter to stare out the side window, which looked out at the scrim of scrawny woods on the far side of the dead oak. The old woman turned to Max again, and Peter Sylvester said, "It's all right," as if he had somehow seen her look at the boy. "Let them go public. Same as ever. Last it was a letter to the *Boston Globe*. Thank the gods we intercepted that one. Next it will be something else."

McKinley. Tchowgosh. There was a sense of faraway places, distant lives, important concerns that rarely ventured to a back-hilled burg like Selleford. The old woman reached over and plucked one of the violin's strings: it sounded frightened now in the big room. The timid note faded, and the old house ticked to itself in the late-summer heat.

The old man turned suddenly from the window, and Max stood up straight, trying to look like he belonged there. "I'm sure all of this sounds very odd to you, young man. We're talking about Leon Czolgosz. People will tell you that he is an anarchist and a louse and an assassin. Human pestilence, they say. But don't you believe it—he's nothing of the sort."

"Well, he *is* an assassin," the old woman said, as if this thought was reassuring. She went over and dropped into a chair near the window; the light glossed her hair and her face from the side, making her look like an aristocrat in an old Dutch painting. "Leon Czolgosz killed President McKinley a few years ago. Pistol under a handkerchief. Got him in the gut. He lingered for a while but thankfully he died a week later."

Thankfully he died a week later. It was puzzling to Max that they thought a murder could have been a good thing. An assassination. He'd been younger when McKinley was killed, but now he remembered: it had been a few years ago, just after his mother and Sig had begun courting each other. Sig had been preoccupied as he read the newspapers, chewing his fingernails to wide nubs. It was still fresh in Max's mind because occasionally the big man would hunch over and pull his foot to his mouth to chew his toenails.

With a withered hand the old woman waved it all away. "We must have you out to the house, young man," she said buoyantly. "Don't be afraid of me, my sisters and I are just old maids. But we often host guests, and we hold the very *best* of parties. We have need of a houseboy for special occasions."

Max didn't know what that meant, but it didn't sound like very much fun. "Yes, ma'am," he said. For some odd reason this woman repulsed him; her affections felt tainted, rancid, oil gone bad. But there was another feeling, not so much an emotion but a terrible certainty, that he would never come to understand that odd *Arabic* book—those strange diagrams, that weird, bulb-headed man, or even how an assassination could be a good thing—on his own. Somehow he was in danger of overlooking an opportunity that was hidden right under his nose, of losing a chance at something that had obscure power and real knowledge and the stirring promise of far places. This woman had something to do with it; he wasn't sure how, but he knew it was true.

"And you will be *well* remunerated," the old woman was saying. She seemed amused by some private thought, and glanced at Peter Sylvester again. "Sunday evening, in fact. Will you bring Max?"

Peter Sylvester made a slight noise of disapproval. He gave the boy a distracted smile. "It's a little early in Max's engagement. We wouldn't—"

"Of course I will," Max blurted. He was suddenly warm, overbalanced; something about annoying the Postmaster made him feel queasy and lopsided, but wisely or unwisely, he ventured further: "I'd love to."

When he looked at them, both Peter Sylvester and the old woman were staring back with a strange, chilly interest. It reminded him of the day he met the old man—bright eyes, silent and filled with obscurities, turned his way. His gambit must have worked, because after a time, Peter Sylvester cleared his throat. "It's a fine time, Lillian," he said amenably. "Of course. All three of us will be there."

The old woman got up and glided over again. She kissed her ringed fingers, and laid them on Max's head, and for a moment her hand trailed down along the side of his face, as if to draw strength from him, or give him some of hers. Then she turned to her quiet young husband, who stood up. Without a word they left the building.

And that was how Max met Lillian Hearst.

THREE: THE SÉANCE

THE NEXT TWO DAYS were uneventful: work at the post office; silent, dismal meals with Sig and Lora and the ever-present bottle of Uranithor; evenings in his room trying to decipher the *Arabic Summoning* book. Every so often he would look up and glance around, as if expecting something to be different; it never was: same old bed, same old bookcase, same old tired table in the corner. Practically all of his furniture had been inherited from his grandmother after she'd died, making it seem like the room housed two people at the same time—an unruly young boy and a fussy old woman. It suited him better than he liked to admit.

By now he had made his way through about a quarter of the book. Latin terms he didn't understand littered the pages like sticks in the snow, along with perplexing references to things like *the Four Elements* and *the Divine Mercury*. There were grand and bewildering pronouncements like, *Do not assume that the world you see around you—the Earth, which is a mere speckle of dust in the Universe—is the Universe itself. There are multitudes upon multitudes of such worlds, and multitudes beyond that; and there are multitudes of multitudes of such Universes in existence within the Infinite Mind of THE ALL IN ALL.* And so on.

But when he woke on Sunday morning and saw the book in the tangled covers at the foot of his bed, he remembered with a nearly audible thump in his chest that the party with the old woman was scheduled for tonight. The rest of the morning was spent in vague, helpless worry, and that afternoon he pulled out his old sack coat and went looking for Ethie to press it for him.

The house was quiet—Sig, thankfully, had taken the horses and the ice-wagon to Atlanta to pick up another load of tonic for the next run—but as Max stood on the landing letting Ethie fuss over his collar and tug his cuffs down from his jacket sleeves, a barrage of coughing came from Lora's bedroom. Ethie excused herself and went to look in on her; when the door opened Max caught a brief glimpse of his mother—feral and wild-haired, staring back at him from her bed with black, barren eyes. Ethie backed out and closed the door.

"How is she?" Max said as Ethie came back.

She went back to tightening his tie. "Illness is hard," she said. "It's a gash in your life. 'Specially if you're on shaky ground to begin with." They went down the wide stairs together. "Give her some time. She's not the kind of woman to fight for herself, not anymore, if she ever was. But she's lucky she has the rest of us to do it for her."

Max hoped she was right. His mother had never seemed very resourceful, even when she was feeling fine; she'd always had the air of a little seabird caught in a fishing net and struggling until someone could come free her.

A full-length mirror stood against the wall leading into the foyer, and he paused to glance at himself. He looked somehow older now, thinner, more solemn. It seemed like a decade had passed since his mother had married Sig, and the years had left him with a queasy, unsettled emptiness—a cavity or cave that got bigger the deeper in he went.

Outside, the twilight was almost blue, the summer air fragrant and balmy as calashes and ice wagons wheeled up and went by, humbled somehow by the shadows. The night, Max thought as he waited at the bottom of the driveway, makes cowards of us all.

When Peter Sylvester's mail carriage rattled up, Max climbed onto the jump seat between the Postmaster and Addie, and they set out for Lillian Hearst's. She lived in the woods, up in the low hills that ranged along the north side of the county. Before long, they were beyond the edges of the neighborhoods and into the early dusk, bouncing up a small dirt road into the trees.

"Where in Scotland are you from?" Max said. With the ride ahead, he had decided it was as good a time as any to risk a couple of questions. The woman, Addie, chuffed out a little laugh. She was wearing a fancy maroon dress, low cut across her bountiful chest, with a matching scarf and jacket thrown around her shoulders. "I mean, you don't sound like you're from here," Max clarified. "It's the first thing everyone notices."

"All right," Addie said in mock surrender. She glanced at the old man, whose angular profile seemed not to listen, but only stared stoically out into the night woods. "Glasgow, we're from Glasgow. But we've lived places. Barcelona. Westminster. Staten Island. Now here."

Max had never met anyone who had been to all those exotic places, let alone anyone who'd lived there and then left them for this tiny backwoods dunghill. He couldn't imagine somebody choosing Selleford for any reason other than they had been shackled to the place by birth or family. "Why come here? Nobody comes here."

"Everybody lives somewhere, right?"

"Most people live here because they have to." Max held on as the carriage's hard wheels bounced through a rut. "Nobody who leaves here ever comes back."

"If that's true, that is a real shame. This lovely place. All these lovely hills. Selleford is as sacred as any place on earth. Reminds me of where I grew up. I wouldn't wanta live anywhere else." In the moonlight, the road was a straight, sloped hallway, the pines drifting past rhythmically, as if they were some kind of scrolling panorama in a theater. "Everywhere's somewhere, right? Sacred lands, sacred rocks, sacred trees. Sacred dirt." Even in the moonlight Addie's face was tanned, with generous laugh lines still pale, as if she smiled so much the sun never saw that part of her face. "We're all the same under God's divine moon, yes? Trinities of spirit, soul and body transmigrating through worlds of material creation, yes?"

Max didn't answer; he didn't quite know what she meant. A vivid moon flickered through the branches, and there was a chill in the woods, a hush that seemed to rise from it like mist.

"Now, Max, let me tell you about tonight," Peter Sylvester said. "This may be the first time you will be exposed to something like this, and we should prepare you. Lillian Hearst is one of three sisters, a family, who maintain an interest in...shall we say, esoteric activities."

Addie said, "They hold séances for friends and family. Among other things."

"It's a private obsession," the old man explained. "And tonight, the sisters are hosting a family from the downcountry. These people have been experiencing...oh, odd phenomena, and hope to have it explained to them."

Odd phenomena. A pulse of dread and curiosity shuddered through the boy. "Like what?"

"The family has two young daughters," the old man said. "First they started hearing noises—knockings and such. They thought it was fun, and claimed to communicate with the spirit, who they said identified himself as Mister Splitfoot."

Addie Sylvester drew in a sharp breath and clutched the collar of her jacket. "Mister Splitfoot is the wrong spirit with which to communicate," she said.

"Why is that?"

Her words seemed hard to find. "Mister Splitfoot is...shall we say, somewhat, ah—"

The Postmaster broke in: "It's not Mister Splitfoot they're communicating with, I can assure you that. Rather, a being *claiming* to be Mister Splitfoot. A rather different prospect."

A being? Max sat up straight. In the darkness the trees melded with the shadows, and the hills dipped and rose, steeper now.

"The girls—Jocelyn and Marie, I think they're called," Addie said, more solidly this time, "claimed the spirit was talking to them. It was a lark. But when they dismissed him, Mister Splitfoot, or whoever it was, didn't *want* to go away. In their bedrooms late at night they would wake to find themselves rising, drifting in the air up to the ceiling. In their schoolrooms they were apparently surrounded by something knocking on their desks. Reports began circulating that the spirit had taken over their limbs, hoping to skewer a fountain pen right into their own eyes."

A dizzying image came to Max—a wailing girl, a pencil in her tight fist, sobbing as she fought to keep from stabbing herself in the face. He glanced out into the woods. The trees, the night forest, had always been a place of comfort for him, a source of pleasant mystery and curious wonder. But tonight they seemed strange; baleful and sinister and malevolent. He wondered if he were just now seeing their true face.

Peter Sylvester's gaze was only a glint. "Apparently, what was once a fanciful way to pass the time became frightening, and the girls are now in near-constant hysterics. So Lillian Hearst and her sisters have requested a noted occultist, a fellow named Daniel Pepper, to come and meet the family and get to the bottom of it all."

In the distance, dim lights blinked reassuringly through the woods, and gradually a grand house, crouching among the trees and spotted here and there by torches, revealed itself. The old man snapped the horse's reins.

It was a ragged, damp-decayed Victorian-style mansion, with heavy fir branches drooped over mossy roofs and gables. In the front, two sets of stairs curved up to a grand porch, over which a central circular turret stood watch. A light burned in the turret's single window, but Max could barely see it through the messy weave of trees: the canopy hung so heavy and thick the house might not have seen sunlight in years. The mud wagon rolled in among the stylish and gleaming broughams and cabriolets crowded into the space at the front, looking as dull among the others as Max felt. Several waiting coachmen nodded at them, their horses turning listlessly to watch as the newcomers climbed down and the old man tied his own gelding to the post.

Inside, the house was all dark, polished oak and smoky gas lamps. High, tin-stamped ceilings, a balustered staircase tilting up. Heavy curtains pulled back from oriel windows, which looked out into the claustrophobic darkness of the trees. Doorways and corridors beckoned to other rooms, and people milled about—women in gowns and furs and gaudy pearl necklaces, men in tuxes, their mustaches immaculately waxed. Hands clutching tumblers of bourbon, glasses of wine, smoldering cigars.

Max and the Sylvesters stood on the threshold, taking in the scene. The Postmaster leaned down to whisper in Max's ear, "They're counting on your help, sonny boy, so why don't you find one of the attendants to take you into the kitchen?"

Max nodded. His nerves singing like angry bees, he made off for a far door. He wound between elegantly dressed adults, looking for the kitchen, but before he could get very far he saw a teenage girl coming toward him. She looked a year or two older than he was, with wavy, sandy hair cut shorter than most girls at that time, and she grinned at him with broad, rosy cheeks and wily brown eyes that shone not with kindness, but with a sly sort of self-importance; as if all these people were her supporting characters and hadn't found it out just yet.

"Max?" she said. This made him a little less nervous, but he still had to force a smile. "You're late." She took him by the hand and led him through the crowd.

And that was how he met Harriet Blackwood.

The kitchen was unexpectedly open and well-lit, and felt worlds apart from the crowded, smoky room from which they'd come. A middle-aged woman, her hair cinched back tight against her head and her cheeks gone fleshy and loose, was leaning against the sink. As they approached she dabbed sweat from the corners of her eyes with a weary middle finger. "Max, is it?" she said. He detected a slight accent.

"Max Grahame, yes, ma'am."

"Miss Yva. You are helping me tonight."

In the far corner of the room, two young girls huddled with an older woman. All three were wearing what looked like their Sunday best, but were weirdly haggard—strangely vigilant, all matted hair and marble skin and dark, tormented eyes. The youngest one clutched a shabby stuffed giraffe. Max realized they must be the girls from the downcountry, who travelled here with their mother to seek help from that Splitfoot spirit-thing. An escort, a thin, fist-faced young man with close-cropped black hair, stood silently nearby, looking like he was an older brother or a farmhand friend of the family. Max wondered why they waited here, rather than at the party or some soft, snug back parlor; maybe they were too terrified to be alone.

"Gonna get hot in that getup," Miss Yva said, frowning at him.

Max took off his jacket and laid it across the back of a chair, and he was handed a silver tray, which had pre-poured brandies and individual *hors d'oeuvres* placed on it—what looked to be creamed mushrooms on toast. He took the tray and, being a novice steward, immediately bobbled it for a terrifying moment. Harriet stifled a giggle. After a brief explanation of how to pass food and drink at a party—to his unpracticed ears, he imagined Miss Yva's intonation sounding vaguely Russian, or Eastern European—he was shooed outside. With a quick, helpless glance at the still-amused Harriet, he went back into the main room.

The gathering had gotten more crowded. Max wove through the people, hearing fragments of conversation:

"—and every morning before leaving the house, I always consult with God on whether to take an umbrella or not—"

"—Swedenborg, Mesmer, I don't care, neither of them gets to the essence of what we're talking about—"

Jeweled hands reached at him and took the edibles and brandies; dark-lipped women smiled and winked; men nodded sternly, placing empty snifters as he braided by. A lively anticipation hung in the air as the mass of guests laughed and smoked and munched appetizers, but below it there was a skittish, vibrating restlessness—the town's intellectuals and sophisticates coming privately together to learn more about the wonders and terrors of the spirit world. Max hadn't realized there were so many spiritualist seekers in dull little Selleford. His service went on for some time, and he went back to the kitchen twice more for fresh supplies. When no one was looking he downed a few bites of the appetizers, but they sat uneasy in his stomach, as if the butter had turned. Across the parlor he saw Harriet, playful and fetching, serving people in the same manner, though with a good deal more warmth and affection delivered her way.

Then someone chimed a spoon a few times against a wine glass, and the buzz of the crowd fell quickly as Lillian Hearst stepped up on the wide hearth to catch everyone's attention. With a jolt of surprise Max realized it wasn't Lillian Hearst at all, but a woman who resembled her almost exactly.

"Welcome, my good people, welcome!" the woman said. Weirdly, Lillian herself stepped up beside her, and so did, on the opposite side, another extremely similar woman. Identical triplets: they were grand and patrician, but somehow too gaudy and garish even for this overdressed crowd; Max could hardly see their bony forearms for all the bangles. There seemed to be more jewelry between the three of them than the rest of the ladies in the room combined.

"Thank you for coming, dear, dear friends!" the woman in the middle announced. "It is so good to see you again. I am Louise Hearst, and these are my sisters Lillian and Loretta. We are here to assist a family from down east. They have been visited and—"

"—need our support," the woman on the far side interrupted. "Several weeks ago, they appealed to us, knowing that maybe we had the means—"

"—to help them where few others can," the third sister finished. "They have been terrified for over a year now, and are quite—"

"—desperate to get to the bottom of it all. Now, are we ready?"

A commotion bubbled in the rear of the room. Max turned to see the nervous woman and the two harrowed girls from the kitchen being led through the crowd. As they passed, a slight susurrus rose up, as if multiple hidden people were suddenly furiously whispering, and from somewhere he felt the cool wisp of an open window. The three made their way through the people and onto the hearth to stand meekly with the three Hearst sisters.

"These are the Burke family," Loretta said, "Marie, young Jocelyn, and their mother, Helen. Their father Jesse passed away in a farming accident, Lord bless his soul, almost a year and a half ago, and—"

"—soon after, the girls began experiencing visitations from unseen presences." This was, Max thought, Louise; they were hard to keep straight. "Now, we have all had moments when we understand that there is something—"

"—or someone, about." Lillian again. "But these beleaguered ladies are exhausted now, and terrified. They reached to us for help, and we agreed to see if something can be done."

Loretta squinted at the gathered crowd. Nests of tobacco smoke curled up near the ceiling. "Is Daniel here? Mr. Daniel Pepper?"

No answer. People glanced around, to see if he might be among the guests, but no one came forth.

Then—from the side of the room, a woman's gasp drew everyone's attention. She pointed upstairs, and the crowd turned in unison to see a tuxedoed man wearing a turban in the manner of an Indian swami, descending the stairs. But he wasn't walking down—he was sitting cross-legged, also like an Indian swami, *levitating* slowly down to the lower floor. His face was lost in concentration, his arms crossed corpselike across his chest.

When he reached the bottom, the crowd parted to let him through. The man floated past the window as curtains raked along his body, and Max's nerves jangled, his eyes darting to the other attendees—their faces were like his, no doubt, stunned and fearful and rapturous all at the same time. Blood pumped loud in his ears; this was no claptrap silliness, nor was it part of the Breakaway Plan. This was something different altogether. Through the phalanx of people Max caught a glimpse of Harriet, who was propped against the kitchen doorframe with a look of mild amusement on her face.

The man levitated down the dark hallway and out of everyone's sight. The crowd leaned over each other to see where he had gone. A woman near the steps fainted; someone bent quickly to attend to her. Plumes of smoke wafted furiously up from the crowd. The room grew quiet again; then, a gasp from the back, near the door. From an adjoining hallway the floating man returned, but now with a huge and preposterously ornate ladies' hat tilted just so on his head—all fake flowers and feathers and taffeta, and a scarlet ribbon tied in a bow under his chin. A patter of relieved laughter and clapping rose from the attendees, which brought the slightest, merest smile to the man's face.

When he reached the center of the room, he opened his eyes and put his feet to the floor, bowing as the guests applauded. He stepped up to the hearth, untied the ridiculous hat, and spun it into the crowd. There was a scuffle as several women fought for it.

"Good evening, gentle folk, I trust you are well," the man said in a stagey voice. His pomaded hair and fine features gave him a studious, clergyman's look. "My name is Daniel Pepper. We are here to assist the Burke family. Gentlemen?"

The crowd parted again as several men brought in a small table and four chairs and put them near the hearth. Daniel Pepper stepped back and gestured for the mother and the Burke girls to join him. Max felt something brush by him then—unsettlingly small and fast, like a child—but when he turned, no one was there. He did see Harriet, however, now eyeing him from across the room. She noticed him looking at her, too, and she started winding through the adults, making her way over.

At the table, Daniel Pepper and the family stood around it, holding hands, their eyes closed in prayer, as he droned out a kind of incantation:

"Almighty, eternal God, Father of Light,
from Whom all good things and perfect gifts come to us,
I beg You, for the sake of Your infinite mercy,

let us recognize Your eternal wisdom,
that which surrounds Your throne,
which has created and made everything,
which guides and maintains everything.
Send it to me from Heaven, Your sanctuary,
and from the throne, Your glory,
that it may enter me and work within me.
For it is the mistress of all heavenly and secret arts,
which opens up the knowledge of and insight into all things..."

"This place is packed," Harriet whispered in Max's ear when she came up to him. "There's not usually this many folks."

The prayer continued, but Max was more interested in the girl. "You know these people?"

With a jut of her chin, she indicated the Hearst sisters, who stood off in a line clasping bony, blue-veined hands to their bejeweled sternums. They looked like they were playing a child's game: *Red rover, red rover, may ghosts and ghoulies come over.* "My godparents," Harriet said. "I was born into it."

Max turned to her. "What does that mean?"

"Just what I said—I was raised to speak to spirits and haints. Don't be daft."

The people at the table were sitting now, and had fallen into silence, their eyes closed, their faces stony except for the younger girl, who seemed on the verge of tears. The crowd was quiet, their heads craned to see the seated people.

Just then, a knocking came from the side of the room—a window shaking in its sill, rattling loudly, then violently. "Is this Pap?" Daniel Pepper asked in a raised voice. "Pappy? Are we speaking with Jesse Burke?" The sill kept rattling.

Harriet leaned in to whisper. "They're worried it's Mister Splitfoot, but we think it's the girls' father."

"Who's Mister Splitfoot?"

Harriet crinkled her nose. "You don't want to mess with him." Max studied her face for more clues, but couldn't find any. "Come here," she said, and took his hand and pulled him through the crowd, back into the kitchen.

They went to a table, piled high now with dirty serving trays and food-crusted saucers and glasses. Miss Yva was nowhere to be seen. "I've been coming here for years," Harriet said, sitting and poking over the remains of someone's snack. "Since I was a baby."

"Are your parents here?"

"They travel. Sri Lanka right now, I think. Sometimes I stay here with the sisters. They're weird but they're kinda fun." Max didn't know what to say; Harriet's experience was so unfathomable, so alien from his own, that he couldn't think of a single question to ask. "What about you?" she said. Her big eyes roamed all over his face, and he felt a tart twinge of self-consciousness.

"I don't know. This is my first time at a...uh, a séance."

"I thought you came with the Sylvesters? They know spiritualism and a hell of a lot more, too."

"I—I started not that long ago. I don't know much about this whole...this stuff."

Harriet laughed, a sweet fluid thing which made Max's pulse quicken. Finally a question came to him, but it was so inane he regretted asking it immediately: "Have you been...visited?"

"Visited, ha! Well. My baby brother Virgil died in childbirth, if that's what you mean. Sometimes I talk to him." Harriet picked up a snifter half-full of brandy, smelled it, and took a sip. "But he can be kinda silly."

"I still can't believe you know these people."

"Well. My mother's a medium. She's teaching me everything she's learned. And the Sylvesters—from time to time I study with them too. And the Hearsts, of course. There's a lot more to them than they let on." Harriet's sharp, pale profile glanced around the room; a flock of contradictory, fleeting sensations—fear, curiosity, dread; a queer heartsick wonder at talking with this strange new girl—darted through Max before he was able to hide them away.

"Isn't it funny," she said, "those people in the other room—most of them have no idea. There's a hidden world going on all around us, yet they're asleep." Max glanced toward the doorway, not sure what she was getting at. The people in the other room certainly seemed like they knew what they were doing. "Not ready to know. Many of them don't want to know. Some in quite literal terms couldn't handle it."

"Couldn't handle what?"

"You ever hear of Hermes? Or Mercury?"

Max had read and re-read the *Bulfinch's Mythology* on the bottom shelf of his over-crowded bookcase. But not recently. "Um, I think so. Greek and Roman mythology, right?"

"Same guy, more or less. Kind of a big deal. Hermes—*hermetic*. I bet you don't know what that means." Max thought that he did, but he wasn't one hundred percent sure, so he only shook his head. "It means *quiet*," Harriet said. "*Closed. Hermetically sealed.* Hermes is often depicted with his finger to his lips"—and she did it—"Sssshhhhhhhh...

"This stuff comes to those who are ready," she went on. "Those who aren't—they live in ignorance. It's like being illiterate—you see the scratchings on the page, but you have no idea what they mean." She looked suddenly bored with her own point. "Say, could I ride home with you and the Sylvesters? I've been out here all week, and it would be nice to get back into town tonight."

Max started to reply, but at that moment a collective gasp rose from the other room. The two teens stood and hurried back to see the crowd in commotion. Women winced with hands over their mouths; men gaped. Max shoved his way around a block-shouldered fellow to see the people at the table—Daniel Pepper grinning stiffly, his eyes wide; the girls' mother sobbing and reaching to her daughters. The older girl recoiled from the younger one, and

Max saw the last girl—the little one, still seated, still clutching her giraffe with a dazed look on her face. Blood seeped from both of her eyes and her nostrils, but it seemed not self-induced; the girl was as startled as anyone. The blood pattered down the flat bodice of her white dress, making her look like a bizarre bridal sacrifice.

Someone tugged on Max's shirt, and he turned to see Peter Sylvester standing there. "Let's go," the old man said. "Addie isn't feeling well."

"What? We're leaving?" This was sudden. Max was just starting to enjoy himself. And then there was the matter of the people at the table, which was terrifying and fascinating at the same time. And also the matter of compensation. "I mean...I was supposed to get paid."

"Yva knows," the old man said. "I'll make sure you get it, don't worry."

Max saw Addie across the room, standing by the front door, her jacket clasped in her arms. She looked miserable. He turned and searched the room for Harriet. She'd been right there, but now she was gone. "I think that girl—Harriet—wants to come with us. Is that okay?"

"She'll be staying here tonight." The Postmaster clapped him hard on the back. "We'll be out with the horses."

The ride home was quiet, but the tense, nervous edge remained. Max sat on the far end of the bench while the Sylvesters huddled close for warmth. The cool of the night air on his face, the lope of the gelding, the low murmur of the woods around them all mingled into one long abstracted reverie; the image of the little girl bleeding from her eyes had seared itself into his retinas, but he was so tired it seemed to have happened a long time ago. Finally, Addie raised her head from her husband's shoulder and studied the dark ribbon of road ahead of them. "Did they ever find out who it was?" she said. "Their father, or Mister Splitfoot?"

The Postmaster didn't reply. Maybe he didn't know. After a moment, Addie put her head back down and closed her eyes.

When the carriage clopped up to Max's driveway, the house's windows were dark and closed. It looked cold inside, shut tight and as impervious to the seasons as ever.

Max climbed down and stretched the trip from his shoulders. "Thank you for letting me come," he said. "It was a...a very interesting evening." He gave them a half-wave and started up the drive.

"Max?" the old man called. The boy stopped and turned. Peter Sylvester put his finger to his lips and said, "Ssshhhhhhhh... What we saw tonight is not for everyone. Yes?"

"Yes. Yessir."

"And Max?" The Postmaster gave him a smile. "You did good."

Max nodded and went up to the house.

FOUR: MAX AND SIG

THE NEXT AFTERNOON SIG came home from Atlanta. He was quieter and moodier than usual—something about the bulk price of Uranithor having gone up over a third of a penny per ounce—and Max did his best to avoid him even more than usual. They passed each other only on the stairs, or in the kitchen, where the boy was spending a little free time helping Ethie with the meals.

When he wasn't at home or at the post office, Max huddled in his room and thought back over the previous weeks and tried to make sense of what he had seen and heard. *Tchowgosh* the anarchist; choosing between the struggle of life and the peace of death; Buddhists going public; President McKinley thankfully assassinated with a pistol concealed inside a handkerchief. It was enough to make him jumpy, this business with the snobby, overdressed people and the weird old house and the crazy old ladies. But then there was the book, the darkly restless yearning of it. The levitating man. The bloody child bride. The susurrations and the dashing spirits and the knocking windows. And the girl. There was the girl. Harriet.

Two days after Sig had returned, Max was in his bed studying the *Arabic Summoning* book when Ethie's quick rap came on his door. She opened it.

"Hey, pretty boy," she said. He lowered the book so she couldn't see the title; Ethie's sober practicalities would never have been able to make proper sense of that strange bulb-headed man. "Something up with the horses. Sig needs you."

Max raised up on his elbows. "Let me ask you a question. Do you know anything about McKinley?"

Ethie stepped inside and frowned. "McKinley? William McKinley? The president?"

"I think so."

"I know he was president."

"Do you know what happened to him?"

"Goodness," Ethie said. She gathered her skirts and came over and sat thoughtfully on his bed. "Got himself offed, didn't he? Some boy, some dark-haired immigrant boy waiting to meet him. Shot him twice. Only one got him, but it was enough—he took infection and died."

"Do you know anything about him? The killer, I mean?"

"What is this, another one of your silly little diversions?" She was referring to a game she and Max played in the kitchen: he loved food, for some reason he enjoyed cooking, and he usually tried to make his own simple breakfasts at home—omelets, bacon, drop biscuits, tomato sandwiches. She was teaching him several basic recipes, but he never mentioned that it was because he felt a need to gain early independence from his family; it was part of his Breakaway Plan before there even had been a plan. To his surprise he found the making of a meal was a kind of creative reverie—the combinations of handy ingredients coming together to create something new and unique. Ethie had taken to letting him help her with the dinner preparations, describing exactly what she was doing and why, and letting him finish it. It had become a fun little sport between them.

But now Ethie didn't wait for his answer; she only clucked her tongue and pushed herself up. Presidential assassinations were clearly too violent and darkly difficult for her. "What's serious is that you'd better get your head out of them clouds and get out there and help your stepfather—that's what I know." She left.

Reluctantly, Max put on his shoes, and in his pajamas bottoms and a dirty shirt he thudded down the stairs—taking care to step on the pyramid—through the kitchen and out to the driveway. The night was moonless and cloudy, and he went up the grassy slope to the barn as much by memory as by sight. Sig's stables loomed in the dark, and Max edged around the corner to see the big man there in the carrot-orange glow from a lantern he'd hung on the wall. He was kneeling next to their gelding, Jefferson, who lay in the door of the barn.

"Lookie here," Sig said. A bright pang of alarm jabbed Max as he stepped closer. A frightening gash scraped down Jefferson's long nose—still seeping blood, with a wad of raw flesh hanging off the side. He knew immediately that Sig had struck Jefferson with something, had punished the horse for some behavior he didn't like. Jefferson groaned softly and started convulsing, his quivering legs held rigid and straight like some oversized toy version of himself. "Having a seizure," Sig said blandly.

The horse needed attention, and right away. "Do you want me to go get Dr. Machen?" Max said.

"Won't help." Sig stood up with a grunt. "Nothin' he can do. Might be bleedin' in the brain."

"How can you tell?"

"One pupil'll be bigger than the other. Only thing to do is watch for it." The horse convulsed in the lamplight, his hooves thumping spastically against the wood floor. "Where did you go the other night?" Sig said in an offhanded tone.

"What?"

"Where'd you go? When I was gone."

It took a moment for Max to answer; the sense of alarm for the horse had been joined by a sudden numb distress for himself: *Sig knows about the séance*, a faraway voice shouted somewhere in his brain. "Nowhere," Max said, trying to sound cool and unconcerned. "It was with the Postmaster. For work."

"Work? What kinda work?"

"Uh. I don't know." A vision came to him of the party—all those elegant people, hungry for hidden knowledge. The Postmaster telling him

Ssshhhhhhhh... He felt another insistent need to keep quiet—to keep it all to himself. He shrugged in the glow of the lamp. "Some...I dunno, people or other."

For the first time in the days since Sig's return from Atlanta, Max felt the big man's full, corrosive regard. In the dim light from the lamp it was plain he was struggling with his temper—lips curled in resentment, eyes blinking a dispatch of barely restrained rage. "What's so goddamn important that you won't answer my question?" he said. "These people are from fuck knows where, and you start goin' off with them without even asking nobody?"

The séance at the house in the woods had been disturbing, but it was important in a way Max couldn't articulate. That was part of its creepy attraction, he supposed—he couldn't explain it until he had figured it out for himself. "It's nothing," he said, "I promise."

They watched as the horse's convulsions slowed and, at least momentarily, stopped. "Where was it?" Sig's voice was colorless, deprived of emotion. He was quelling his temper now, choking it into submission.

"I, uh...I'm not sure. Somewhere out in the woods. West, maybe?"

"So these people, these catlick people, are living in our town, taking our money, and now you're pallin' around with them and leavin' your mother alone all night." Air whistled through Sig's nostrils. "This is your gratitude for me taking you in?"

"I don't know," Max said, hoping some sense of reason would come over Sig merely from the pleading tone in his voice. He looked at Jefferson, who lay on the floor, legs stiff and splayed out, a menagerie figurine that had tipped over. "They don't tell me anything. I'm working there, that's all. I help out. I'm a helper."

Sig hitched his pants; his belly bulged out like a melon, and his trouser legs drifted three inches above the tops of his shoes. Suddenly his hand swung up and struck Max—a hard-knuckle slam to the underside of the chin. Max's head was thrown back, and he staggered to keep from falling. Then Sig was upon him, grabbing his collar and chuffing tobacco and sweet cloying sweat in his face.

"THIS! IS NOT! HOW WE DO IT!" Sig's face was crowding so close that the boy could see only a part of it—one of his eyes, a mottled temple, a cauliflower ear. "Your mother and I work hard every day to give this family some *stability*, and here you are doing your best to *undermine*, to cause *trouble*! To *disobey*!" Sig shook him in time with his words. "Keepin' secrets from me! And for what? For *what*? A bunch of goddamn catlicks?"

Sig pushed him and Max caught himself on his haunches, his mind already calculating the best routes out of here. But maybe it was best just to take it—running away right now would just put it off for something worse.

"All I know, they been having all manner o' lewdness out there." Sig glared at him and spat in disgust. "Men in petticoats and syphilis and sleepin' with boys." He kicked a hatchet buried in a stump, and it came loose and skittered toward Max; the chipped blade pointed his way like a threat. "Jefferson's gonna need somebody," Sig snarled. "*Watch him.* He stands up and falls again he's gonna hurt hisself worse. You stay here with him and keep him down."

As if on cue, the horse did try to stand, his front legs flaring out, awkwardly seeking purchase in the loose hay. "Get *down*," the big man snapped, and stamped the horse hard with his foot. Jefferson fell back, blinking up at Max, his brown marble eyes helpless. His sweaty flank rose and fell in the dull lamplight.

Sig turned his moist face to Max, red even in the low glow. "You stay here. All night if you got to. Muck the stalls. I gotta big day tomorrow and the wagon'll be out and I need you to watch him for me and muck the stalls."

"Tomorrow? Jefferson's not fit to do anythi—"

"*Muck!*" Sig kicked the hatchet again for good measure. "Water buckets cleaned and filled. Then stalls—lime and re-bed. And the tack room. And keep an eye on Jefferson. His seizure gets worse, come wake me up."

"Why can't we get the vet and get him some proper care?"

Sig ignored him. "You're tired tomorrow, you tell your postal assholes you been busy off at orgies in the woods." He hitched his pants again, rubbed his neck with a beefy hand, and, elbows swinging, stalked back down to the house. "And this job you got?" His voice floated up at Max in the thick night air. "You might wanna start thinkin' about gettin' another one, bucko."

Max stayed with Jefferson for hours, soothing him, trying to keep him down. But sometime in the cool early darkness the horse staggered up and Max didn't have the heart to fight him anymore. Jefferson swayed drunkenly, thumping into the walls, staggering from side to side as he made his way into the barn. He wheeled in his tight stall, and stepped head-first into the cross-tie with a painful thump. Max wondered what Sig had hit him with—maybe a pitchfork, or the poll of the hatchet, God forbid. In the darkness he examined the horse's pupils, not sure what to look for, but everything certainly seemed normal. He found a rag and wet it in the trough, and cleaned the wound as Jefferson stood squinting in his stall, his eyelashes feminine and impossibly long. A vicious welt had formed down along on the left side of his head and between his eye and his left ear.

Deep into the early hours of the morning, there was nothing more to do, and Max decided finally he was finished for the night. If Sig had a problem with that...well, they would have problems. Back in the house he climbed into his bed—it must have been sometime between three and four in the morning—and like a cliff diver leaping off into the sea, he plunged immediately into sleep.

When he woke, the room was bright and hot. It was late. He jumped up and rushed out to the barn and saw that it was empty. Sig had already taken both horses out for the day. Max hoped Jefferson was fit for it. He dressed in a hurry and, his heart pounding with panic and feeling as if the oxygen were draining from his body, left the house and raced on his bike up to the post office.

The Postmaster and his wife were talking in the main room. The old man was sitting on the stool behind the counter, while Addie Sylvester leaned across from him, cradling, of all things, a small bird. A pheasant. Or maybe it was a quail or a partridge. She had one arm around the bird's body and the other hand soothingly caressing its breast.

Max went breathless up to them, unmindful of interrupting. "Sorry I'm late. Our horse was injured and—"

"Yes," the old man said to Max, "it's—"

"And I'm not sure if the horse was okay to—to... But I'm—I was—I was up all night with him—with—"

"Sssshhhhhhhh," the old man said. "It's all right. We know what happened."

Max stopped. As if his brain itself had snapped closed. "What?"

"We know who your stepfather is. It's okay." Max didn't understand; he felt kicked in the gut. They knew Sig? How did they know who his stepfather was? "This is a small town, Max, everyone knows everyone. But if you'll excuse us, Addie and I have something slightly more pressing."

Max stepped away, and as Peter and Addie Sylvester went back to their conversation, he retreated uncertainly across the room to the table near the window. He sat fidgeting, wanting to look interested in the yard outside and trying to listen without seeming to; the words *convocation*, *adepts*, and *sacraments* came skittering in whispers across the room. Addie nodded, licking her lips and calming the bird, seeming slightly anxious herself.

After a time, it became clear the two were planning some sort of meeting soon. Maybe even tonight. It would, Max knew with a sudden lurch in his bones, take place in the room upstairs. The room with all the books.

The room upstairs with all the books. By now that spooky chamber had taken on an almost mythical feel. There was something inexplicable about it—private and perilous and deeply seductive. It pulled at him like a vicious undertow, and he wondered why they were being so secretive about this meeting or whatever it was. He worked here, did he not? He was their so-called secret weapon, was he not, the only employee other than the Sylvesters themselves? He was practically goddamn *required* to be here.

Conflicted, but not enough to stop himself, he broke in: "Let me help. I can do it."

The two older people stopped and turned. They stood blinking at him, caught off-guard but somehow not entirely surprised either. In the silence, Max swabbed his clammy face with the crook of his elbow. "You told me I could work here, so it's my place to do it."

It was then that he realized the original strategy he'd come up with—the Breakaway Plan, to get out, to get away from Sig's reach—had mutated somehow, had become something altogether more odd: to apprentice with the Sylvesters as Harriet had apprenticed with the three weird sisters. To study from them and become like them. To learn their secrets.

Addie turned to her husband. She seemed to be taking a stand in some unspoken debate. The old man frowned.

"Addie and I are hosting a small group of local people," he said, "as well as several guests coming in from out of town. We need to decide what to do about that letter."

"It's quite sudden," Addie explained. "An attendant will be helping us— secure the animals, fetch wine, fetch water. We've asked Harriet to do it."

"Animals." Max took a calming breath. "I know horses. I know animals. Let me do it."

"This meeting, Max, it will go quite late. It's quite involved."

By now Max had collected the pieces of himself and put them back together. "I can work late. I want—*I will.* Of course I will." His gaze skipped from face to face, trying to appear as if he were capable of great talent and discipline. The two older people glanced at each other, and something wordless passed between them, some assent or cautious warning.

The Postmaster nodded toward the door. "Why don't you go find your stepfather and ask him if it's all right for you to stay. We would hate for him to be unhappy with us."

Without a word, Max rushed out to his bike.

The town flashed by as he pedaled hard. The sun was higher in the sky by the time he skimmed up to Sig's storehouse, a low building edged on both sides by symmetrical platoons of dead pecan trees, and he dashed up the leaning wooden stairs at the end of a concrete loading dock two at a time. Inside, Sig's only employee, a man named Alfred Byles, sat sullenly at the desk, his bald forehead polished and gleaming in the glare from the loading bay. Cigar smoke coiled above him in the air.

Max was breathless: "Is Sig here?" He felt Alfred considering him, felt the man's sluggish animosity radiating out—toward himself, toward Sig, toward the job, toward the world. It was dulled from overuse. Alfred shook his head.

"Do you know where he is?"

"Left to go on a run, didn't he?"

"Is he coming back?"

Alfred shrugged. Somewhere outside, a dog barked frantically.

"Did he say where he was going?"

Alfred took his cigar from his mouth. The end of it was sloppy and wet, and he shook the spit from it in an arcing plash of saliva. "Up the hill, maybe. Near the Shelf."

The Shelf was a high limestone cliff on the eastern border of the little town, a place for the local kids to play *Tom Sawyer* and *Treasure Island* and dig up fossils. There had been a few suicides—ruined bankers, discarded mistresses, jilted young Romeos jumping to their deaths—but there was a scattering of nearby homes outlying the area. These people were some of Sig's best customers; Max knew the route well. "Thanks," he said, and jumped from the loading bay back down to his bike.

He rode fast up the lane, then cut through a yard onto another road. He didn't have a clue what he was going to say. Sig had never listened to reason, and seemed incapable of following any logic other than his own, but it was worth a try. He took a right turn and hurried down this lane until it sloped gradually up into a steep hill. He rode hard, standing on his pedals, grinding up the slope, past a tiny outlying homestead and several slumping barns that were in danger of being swallowed by monstrous, chaotic honeysuckle thickets. The Shelf—grey and striated and bright in the air—looked down upon him through the trees, growing ever higher as he got closer. Just as he came around a bend, Max caught sight of Sig's old ice-wagon. Even from here, the sad sight of Jefferson's head hanging low clenched his heart.

He rode up just as Sig hopped from the wagon and went around to the back. The big man didn't give the boy half a look. "You ain't at work," he muttered.

"No, sir, I am." Max went to Jefferson, who raised his head woefully. He was panting, his nostrils flared, and a gooey sheen of sweat had gummed under his harness; the raw place on his head was crusted over, but drops of blood seeped out here and there, like jelly squishing from the edges of a sandwich. "The Postmaster asked me to find you. He—they need me tonight. I'm helping them with a meeting. They want to make sure if it's okay with you and mother."

Sig picked up a crate of Uranithor, the bottles clinking brightly. "Tonight?"

"Yes. Yessir."

With his arms full, Sig shuffled over to a set of steps cut into a steep hill that sloped up to a weathered private home. The stairway was lined by mossy rocks, and one of the stone walls leaned worryingly inward on itself, but had so far resisted collapse. "No, you're not," he said.

"But—please—"

"Work's for the day. Chores for the night. And studying."

"Studying? It's August! School's not until next month!"

Sig paused halfway up the stairs, and there was a kind of interior gloom on his face. All at once Max could see the little boy inside him—a tender, tuber-headed child who'd been scolded for something he didn't do, beaten for some offense he didn't commit. He gave Max a glance that was mostly turned inward, which seemed equal parts derision and self-hatred. Max almost felt pity for him.

"I said no," Sig gruffed. "Now leave me alone, 'less you want a bottle broken over your head and have to pay for it besides."

Sig continued up the stone stairs. As he went his entire demeanor seemed to change, step by step, evolving into a warm, smiling presence in little more than five seconds. He stood straighter, and the darkness rose from his face like a stage curtain. "Hello?" he called, soft and meek, when he got to the porch. With one hand and a knee he balanced the crate, and with the other he knocked on the door. "Sig Sigfried and Associates! Tonic's the ticket, you know…"

FIVE: THE CONVOCATION

FROM THE MOMENT LORA told Max that she and Sig were planning on marrying and building a life together in that big house, so murky it seemed submerged in river water, a darkness had settled into Max's gut. When Sig was courting Lora, and Max and he had occasionally met—the big man smiling too broadly in cramped suits, his puffy hands and fingers like sausages from Boyd's Butcher's Market—his presence was merely tense and uncomfortable. But as the boy had gotten to know him better, his distaste spilled closer to full-on animosity. Max occasionally wondered what sort of insults he could sling if he had been smarter, cleverer, wittier; these taunts—defiant, scornful, funny in a bleak way—would stupefy Sig so much he'd be left sputtering in shock. But Max, who was neither clever nor witty, and who was generally so shy that making his great plan to break away from Sig had practically been an act of self-defiance, could never do that. He was left with his fists and his dumb, brute bravery, which would only get him beaten, and make his mother homeless and destitute. And so he suffered his losses in silence.

As they sat around the table eating dinner that night—they were eating outside on the porch now, sitting low in wicker furniture with no reason or explanation—there were no sly insults, no outbursts of emotion; Max kept his eyes mostly on the tablecloth, or on his plate. Every once in a while he stole a glance at his mother; a kind of welted rash was rising now up her neck and her cheeks were withered, and her red-rimmed eyes looked out from a face like a trapped animal. Sig was silent and made conversation with no one. Max knew Peter Sylvester was counting on him to be at the service. The Breakaway Plan was working; he was making himself necessary. And both of the Sylvesters had given him a respect and a warm sense of belonging—a new feeling, one that he had never gotten at home.

After dinner, he went upstairs to his book. He paged through it as a muffled murmur of voices drifted up from downstairs. After a time, as he knew they would, they solidified into the CLOMP CLOMP CLOMP of heavy footsteps coming up to the second floor. Max swallowed and drew in his knees and waited for the door to open.

It did, and Sig stepped into the doorway, his face cast in darkness, his vast contours radiant from the lamp in the hall as he settled himself into the threshold. This house belonged to him; even in Max's room, he took ownership.

But his voice was quiet. "You think I'm hard on you, Max, but you'll thank me one day. This kinda thing's easy to learn, but it's hard to know. My father was tough on me, and now look where I got." Not wanting to give him the satisfaction of looking at him, Max kept his eyes on his book. It was opened to the engraving of *Abu Yūsuf Ya'qūb ibn 'Ishāq as-Sabbāh al-Kindī*. Max didn't care if Sig saw it or not. The big man stared at him for a long time, as if he was working up the will to say something. Then the moment passed.

"Goodnight, Max," Sig said. He pulled the door closed.

The house was chilly and dark when Max opened his door and slipped through, clicking it shut with an expert's feel for wood against wood. He crept quietly down the stairs, step by step, ready for any surprise. In the shadows the house felt more oppressive than usual, the stale air heavy with grief and hostility. The chandelier watched him as he passed beneath it.

The post office, on the other hand, practically shone. As Max sailed up on his bike, its jack-o'-lantern windows were as bright as he'd ever seen them; even the rarely used upstairs was glowing. He stowed his two-wheeler against the oak as the Postmaster came out onto the porch. The old man was dressed in a suit, his wiry beard spilling over a trim vest and string tie, just like when Max had first seen him. A watch and chain was tucked smartly into his vest pocket. The boy felt a wash of deep affection; when he was older, he wanted to be just like this.

"You're late," the old man said. "Everything worked out?"

"What can I do?"

"The guests are coming. Why don't you go in and see what the Missus needs?"

Max went inside to see Addie Sylvester, her short hair fluffed up and wearing the same maroon dress she had worn at the séance, setting out freshly brewed coffee. The room seemed larger, there was a thrumming sense of anticipation that Max had never felt here before. He went to her and presented himself. "Sorry I'm late."

Addie had a man's bow tie wrapped around her wrist, and, smiling sweetly, she flipped up Max's collar and knotted it expertly around his neck; they shared a private soothing moment, just the two of them. "Very smart," she said, clapping his shoulders. "Now go up and help Harriet arrange the room. Semi-circle works best. Fifteen chairs at least, maybe twenty."

A clatter came from outside, and Max peeked through the lacy curtains: a man, not quite as old as Peter Sylvester but close, was arriving on horseback. He dismounted easily and went to the Postmaster and wrapped him in a sturdy bear hug. Behind them, a sleek black brougham rumbled up, and more gracefully dressed folk climbed down and clustered around the two—the men warmly regarding one another, the women laughing and kissing each other's cheeks.

Upstairs, Harriet was already in the room, pulling chairs this way and that. She looked almost impossibly smart and sweet in a dapper blue dress, her white socks pulled high. Her short hair was tousled, and it fell pleasantly, divinely, along the sides of her face. When she saw the expression on Max's face she laughed, an unfettered birdsong that scattered away into the corners of the room. His heart leapt; right now, he wanted nothing more than to work by her side, to be her equal, her collaborator, her cohort. Even this glum room had a new, brighter sense of itself.

The night was busy: the teens greeted the visitors, all of them impossibly elegant and gracious, none of whom Max had seen before; though many of the people looked to be in their late thirties or early forties, some were significantly older. There were as many women as men. Max and Harriet took coats, helped with coffee, assisted the elderly upstairs and into the ceremonial chamber. At the door, Addie had laid out a basket of odd trinkets, curious items—each one a severed bird's foot twined with twigs and a carefully tied white ribbon—which Max puzzled over for a moment, and as the guests filed in, he made sure each had their own.

The battered wooden table at the front of the room was covered now with white linen, with a large clear crystal sphere balanced on a delicate wine glass. Six tall candles surrounded it in a circular pattern, with flowers and an incense burner just off to the side. At some point Harriet had pushed a great number of robes into Max's hands, and he went around the chamber handing them out—thin, shapeless, black-hooded vestments that looked like they'd been swiped from a poorly-funded church choir. The guests laughingly struggled into them, trying to keep their ties straight or their hair just so as they adjusted their hoods.

Then everyone—there must have been sixteen or seventeen of them, only three of the chairs were empty—took their seats in a loose semi-circle around the table, each grasping the left thumb of the person to their right. Feeling proud and oddly valuable—it was a new emotion for him—Max pulled a robe over himself and shut the door. He moved quietly to the rear of the chamber, next to Harriet, where he leaned against the wall. He licked his lips and surveyed the room. He'd hardly had a moment to consider the purpose for this sudden meeting, but now he realized that he had no idea, not a single clue, what they were here to do.

The Postmaster stood behind the table, and when everyone had quieted down he began reading from one of the books from the bookshelf. The first part was in Latin—Max was slowly getting a handle on the basics of the language, thanks to the purloined book, which made generous use of it, among others—and went on for some time. The attendees sat quiet, some of them with eyes closed. Addie, near the table on the side, turned and pulled back her hood and offered the teens an encouraging smile. None of the other people said a word.

Then, without a breath, the old man broke into English. "*He will pass during a rainstorm and not a drop will touch his body,*" he read slowly. "*The wind will not disturb a fold of his raiment. He will pass through fire with no sear. For he can, by virtue of the imperial human will, control and direct the intelligent forces of nature and change or arrest their effects. No thing is impervious; to think is to manifest. And when he—"*

With a sudden bang, the door at the rear of the room slammed open, startling the attendees. A few cries of "Oh!" came here and there. And everyone turned to see Sig saunter in.

Max's heart felt like it had fallen from a great height. The big man stood in the doorway and hitched his pants. His breath hissed radiator-loud in the room. The robed people all gaped dumbly at the outsider. Sig's intrusion was beyond a simple breaking of decorum; it ripped the fabric of propriety itself. He stood rooted and took in the scene—the people, the robes, the table, the candles, the crystal sphere. A barely contained violence emitted from him like sparks.

"Well, look at this," he said finally. "Buncha people here."

Max shrank back against the wall, trying to melt into it. Harriet's presence by his side was like a scorching brand, hot and bright in the shame he felt. Her shocked gaze moved back and forth between him and his stepfather.

Peter Sylvester lowered the book. "Sir, I'm sorry, we—"

"People in town know about this?" Sig looked ill at ease. "They will in the morning."

The old man smiled and came from around the table. "Mr. Sigfried, can I—"

Sig cut him off with a forceful sniff. "How do you know my name? Where's my boy?" His hot gaze scanned the room, the baffled faces, and settled on Max in the corner.

Peter Sylvester approached Sig. "Please, sir, if you would—"

"*Don't touch me!*" Sig yelled. His voice was like a detonation in the room. "*Old man!*" He stomped over to Max, and snatched him by the hood, pulling a yankful of hair underneath. "What the shit is this?" He jerked the boy from his place against the wall and bum-rushed him across the chamber. Max caught glimpses of the horrified guests, their eyes and mouths little open knotholes in his peripheral vision.

"He's done with you," Sig insisted. "All o' you! Don't bother us with your sicko shit ever again!"

As he was shoved out the door, Max and the Postmaster locked each other in a quick, loaded glance. Then he was down the hall, down the stairs, across the shadows of the main room and into the dark damp air outside.

The stars overhead were as bright as Max had ever seen them. As the ice-wagon trundled down the lane, the homes on either side were dark, the branches overhead girders bracing up the heavy night sky. Sig drove the horses slowly, without saying a word. There was no point in trying to engage with him; the big man had drawn his anger around him like a greatcoat. He kept licking his lips and blinking rapidly, as though he were having some private squabble about how to handle this latest offense. Max sat ready for Sig to clap him hard in the temple, or in the face, but he never did.

When they got home, Sig followed him into the night house, trailing a wake of quiet rage. Max pulled off his robe and tossed it onto the floor; Sig shrugged off his own jacket and hat and took a moment to arrange them carefully side by side on the couch. Max's nerves sizzled: Sig never did this. Usually his clothes were tossed into a pile that Ethie took care of later on. "What were you doing up there?" Sig asked, his voice quiet.

Max wanted only to escape, to flee up the steps to his room and lock the door. Instead he backed away, knowing the dreadful moment had come. It was better to get it over with now. "Sig—"

Sig approached slowly, his frame huge in the darkness. He drew off his belt.

"Sig," Max implored, "the Postmaster needed—"

"THE POSTMASTER! NEEDS! NOTHIN'!" Sig's voice thundered in the room, and he rushed almost on top of the boy, looming like a troll from a fairy tale. "What was that fucking fruitcake shit—*what were you doin'*—" and he slashed the buckle of his belt at Max's legs, one swing for each word—"AT! THAT! FUCKIN'! PLACE?"

Legs stinging, Max skittered away. Sig moved closer, trapping him in the corner by the fireplace. "WHAT! WERE! YOU! DOIN'?" He didn't want an answer. The buckle came hard and swift, thrashing Max in the thighs, the knees, his waist, his upraised arm.

There was movement above, and Max caught a glimpse of his mother standing at the top of the stairs, her hair wild, her nightgown mussed. "Sig?" she slurred dreamily.

But Sig swung now with his other fist, too, thudding blows that at first were numbing and then ached worse than the belt. "I! TOLD! YOU! NOT! TO! GO!" His lips snarled back from his teeth, his earthworm tongue working back and forth. Max kept silent, his arms upraised, warding off the blows as much as he could. They came fast, and for one strange second he felt himself detach from the scene and stood off to the side, coolly watching the episode, no pain at all; his phantom gaze went over to the darkened fireplace, where a soot-black fire poker leaned against the wall; in an instant he saw himself taking up the poker and braining Sig over the head with it, the little hook on its side piercing deep into the big man's skull. But he knew it wouldn't work. Sig was stronger and bigger than he was; in the heat of the fight, the fire poker would only be pried away from him and slammed into his own thick head. And then he was inside himself again, curling up as Sig's fists pounded his arms, his shoulders, his neck, his body on fire.

Lora stumbled down the stairs and across the room and tried to pull Sig away. "Stop it! Sig! Please, stop it!"

But Sig didn't stop. He spun, fist raised, spittle flecking at his lips, and with the belt whipped Lora full in the face.

When Max thought about this moment later, he knew there had to be a sound, had to be air in the room: Sig's big chuffing breath; his own panting; the night wind outside rushing against the house. But in his memory, everything became very quiet then, almost peaceful; no one, not even Sig, took a breath. It was as if the house itself had gone numb.

Lora slowly brought her hands up and held them there, like a weeping angel memorial in a cemetery. "Mom?" Max asked. She didn't move, didn't seem to hear. *She's hurt,* the faraway voice called, *he's put one of her eyes out.*

Sig sucked in raspy air. "You'd better stop, you bitch," the big man growled, "or I'll beat you like I did your boy."

Lora lowered her hands, and Max was relieved to see both of her eyes were still intact. She stood stunned, face frozen, mouth open, maybe not quite grasping what had happened. A red welt was already burning its way across her nose and cheek. Max looked over at the fire poker: it sat there, so cold in the shadows, so ready. *Yes, this is it,* the faraway voice said. *Yes. But now is not the time. Later, later, later.*

He stood up slowly. In his vision the corners of the room were dimming now, in and out, and he realized he was close to fainting. Sig, his anger starting to cool, or at least going somewhere else, fixed the boy with a nasty, baleful look. He spat on the floor, dropped the belt with a heavy thud, and turned and plodded up the stairs.

Max couldn't sleep. Agony sliced through his body. The welts and bruises on his arms and shoulders thrummed with every heartbeat, his bottom lip was cracked and swollen, and his right eye was puffy—not shut, but nearly. Turning over in bed was a special hell, and the marks on his thighs throbbed with a deep, edgeless pain that seemed to spread all the way down to the bone. But worse than the pain was the white-hot burning rage and grief and resentment. Sig had belted his mother. Max would never again let that happen—no matter what he had to do, neither he nor his mother would ever again suffer Sig's rage. Not even once. He kept wanting to be furious with his mother. Anger was such a perfect emotion, knifelike and sleek, but in truth he couldn't; between being an infirm parent to him and being Sig's partner, Lora was caught as firmly as a moth in a web. There was nowhere for her to go. Her presence lately had grown even more wraithlike—she haunted only the parlor and the kitchen and her bedroom now, with little connection with the outside world. She was to be condoled, not despised.

No, Max was on his own. It was him and the fire poker. There was no other way.

He got painfully out of bed and slipped into his pants. He limped across the room, and in his sock feet he eased the door open and crept silently and weightlessly across the landing. Down the stairs—he could feel the pyramid through his socks—to the bottom floor. The house brooded around him. Dark, polished mahogany gleamed in the moonlight; floorboards squeaked under his feet. He went to the fire poker, and hefted it. The iron was solid and cold. He swung it and a stitch of pain cut through his side, almost making him groan out loud. One of his ribs was cracked, he was sure of it. He took the poker in both hands, and turned the handle so that the little barb hooked outward. He saw himself, iron in hand, slipping quietly inside the master bedroom and standing like a bogey over the bed as Sig and his mother slept. The poker's barb was three inches deep if it was one; with a good swing, he could put it into Sig's skull before the big man knew what was happening.

Yes yes, this is it, yes, now is the time, the faraway voice said. Max's heart beat like war drums.

He was halfway up the stairs when—*BOOM BOOM BOOM*—an assertive pounding came from the front door. Max froze; for an anxious moment the house held its breath, a deeper quiet than before.

The pounding came again. And again.

Before Max could react, the door to Sig's bedroom upstairs opened and shut. He heard the big man grunt to himself as he came down the hallway, and he hurried silently back down the stairs to the kitchen, and peeked around the corner.

"What's this mess?" Sig's footsteps pounded down the steps and across the room and out of sight into the foyer. Then the front door opening. Voices, which he couldn't hear well enough to understand. One was Sig, of course, and the other was—oddly—a woman. From the tone of things, quite a young woman.

A girl, this time of night—an odd occasion to say the least. Max leaned around the kitchen door. He couldn't see anyone, but their voices were more distinct now. Shadows moved in the foyer. Sig's voice was annoyed: "You one of those postal people?"

"May I come in?" The woman's voice, in perplexing contrast to her pounding, sounded bland and unemotional.

"What—*no!* What do you want?"

"I need to speak with you. It is urgent. Please." Her tone was odd, the intonation flat, like someone who spoke English only as a second or third language.

"I told them people to leave us alone. That wasn't even a bunch of catlicks, it was—" Sig stopped, followed by a long silence. Max listened; there were no sounds now, except for a windy rustle in the leaves of the trees outside.

The young woman mumbled something Max couldn't hear, and Sig spoke up again, his voice a bit more at ease. "Yes, all right, yes. All right, but be quiet. In here."

With the fire poker still tight in his fist, Max peeked around the door. Sig and the young woman, the latter in a hood and cape so green it was almost black, went through the dining room and into the parlor. The big man pulled the heavy sliding door shut behind them with a hiss and a thud, and their voices were muffled again. This was odd, exceedingly odd; if the woman was one of the people from the post office, Max certainly didn't remember her. The sophisticates had all been older, but from the pitch and timbre of this lady's voice, she was barely in her twenties. More muted conversation, now; cautiously, Max left his hiding place in the kitchen and prowled toward the closed parlor.

From the other side of the door, Sig was hesitant: "This time of night? About what?"

"About this." That flat voice.

"Oh! I don't—that's not what we should—"

The woman said something Max couldn't make out.

"What were they doing up there in that—"

More whispered, unintelligible words; the woman was hard to understand even without a closed door in the way. Max drifted closer, head tilted in rapt attention.

"Would you—rather—" Sig was jumpy now.

"This, sir. I'd rather this."

"Whoa! You're quite bricky! Do this often, do you?"

"And this."

Their words fell into a series of affirmations and breathy utterances. Max thought: *What in heaven?* In the years Max had known him, Sig had never flirted with anyone, not even pretty girls; he seemed oddly asexual, as if his inner rage had a castrating effect. But here he was, in his parlor with a strange, oddly assertive young woman in the middle of the night.

"Ahhhhh...yes!" the woman warbled. Her voice had an enthusiasm, a rippled edge, that it hadn't before; Sig's own murmurs grew intense and furious. Buttons popped, a whisper of clothes sliding to the floor.

"Here..." Sig was saying. "Let's—whoa, okay, okay, I never."

"Yes, this—this is what I wanted!"

The talking stopped. Max's eyes distractedly traced the tarnished brass fittings of the door handle, the fire poker forgotten in his hands. By now the breathing had slid into a succession of snorts and carnal gasps. Sighs, flutters, exhalations.

"Oh!" Sig said then, amazement rising in his voice. *"Hunnh!"*

"This is it!"

"Goddamn! You're off your chump!"

And then—astonishingly—the woman's speech changed, and spread—grew guttural, and broad and thin, like the rasping of cicadas: "This is *iii-iii-iii!*"

Max stepped instinctively back, his jitters sparking now like fire.

"Ah—*Stop! St—*"

There was a ripping sound, but it wasn't cloth. Then a rumble—a slamming on the walls that made Max jump back from the door even more.

The woman's cicada chatter terrified him: "*Rii-iii-iii-ii-hhhhhhhh!*"

Max couldn't take it any longer: He went to the parlor door and allowed himself heave it wide. What he saw there would be marked in his memory for the rest of his life. In the dim lamplight, Sig was reeling back, his throat spilling blood and spurting onto the woman and the Persian rug under her. His pants were wadded around his hairy calves, and he collapsed onto the spattered davenport, hands fumbling at the spurting wound on his neck.

The woman crouched on one knee with her back to the door. Her thin fingers fluttered in the half-shadows. She seemed aware that Max was there now, and turned slowly to meet his gaze—

—and he saw that her mouth and cheeks had been chewed away to reveal misshapen, broken teeth, her lips and gums black with Sig's blood. Irregular mottles stained the flesh of her face, her hair hung thick and fibrous and stringy, and one of her eyes leered bigger than the other, as though an invisible hand were squishing the face of a beautiful girl. Her bloody lips twisted into a gap-toothed smile as she spat a wad of half-chewed flesh onto the floor.

Max stood rooted, unable to move. His brain wasn't communicating with his body.

Then the woman's index finger went to her wound of a mouth. "*Sssshhhhhhhh...*" The room was caught in silence, as if in a photograph: Grandfather clock still and tall in the corner, curtain at the window caught mid-sigh in a night breeze. In the horror of the woman's presence, Max's thoughts funneled down. He could think only of the dusty, overturned wine glass on the floor near the couch, forgotten from some other evening, some other revelry. *Ethie must have missed it*, the faraway voice said. *Pick it up and take it to the kitchen yourself, boy.*

Without a word, the woman stood and pulled her hood over her head, obscuring her ruined face. She paused for a moment, then swept past Max frozen there in the threshold and through the big room and out the front door. The house shook with the thunder of the front door slam.

With a brassy *clang!* the fire poker fell from his numb hands.

Sig on the couch, grunting, his pajama pants down. His throat a bloody mess. It took Max a moment to realize blood seeped also from the big man's groin. His phallus was gone, his crotch a stew of ripped meat. Sig leaned back and regarded the boy with startled eyes that gradually seemed to lose interest. Saliva burbled at his lips, and he fell still.

Outside the window, there was movement. Max dashed over and pulled back the curtain to see a lone figure gliding down the middle of the moonlit lane, her cape flowing behind her. She was tall, walking with shoulders thrown back, not yet humbled by gravity. The shadows of a large sycamore swallowed her up, and for a moment she disappeared.

Lora's voice came distantly, groggily, from the other room, at the top of the stairs: "*Max? Maaaaaaax!*"

Max watched, breathlessly waiting and waiting, but the hooded young woman never emerged from the darkness.

SIX: THE PLAIN-CLOTHES MAN

THE HOURS AFTER SIG'S death were an endless assembly of screams, gasps, much dramatic fainting from Lora, and a great strained-gut steadiness from Ethie. Max remembered only moments, like thumbing through a photo album: Policemen in the house, crowding every corner, most of all in the parlor; orderlies in smocks draping Sig with a white cloth which bloomed maroon stains in two distinctive areas; men removing a body on a stretcher. And later, Lora and Ethie, sitting in the big kitchen, bleakly answering an officer's questions.

Max sat at the top of the stairs, still trying to make sense of it. He was coming to understand a strange fact about the human brain and its ability to adapt to difficult conditions. He saw how the mind sought to deal with unusual and disturbing phenomena—something exactly like Sig's ghastly death, for instance—to contain it, analyze it, cope with it, all the while getting on with the mundane affairs of daily life. Some people, he supposed, went insane after things like this, walling themselves off in grief or straitjacket paranoia. Others merely went on with the daily mundanities of their everyday lives. He'd heard raucous laughter at the grimmest of funerals; he knew of miners who'd lost colleagues in dreadful accidents, then shown up, lunch pail in hand, ready for work the next day.

So, feeling hazy and blurry as much from a lack of sleep as anything else, Max sat on the pyramid gouged in the wood of the stairs and decided this was his new purpose: to keep everything running smoothly, to get back to real life. An idea was itching at him now—with Sig gone, there was no more time for childish things. If it needed doing, he would do it. He stood and went into his bedroom, and made a face in a little mirror on the wall his grandmother had left behind. His eyes were fierce, his teeth were clenched, tendons bulged at his neck. He was the Man of the House now.

His own interrogation had happened at dawn. A policeman from the station—Parrish was his name; he introduced himself with a genial handshake that said, *I'm on your side, unless you give me a reason not to be*—sat with him on the house's wide front steps. The rising sun spilled through the sycamores as he asked Max again and again about what had happened. He was most interested in the bruises on the boy's face, but Max assured him the beating was typical, and honestly unconnected to any abnormal events. He didn't mention the fire poker, but he did tell Parrish everything he had seen of the weird, awful woman. The cop took notes and seemed unimpressed with the strangeness of Max's story, while nodding and affirming in mild, reassuring tones.

Inside, one of the cops, a commanding officer from what Max could tell, the boss of them all, stood near the closed and cordoned doors of the parlor, wearing white cotton gloves smeared with blots of rust red. He whispered with another man who had recently chugged up in a formal and impressive-looking motorcar with *Atlanta Metropolitan Police* painted on the side. Atlanta was hours away, even by motorcar, and yet here the man was, dressed in street attire, with eyes that seemed to pull in everything around him, like a fisherman with a net; in his gaze, every detail of the house, no matter how small, seemed to hold equal, deadly significance.

Lora huddled on the couch, her lap piled high with three of the couch's throw pillows, as though she were barricading herself behind them. She looked at Max as he came down the stairs, and she smiled stoically, her face a graveyard shamble of grief and shock. "You haven't slept," she said, her voice shaky.

"Have they got anything?" Max sat on the arm of the couch and studied her, watching her grow visibly older before his eyes. The need to say something, to somehow dispel the poisonous shock that had leaked into the room, lay heavy on him. "When are we gonna...you know. Clean up?"

Lora brought her fingers up to touch the veiny globes of her closed eyes. "Ethie's gonna bring in some people, but—"

"Max?" It was the captain, or whoever he was, calling to him from the other side of the room. Max stood up to see him coming over, the other man in street clothes following with a faint but troubling smile on his face. His gaze focused readily on Max's cuts and bruises, as Max knew it would. "I'm Beckman. These are my boys. Where've you been?"

The sharp tone caught Max off guard. "Nowhere. I've been right here."

"Well. Let's keep it that way. Nobody leaves until I say, all right?"

A swift defensiveness came over Max. Why was this man angry at him? He didn't do anything. "I've already talked to your man. Answered all of his questions."

"*All* of his questions?" Beckman said grandly, his voice too loud even for this big room. He was a small man—not just short but small, with a delicate face and precise mustaches; his tone of voice seemed intended to make him sound larger than he really was. "Ha! I certainly hope so! You were here at the incident! The only living witness!"

"These questions are just getting started, son," the Plain-Clothes Man said. His face was unreadable in a way that made the boy nervous.

"Yessir."

Beckman gestured to the other man. "Max, this is Inspector Stoppard. We called him in special from Atlanta." Stoppard stood tall, with salt and pepper hair thick at the temples but thinning up top. With his careful gaze taking in every detail, Max found it hard to look him in the eye. "I'm happy to say that Stoppard here has never left a case unsolved. He's got every man he's ever went after. So we'll get your whoever it is. Don't you worry about that."

"Now, Max," Stoppard said, "you told Parrish it was a woman—a young woman?"

"Yessir."

"But you didn't know her."

"No, sir."

"And you heard them—what. Talking?"

"Most of it was them...um. Breathing on each other. Touching each other." A sudden vision of that strange woman kneeling in front of Sig in the parlor came to him: her mouth working...and...and eating. From the corner of his eye he saw his mother put her face fully down on the uppermost pillow. The cushions rose and fell with her breath.

Stoppard caught Beckman's eye, and a silent shorthand communication seemed to hover between them. Beckman tucked his chin into his chest and considered for a moment. "Well," he said. "You people are exhausted. I think you need to rest before we'll be able to get anything of any use. Take care of her, son, get some quiet. I know Parrish already got your statement, but we need to talk to you firsthand."

"Yessir." Max realized the man was right—he was exhausted. Suddenly his body was very heavy, and he knew that if he didn't soon lie down, he might actually fall down.

"Do not," Stoppard was saying, "go anywhere. We'll talk in a couple hours. Yes?"

Max glanced at his mother, feeling the Plain-Clothes Man's harsh gaze prodding at him. "Yes. Yessir."

A few hours later the house was hot from all the people; doors were wedged wide, curtains were tied back, the sun burned in and police moved here and there with the collective focus of ants in a colony. Corners of the house that hadn't seen sunlight in decades were bright now, and revealed their shabby secrets: scratched floorboards, mouse droppings, elaborate and dusty spiderwebs, dead insects. All of it made Max's head hurt, and he wondered how his mother was holding up. He went up the stairs and stood in the shadows of the hallway for a time, taking deep breaths and working up his courage. Then he nudged open the door to her bedroom.

The windows were closed and drawn. A kerosene lamp on the side table threw chiaroscuros across the floor. Apart from the main chamber downstairs, this bedroom was the biggest room in the house, a fact which Sig had boasted about every chance he got. But Max hadn't been in here in years; it wasn't at all as he remembered it. Now, clothes littered the corners. A bulky, mirrored highboy, one of its doors half-open, stood aslant against the far wall and a rococo chaise lounge had been butted up against the end of the bed. In the shadows, the floral designs on the dull yellow wallpaper were like cobwebs drifting in the air. Lora lay awake among twisted blankets in the bed, her hair as wild as one of those tortured, tragic heroines Max had read about in his

Greek and Roman mythology.

Softly, he cleared his throat. "Mother? How you doing?"

She lay there, blinking at the ceiling. He went over and sat on the edge of the bed. Her face was puffy with grief. The empty space next to her where Sig had slept was hollow and bare, and it wrenched up a strange feeling in Max—the sudden pruning, the terrible finality of it. "You okay?"

Suddenly Lora lifted herself, her face knotted in the half-light. "*WHAT HAPPENED TO HIM?*" she screamed, her face inches from his own. He pulled back and saw she'd been scratching herself with her nails, open scrapes crosshatching her right forearm and elbow. It hurt him to see this; he was her only child, and the bond between them was as strong as anything he'd ever known.

"I don't know," he said softly. "We don't know. But try to relax."

There was a footstep outside the door, and Ethie came in, holding a glass with some type of liquid.

"*GET THAT AWAY FROM ME!*" Lora shrieked. "*I DON'T WANT ANY URANITHOR, I WANT—*"

"Sssshhhhhhhh, this is a bromide." Ethie kneeled by Lora's bed. "It's Mrs. Winslow's. It'll help you sleep."

"I don't want to sleep! I want to know *WHO WAS IT?*" Lora shrieked in Ethie's face too, but the maid didn't flinch. She had stores of nerve Max could only admire.

"Sssshhhhhhhh," Ethie whispered again, "let's have some of this and we'll talk about it."

"No more Uranithor! I can't do—"

"We can't do lots of things anymore. We'll not do all that stuff later. We're doing this now. And it's not Uranithor."

Lora levered up again on one elbow, her hair matted and snarled in the back, and sipped. Ethie looked at Max, eyebrows knitted. He took the hint and got gently up from the bed, and excused himself from the room.

"Yes yes," he heard Ethie murmuring to his mother, "right right, that's right."

When he came down the stairs, the open space of the big room pressed in around him. Despite the activity and the open doors, the air was dead and still smelled stale—old cigars and turpentine and mold. But there was something new, something eggy and sickly sweet, like an animal had crawled between the walls and died. A single thought, cold as an icicle, jabbed itself into Max's mind: the woman had targeted Sig. For some reason, Sig and only Sig had been her prey.

A babble of voices came from the parlor, and Max went over to see several women, maids for hire evidently, kneeling in there, scrubbing and scouring the floor with rags and buckets of soapy water. One of the women looked up at him with queasy eyes. Max had a vague memory of meeting her before; she was one of Ethie's friends.

Then there was a presence behind him, and Max turned to see the Plain-Clothes Man standing there, hands dug into his pockets, rocking back and forth on his heels. Another policeman crossed the room and stationed himself in front of the foyer door. "Hi, Max," the Plain-Clothes Man said, his voice ominously cheery.

The man's name was Stoppard, Max remembered. He had rushed up from Atlanta, his eyes took in everything, and right now there was a gun in a shoulder holster inside his jacket. The handle caught the light coming in from the front windows.

"This is just peachy," Stoppard said. "Your mother complained about us quite a bit, she did." He grinned, a smile which seemed to rise to the surface from below, like a belch. "Evidently doesn't get out a lot."

"What—"

The Plain-Clothes Man stepped closer to Max; Max took a step back. In the silence he heard the kitchen door behind him whisper open. *They're closing you in,* the voice said. The cop—not Parrish, not him; Parrish had mostly been nice—came out from the kitchen and stood flat-footed, blocking the stairs. The rasp of his hands rubbing together sounded like wasps rustling inside a nest. A rising sense of alarm came over Max, a new emotion that was equal parts panic and a numb, disconnected sense of amusement: *They think you did this.*

"Time to talk," said Stoppard.

Beckman sat at the kitchen table, and Stoppard went to stand with his hands clasped behind his back and stared out the window. Another cop was stationed by the kitchen door to the driveway. "Edgar, leave us alone for a little while, will you?" Stoppard said without turning around. The cop excused himself while Max slipped into the chair opposite Beckman.

"You have more questions?" the boy asked, feeling as if whatever he said would somehow be the wrong thing.

Beckman took a moment to smooth his already precise mustaches. "We don't know what happened here, Max. Obviously somethin' did. Kinda thing we don't see a whole lot around here. We get payday brawls and bar fights and horse theft. Sometimes we'll get something worse—husband goes kablooey and guns down his wife, some tramp shivs her john, stuff like that. But we ain't never seen where a strange woman chomps a fellow's johnnie and spits it out while the fellow's kid was watching." In the silence that followed, he leaned back and took out a handkerchief and blew his nose mightily. Max didn't say anything; the tips of his fingers had gone numb.

At the window, Stoppard stood with his hands still clasped behind his back. But something in his manner gave Max the impression that, if he needed to, he was ready to spring into action. *They think I might try to run away*, Max thought coolly. And he realized with a mild detached surprise that the idea of bolting up and dashing out of the house did sound oddly inviting. *But you didn't do anything*, the faraway voice said.

"This is serious stuff, Max," Beckman was saying. "A violent death."

"A *murder*," Stoppard said to the window. He turned and faced them, looking like a man readying himself for enjoyable work. "Lone witness. Claimed it was some 'crazy woman,' nobody else has seen. And I mean *nobody*. We ain't been able to get behind that in any way."

"Stoppard brought forensics up from Atlanta," Beckman said. "Told us the teeth was more canine—or feline, maybe—than human."

A buzzing dread rose up inside Max. They couldn't be serious, could they? Did they really think he was part of this? He tried to understand their line of reasoning: How could he have done this, how could he possibly have anything to do with it?

"This stepfather thing ain't your average hothead killin', is it, Max? Somethin' here you're not tellin' us."

The boy's mind raced through the recent events—the odd conversations, the séance, the gathering above the post office. All the things he knew he shouldn't mention. He saw the cruel woman put her finger to her chewed-off lips: Ssssshhhhhhhh... And then his own wicked relief, glittering like a spiteful jewel—*It was good that Sig was gone*. He tried to come up with ways of spilling only part of the truth, but couldn't. "What I know is what I told you," he said, hoping to sound stronger and more defiant than he felt.

Stoppard crossed his arms and leaned against the sink. "Look. There are some other things we need to get clear. This post office thing you've been working at. I've been brought up from the big town not because this was just a murder. We see that all the time." Something like arrogance was lighting up his face; he really was enjoying this. "I came up because this was a ritual murder." Max didn't answer. He felt his heart skipping, trying to catch up, but he stayed silent.

"For two years now I've been studying the...uh, so-called activities of various spiritualist groups across the nation, Max. Seeing how this one's so close to home, this is the first time I've had the occasion to actually visit the scene of the crime in person. Usually it's just me and my desk and a bunch of maps and photos." He pulled out a chair and sat down. "This guy Sylvester is not who you think he is, Max. This killing is no small deal."

Max thought of the convocation—all those glittering, elegant people who seemed to come out of nowhere. Same with the séance. They were just...there. But who really were they?

"Now, I gotta admit, they're pretty good at hiding in plain sight. We had no idea they were here. They're good at what they do. But we think he's one of the higher ups of a large spiritualist faction. A large 'cult,' if you want to call it that."

Max stared blankly. That word: *cult.* It suggested blind followers and sham leaders and people doing things they shouldn't for reasons they couldn't explain.

"Don't kid yourself, boy. These people may look innocent, but they're not. We don't know the full extent, but we're working on it. They're good at keeping quiet, but once you connect the dots it starts to make a lot more sense."

"What does this have to do with me?" Max said, trying not to think of *Tchowgosh* or fortuitous assassinations. "I don't really know these people."

Stoppard looked at Beckman, and the Colonel shrugged. "Well, this is where it gets sticky. You have a choice, Max. You either help us or you don't. If you do, we'll make it worth your time. If not, we'll do everything we can to make sure you spend the rest of your life behind bars. We can pin this one on you. It's easier than you think. I've done it before, and we've got lots of friends in these parts." An uncomfortable sensation, like an acid burn, roiled in Max's gut. "You'll start at a boy's camp," Stoppard was saying. "Then once you're eighteen—what is that, three years?—you'll move up with the men. There may even be a hanging in there, if you get the wrong judge. I'll do my best to see that you do."

Max's acid burn bloomed now into full nausea. "Why would I still be here if I was the one who did it?"

"We're not saying you did it, Max," said Stoppard.

"We're only trying to get clarity here," Beckman assured him.

We're not saying you did it, Max. But we'll blame it on you anyway.

The air in the room had grown thick. Thoughts and worries tumbled in the boy's head in a storm of problems with no solutions, a rage of faces and smiles and uneasy moments. And he kept circling back to this central snag: *This guy Sylvester is not who you think he is.*

Easy to learn, the faraway voice said, *but hard to know.*

"I may be young," Max snapped, surprising even himself. "But I'm not an idiot. If you want to jail me now, do it. Otherwise, leave me alone." Willfully—but slowly, so they wouldn't think he was running away—he stood up, leaving Beckman and Stoppard to watch him go out the kitchen door and across the family room. Not out the front door—there was a cop blocking that, standing flat-footed there and dourly watching him—but back upstairs. Back to his room.

A *ritual murder.* What did that mean? And who was Peter Sylvester affiliated with, anyway? Those bizarre names again—*Tchowgosh. Mme. Z—.*

Max lay on his back in his bed, his head at the foot and his sock feet on his pillow, staring out the window at the dimming, upside down sky. He'd been having strobing visions of that woman's red, ruined smile. And then this man—this plain-clothes man, a specialist in cultists, whatever that meant—threatening him with prison. With hanging.

Footsteps came plodding up the stairs, toward his own closed door. It was one of the cops. The steps paused outside; Max held his breath. The cop remained outside the door.

A guard. They were confining him now. He was not only a prisoner in his house, he was a prisoner in his own room.

He got up and slipped on his shoes. Quietly he pushed the window open. The driveway below was empty. By now it was almost dark, and most of the cops were either inside or had returned to the station. The big poplar near the house had been Max's steady companion for several years, and now it provided him with a decent, if spare, ladder down. With a quick glance over at his mother's own dark window—Max sent a quick prayer, *I hope you're okay, please please be okay*—he jumped painfully down the last eight or so feet, snuck around the corner, and climbed on his bicycle.

The ride to the post office was fragmented and harrowing: the twilight gave everything a ghostly, paranoid edge, and as Max coasted down the lane, unhurried, thinking he should take his time to not draw any unwanted attention, he noticed people occasionally staring at him, townsfolk whose curious glances lingered longer than usual. Maybe it was the bruises on his face. Maybe the news about Sig was starting to get around.

At the post office, the only evidence of the broughams and calashes from the previous night were the ruts and hoofprints in the uneven grass. That was a lifetime ago. Max laid his bike down and looked up at the old building. Its windows stared back with a kind of guarded sentience. Inside, the Postmaster—*not a Postmaster*, Max thought, *but* the *Postmaster*—was closing up behind the counter, looking trim in his suspenders. He seemed slight, though, somehow more frail than he did last night. When he noticed Max he smiled, seeming to ignore the boy's black eye and split lip.

"Good evening, Max! How are you?" he said, squaring and stacking several envelopes. Max stood in the doorway, not knowing what to say. His thoughts wheeled round and round, a wake of vultures circling but unable to land. He glanced warily about the room. Now that he was out of that awful house and back at the post office, everything had taken on a glassy, narcotic feel. Too many doubts crowded together in his head. Omens and intimations lay scattered everywhere—in the haphazard stacks of letters, in the posts tacked to the walls, in the spiraling galaxies of dust crowding the corners of the hardwood floor. But inside he felt stoic, hollowed out. He needed to talk.

Addie leaned in from the kitchen, glancing at her husband, but the Postmaster turned and shook his head. *It's all right*, he seemed to say, *I'll handle it.*

"We missed you today," the old man said. His voice was cheery but low, his eyes somewhat sad. He went back to the letters. "We all lose someone once in a while, you know. Happens to everyone. Only thing to do is keep on."

Max opened his mouth to say something, but stopped.

Peter Sylvester raised his head to look at him, his face half-turned, as though trying to see the world from Max's newly slanted point of view. Then he put down the papers and slipped from behind the counter, and went to stand in front of the boy.

"When we first met you," he said gently, "Addie told me, 'This is the one.' And sure enough, you were, Max. You really were." He put his hands on the boy's shoulders. It wasn't a hug, but it seemed to crack the shell of Max's stunned trance. His eyes watered and tears started to come, slowly and then all at once. He wasn't crying for Sig—he didn't think he could ever shed a tear for that distasteful man, not even a single one—but for something deeper that he didn't fully understand, a tectonic shifting in the firmament beneath him that pulled him further away from everything he had taken for granted. He felt suddenly, frighteningly, adrift.

"I'm sure you have questions," Peter Sylvester said a few moments later. "I certainly would." They had made their way up into the ceremony room. Now there was no sunlight trying to slip in through the curtains, no babbling crowd of sophisticates; the glum stillness of evening had settled in unopposed once again. The old man pulled two chairs into the center of the room, and they sat opposite each other, nearly knee to knee.

"First, the unfortunate incident with your stepfather. You may have wondered if I was the one behind it all." Max's gaze dropped to the papery skin of the old man's hands, the blue veins there. His tried to push his mind into a purely receptive place; he was not yet ready to shape the formless mass of his confusion into actual questions. "You would be incorrect—although I do know who it was. Either way, causation is impossible to prove."

There was a dazed silence. Neither of them spoke. The moment grew long and painful, and then the old man leaned in to whisper in the boy's ear: "For you, Max. We did it for you."

Peter Sylvester pushed himself up and went to the battered bookcases. "Many solutions were considered. First it was a will o' the wisp. Such a lovely way to go. Many times the party in question is never found, because they had been led into a swamp and their bodies simply mired under the muck. But your stepfather seemed not to have the inclination—or, frankly, the imagination—to wander into uninhabited areas." He pulled one of the bookcases out from the wall and began shouldering it toward the corner. "After considering several other solutions, it was settled. The Moorlander, we call her. She has other names, other designations. She could have chosen merely to inhabit your stepfather, make him think thoughts that weren't his. Terrify him to no end, and then follow him for the rest of his life, which would have been spent in constant dread. Most likely he would have died by his own hand. In that sense, what did happen was merciful. Certainly it was quick."

The Moorlander. Max said it to himself, feeling the bones of the word. By now that terrible episode seemed to have happened a long time ago—threats from cops with guns tended to have that effect, he supposed. But with this new information, the idea of that woman, the very existence of her, unsettled him in ways he couldn't explain.

"Have I answered the question?" Peter Sylvester said from across the room. He'd squared one bookcase up with the corner and was swiping the toe of his boot at the scuff marks he'd made on the hardwood floor. "The one you never asked?"

Max licked his lips. The back of the chair felt good and solid against his spine. He said, "They told me about you. About your group. They brought somebody up from Atlanta. An expert."

The old man stiffened, straightened up; his nostrils flared. "What did he say?"

Max told him about the cops—about Parrish and Beckman and Stoppard. How they seemed to know about the old man's group—the old man's "cult," they had called it. He told the Postmaster about how they told him he couldn't go anywhere, and how he had slipped out anyway, from his second-floor window.

Peter Sylvester gave the boy a measured smile. "Did you tell them anything about us? About the things you've seen?" When Max shook his head, he said, "Very mature. We do like our privacy, after all. But these reprobates are looking for you now, no doubt. And no doubt they will come here."

This was an unsettling idea. The old man came back over and sat down with a sigh.

"I should tell you this much. Partially, they are right. There is a faction, as they might call it. A *cult.*" He gave a tired smile. "We prefer to call it a brotherhood. The Brotherhood of the Aurora, as a matter of fact. We are a loose connection of like-minded individuals who maintain an interest in so-called 'occult phenomena.' For the purpose of bettering the world. You have seen us very much in action. There's nothing nefarious about it. We're quite boring, actually. We try to help. But the scunners interpret our discretion as sinister, while we see it as a way to do our best work unheeded."

"But what about that—that woman? The Moorlander?"

The Postmaster didn't look like a dashing Civil War general now; he looked every minute of his age. "She's a fearsome sight, isn't she? A last resort. Or at least a quick one. Sometimes one must employ indelicate tools to do necessary work. We're gardeners, Max, tilling the soil. Sometimes we fell a tree for the betterment of the crops at large."

The room was strangely silent now; the heavy curtains seemed to gather up and keep all the noises of the little town outside. Max felt lost. After all the activity of the last eighteen hours, his brain wasn't working so well anymore.

"All right," the old man said. He pushed himself up again, went to the other bookshelf. He positioned it so it lay perpendicular across the corner of the room. The two made a kind of nook behind them. "Tell you what. Come here."

Max got up and went over. The corner behind the bookshelves was just big enough for a person to stand behind. Or sit in.

"You stay here," the old man said. "You're safe here. They won't come up here just yet, and if they do, you'll be out of sight. I'll have Addie bring you anything you need." The Postmaster leaned closer. "I would think you'd be exhausted right about now. Why don't you try to get some rest?"

Max nodded vaguely. Not at the thought of sleeping, or at the old man's line of logic, but at the wonder of what had happened, the weird inexplicable horror of it all. He slid behind the bookcase. Peter Sylvester extended his hand around the corner, a disembodied thing, like a slightly repulsive sea creature, and Max took it. It was sturdy and stronger than it looked, and it gave him a firm shake. Then he pushed the edge of the bookcase against the wall.

For the next few hours, Max sat cramped and exhausted behind the bookshelves, still too tired and jittery to sleep. Visions of the weird woman—*the Moorlander*—flickered behind his eyelids. Sig's slack face staring at him; the house hectic with policeman, all of whom seemed to have a secret hostile need to see him hang for it all. The back of the bookshelf, as scarred and blemished as the night sky. Hours passed. Twice Max slid the bookcase away and took stealthy trips to the lavatory down the hall. With his stomach rumbling from hunger—he hadn't eaten since the afternoon of the previous day, a quick apple and a piece of cheese—he removed the stacks of pamphlets, and urinated bright yellow into the dry, stained bowl.

At some point he heard voices, men's voices, in the main room down below. He couldn't tell if it was Stoppard and Beckman or anyone he knew. Once, the voices came upstairs and paused in the doorway, obviously looking in at an empty room. Then Addie pushed them along their way. Finally, as the hours grew early, Max heard the door to the ceremony room open again. There was a soft, uncertain pause. Then: "Max?"

He slid the bookcase away and peeked out to see Peter and Addie Sylvester coming in, followed by the three old Hearst sisters and—startlingly, astonishingly—Harriet. Max gaped at her. Instead of looking worried, she seemed not to notice him at all. She shut the door behind her and went to wait at the rear of the room.

"What time is it?" Max climbed stiffly out, ashamed to be caught hiding. "What's she doing here?"

The Postmaster was distant and preoccupied, which was not at all what the boy expected. Lillian, Louise, and Loretta fanned out toward the ceremony table, and Addie went to stand beside them. The four of them made an odd image—three thin, leering beldames, and one middle-aged matron, glowing with genuine warmth and concern.

"Max," the Postmaster said in a formal tone, which made the boy even more uneasy; he had seen Peter Sylvester slip into a firm leadership role more than once by now. In his experience, that was when bad things happened. The old man shrugged himself into a crimson robe that exactly matched the color of the rug, making his head look floating and disembodied in the gloom. He nodded at the boy. "Approach, please."

Still in his filthy clothes, the ones he'd been wearing since the day of the murder—*Was that yesterday, or the day before?*—Max limped across the room, as though he was walking to his death. He stopped before the altar.

"Harriet. Approach." Harriet also came forward, holding the skirt of her dress. She stopped next to Max, hardly seeming to notice him.

"First: Max, we are proud of you," the Postmaster said. "We know what you have been through, and how terrifying it must have been. We know also that it was not your fault."

Sure he looked a shock in his rumpled clothes and bleary eyes, Max glanced at Harriet, but her soldier's gaze stayed fierce and focused. His hands wanted to hide themselves in his pockets, but he wouldn't let them.

"We are sorry for your stepfather's untimely demise. For this, we mourn."

Max thought of Sig on the settee again, his eyes flat and empty. The image distorted, warped into grotesquerie, faded to black and white, an illustration in a book of fairy tales. *I'm not mourning,* Max thought, *I'm not. I'm glad he's dead.*

"In light of these events, however, we must adapt and make new plans. Haste is never a preferred method of choosing, but occasionally our hand is forced." His expression seemed harsh. "There is a community in the Midwest, an academy of sorts, with whom we maintain a tight alliance. It will be safe, and most of all it will be secret. In light of what I have told you about our Brotherhood, you have a choice to make."

Peter Sylvester turned to Harriet. "Miss Harriet, as you know, for some time we have intended for you to go there and begin your education proper. Many times you have proven you have the talent and the drive and the ability." Behind the old man, the chorus of sisters—Lillian, Loretta, and Louise—beamed the same bewildering, gummy smile. "But given the events of the last few days...we have no choice but to offer the position instead to Max. To attend in your place."

Harriet's face fell. "*What?*"

"Please hear me," Peter Sylvester said. "We know you were expecting to attend, and for good reason. But you must understand—through no fault of his own, Max has now been implicated in a crime. He is being hunted by bad men. For his sake—for the sake of our elders, for the private community, for yours and also ours—Max must disappear."

"*But Max hasn't—*"

"He is stronger than you know, dear child. Stronger than he knows." The Postmaster turned to Max. "We won't force you to go, young man. You can choose to stay and face whatever consequences may come. We will deny everything, of course. The nature of what we do depends largely upon stealth and silence. No single member is above that."

Max's thoughts came stumbling and slow. He felt as if he had been mesmerized, and wished somebody would snap their fingers in front of his face and wake him up. "I...don't really know what we're talking about."

"We are talking about an academy. A school. You can go and begin your studies in earnest with the Brotherhood. Or you can stay and face whatever may come from these..." The old man's lips curled in derision. "So-called authorities."

"But that's *my place*," Harriet hissed. "It was for *me*."

"No other option, Harriet. We won't insist that Max go, but we must offer him the choice."

Max licked his lips, thinking of the Plain-Clothes Man. That smug smile. That gun in his jacket. "When would I leave?"

"Tonight. Immediately."

"But—what?"

"They are looking for you as we speak, young Max. They've scoured the streets of Selleford. They've even come upstairs into this very room, despite the protestations of Miss Addie here."

Max groaned. "My family—my mother—Ethie..."

"We have arranged," Lillian Hearst said.

"—for a train," Louise added, "which—"

"—leaves very early," Lillian finished. "In darkness."

Harriet stomped over to the side of the room and collapsed into one of the chairs. She buried her face in her hands, which sent Max into another spiral of despair. How could he ever hurt this wonderful creature? "Sir—" she said, "I know, I know why you—"

But the old man held up his fist, closed now. The girl fell silent. "Harriet— I'm sorry. Our decision has been made. It's up to Max."

Max felt everyone watching him. "Will I be able to say goodbye?" he asked weakly. Peter Sylvester shook his head, no. The three old sisters leaned in to

Max. Their smiles, if it was possible, grew even wider.

"You—"

"—must—"

"—go!"

It was a terrible choice. Max looked over at Harriet, who glowered from the side of the room, her eyes bloodshot. A dribble of snot had trailed down from her nose and sat glistening in the half-light on her upper lip. He thought of his mother, the wild harried thing at the end of the hall. She didn't seem rational anymore, and he wasn't sure whether or not she would be coming back from this latest tragedy. He thought of the book, *The Worm at the Heart*, and *Abu Yūsuf Ya'qūb ibn 'Ishāq as-Sabbāh al-Kindī*'s diagrams and legends and algebraic formulas. Despite all the turmoil of the last few days, the riddle of it still pulled at him, the stark, stripped-away need to understand. The dark promise of the Brotherhood of the Aurora, whatever that was. Max looked at the Postmaster with a face of despair. A flash of himself appeared—older now, his mother long dead, jouncing along the streets of Selleford in an old converted milk-wagon; behind him were crates of clinking bottles of Uranithor. He saw himself climbing mossy stairs, up to a house—his posture slowly unfurling until he was no longer what he was, but instead the picture of a happy strong family man with a thriving business of helping people in a small textile mountain town in the toenails of the foothills of the Appalachians. His fake smile at the top of the stairs would be dazzling.

Harriet stared back at him with a teary desperation. Max tried to find some sense of justice in the moment, some fairness or mercy, but couldn't. He turned back to Peter and Addie Sylvester. Slightly, uncertainly, almost imperceptibly—he nodded.

An hour later, he was sitting in an empty brougham, staring at the night outside his window. It was the nicest carriage he had ever been in. He did not know the coachman, had never seen him before. They were headed to the vast train yards of Atlanta.

But his mind was back in the dim ceremony room, as the three sisters led him arm in arm toward the door. A strange afterthought pressed itself in, and he was reminded of Sig pulling him, marching him, from the very same room. The sisters' soft but insistent ushering had been every bit as firm. Peter and Addie Sylvester had watched him go.

And Harriet. She stood teary and red-faced beside them, her expression a mask of anger and despair. Just before he passed the doorway, she and Max had locked eyes: she watched him, her gaze as savage as a feral child's—all wordless resentment and confusion and rage. And then he was gone.

BOOK TWO

THE AURORA

SEVEN: STEPPELAND

THE PASSENGER TRAIN WAS headed west, to Nebraska.

It was a mainline day coach, with red cushioned seats, ornate mini-chandeliers rattling overhead, and broad windows in which the moonlit darkness slid past the blurry reflection of Max's face looking out. It meant he would sleep in his seat for the duration of the four-day trip. At first he thought this would be easy—each seat was a decent width, and for the first couple of hours he rolled his jacket into a pad and dozed against the window. But sometime in the early morning, with the landscape outside the window mostly black and formless (vague geometries of passing buildings; pinpoint lights blinking by in the far distance), he got up and went sleepily down the swaying aisle to use the water closet. When he came back he found his seat taken by an older woman who slept with her mouth as roundly open as a birdhouse hole. In his dreamlike state he half-expected to see a wren or warbler hop out and perch on her nose.

So he had to find another seat, and ended up with one on the aisle, which was not nearly as comfortable; at the window, he could slump hard against the cold pane of glass, but in the aisle the train inspector and the newsboy and various passengers brushing past him at all hours made for a miserable night's rest. When he did sleep, broken fragments flickered across his mind, glimpses caught in the shards of a shattered mirror: the little Burke girl, blood seeping from her eyes and spattering on her dress; Sig's blank stare, the terrible ripped wound at his crotch; the weird woman, chewing and spitting from that ruined mouth. The way she had slipped into the shadows of the sycamore, but never came out. Max woke, stiff in the darkness, wiped his face with a clammy hand, relieved to be free from his nightmares.

It was morning when the train stopped outside Birmingham, and he got off, feeling unmoored from himself in the pale light of the rail fields. The city was vast, steaming and clanging in the moist air, and gravel and charcoal crunched under his feet. When he thought of Harriet, his heart twisted itself in knots. She was clearly devastated by him taking her place at this academy, or whatever it was, but he'd had no choice.

But then his poor mother and Ethie. Sig had been murdered, and now her son was simply...gone. They would have no idea to where. No doubt Peter Sylvester and his associates were keeping quiet. Beckman and Stoppard would be tormenting Lora and Ethie with a thousand questions, scouring the area, searching the woods. Maybe even dredging the local lakes. If he went back now, he would be snatched away to some stinking boys' reformatory or some brutal men's prison. Or, if the Plain-Clothes Man got his way, hung to death.

Max snuffed snot, spat into gravel.

He got back on the train just before it pulled away, knowing, reluctant as he was, he had taken the only realistic option available. He trusted Peter Sylvester. He had seen the wondrous and terrible things that he—that they—could do. Being on this train was the only path now. Max took his seat on the aisle again and told himself he would contact Lora and Ethie as soon as possible. To let them know he was okay.

Evening in Arkansas looked much like Georgia: lush trees, pleasant hills, train trestles spanning wide, polite rivers. The train stopped three times, the last to let on a family of what looked like Amish—an older man, a woman, and three young children, without a single properly fitting garment between them. They shoehorned themselves into the row of seats in front of Max, and one of the little ones, a choppy-haired boy of about four years old, kept staring at him over the back of the chair. At first it was funny—they played little games of peekaboo and made faces at each other—but soon Max just wanted the boy to leave him alone. Every time his mother nagged him—*Beanie, stop that! Beanie, leave that young man be!*—it lasted for only a few minutes before Max could feel the press of little boy's gaze on him again, his tuft of hair above the seat, the shiny beads of his eyes like the black pebble stare of a crow. A cruel part of him wished for Daniel Pepper's ability to talk to spirits; he could maybe call them up to torment the boy and put an end to this nonsense. The passing hours would have been more interesting, at least. Max closed his eyes and slipped into a shallow, fretful nap. When he woke, it was Tulsa.

Tulsa: reeking of the briny stink of too many cattle in too little a space, it was dusty and airless and dry, even down by the withered, rocky river that bordered the town. Indians ambled from sidewalk to sidewalk—sad, chisel-faced people who were outwardly stoic but plainly dying on the inside. Taking a stroll outside the station, Max came upon scene after scene of cruelty toward them—boys throwing rocks at an old Choctaw man, a pair of dusty cowhands harassing an Osage cleaning woman, a tight-laced matron chiding a Creek girl's handmade frock. Max fled back to the train and went to the cramped water closet and locked the door; with the lid down, he sat on the toilet and studied the woodgrain of the paneling, trying not to think, or at least to think of nothing. His hands shook and his brain was having trouble now separating the phantom visions in his head as they melded horribly together into new, ever more delirious patterns: Sig bleeding from his eyes; his mother shushing him with a bloody finger to her ruined mouth; Harriet in a black-green cape, disappearing into the shadows.

Addie Sylvester had given him four dollars for the journey, so once a day he went to the restaurant car and wolfed down egg sandwiches with pickled red onions and spicy tomato catsup. Though the eggs were bland—Max had a notion to find the cook and let him know if he would add just a pinch of tarragon and salt the flavor would spring to life—he could have eaten three of them at a time. But with so little money, he mostly sat at the table and sipped lemon water, his stomach growling at him as he stared out the window. Eventually, the hills outside smoothed out like air pressed from a pillowcase: the Kansas horizon opened up for miles, and the dome of sky overhead was the biggest he had ever seen. The new perspectives helped clear his head; the Georgian hills and trees were lovely, but this was something else—golden flatlands that never ended, fading out in the diamond purity of a late-summer morning. The only reason he couldn't see further was because of the curvature of the earth itself. With his crowded, delirious imagination, this idea somehow calmed him.

Finally, the train slowed for the last time. The inspector, on one of his ramblings up and down the aisle, tapped Max on the shoulder. "North Platte, Nee-braska," he said, his breath smelling of black licorice. Max sat up, wiped the sleep from his eyes, and slipped into his one possession—the rumpled jacket.

The train rattled to a stop. Feeling exhausted but relieved, he tottered down to the platform. It was late afternoon; the world around him was as flat as a floor, and the station stood alone, with a few other low buildings huddled off by themselves. The sun blazed hot in the sky, and he squinted against it, looking around for anyone who might be expecting him. He had assumed there would be someone here to meet him. Peter Sylvester had certainly treated his elopement with great urgency and a grand sense of importance. But though people milled about outside—a broad-shouldered farmer hoisting a young girl high on one arm, a stooped and very sweet older couple who needed help getting down the last long step—but no one's eyes settled on him.

The train station was a one-room affair: high ceilings with exposed rafters still smelling of tree sap, and lofty, domed windows which let in bright shafts of sunlight. Max went to the ticket booth and got in line. When his turn came, the teller glared at him as if he were one of those sad Tulsa Indians.

"Hi, my name's Max Grahame," he said. "I'm supposed to meet someone here."

"I can't say," said the man behind the glass. The lenses of his *pince-nez* were dusted with dandruff, and his lips were hidden underneath a fleecy brown mustache. When Max hesitated, the teller waved him to the side. "Young man, I really cannot say," he said again, slightly louder this time.

There were two opposite-facing polished wooden benches in the center of the room, and Max went and collapsed into the closest one, feeling as if he was back on the train all over again.

Hours passed. His mind was blank. Every so often he got up and wandered around the station. No one came to him; no one introduced themselves. He studied a lopsided newspaper wall map tacked in the far corner and learned he was just over 200 miles outside Lincoln. Outside, the horizon line was broken only by grain silos, the cluster of one-story buildings, and a lone house as grand as a big city bank. Max went inside and sat again and watched the light crawl across the walls. In a few hours, the sun reached the ceiling and shaded out; heavy electric lights, trimmed in brass and wood, sputtered on. Max's stomach growled, but there was nothing to eat. Just the ticket counter—the teller now long gone—the crooked map in the corner, and those polished benches.

Late in the evening, more trains arrived and the station flooded with travelers—families, grandmothers, ranch hands, serving maids with baggage. The room hummed with the chatter and buzz of too many people. Then, as suddenly as if a stopper had been pulled at the bottom of a drain, they were gone: Max was alone again. He could see his heartbeat in his shirt.

Even later, he was lying on his back and trying to sleep in the far corner when the room filled yet again. Faces grinning, couples hugging, beards laughing, knuckles on shoulders, hands adjusting worn suspenders. Then it drained once more, and gradually, like a mist burning off, Max realized he wasn't alone: a single last man leaned against the far wall.

Max sat up. The man was slim but solid, clean-shaven and formal in a brown banker's suit, with a derby hat and squinty, buggy eyes under prominent brows. Max stared at him and the man stared back. Then the man lifted himself from the wall and left the building.

Max lurched up on legs that had fallen asleep and tottered after him, feeling relieved and also trying not to sink into the lower depths of a dread like he'd never felt before. *You made the right decision*, the faraway voice assured him. *You did what you had to do.*

"Mister!" he called. "Sir! You looking for me?"

The man didn't answer. He went to his carriage, a simple, battered buckboard, and climbed onto the jump seat. When Max did the same, he didn't say a word. He only hitched his horses, and together they set off into the flat, starless morning.

For several hours, they rumbled along, the air cool and thin and dry, not at all like the thick air of Georgia. The man—Max still didn't know his name—hardly said a word. "You hungry?" he mumbled once in a loose, creaky voice, as though he wasn't used to talking. Max was beyond hunger by this point; he was only exhausted. But the ride was too jolty to sleep, and he stared blearily as lights crawled by on the far horizon, scattered dreams gone to seed out in the fields.

After a period in which he was aware only of the dim, moonless streak of road ahead of them, the wagon veered off the main track and onto a rougher one. Max sat up, took a look around; morning had crept closer. Behind him the horizon line was barely visible, the darkness of the plains contrasted gently against a ruddy glow. Out in the fields, waist-high barley stirred in the darkness. Here and there, phantom trees watched over the crops.

Then, in the dark expanse ahead, a lake, and then a dim building looming

at the far edge of the water. A few lighted windows glimmering off the surface.
As they got closer a large structure emerged, as if it had stepped forward from
the gloom—finished in rough stone, surrounded by gently rolling lawns and
apple trees that hadn't been picked for years. Porches, balconies, and terraces,
with gambrels and chimneys and a bright plume of smoke feathering up.
Someone was awake.

The man pulled the wagon up the circular drive in front and halted it.
"This is you," he said. "I've got to run the horses around back."

Max climbed stiffly down and stood looking around. The night was cool
and quiet, aside from the fading crunch of the wagon pulling away and the
disembodied staccato chirp of a nightingale somewhere out in the prairie. A
wide set of stairs rose up to the front door, where a peeling sign proclaimed
Steppeland Mercy Hospital. He felt numb and uncoupled from himself, as if he
were a character in one of the books on his shelf, and he went up the wide
stone steps and pulled open the front doors.

The foyer was roomy, with high ceilings and brass lamps drooping
overhead like insect pupas, throwing a milky glow over the chamber. Max stood
there, dazed and dead tired; he needed badly to urinate. Sad rococo couches
and chairs lined the room, their seats sprung and flat in the middle. Area rugs
slanting across a black and white checked tile floor; corridors shrinking away
on either side; tall windows spilling in a faint pink radiance from the east. The
slip of a footstep behind him caught his attention, and he turned to see a
middle-aged woman in nurse's white coming primly down the hall.

"Max Grahame?" She came and stood before him; tall, with a stretched,
earnest face and greying wisps of black hair curling from behind her ears. "I'm
Nurse Agnes," she said, and wrapped him in a quick, dispassionate hug.
"Welcome to Steppeland."

"What is this?" he asked when she had let him go.

"We help all souls here, from flu victims to mothers giving birth. But we
specialize in glandular replacement. And also remarkable young people like
you."

Max took a step away. Despite her kind words, she had a kind of stubborn
directness that reminded him, and not flatteringly, of Ethie. This was a woman
who demanded, and surely received, proper regard. She said, "You met Tom
Howland?"

"What? Him? Yes, ma'am. I think I did."

Max felt that he could curl up catlike on the floor and sleep for days. She
must have seen this, because her face brightened—"You've had a long trip," she
said—and she waved him down the corridor from where she had come.
Dreamily, he followed. They passed doorways that opened into dark recesses,
dim halls leading to other wings of the building. This one had the feel of a
dormitory, with spartan chambers and tiled lavatories at both ends. She took
him to the second to last room down the hall, opened the door and paused in

the doorway.

"Here we are," she said, and, without waiting for an answer, grabbed Max by a fold in his shirt and pulled him past her into the chamber. Then she shut the door. In the sudden hush, the patter of her footsteps moved away, grew faint in the distance.

It was dark. He was alone. Max stood motionless until his eyes adjusted. The room was sensible, not fancy in the least, with a firmly made single bed, washbasin in the corner, and white curtains drifting from a slightly open window. So tired now that blue-flame coils and sparkles were firing in his vision, his own little private fireworks show, he went and looked out: Beyond a lonely backyard, up a small hill, a long, flat-roofed building sat among the tallgrass like a ship riding ocean swells. At the bottom of the window, a collection of hollowed-out insect husks—moths, houseflies, bottle flies, and yellow jackets, their casings pale and colorless—lay inside the lip of the sill.

Max undid his pants, and urinated out the window for at least a week.

When he was done, he closed the curtains, slipped off his shirt and pants and climbed into bed. He pulled up the covers—musty, damp-dry smelling; obviously unused for some time—and for the next nine hours he knew nothing else.

EIGHT: THE INITIATES

MAX WOKE TO A stiff rapping on the door. He lunged up, wondering if he'd actually heard it or if it was only in a dream. The room was bright; the curtains sighed again, in and out. Somewhere outside, a tin roof pounded in the wind. But there was nothing else, so he laid back and took a deep breath and dug his knuckles into his eyes.

The knock came again: loud, rapping three times.

"Hold on," Max called, and he got up and struggled into his pants and shirt. He opened the door to find Tom Howland standing there, wearing what looked like the same clothes from yesterday. Max noted this because he too was wearing the same clothes.

"Dr. Stout wants to see you," Tom said. His mouth was flat, almost without lips. It wasn't a mouth from which frivolous things came.

"Oh. Should I get my jacket?"

"Boots." Tom Howland waited, staring at the floor, while Max blearily went back in and stepped into his shoes. They went down the big hall together, the high windows on the western side blazing now with light, and Max guessed it was about four in the afternoon. Still half-asleep, everything seemed to him like it was padded, and faraway. Tom led him to yet another wing of the building—*How many wings were there, anyway?*—toward a small, thin doorway.

"Here," Tom said, "but be quiet."

Puzzled, Max opened the door and slipped in alone. It was a passageway—narrow and dark and so low he had to stoop. He looked back at Tom, receding now as he waited in the light from the hall, and Max realized he was strangely relieved to be getting away from him.

The passage opened like a womb, into a kind of chamber he had seen only in photographs: he stood at the top of a tight, inclined auditorium which branched off into a semi-circle on either side. Fixed wooden chairs gazed down onto the floor below. There, in a recessed hollow, a surgery table held an oversized, anesthetized man, naked from the waist down. He was surrounded by several medical professionals in white and wearing surgical masks, who seemed to be busy working on the man's genitals. It was, Max recognized, an operating theater.

Not sure what to do, or who he was there to see, he went down a few stairs and took a seat near the aisle. Down on the floor, one man and three women surrounded the patient—doctor and nurses, surely—but with their masks they were as anonymous as boxcar bandits. For five minutes or so he sat there, feeling numb and still half-asleep and wondering what he was supposed to make of this odd assembly down on the floor. But then the door to the passageway behind him opened and closed, and a figure slipped silently down into the auditorium and stood where he had just been. It was a young man, perhaps a few years older than Max; he propped himself against the railing and observed the surgery below. Max thought he must have been an Indian, or an Arab; his skin was a light hickory brown, and he was lean and almost dazzlingly handsome, with fine, almost feminine features and a glimmer of shiny, blue-black hair.

When Max's chair creaked, the young man turned to look at him. The young man's dark gaze considered him for an uncomfortable moment, then, alarmingly, he came over to sit in the very next seat. His half-lidded eyes blinked slowly, as though nothing worried him, or even interested him.

"You're Max." The young man said it in a heavy accent: *Youad Mex*. He put out his hand. "Durga." *Doorga*. His skin was dark, but his palm was as pale as Max's own. Max took it.

"You know my name?" He was awake now, and fighting an impulse to shrink away, unsettled that everyone here seemed to know who he was, and yet he knew no one.

The young man didn't answer. He put his feet up on the seats in front of him and nodded down at the operation. "Have you met Stout?"

"Stout?"

"You know what they're doing down there?" Bewildered, Max shook his head. "Glands." Durga made a pair of scissors with his fingers and snipped playfully at his crotch. "Goat glands." *Goot glonz*.

"What are those?"

"Testicles—*goot* testicles. He's implanting them in that man."

"Implanting them?"

Durga's smile almost became a laugh, and Max marveled at how graceful he was, almost angelic. "Implanting is one way to put it. Really, he just puts them in people—in men—and sews them back up. No connectivity, no tissue, no nothing. Just drops them in and *voila!*" He dusted his hands together—*done with this*.

Max was at a loss. He was as perplexed by this young man as he was by the procedure going on down on the floor. "Why do they do that?"

"Vitality, I think. Virility. Fortitude."

"Ah." Max considered this for a moment; there was definitely something odd and unscientific about it. "You know medicine?"

Durga frowned, as if this question had been asked many times before. "No no, nothing like that. Well. My father was a sawbones back in Dharwad. Heart surgeon. So I've seen dissections, amputations, this kind of thing. My father is more better, he would scoff at what Stout is doing. But evidently people pay him well for it. So." Durga put his palms together and closed his knees upon them, as if he were trying to warm them up. "Are you going to be here now? With us?"

"I—I don't know. I'm not sure. How did you know who I was?"

Instead of answering, Durga stood up. "They brought you in," he said. "From where?"

Durga's odd phrasing was a challenge; it took Max an extra beat to figure it out. "Oh, um, Georgia. A—a small town. It's in the South." He worked to clear his head of the cobwebs. "Are you part of the...the Brothers?"

"The Brotherhood of the Aurora," Durga corrected him. "You could say that. Or I will be. You will be, too, if you can manage it."

Max didn't like the sound of that. Manage it? Manage what?

"You look a little chomped," Durga said, seeing the look on his face. "But it'll work out. It's a big group"—*beeg groop*—"and we're only a little part of it. Good things. Great things. You'll be quite proud when you settle in."

Good things. Baffled, Max turned back to the procedure down on the floor. *Great things.*

Durga still stood over him, almost crowding his space. "Has Black Howard arrived?"

Max looked up at him. "I...don't know who that is."

"Black Howard. Our *adyaapak*. He may be the very best diviner in all of America." Durga yawned and rolled his shoulders. "All right. Soon enough. Goodbye, Max from small-town Georgia." He climbed up the stairs, ducked his head, and slipped back through the low doorway.

Max sat for a half hour, watching the team down on the floor work on the patient. The man was fleshy and fat, the bearded jowls of his neck like a loaf of bread held between his chin and chest. Occasionally he would wake and groan, and once he even tried to struggle up into a sitting position, but the nurses pressed him down and pushed an ether mask over his mouth and nose and squeeze-pumped him back into senselessness. A nurse stood by, and when the doctor stepped back, she wiped blood away from the incision at the man's groin with a red-soaked rag. Sweat shined on their foreheads. Occasionally one of them glanced up at Max, including the lead surgeon himself, but they never seemed to hurry anything along; if anything, it was becoming apparent the session wouldn't be over for quite some time. But soon Max started to get restless, and in a quiet fit of mood he decided he'd had enough. He got up and went back through the little doorway.

The building—the clinic or school or whatever it was—seemed oddly unoccupied. The corridor was empty and his footsteps echoed as he wandered aimlessly along. Most of the doors on this wing were closed and locked, but more than once he wandered past an open room with a lone custodian in it—an orderly, maybe, or an attendant, dismantling a desk or sweeping dust from the drapes. They glanced back at him with timid eyes, as if he had caught them doing something they shouldn't. Or as if they were afraid of him.

When he returned to his room, a folded pile of clothing was laying on the unmade bed. Several shirts, pants, socks, undergarments, all soft brown and tan and woodland green. At the basin he gave himself a washcloth bath and changed into his new clothes, which were comfortable but plain. They fit, but were scratchy and reminded him unpleasantly of the Amish folks' cheerless outfits back on the train. He made his bed, and sat on it for a minute or two, staring at the opposite wall and listening to his stomach growl. He wasn't sure of the situation regarding food at Steppeland—whether there was food, whether it was free or if they charged by the meal or the pound, or what. But it had been days since he'd had anything of any substance, and he needed something, and soon.

He had just stepped out of his room when he saw Nurse Agnes approaching from the opposite direction. She was also wearing the same outfit as before—starched cap, white dress over a pinstriped blouse. It was as if she had never slept at all.

"Good evening," she said. "I had one of the orderlies bring you some vestments. Are they acceptable?"

He presented himself for her inspection. "How'd you know my size?"

She didn't answer, but instead said, "Have you eaten?" Max shook his head against the rumble in his stomach, and they went together down the long hallway, Nurse Agnes stepping smooth and quick, as though she knew exactly how many steps it took to get anywhere in this maze of classrooms and empty hallways.

Soon they entered a large room, with rows of rough-hewn tables and chairs scattered across the hardwood floor. A grand fireplace caught Max's eye—it was easily big enough for a normal-sized adult to stand in, its stones black and scorched from countless fires. This was a mess hall, he could see, but empty, like a canteen for soldiers who were all off at war. Dim electric lights gave off a dusty, gilded glow. Everywhere he looked spoke of faded glory, and better, richer times—blurry photos on the walls of formal ranks of men, proud and barrel-chested on the clinic's front steps. Women in long dresses pantomiming frivolously with croquet mallets out on the front lawn. Dusty athletic pennants sagging here and there. Max was surprised to see Durga off in a far corner, with a blonde-haired girl; they both looked distractedly over, but when he nodded in their direction, they only blinked at him and turned back to each other.

Max and Nurse Agnes got their food from the kitchen, from a negro woman, listless and shipwreck skinny, and found a table in the lonely center of the room. With her fork Nurse Agnes speared a steamed asparagus and held it up between them.

"The provisions here are healthy, Max," she said. "Purposefully bland, but quite nutritious. Dr. Stout makes sure of it." Max's own dinner was an overcooked pork loin, new potatoes in a watery dill sauce, steamed green beans and pearl onions. All of it seemed to have been made yesterday and left out overnight; the pork looked as tough and dry as a pencil eraser.

"Now, I understand your introductions this afternoon were cut a bit short," Nurse Agnes said curtly. "So let me do the honors. Dr. Stout has a strong practice. He is a respected man—world-renowned, in fact. Two years ago, he was called to Rangoon to perform his services on Burmese royalty." She flashed a smile, and Max felt her sharp intelligence inspecting him, prodding at him, trying in her way to test his reaction. "He is originally from the south, like you. South Carolina, I think. But he chose Nebraska for its...shall we say, *indulgent* medical laws." She held her hand out flat, palm down, as if it represented the great plains, or maybe its lack of laws and regulatory oversight. "He can practice here, experiment here, with very little federal intervention."

She leaned back. "Now, do you know why you are here? What this place is for?"

Max speared an asparagus of his own, and munched it. He was doing his best to not tilt up the plate and shovel in everything at once. "I have to admit that I don't. Not really."

"Well. Evidently you have proven yourself to be worthy of our company, Max, of this unique community. We have a very unusual mission here. A mission within a mission."

"What kind of mission?"

"Let's just say we have hosted other special young people like yourself, to come here, and study. To be trained in...certain ways of thinking."

"Spiritualism, you mean. Séances."

Nurse Agnes studied his face; she was smiling, but her eyes were serious. He had a feeling his answers weren't as important to her as his questions. "What do you know of séances, Max?"

"Um. I watched one. Recently."

"What was it like?"

"It was—scary. These two girls. They had somehow summoned a...a spirit. At first they thought it was their father who recently passed. Then they were worried it was someone called Mister Splitfoot."

Nurse Agnes put down her fork. "Mister Splitfoot! My goodness! As if someone like that would waste time on mere children! What happened to them, may I ask?"

"I'm not sure. The last I saw, the youngest one was bleeding from her eyes."

Nurse Agnes' stiff smile slipped away. "I'm sorry to hear of that," she said, dabbing at the corners of her mouth with a napkin. "News of real human pain is never pleasant. These things do happen, of course."

Over Nurse Agnes' shoulder, Max could see Durga and the blonde-haired girl in conversation. The girl's eyes were hidden; she was either not listening or listening intently, Max couldn't tell which.

"Now, we've been told you're special," Nurse Agnes was saying. "So special that you were invited to come to us after only knowing the Sylvesters for less than a month."

"*Special*," Max said bleakly, around a mouthful of dry pork. He didn't feel special. The situation in which he'd left Selleford seemed special only in the degree of its distress. "I don't know anything about spiritualism. I've never spoken to the dead."

"But you have participated in some very interesting phenomena."

"A séance. Once."

"But with the Hearst sisters, no less. And Daniel Pepper."

"I saw my stepfather be murdered by something that shouldn't exist."

Nurse Agnes drew in a hiss of breath, as if he had flung his food at her. Immediately Max regretted telling her that. "Yes," she said quietly. "And surely even more." She looked down at her dinner. "All of this underlines the point: You understand what we are doing here?"

"Actually, I don't. I don't understand at all."

She leaned forward and lowered her voice to a proud, confidential whisper: "You are here to study, Max. To learn. To grow as a practitioner of your craft."

"What craft is that?"

"The mastery of the universe. It is not a term we use lightly. Nothing less than the manipulation of the rules of the universe in which we live, for the benefit of all mankind." Her face had taken on a sudden beatific glow. The devotion in her eyes was almost frightening. "There is more to creation than you may have realized. We are blind creatures burrowing our way through the universe. Touching the tactile face of God."

There was a pause as Nurse Agnes settled back into her chair. With his pork finished, Max took a bite of potatoes. These were undercooked, and the sauce was terrible—bland and too thin, and clearly they'd used powdered milk instead of cream. He could feel the powder gritting across the inside of his teeth. When he thought over why he'd been chosen to come to this place, he couldn't come up with any reason other than as a means of simply shunting him away from the intrusive gaze of the Selleford Police Department. He'd shown no aptitude whatsoever, and had never once studied with an occultist, not even an amateur. Only in the last month or so had he become aware that mystical arts were something that existed at all.

Nurse Agnes seemed to see his worry. "Peter Sylvester must have thought very highly of you to bring you here. And the Hearst sisters, of course. They have been very generous to Steppeland, and we value their opinion a great deal. Our mission is nothing less than the betterment of Man and the universal benefit of all of our brothers. It's a big job, Max. It requires a rigorous discipline, in which we challenge our students to become the stellar men and women we know they can be."

Max leaned forward against the table, feeling its edge push into his ribs. It was solid and reassuring, something he desperately needed right about now. "There was a girl back home—she'd been born into it. She knew all about it.

She should have come. I know...very little."

"And yet you were chosen. You were the one." Nurse Agnes said this with a sort of finality, as if the fact that he had been selected was itself proof that his selection was valid.

"This is different. I was in trouble and they wanted me safe. Or wanted themselves safe."

She took a sip from her cup of coffee, and her eyes studied him from over the rim. "We do like to keep our anonymity. It's part of what makes the Brotherhood so effective. But they evidently saw something—Peter Sylvester saw something. And Addie, too." She blinked, her gaze turned inward. "Dear, dear Addie. How is she, by the way? I miss her."

"She's fine. She's good. She was nice to me."

"Addie Sylvester is always lovely. To everyone."

"Look, when I left, it was under great haste. I never got a chance to speak to my family. My mother, our maid, who's really more like a—a..." Max shifted in his chair. "I know they're worried sick about me and where I am. There was, you know...a death."

"Of course."

"I need to know they're safe. Protected. And they need to know the same of me."

Nurse Agnes smiled. "Peter Sylvester has made arrangements. They know about your situation. We certainly don't want you distracted, and so their circumstances have been...remedied."

"They're in the big house?"

"Well. I don't know what this big house is, and I confess that I don't know the precise details. But they are safe, yes. Their situation is stable. You are our highest priority, Max, and thus so are they. This is the same arrangement with the families of all of our students."

"But they need to hear from me. And I need to hear from them."

"Very good. I was about to tell you the very same thing. We want you to be connected. Grounded. It's important that our students stay close with their individual families. In this there is power and security. Any correspondence you may have, just give it to me and I'll make sure it gets passed to them."

Max looked across the room to Durga and the girl again. They were still locked in close conversation. He felt a quick stab of envy at their intimacy and their friendship; they seemed to exist in a world completely separate from his own. "What happens when we're—when I'm done?" he said. "With all of this?"

Nurse Agnes seemed surprised by the question—the vulgarity of saying out loud what usually went unsaid. She folded her napkin, corner to corner, and dropped it on her plate. "Whatever you want to happen. Our students have quietly reasserted themselves back into society. Mediums, spiritualists, trance-talkers. Some have gone on to do...interesting things."

Max thought of the people Peter Sylvester had mentioned: Mme. Z—

"splintering off." *Tchowgosh*, the deadly anarchist. President McKinley and his bullet to the belly. It didn't seem to fit neatly into Nurse Agnes' portrait of a quiet happy academy on the peaceful plains of Nebraska, but he didn't press the point. In the end it didn't matter; he couldn't go home even if he wanted to. Stoppard would put him behind bars. Or see him hanged.

Nurse Agnes cleared her throat and slid her chair back. "All right. I've said enough. I have night duties to attend. If you have any more questions, please, you can find me in the infirmary." She stood and gave him a bow of her head, and gathered her mostly untouched food and utensils, and walked off.

Max sat for a time, a crowd of unanswered questions gabbling in his head. He supposed he had been headed here, to this dreary isolated academy, ever since he had taken the job. Ever since he had stolen that book in the upstairs room at the post office. Ever since he had told Lillian Hearst he wanted to work for her. He chose this life as surely as he had chosen to leave Selleford. But as he looked over at Durga and the blonde-haired girl, he couldn't shake himself free from the dread, not even for a moment, which by this point had settled into his bones like a fever. The private crippling things that had happened to him in Selleford—the abuse, Sig's violent death, the Moorlander and the sudden evaporation of everything he had taken for granted—these were heavy burdens. If he had been lost before, he felt lost now in a terrible new way. But he had thrown in his lot with these strange people, and he needed somehow to make peace with this strange place. Before he could change his mind, he stood quickly, leaving his plate and silverware, and crossed the room back to where Durga and the girl sat and talked. He slid into a seat next to the Indian boy.

They both looked up, surprised. Their discussion, whatever it had been about, came to a halt.

"Hi there," Max said. "Hello."

"Hello, small-town Max," Durga said. Max saw he and the girl glance at each other, and Durga raised his eyebrows at her. She turned away.

"I hope I'm not interrupting anything." The smell of their dinner wafted toward him. He was still hungry.

"But of course you are," Durga said. "Every moment is an interruption of every other moment. What is time but an endless cascade of interruptions, a shadow interposed upon other shadows? But this is as it should be. We were wondering if you would come and say hello."

The girl looked up, wary. Her blonde hair draped across her shoulders, a veil to hide from the world, and there was a brittle quality about her, as though she would break if she wasn't careful with herself. Max was struck again by the steady aura of unease at this weird clinic or hospital or whatever it was; hardly a single soul besides Durga and Nurse Agnes had given him as much as a decent smile. It was starting to feel as if the place was enclosed in some enormous desktop snow-globe—a confined atmosphere of murky intentions and recirculating gloom.

She looked down at the table. "Who are you?" she said finally.

"Max. Max Grahame. I'm new here."

"Are you living here?"

"I...think so. I'm not entirely sure, to be honest."

She looked at Durga and then back at Max, considering him through her curtain of hair. "Why?"

Why? Why what? Why wasn't he sure? It was a good question, one that he couldn't really answer, even for himself. "Hi," he said finally, ignoring the question. He held out his hand, and after a moment's hesitation, the girl took it. Her grip was tiny, and he could feel the bones inside, as fragile as a bird's.

"Sage."

"Where are you from?"

She looked down at the table again. "New York. Upstate, Finger Lakes, Pennsylvania."

"Ah. How long have you been here?"

"At the clinic? Almost a year."

"Do you like it?"

She shrugged. "I don't really judge things on whether I like them or not. If I did, I don't think I would ever do anything at all."

"What are you...uh, studying?"

Sage lifted her gaze, and Max had the strange feeling that he had unintentionally offended her. "What are we studying? What do you mean, what are we studying? We're studying everything."

"I'm sorry, I don't—I'm new here, I'm not sure what that means."

"Clairvoyance. Scrying. Invisibility. Astral projection. Communication with the dead. Automatic writing. Alchemy. Divination." Her words weren't so much expressed as spat at him. She wasn't giving him information, she was pushing him away. "Everything."

Durga seemed to take pity on Max. "What were you discussing with Nurse Agnes?"

"Oh," he said, "not much. I'm still a bit, you know...getting the feel of this odd place."

Durga smiled, *Ah*. His teeth were as perfect as a white picket fence. "Odd. It is a bit, yes. Sometimes I get the feeling that they lack a proper understanding of their own affairs. It is the same with any other academy or institution, I suppose. They present a perfectly capable outward appearance, but when you look closer, things are not quite as they seem."

"Like what?"

"Well. As I said in the operating theatre—the doctor's procedures are, shall we say, less than medically sound. And the facility itself—you may have noticed that things are not exactly bustling with activity. We keep hearing of the group's powerful affiliates, but we see no evidence of them at all."

"Maybe that's just, I don't know. Part of the plan. Keeping things hush hush and all that." Max's voice sounded colorless in the large room, dead and devoid of the air needed to conduct it.

"We were talking about the missing race," Sage broke in.

"What?"

"Sage seems to think that there was a race of ancient, advanced beings," Durga said, as if in wonder he had found himself surrounded by erratic, childlike idiots. "A highly developed people, maybe not even human—living here on the American continent before anyone else."

"Not everywhere," Sage said. "New York." Beneath her cowl of hair, Max saw she was quite pretty, with thin lips underpinning a sharp nose and bright green eyes. In the glow of the lamps, the skin of her face was milky and delicate.

"I think you are talking about your own so-called Indians, my dear," said Durga. "Your Native Americans. Your indigenous people."

Sage answered, some comment or other, but Max had stopped paying attention. Something about the hospital was still bothering him. What Dr. Stout was doing—putting goat testicles into men's bodies—felt weirdly, drastically, unscientific. But then again, so was Sig's Uranithor. So were séances. So was the Moorlander herself. And yet he had witnessed them all with his own eyes. Absolutely nothing at all felt real anymore.

"Max. Where are you staying?" It was Durga.

"Hm? Oh, the dormitory. One of the wings."

"But you're not in with the rest of us. You should be with the initiates."

"I don't know anything about that."

Durga didn't answer; he looked at Max for a long time, gears of sympathy turning behind his eyes. He stood up and grabbed his plate, and Sage's as well.

"Here. Come with us," he said. He took the plates back to the kitchen and put them in a large industrial sink, and motioned for Max to follow him and Sage out a side door. It opened into a tight back hallway, dim and red-bricked.

"So how did you get here?" Max asked Durga as they walked.

"Me? I am from a small town in India, from Karnataka."

"But—but how did you come to be *here*? To this clinic, I mean." There was a door at end of the hallway, and without stopping, the three of them went through it and outside. The night air was thick and loamy, but cool with an early fringe of autumn. The sky was brilliant with stars—much brighter than the ones Max had seen in his little town. All around, the land swelled and dipped; it was hard to tell where the clinic's campus stopped and the wild prairie began. On this side of the building there were hardly any trees, or any other lines of demarcation, just endless oceans of tallgrass and the gentle surging of the slopes.

"Ah yes, my past," Durga said. "All was good for me and boringly normal"—*bordingly nordmal*—"until as a small child I contracted malaria. From that day, I was told something in me changed—I became dreamy, and odd. I don't remember. But when my father took a job with a British hospital in Dharwad, one of the doctors working there met me and happened to read my aura. It was most unusual, he said." Durga smiled at the memory. "The man told my family. They had thought me somewhat dim-witted, I think, but really I was just different. Pensive and quiet. Evidently the man realized I was special, something very rare, and he took me in. Mentored me. I was tutored in the western classics, and mathematics, all the while enjoying a lavish lifestyle at his *haveli*, living with his people in a kind of...what is the word, *communal*? But it was when I showed an affinity for languages and their mystical teachings—a mastery, really, like a savant—that they decide to bring me to the United States."

"Languages? How many do you speak?" They were following a path through the tallgrass. Durga grinned shyly. "How many?"

"Some," he said, reluctant.

"How many is 'some'?"

"Seven." He grinned again: *you asked*. It didn't make Max feel any better.

It was then that he realized they were alone; Sage had stopped just outside the door. They saw her standing back there, a ghost under the soft electric glow of the clinic, flat-footed and frozen with her face arched up to the sky. Durga raised an eyebrow at Max in confidential amusement—*here we go again*—and went back for her. Max followed. He watched as Durga went to her and stood quiet, waiting patiently. Sage didn't react; her eyes were fixed only on the heavens.

"What's happening?" Max whispered.

"Augury. Divination. It comes upon her at odd times."

Sage didn't blink, and hardly breathed. She stared up into the sky, rapturous and lost, as if the constellations were whispering in her ear.

"What do we do now?"

"We wait."

Durga and Max stood silent for several minutes, shifting from foot to foot, staring up at the clinic's windows, at the rolling sea of tallgrass, at a low congregation of trees out on the far horizon. Occasionally the two boys would catch each other's eye, and Max caught fleeting wisps of the Indian's sympathy and good humor.

Finally, Sage took a deep, ragged breath. "*Seven sisters*," she said, her voice not quite her own. "*The Pleiades*."

"What is it?" Durga asked her gently.

"*The seas are rough. The sailors use the seven sisters as guides and now they've run upon the rocks*." A tear formed in her eye, glistening faint in the light. "*They're drowning*."

"*What?*" Max said. Her words alarmed him—he'd never heard such a thing.

Durga took his elbow. "This is a long time ago," he whispered. "It's already happened."

"A boy," Sage was saying, "A boy has stowed away in the hold. Barrels of wine. And water. Water pouring in through a gash in the side." Suddenly she turned to Max, took his hand, imploring him to live the awful experience with her. It was the first time she'd made real eye contact with him, and it was all he could do to not look away. "He's dying. He stowed away and now he's dying before he ever got a chance to live."

She let out a whimper, and dropped his hand. Her eyes went back up to the sky. "His bones lie now on the bed of the Mediterranean. Near Pantelleria. He had a sister. Rosa, who married a man. Who hit her. Who broke her shoulder and she slit his throat in his sleep with a boning knife."

Durga stood listening, fists fidgety in his pockets. The wind gusted through the weeds, and a restless hissing came in response, a million seed heads speaking at once.

"She had a son who also drowned, but not near Pantelleria. This young man drowned in a lake. In a shallow lake." Sage turned to Max again, her eyes glossy with tears. "He never knew love, he never knew a woman's touch. When he died, he was crying out soundlessly for his mother."

She fell into sobs, and Durga moved in to hug her. "Okay, it's okay," he said. Her face was buried in his collarbone. "This was a long time ago, Sage, long, long ago. There is nothing we can do about it now."

The two of them stood for a time, twined together, and in a moment Max saw from the breath hitching in her body that Sage was back with them. The spell was broken.

"Sage?" Durga asked gently. "We were showing Max where we live. Will you come with us?" Still cradled in his arms, her face tucked away, she nodded. With Durga's arm around her, the three of them went off, out of the clinic's light and into the darkness.

They walked wordlessly through the trail in the tallgrass, along the frayed edge of a small creek, to a string of cottages. The cabins reminded Max of workers' housing—all of them flat-roofed and identical, made of bricks once painted white but now weathered to a dull watery grey. Several of them were attached and strung in a line, but others squatted petulantly off by themselves. Durga opened the cabin at the northernmost end and ushered them in.

He struck a match, and lit candles that had been placed upon practically every flat surface in the room. Sage sat on the floor, staring wordlessly into her lap. The smell of incense was strong. When the candles were lit, the room seemed larger and more appealing than Max had expected: oriental rug underfoot, woven silks on the walls, Persian-looking floor pillows and poufs dominating one corner. It looked to Max like something out of *One Thousand and One Nights*—all swirling paisley and mandalas that reminded him of the shimmering, geometric landscapes he saw when he closed and rubbed his eyes. "Have a seat, have a seat," Durga said.

Max sat on the floor next to Sage and looked her over—flushed cheeks, as if she'd been working, skin radiant with a thin sheen of sweat. "You okay?" he asked. She didn't reply, but only lowered her head and quailed back into herself even more.

Durga dragged a pillow opposite them and fell onto it. "Want some water, Sage? Or tea?"

When she didn't answer, Max ventured a question: "What are these places?"

Durga looked around his quaint little home. "At one time these housed some of the clinic's servants. The landscape was slowly reclaiming them, so they let the initiates take over." He pulled at his collar as though he were loosening a tie. "Could be worse."

"What does that mean?"

"When I first came to America, it was California. Morro Bay. They housed me in a fruit-picker's cabin. I'll never forget the stink of rotten oranges. Bitter and sickly sweet. And so this"—he elbowed the brick wall next to him—"trust me, this I can take. Wood stove for the winter, well not too far outside. Outhouse is close. We take baths in the creek. Even in the winter. Even in the snow."

The tapestries, the mandalas, the fierce Ganesha glaring back at him from the opposite wall—they were exotic and alien, but not exactly unfriendly. "You brought all this stuff from India?"

"Sailed on a steamer. Truckloads of gear."

Max turned to Sage, looking for some sign that her mood had improved. There was none. "Is she okay?"

"I will watch her tonight."

"Watch her for what?"

"Sage often travels in the Akasha—in the æther. Without proper care, it is easy to lose one's self. There are stories of people roaming too far and never finding their way back. So I sit with her. Keep her close."

Max stared at the girl, suddenly worried now. "What happens if they don't make it back?"

"Their bodies wither and die. Empty vessels. Seed pods with no seeds."

Max sat quiet, feeling the tension pooling in his bones, as if the spigot of dread in this place had been opened even wider.

"Do you want to pick out a room?" Durga said. "Better to do it before the others arrive."

"There are others?"

"More will come. Sage and I have been wondering when someone would arrive." He opened his hands like a book, showing pale palms. "And now you are here."

As they stood, Max tossed Sage a worried glance. Durga shrugged. "She'll be all right for a moment." The two of them went outside and waded into the tallgrass, toward the rest of the cabins, shadowy mausoleums hunkered among the high weeds. "Sage stays here," Durga said, pointing to the third cabin; aside from that, there were three more, along with two unattached structures drifting off to themselves. "And the rest are for you."

Max nodded at one on the far end. "What about that one?"

"Yes, yes. The girl who lived there was quite interesting. Florence. Maybe she will haunt you."

"She *died?*"

"No, no, nothing like that. She left suddenly last year, some kind of personal thing. But she was adept particularly at speaking to spirits, and angels. The dead." The door was already partially open, and the room inside was as bleak as a cell. In the shadows Max made out a bare, lumpy bed pushed against the wall and a dresser, now almost ruined by weather, with a large, age-speckled mirror and a wooden desk with a chair in the corner.

"Is Sage okay?" Max said. "That was kind of...scary."

"We are used to it. The next day it is like nothing ever happened." In the moonlight Durga looked like a spirit himself—angelic, saintly, only half-real. He stifled a yawn. "All right, Max. I am finished. You'd better get some rest." He sloshed his way through the high weeds, back to his own cabin. When he got there he turned and looked back.

"My stuff's in the clinic," Max sighed. "I have to go back."

Durga shrugged. "*Shubharātri,*" he said, and went inside.

Max glanced at the hospital in the distance. It stood up on a gentle rise, black against the evening, like a once-elegant hotel—mostly abandoned now, with hollowed-out hallways and only a few of its windows lit, like squares of moon-yellow. Even from here he could see most of it was falling into disarray.

NINE: BLACK HOWARD

THE NIGHT WAS BRUTAL. Max spent the early hours shivering in layers, his old dirty clothes pulled over his itchy new ones, huddled into himself on the cabin's bare, musty mattress. Half-remembered nightmares tangled up in his sleep—anxious missions, strange rooms, tense encounters, delayed arrivals. The Moorlander and Sig were in there, somehow impossibly conspiring together, both of them stalking the halls of Sig's house like minotaurs in a maze. The little Burke girl was there, too—her eyeless sockets darkly weeping as she trudged after him, her stuffed giraffe dragging a sloppy trail of blood on the floor behind her. Even his mother made an appearance, though she wasn't his mother at all, not anymore.

In the cold early morning, Max got up and went out to the creek. In the high weeds he found a little private area, out of sight of both the hospital and the cabins, and pissed. Despite the chill he stripped down to his underclothes, preparing to wash the dirt and itch out of his garments in the water, when he saw an odd sight—Tom Howland, with his banker's suit and tie and bowler, stepping high and stork-like toward him through the tallgrass. Weeds slapped at his legs. When he got a little closer, he called out, "Mr. Grahame, Dr. Stout would like to see you."

Max, standing half-naked by the creek, didn't answer. How did Tom know he was out here? He'd told no one. Stolid as ever, Tom surveyed Max's skinny, plucked-goose body. To what conclusion he came, if any at all, Max couldn't say.

"Five minutes. Stables," Tom said, and then he went gingerly back through the tallgrass.

From outside, the barn looked clean and tidy, cleaner practically than any place else in this facility, and when Max got there he paused for a moment to collect himself. He'd always been shy—painfully so, too sensitive and withdrawn to be good at much of anything, other than laying in his bed and losing himself in book after book, that is; he was quite excellent at that. But so far this Steppeland place, this weird clinic or academy or whatever it claimed to be, made him feel small and rudderless and out of place. And people like Durga and Sage and Tom Howland—confounding and unnerving folks whose talents and worldly experience he could only imagine—made it even worse.

There were no horses in the barn, but there were plenty of goats. Twelve or fifteen bucks and nannies clustered just inside the door, stamping and bleating almost in unison. They stared imploringly up at Max with their flat, alien pupils and their huge, flapping ears, somehow adorable and sinister at the same time. And there was a man in the back, outfitted as though for a safari: double-breasted Norfolk jacket, breeches and boots. Max recognized him as the lead physician from the operating theater. He was chubby and had one leg propped up on an empty hayrack, sighting down the barrel of a shotgun. He looked over and pocketed his shells as Max stepped in.

"Ah! Hiya, hiya, good to see ya!" He grinned at Max, his face wide and ruddy. When he smiled, his broad bare cheeks touched and raised the bottoms of his wire-rimmed glasses. "You must be Max! Settlin' in?"

"Yessir, I'm good, sir."

"I'm William Stout." He leaned down to restring the laces of one of his boots. "Fancy a little huntin'? Grouse is busy this time of year. Good way to relax. Good way to talk."

"Yessir. Sounds fine."

Stout waved him through the open door in the back of the barn. They stood outside a moment, looking off into the vastness of the open fields. The sun was lost behind a film of sheet metal clouds, but Stout shielded his eyes and squinted out, like a sea captain over the waves; the swells and slopes seemed to go on forever, the diffused morning light making them look lit from underneath. "The Sand Hills," he said proudly. "Part of the High Plains. You ever been out this way?"

"No, sir." Max had never left north Georgia before a few days ago.

"Nothing'll grow, no crops hardly but wild grasses and weeds. Just a bunch of sand. But the lack of cultivation is what's kept it wild and unspoiled. Lots of birds. Lots of grouse." Stout broke his shotgun open and loaded a shell, and snapped it closed. "Ever seen a grouse? Fascinatin'. Lovely. Tasty, too. But a hard, hard life."

"Why is that?"

"Don't tolerate snow too well—they burrow into it to keep warm. In the spring, heavy rains kill the chicks. Then drought in summer—destroys their food supply and makes it hard for the young ones. And, of course, huntin's got their population scarce."

Max looked over. Stout didn't seem too bothered by this line of reasoning. They started wading out through the tallgrass straight out from the stables, going down into the shallows and up over mounds and hillocks. The weeds and stiff pulling tallgrass made every step deliberate.

At the top of a rise, Stout stopped and gazed out over the savanna. He was like a man in love. "Max, I'm glad you're here," he said, with an exaggerated hint of devilry in his voice. "We can always make room for another talented young'un. Now, we're both busy men, so I'll get right to it. I was told that you had some medical experience. Is this true?"

"What?" Max was perplexed. "No sir."

"Radithor, Ranithor, something like that? Radium tonic, at any rate."

"Oh! Uranithor! Right. My stepfather distributed Uranithor. That's how he made his living."

Stout squinted at him, frowning slightly. "Did he take it himself?"

"My mother did. She was...unwell."

"How's she doin' now?"

The boy felt a wash of shame. "Uh, I don't—honestly, I don't know. I left in a...bit of a hurry." Stout looked at him strangely, so he said, "When I arranged to come here, the circumstances were, uh, not ideal. Sir."

"It's always like that, isn't it?" They started walking again. Up ahead was a great bramble, a thicket of thorns and woody tangles taller than a grown man. They were headed straight for it. "And you had experience at your local post office, yes? Peter Sylvester and all that, yes?"

"Yessir. I did do that."

Stout reached into the breast pocket of his jacket and pulled out a thin silver flask. He uncapped it and took a long swig. "The reason I ask is I'm gonna need some help," he said, and smacked his lips. He took another long swig of the flask, capped it and slipped it with practiced fingers back into his jacket. With the shotgun propped in his arm, he patted himself down, pocket to pocket, until he finally found what he was looking for—a folded piece of paper, a tattered pamphlet of some kind. He passed it to Max. The pamphlet was light blue, with elaborate script reading, *Electricity–Nature's Chief Restorer!* A drawing of lightning bolts bursting from planet Earth filled the middle of the page. Below that, it said, *Self-applicable for the cure of nervous and chronic diseases without medicine. Electricity is life!* It reminded Max of the Uranithor label, with its coils and sparks of energy.

"You heard of the War of the Currents?" Stout said. Max shook his head. "Okay. Edison and Westinghouse had a bit of a disagreement regardin' the use of direct current versus alternating current. There was a battle in the public arena about it. Most people think Westinghouse won, and now they've started executin' criminals and prisoners using a chair, of all things, in which a man may be shocked to death merely by being strapped into it."

Max wasn't sure why Stout was telling him all this, but he tried to look interested anyway.

"The point I'm tryin' to make is, like that war of the currents there are quite a few new remedies on the medical scene now. Many of them hopin' to gain a foothold. A battle between the cures, so to speak. People trying to put us—tryin' to put *me*—out of business. And that's where you come in." He put the butt of the shotgun to his shoulder, sighted down its barrel again. "Ever go plume huntin'?"

"No, sir."

"Well. That's not what we're doing today. Plume huntin's all about keeping the carcass intact—not destroying the feathers, mind you. This is just for fun." They started walking again, and as they pushed through the grass Max looked down and saw the legs of his pants were covered in burrs. "Anyway. Everyone here works for their room and board, whether it's in the kitchen or moppin' hallways. Work's one of our requirements, you know. Idle hands and all that. But with your sense in both the medical field and the postal background, I feel it's a good idea for you and me to work just a bit closer."

"Closer?" This didn't sound very appealing.

"Me and you."

"But I know stables," Max suggested helpfully, "and also I like to cook. I'd probably be better suited to work with the goats or in the kitch—"

"Everybody knows stables and kitchen. Anyone can do that. But not everyone can do glandular. Great boomin' ground up here."

"What?"

"Boomin' ground."

"What is that?"

"The birds are territorial. The males put on a display for the females."

"But at the post office I was never even an assistant," Max said. "That was the Postmaster's wife, Addie. I was more of a...an errand boy."

"Okay. That's good, too. I'll need errands here and there. Point bein', I need you to stay a little closer in and help me weather these tumultuous times. Somebody who's been there, least a little bit. Hang around the office when I need you. And you'll have a way to make your board. So I'm killin' two birds, same shell." He smiled; his glasses raised.

They went down another little rise and lost sight of the big thicket, but when they came up they were almost upon it. They paused and listened; a rustling came from somewhere inside. Max hung back, not saying a word. "So what do you think of that?" Stout whispered.

"What?" It took Max a moment to understand what Stout was asking. "I really do think I could be better used in the kitchen. Cleaning and all that. Washing dishes."

"Don't worry, you'll be witness to some of the most extraordinary things this hospital has to offer. You'll get to see how it happens down in the theater."

Max pulled his eyes from the thicket and looked at Stout. "The theater?"

"No better way to learn. Firsthand and all that." Stout took out his flask again, uncapped it and swigged. He put it away, and both of them turned to the thicket. "You ready?"

"I...I don't know."

Stout pointed his gun into the air and fired it. BOOM! The sound ricocheted off the slopes and the hills and up into the sky. From the thicket came a sudden flutter of activity, and several large birds flapped out, terrified and disoriented. Stout ejected his shell from the gun and loaded it again. He sighted one of the grouse as it made a fatefully poor choice to fly over them—a brown and white-striped fowl the size of a chicken—and he pulled the trigger again. BOOM!

Feathers fluttered and the bird was blown maybe twenty feet away, out of sight and down along the far rolling slope of a hill. Stout said, "Yessiree, all right."

The grouse wasn't dead. As they topped the rise they saw it flopping and flapping against the grass in a messy splay of feathers. They went to it, and stood looking down at its struggles. One of the bird's legs had been completely destroyed, and the other was bent unnaturally back. Its tiny black eye blinked at them. Max was reminded of little Beanie on the train, staring from between the seats.

"Certain amount of pressure in the operatin' chamber, though," Stout said. "Even for blood boy. Things happen fast." The doctor's gaze was hidden by the reflection on his glasses; all Max could see in them was the watercolor wash of clouds on the horizon.

"Blood boy?" Max glumly watched the land around them; it seemed to go on forever. *Blood boy* didn't sound very good at all.

Stout looked down at the flapping bird, and put his foot on its body and held it down. "It's a big job, Max, but I think you'll be better served by workin' a little closer in with me."

He raised the solid wooden stock of his gun and smashed it down upon the bird's head.

⁕

The infirmary was a long, high-ceilinged room with a row of beds along one wall. Max had gone there to find Nurse Agnes, to ask her for a pen and some paper to write a letter to his mother and Ethie. But the only staff there now was a tiny, middle-aged nurse, her skin mottled and shiny, like smoked turkey. She sat at a desk in the front corner and glared at him as he came in, somehow already annoyed, but before he could speak, a patient about half-way down the row of beds started moaning and grasping feebly at the bloody bandages covering his crotch. The nurse jumped up and dashed down to him, and Max stood there, stammering alone. After waiting there for an interminable wordless amount of time, he drifted away.

He went back to the main part of the clinic, thinking he would roam the halls and search the place himself—wing to wing, room to room, if he had to. He moved through vacant hallways, trying to picture what the clinic had looked like in former, grander days. He couldn't. Even in the afternoons, when the sun burned bright through the western windows, there was a pervasive gloom about the place, as if it had been built that way by design. Loneliness seemed baked into its bricks. He came across a few people here and there—orderlies smoking and whispering at the bottom of an empty stairwell; an old, leathery-skinned Lakota cook, as slumped as a human question mark, headed glumly into the mess hall—but his search only turned up more empty classrooms, more custodial closets, more dark offices lined with bare bookshelves and stained drapes.

Finally, on the second floor of the north wing he came upon a smaller, windowless area, like a hallway that went nowhere, and inside an old desk there was a pen and a rumpled stack of stationery. The paper was yellowed and had a circular stamp in the top right-hand corner of each page that read *Republica Argentina 5 Centavos* around the circle's rim. The pen was an eyedropper design, and Max unscrewed it to miraculously find the barrel almost a third full of rich, glistening, wondrously black ink. With his heart banging in his ears—he had no idea what to say, but he felt the need to say it anyway—he knelt down and filled the nib and, in the light spilling in from the corridor, wrote a letter to his family.

Dear Mother and Ethie, he said in his familiar little blocky scrawl, *I am happy to write to you and say hello to you. How are you? How is Selleford? Any news? I am fine. Though I am probably not supposed to tell you this, I am at a very well-known glandular clinic in central Nebraska, where I am learning all kinds of things. We are busy here, which is good, because I like to be busy, ha ha.*

He chewed the dull end of the pen, which someone else, long ago, had already chewed. Was it okay that he mentioned Nebraska? The worry over his disappearance would have pushed his mother even closer to the edge of sanity, if that was possible. No doubt Ethie would have both hands full just keeping her together. Max lowered his forehead to the desk; a sadness came over him, sudden as a summer squall, and he felt himself flush with guilt. There was no real way to address the pain of his decision to leave them, to come here and start a new life. He had abandoned them, as surely as if he had gone west to become a cowboy or gotten lost inside an opium addiction in some sweltering coastal city. They were alone now, because of him. The man of the house had run away.

Feeling more hopeless than ever, he lifted up, and put pen to paper.

I am sorry for...

He stopped again, staring at the scrawl of words on the paper. What was he sorry for? He was sorry, yes. He was terribly sorry. For all of it, for every goddamn thing.

He wrote, *everything that came about. I miss you. Life is fine here, there is a horse barn but used mainly for goats. A row of cabins which I picked out my very own from. I have been asked to help the doctor in his glandular operations, performed in an operating theater like you see in books. I am learning a lot. Everyone is very nice. The plains are flat and endless and the sky goes on forever and the food is nutritious and tasty. I will write again as soon as I can. Love to you both, yrs, Max.*

A shadow fell over him then, and he looked up to see the tall silhouette of Nurse Agnes standing in the doorway. "Max?" she said. "What are you doing here?"

He was weirdly reluctant to tell her, but did anyway: "Writing a letter."

"I've been looking for you."

He capped the pen. "I was looking for you, too."

"Will you meet Tom Howland out on the front steps?"

He hesitated. There was something he didn't like about Tom Howland. Something sort of...off. "Of course," he said, after a moment. "Why?"

"You and he are going to pick up Black Howard."

From out in the sea of tallgrass came the chorus of autumn crickets, an irregular buzzing with pulses of higher-pitched trills and clicking and purring that came and went behind it. Max waited up on the front stone steps, listening to the clatter, trying to pick out where it came from, but it was coming from everywhere. The bugs were all hidden in the grass, and there was not a single person in sight, not a single movement: Steppeland was as still as a watercolor.

Earlier, Nurse Agnes had taken him back to the infirmary and given him a stack of envelopes. She reminded him to properly direct his letters, but to not be too specific about the return address. "We are still trying to be a little, well, *sly* about the young people here. It's not for everyone to know, you understand." Max told her he did, and she said he could leave them in her outbox on her desk—a little rusty wire tray, the contents of which got emptied and processed at least three times a week.

Now Max heard the buckboard wagon coming around the south edge of the building, and looked up to see Tom Howland sitting high in the jump seat, pulled by a muscular brown Shire. Tom slowed the cart in the circular driveway, just long enough for Max to pull himself up. Then he hitched the reins and they took off.

Soon they were back on the roads that had carried them that long, surreal night, except now it was daytime and Max could get a better sense of the prairie. The dirt road cut a mostly straight line through, and as it rose and fell from the undulating hills, the grass shaded from pale green to honey blonde. The spindled tips of the spikelets glowed as if some careful, celestial painter had highlighted every one.

Tom Howland was as inexpressive as ever. Max worked up his courage to press him a bit, see what he could get out of him. "We're going to the train station?" Tom sat without a word, lips pursed as if he was deep in thought. "Why did you want me to come?"

After a long pause, Tom said, "I didn't."

Max decided to try another approach. "How long have you worked with Dr. Stout?" Tom didn't answer. He stared at the road ahead, the lip of his hat raked low over his eyes. "Those glandular operations—do you help out? Do those things actually work?"

Tom stayed quiet. When he shifted his feet, his shoes caught Max's eye. They were clean and fancy, more what a city gallant would wear out on the town, rather than a tight-lipped tough guy on the windy plains of rural Nebraska. But there was something even odder about them, and Max realized with almost physical start that Tom was wearing them on the wrong feet.

More unsettled than ever now, the boy sat back and gave himself over to the silence. For the next several hours he only looked out at the rolling flatlands and the endless sky as they bounced their way into town.

It was early afternoon by the time they reached the train station. Children chased each other, ladies in hats and parasols flitted about in the sun. Tom Howland banked the wagon and he and Max went wordlessly inside. Tom found a place on the polished bench and sat motionless, staring straight ahead at the opposite wall; Max paced and went back outside to look around and kick gravel toward the empty tracks. Finally, after more than an hour, a far-off whistle fluted from the east. Everyone filed outside and leaned in to watch the train appear on the horizon, as if their leaning could bring it quicker. Kids clapped and hooted, wives beamed and fluffed their hair, and soon the train pulled in and drifted to a noisy, steamy stop. Even Max was caught up in the thrill, curious and a little nervous to meet this Black Howard fellow. All he could think about was what Durga had said: *He may be the very best diviner in all of America.*

A stream of people poured down from inside the train, and the crowd scanned each new face appearing from inside the cab: gristled farmers' wives, lanky ranch hands, an occasional oily, overfed businessman or two. Then, toward the back of the line, a middle-aged black man appeared, a gentleman bachelor wearing a city dandy's hat and a bright blue scarf and carrying a gilt-handled cane. He hopped down to the platform and stood scanning the crowd. He looked like a college professor from some East Coast Ivy League school; he was a big fellow, broad-chested and tall, the skin of his face like creamed coffee, and wrapped by an open, agreeable air. Prominent laugh lines were carved around his mouth and eyes. The lenses of his glasses were so clear Max thought he could put his finger right through them.

The man spotted Tom Howland and broke into a grin. "Tom!" he called. "Tommy-Tom!" He dropped his bags and took the quiet man in a big bear hug. Tom remained as expressionless as ever, but he did allow himself to be embraced. Max searched for signs of affection in Tom's face, or any sense of a shared past between them. There was nothing.

The black man turned to Max. His gaze was instantly—bracingly—astonishing. In his eyes there were worlds: unexpected vistas, mosaics, violent floods; ravines and combes, night stars, riverbeds, lynchings, fuckings; alleyways, skylines, knotted medinas, caravans and sloping graveyards; the S-curve of a naked woman's hips.

Stunned, Max took a step back.

"Who's this young buck?" Black Howard said cheerfully.

For a moment, Max couldn't speak. "I'm...Max Grahame, sir."

"Sir? *Sir!* I like you, son! Keep it up!" He turned to Tom and laughed, and Max saw the glint of gold in his mouth. The tall man rolled his shoulders, cricked his neck. "Goddamn, that was a long trip! You hungry? Who's hungry? Let's get some scoff!"

When they'd retrieved his bags, Black Howard slung them handily into the back of the wagon. "How 'bout one of them places over there, boys," he said, and pointed his chin toward the low scattered buildings. Presumably there was a restaurant there. "My treat." He gave Max a jaunty wink.

Indeed there was a café, a place near the far end called Joe Miller Joe's. Inside, it was rough-hewn and smelled of paraffin wax, but mostly it was shadows; a single group of old men, six or seven of them, roosted around a cluster of tables near the door. They were chatting over cups of coffee, and a hush fell as the three came in and took a seat in the corner. Across the room, behind the bar, was a barman—Joe Miller Joe, maybe. He was turned away, but watched the newcomers in the mirror with visible concern. For a moment Max was confused, but then he realized, of course—Black Howard.

Joe Miller Joe came over slowly, reluctantly, as if marching in a funeral procession. He was dressed in smeared kitchen whites, bottom-heavy with a bald, lightbulb head and mustache plucked so thinly it seemed drawn on. His forehead was notched with worry lines. He glanced at Tom Howland and Max, but winced visibly at Black Howard. "I'll serve you boys," he said. "But not him."

"We are together," said Tom in his flat voice.

"Mister," the man said, restlessness in his voice, swiping his fingers against his apron. "It ain't me. I got no problems with nobody. I love ev'body. But I feed this negro, ain't nobody gonna come in here no more."

With a squeak of his chair, Black Howard stood up, causing Joe Miller Joe to skip back a step. But the tall black man only dug in his hip pocket for a slim wallet. He pulled out and slapped down an impressive fold of money. "What about if I pay twice't?" he said.

The group near the door had taken notice. If the place was quiet before, Max could now hear the creak of their chairs. Joe Miller Joe stared at the money, fingers still going. He looked over at the men, and down at the folded cash. But then he said, "I ain't got nothing 'gainst you, boy. I got no problem with your breed. But I'd be hard pressed—"

"Thrice't, then," Black Howard said, sounding defeated, like a poker player who'd been outmatched fair and square. "Dammit! Just a coffee and a water and a chicken fried steak's all I want. A biscuit if you got one gettin' stale in the back. And whatever these boys want."

Joe Miller Joe looked at the money again, his lips pressed tight. "Three times the bill? For ev'body?" Black Howard sat down. Joe took a deep breath, and pushed it out. "Okay. Whaddaya want?"

Black Howard grinned and looked at Max and Tom and cocked his thumb at the owner. "Hoo-whee, this here man's a genu-wine phil-an-thrope. You boys order anything you want—and I do mean, anything! Eat up! Let's give this ben-

evolent hum-ani-tarian some goddamn *bidness!*"

So Tom and Max ordered. A bowl of oatmeal, three eggs, bacon, sausage, toast, ice cold milk, and two blackberry muffins for the boy; boiled sweetbreads, beefsteak pie and calf liver with ham and eggs, hold the toast, for Tom. Black Howard chose his own meal—chicken fried steak, a stuffed tomato salad and caraway seed biscuits—and while they ate he kept them entertained with a scattered and lively range of conversation: where to get the best tailored suits in Baltimore, the breeding habits of stage hares, which islands off the coast of South Carolina were the true home of a curious people he alternately called the *Geechee* and the *Gullah*. The complicated role one Chicago gin mill—Mackie's, on Armitage Avenue; here Black Howard crooned a bit, his arms conducting silent music—played in the life and culture of the nation's working class. The oysters from Baltimore's Inner Harbor, crispy and light and buttery enough to make you cry. Even Gainesville, Georgia—back to the Geechee again—where he'd romped with the ladies in their ring-shout dances. Max ate, charmed and fascinated; his own food was good and fresh, if a little greasy, but it was the first proper meal he'd had in over a week.

Finally Black Howard wiped his mouth and sat back from the table. His belly pushed at the buttons of his vest. He drained his coffee and then his water, and tossed his napkin on his plate. "*Haw*," he said, checking his teeth in the reflective surface of a clean steak knife, "you boys ready?" He waved the owner over. "We're ready, boss."

Joe Miller Joe tallied it all up, then paused, frowning at Black Howard under his lightbulb head. "Times three. Just like you said."

"*Yessuh*," Black Howard affirmed. It came to almost eleven dollars, quite a bit of money, more than Max carried in a month's wage at the post office. But the magician paid for it without hesitation, slapping the bills on the table with a theatrical flair. "You got me, boss. Count it to make sure I did okay, you know how us black folk get. And plan on me next time, too!" He put on his hat and tipped it. "Thank you, suh."

Outside, the sky had become a low rippled sheet of grey, and the afternoon air brought hints of the chilly night to come. They got onto the wagon, Tom Howland and Black Howard in the front, while Max found a place in the buckboard among the luggage, and started trundling their way back to the hospital.

They were silent for a time. Then Max said, "Does that happen a lot?"

Black Howard turned to him and shrugged. "More than you know, buddy boy, more than you know." He held up his right hand so Max could see it, and with a sudden flip, a wad of bills appeared—all of them ten dollar notes, with a bison on the front, fanned out like a deck of cards. With a quick twist of his hand the money became simple decorative paper, verbena purple and hydrangea green. Then another twist—back to money.

"It ain't good for nothin' no how, that cash," he said, "'cept maybe to clean your quim. Gonna turn back to toilet paper any minute now." With a satisfied grunt he tossed the bills in the air, and they went high above the wagon and billowed down as the carriage passed. Behind them, Max saw a bright scattering of colored paper in the road.

There was a low, lumbering, surprising sound then, and Max looked over to see Tom Howland laughing. Black Howard started laughing, too, a joyful braying that seemed out of place in the stark landscape all around. And Max laughed, too: Their bellies full, their thirst quenched, the three of them laughed and laughed as they bounced their way back to Steppeland.

TEN: THE PLEASURE OF THEM WHO LONG TO CROSS THE HORIZON

"MEET ME AT THE lake," Black Howard said. Tom Howland was pulling the wagon around the circular drive in front of the clinic. The big man turned around, elbow over the seat, addressing Max. "'Bout an hour?"

Max nodded, unsure but willing. He watched Black Howard hop down, snatch up his bags, and take the stairs three at a time up into the hospital. By now he had learned not to expect much from Tom Howland, so he jumped down without a word while the other man waited. He stood and watched the Shire rattle the buckboard around the edge of the building.

With an hour to kill, he took a stroll around the estate, exploring the eastern side of the clinic. There wasn't much to see. That side of the facility was flanked by the endless ocean of tallgrass, the lake with the copse of trees beyond it, and that was pretty much it: nothing for miles but the billowing hills and the pressing-down sky. Here and there the late sun tried to poke through as the clouds broke up.

But the lake was lovely, luminous in the glow of early evening. It was formed roughly in the pear-shape of a guitar or a cello, with a taper squeezing the middle into two bulging ends. From the promontory, the closest opposite bank lay a hundred yards away, where a grove of maple and hickory trees crowded along the far side. Cattails waved from marshy banks, and the water pleated gently as the breeze drifted through shivering leaves. Max knelt and brushed his fingertips in the cool water and watched the fleet of evening clouds sail in over the trees.

Behind him there was a voice. "How ya doin', boy?" Max turned to see Black Howard sitting on the old weathered table on the bank. He hadn't heard the man come up. "Relax, sonny, we're in this together. I ain't tryin' to git no one and no one's tryin' to git me. Come here." Max stood and went over as Black Howard dug in the breast pocket of his jacket, and he pulled out a hand-rolled cheroot and a box of matches. "Grahame, right? Horrible with names. I know lots o' everything, but how to remember names ain't nothin' I ever figured out." He took a moment to light his cigar, and flung the match out into the wet weeds of the lake. "What is that? German?"

"Grahame? I think it's Irish. Or Scottish."

"Well, tell me, Scotty. What kinda things you here to learn?"

Surprised by the suddenness and also the depth of the question, Max didn't have an answer; he could only stare back.

"You honestly not sure, or are you one of them 'I'll know it when I get there' kids?"

Max could only feel how the crazy jumble of this place was tying his stomach in knots. "Uh. I think I'm the second kind."

"Well then, we're both in the right place. Them kinds is my favorite." Black Howard pushed his hands into the pockets of his blazer. "Now tell me what you did to get yourself on the run."

Max took a breath. Could he trust this man? He wasn't sure he could tell it all again. By now the horrible memories had taken on a kind of storybook feel, like he had read about it or dreamed it. That ruined smile. The chunk of chewed flesh on the floor. The gleam of the gun in Stoppard's shoulder holster. Max's heart banged in his ears and his jaw and all the way down to the tips of his fingers. He hoped the fear and shame of having made the wrong choice to come here didn't show on his face.

— *You were right*, said a voice in Max's head. *You did the right thing.*

Max blinked, confused; it had sounded like the wind.

— *And I will protect you as I protect all of my ward. I give you my vow.*

Black Howard smiled at him, and inside his grin a gold tooth caught the fading light. He hadn't said a word.

"Come walk with me," he said, his voice dense against the silence. He got off the table and put an arm around the boy's shoulders and guided him along the muddy bank, toward the trees on the far side of the water. With Black Howard at his side, Max felt suddenly—almost peculiarly—safe. Safer than he had in months, and certainly since he had unleashed the strange and terrible forces in his own life by stealing that weird book and by following the urges it had raised in him. There was something unknowable about Black Howard, something dangerous and deadly competent, but there was a sheltering quality in him, too. Maybe that's why, when they stepped through the threshold of trees, the high canopy of leaves overhead just beginning to darken with the rising nightfall, Max found himself telling everything, his story spilling out of him as plainly as water from an overturned jug. He told it all—Sig, his mother, Peter and Addie Sylvester; the book and Daniel Pepper and the Hearst sisters and the séance and the ceremony that Sig interrupted. The Moorlander, Sig's awful death; and then the cops, with their charge that Max himself was to blame, even if he wasn't. The forest was larger than it looked—as they walked the underbrush fell away and the sanctum grew, along with the autumnal scent of life squirming and moving and changing. Telling his story, Max became aware of the energy pulsing around him in a thousand different ways—the great upswell and downswell of being and breath: respiration, transpiration, expiration. He felt himself becoming part of it, too.

Through the trees up ahead, there was a flash of deep red and bedsheet white. Stripes, giddy and bright, like a circus tent. They stepped out of the woods to see a pavilion, startlingly large, set into a still-sunny glade. The trees surrounding it were tall and pillar-straight, with green grass underneath, reminding Max of an illustration he used to study in his encyclopedia—a ruined, roofless Benedictine abbey, the gothic columns rising from a jarringly tame carpet of soft grass. From the pavilion's crest a triangular flag flapped merrily, and the bright colors glowed in the late sun. Questions sparked in Max's mind—who put this thing up out here? Had it been here all along? Black Howard lifted the flap for them to enter. "Step right in," he said with a grin.

Inside it was murky, everything tinted red from the light. Byzantine patterns were painted along the interior canvas walls, with trunks and armoires and even chairs around the room draped with green and gold tapestries. Musical instruments hung from the posts—scarred banjos, ragged parlor guitars, snare drums, trumpets, and tambourines. At the front of the room, up on a Persian rug-covered riser, was a large rococo chair which could only be called a throne. Faded desert landscapes with palm trees and ziggurats were embroidered onto the cushions and the padded headrest. Muscular wooden arms curved out and ended in a flourish of what looked like lion's paws. Black Howard guided the boy up there, and, to his surprise, sat him down.

"How does it feel?"

Max held his breath. He was dwarfed by its size, and like a child his feet barely touched the floor. But it was comfortable, the way it made his body want to regally mold itself and look down upon everything around him, as if he were perched high on a camel's back or in an elephant howdah. A person could sit there for hours. All day, really. Maybe a lifetime.

"It's odd," he said, admiring the worn wood. "But interesting." He put both hands on the arms of the chair, tasting its power. It was hard not to feel special sitting in this.

"All righty, now get up and get out," Black Howard said. "This one's mine. Maybe you'll get your own someday."

Max scooted out and went over to a fancy padded footstool, while the black man perched himself cross-legged in the big seat. Instantly, it was as if he had been born there.

"Now, listen on this," Black Howard said. "You gave me the gift of your story, so I'm gonna give you the gift of mine. Man to man. At least part of it— who I am, and why I'm here with you." He dug in his breast pocket for matches again, and lit what was left of his cigar. The smoke ribboned lazily through the fading slants of red and white light. "Now. I was born in Virginny, and came to learn how to read minds and ward off spirits—tricks of the *Sangoma*, them old Zulu witch doctors. My grandmother's father taught her, and she taught me. My mother and father was dead by that time, so it was just me and her, and there weren't nobody to stop her. In the next two years she gave me everything she knew."

He sat back, coughed sharply into his fist and reached down for a glass of water on the riser that hadn't been there a moment before. He held up the water like he was proposing a toast. "Left home at fourteen. Then I was touring the regional—card tricks, stage tricks, parlor games, spirit mediums, psychic readings, that whole kit and caboodle. Many adventures. Everybody loved me—still do." He smiled at the memories. "I ran the Chitlin' Circuit in the south and the Sawdust Trail out west. Then St. Louis, Jersey, Chicago, Philly, Harlem. I go here and I go there, circlin' back around every seven years. Got my props, got my toys. For the payin' folks sometimes I die and get buried and get my way free and come up in some skinchy cemetery on the outskirts of a town I ain't never been to. And I ain't t'only one doing this, neither—there's plenty of others. Prince Dante, Trickyboy Lawrence, Creole Mahatma. But everybody think I'm like all the rest—a voodoo charlatan. An illusionist. Cep'n there's one thing, Scotty boy."

Black Howard paused, then leaned forward and put his palm on his knee and cocked his elbow. He fixed Max with one cavalier eye, his face half-turned away as if he were posing for a publicity poster. "They's faking it. And I ain't."

He let that hang in the air. "I believe you," Max said finally. And he did.

"*Never forever*," the magician said, and leaned back into the chair, as if some unspoken voice had accused him of lying. Water sloshed from his glass. "Listen to me: *I am the real thing, boy.* None of them others got what I got."

"What...do you have?"

"*Tamkarra*, Max. *Azemtaw.* Miracles. They call me The Doctor. Want me to be a healer, like some South African bone-in-your-nose *inyanga*. But that ain't it. It's *tamkarra*, from the great deserts of the north." He giggled suddenly, and through his teeth Max saw the pinkish wedge of his tongue. "One of my grandma's uncles had it, too. It was born in the Siwi Oasis, Ammonium, the Field of Trees. An ancient empire stretching from Egypt to Morocco, a thousand languages and dialects. The Cult of the Dead. Books by cartographers and gravediggers. *The Book of Journeys Into Faraway Lands*, or *The Pleasure of Them Who Long to Cross the Horizon*. That's me, young man." Black Howard turned his face to the side again, and stared at the boy with that same wild, clear eye. "And that's you, too. That's why you took that book. You had it burnin' inside you and didn't even know it."

Max felt a thrill dart through him. The big man went on. "We worship the air," he said, "and the moon and the sun. *Baal Hammon.* Isis and Set. Osiris and Tanit. The Ram."

To Max, these names were vaguely familiar, mainly from reading *The Worm at the Heart*, with all of its lesser gods and goddesses. No doubt that book was now in the possession of the Selleford police. "How did you come to be here?" he said.

Black Howard set the glass down on the floor—he had yet to take a sip—and righted himself slowly. He laced his long fingers together in his lap. "That's a tale for some other time," he said. "A tale for a cold night. Complicated, half-remembered, half-forgotten. *Intentionally* half-forgotten." He looked suddenly over into the corner, as if a voice had called him. "Let's just say this—in the end they offered me a deal. They asked me to instruct, to *deliver*—to guide folks who

also got the *tamkarra*, to show them how to let it come out. It's like any talent—
you find it, you work it, you feed it. Like a dog. You let it sleep in your bed, you
share your food. You do that, it'll be your friend and serve you any way you
want."

Max laughed, surprised at how easy it sounded.

"So here we are," Black Howard said. "Teacher and student, student and
teacher. But which one's which? I know you's had a hard time, Max. But then
again, we's all had a hard time. I could tell you stories, things that would keep
you up at night, things that once you heard 'em, you wouldn't never look at
nobody the same way again." Max nodded vaguely. He was close to that point
already. "The point is, you're not alone. You're special, *but you're not alone*.
You're gonna rise above that hurt and you're gonna give people somethin' they
ain't *never* goddamn seen before. You hear me?"

Max hugged his knees. He had heard.

"All right. I been gabbin' plenty." Black Howard grabbed the arms of his
chair and pushed himself up. Max stood with him. "First thing tomorrow
morning, I want you out here—you and them others. We gonna do some
learnin'. You got the *tamkarra*—it's inside of you, Mac, curled up in there like
some kinda parasite worm." *The worm at the heart*, Max heard the faraway voice
say. "If you don't get it outta you, it's gonna eat you up from inside your guts."

But there was a persistent thought tugging at him. The other young people,
Durga and Sage, seemed so much more talented, had much more—what was it?
Tamkarra?—than he did. And Harriet. This place had been meant for her, until
he had snatched it away. The simple fact of his presence at Steppeland made
him nervous; he was here with these strange and gifted people, and she was
not.

Black Howard put his arm around the boy and looked him in the eye. Even
in his shame, Max couldn't look away. "They was right about you, Max, I
promise," the big man said, his voice gentle. "So you make sure you give 'em
everything you got."

Max nodded gravely, and started away from the riser and the big chair.

"Hey, sonny boy," Black Howard said. "You goin' the wrong way." Max was
headed toward the flap that led outside and back through the trees, but the
magician nodded toward the far corner of the pavilion, where a small wooden
door was set. Max hadn't noticed it before. He went to it; the knob was dull
and scarred, as if it had come from a much older structure, a barn or an
outhouse. He looked back at Black Howard, who leaned against one of the
poles, arms crossed in the striped sunlight, watching and smiling.

He went through the door, and stepped immediately into one of the
hallways of the clinic: it was the northern wing. Not a soul around. The sudden
quiet, the stillness of the air, made him dizzy. The sun had gone down; it was
full night now, and electric lights glowed all along the hallway. Closed doors
slanted away into shadow. Max turned back, but the door behind him had

already shut. It looked exactly like every other door in the hall. He tried the knob, but it was locked.

Outside, the air was heavy and chill. It was only going to get worse during the night, but Max still hadn't gotten a chance to find any bedclothes for his bed, and right now he couldn't muster the energy. So in his cottage he huddled on the bare mattress in his layers of clothes, feeling—despite Black Howard's words of encouragement—a swarm of worries and fears flitting like angry wasps above his bed. Closing his eyes didn't seem to make it any better. Max curled into himself and tried to will it away.

The next thing he knew, he opened his eyes. It was still dark. The collar of his jacket was pulled up like a blanket and his breath fogged out into the night air.

Someone was sitting at the foot of his bed.

It was hard to see in the darkness, but there was enough moonlight to make out who it was. A young man, maybe 25 years old or so, thin as a colt, with a blackish knobby head that seemed to want to grow a dense thicket of hair but was instead shorn close. His knuckleface was bony and big, as if he'd been jailed and kept hungry for a long time. Slits of eyes and a root of a nose. Bare feet poking out from ripped pant legs, ending in oversized muddy toes, and his shirt was several sizes too small, his shoulders bulging out of it like a rugged Nebraska farmhand who'd snatched some little girl's dress from a clothesline and slipped it on for a laugh. Max watched, not frightened or alarmed. At first he thought it may have been one of the previous tenant's ghosts—Florence, or whatever her name was—some phantom-echo memory from her stay in the cabin. He had a strange feeling he had seen the young man before, but he couldn't remember where.

"Hello?" he said tentatively.

The young man's smile got bigger, and Max saw he was missing one of his front teeth. It made him look like an overgrown child. "Hey there," the young man said, his voice hoarse and heavily accented. *Hay thayer.*

"Hey. Are you one of the...new people?"

This caused the young man to laugh, a looping, loping sound that was part hilarity, part insanity. "Thass a good one," he said, eyebrows raised in a smirk. "You're a real funny boy, you are."

If Max hadn't been half-asleep, maybe he would have—should have—been terrified. He knew it wasn't a nightmare, there was too much ragged clarity for that. But as it was, all he could muster was a mild, benumbed alarm. "Are you with Black Howard?" he said.

"That coon? Hell *naw*! That idjit wouldn't loan me a cent even if he had it—which he *don't*!" The young man's pupils lost their moorings and drifted slightly apart in the white jelly of his eyes. He leaned toward Max, his breath warm and sweet. "Naw, I'm here to see *you!*"

Max almost pushed him away before the young man could put his face in his own. But he didn't—something told him that touching the man would have been a terrible mistake. Instead he scrambled up and backed away toward the wall. "What do you want?" he said, scared now, his shoulders flat against the brick behind him.

The young man settled back. His tongue probed thoughtfully at the gap in his teeth. Max could hear it squinch back and forth.

"You just woke up," the man said. "Woke up to the ways of the world!" *Wer-uhld!* "You better be careful, Maximilian Grahame!"

"Be careful? Why?"

"There's things out there—*things in here,*" and he tapped his temple with a dirty finger, "that don't act nice't. Thems ain't your friends. Thems don't have your bestest prosperity in their hearts."

"Who are you?"

"I ain't your friend, neither. Matter of fact, *I could just eat—you—UP!*" He leaned into Max again, his mouth square and huge, his breath balmy, sickeningly sweet, the smell of rancid fish and hay gone moldy after too much rain. A cold wash of fear flushed through Max's body, from his heart down his gut; he felt his bladder trying to go.

"You—wouldn't do that." Max's breath was starting to come in hitches. "That's just a—" He stopped, not sure what to say, or if he should say anything at all.

"Well, I ain't like them, that's fer sure," the young man said. His voice was like a moan. "I'm *worser.* And I'm watching *you,* Maximilian Grahame!"

Then, like a snake charmer, the young man grew still and his gaze held Max's own. For an incomprehensibly long time—it might have been seconds, or minutes, Max couldn't say—their eyes never left the other. Max knew his night visitor would do as he liked, so he didn't try to make the situation any worse or any better—he wasn't sure which was which, anyhow—and he was lost, beyond lost, he was in uncharted territory. The awful stories he had read in books—the Poe and the Verne and the Wells—were coming true, were peeling themselves from the pages and coming after him now. Max kept thinking, *Don't move, don't make a sound, don't make him mad.*

But then something changed—maybe the moon went behind a cloud, or the wind picked up; whatever it was, something in the man adjusted, slipped, fell into place. He nodded at Max, and stood up. The bed didn't rise—his weight had never caused it to sink.

"I'm watching you!" the man moaned. "I surely am! You better watch for *me,* too!" He let out another loopy giggle, and dove suddenly at the dirty frame of the old oval mirror. Max flinched, expecting the glass and wood to shatter, to splinter, but nothing happened. The young man passed cleanly through it—or, rather, into it. As if in water he seemed to disappear to the degree that he went in.

In less than a second, he was gone.

The room was still again; except for the disturbed motes that drifted and tossed in the air, it was as if he had never been there at all.

Then Max remembered where he had seen the young man before. He had been the young girls' attendant at the Daniel Pepper séance. The companion traveling with poor, beleaguered Jocelyn and Marie.

Max felt his stomach tilt and he leaned up and vomited over the side of the bed. Chunky liquid spattered across the floor and under the legs of the desk. When he was done, he wiped his mouth and tasted bile, and he put his face on the cool mattress and tried to do nothing, to think of nothing but breathing in and out.

From the corner of his eye he caught movement.

And there he was again, the young man, now in the darkness outside the dirty window. But it was the window in the mirror. He was grinning. When he saw that he had Max's attention, his maniac smile grew wider. Max turned and looked out at the window, the actual window, but it was empty.

Through the reflected windowpane the man pointed at him with a grimy middle finger. But then the man turned, and with a spasmodic glee he loped off into the mirrored sea of tallgrass. In a moment he was gone. His laughter rolled away in the darkness.

Max laid back, his breath wheezing raggedly in and out of his chest; he was trembling. Outside the window, off in the distance of the vast Sand Hills, came the burbling call of a male grouse looking for a mate.

And that was how he met Mister Splitfoot.

ELEVEN: INDOCILIS PRIVATA LOQUI

"WHAT'S WRONG WITH YOU, boy?" Black Howard said. Max had just come into the pavilion, his face ruddy, sweat dripping, a razed look in his eyes.

He'd a hard time in the clinic finding the door back into the glade beyond the lake. The sudden appearance of Mister Splitfoot had unsettled him deeply, had unraveled any confidence he'd managed to assemble at this place, and he'd spent a sleepless, heart-pounding night staring at that old mirror and seeing faces in the dark window; every birdcall caused him to start, every gust of wind was another worried glance. When morning came like the end of a bad dream, Max went up to the clinic, hoping the exhaustion and stress didn't show on his face. It was the first official day of his new education.

He tried several doors along that north wing more than once, including the one he was sure he'd come out from—seventh door down, on the right—but they were all either locked or opened into an empty office or classroom. So he decided to find the pavilion the old-fashioned way—by hiking out to it. But the copse of trees beyond the lake was unfamiliar now; modest, weirdly thin, nowhere near the ancient forest he'd been in last evening. In less than five minutes, he'd found himself on the far side of it, staring at another endless sea of tallgrass. After the frantic trip back to the clinic, and the north wing again, he spotted Sage down the hall, going in the door, and dashed over to catch the knob just before it closed. Sure enough, it opened into the warm red radiance of the pavilion, and he came in, hoping no one noticed the state he was in.

But now Max didn't know what to do with Black Howard's question: *What's wrong with you, boy?* "Nothing," he lied. "Sorry I'm late."

Durga was already there, perched in a rickety wooden chair so rough-hewn it could have come from a Tennessee mountaineer's log cabin. And another girl Max didn't know—a black girl who looked about his age, her head covered in a white wrap, with a constellation of dark freckles scattered across her nose and cheeks. A billowy blue and white-striped gown was draped around her casual frame like a caftan. Sage took a chair amid the semicircle facing the front of the tent, and Max fell into the seat next to her.

"Don't be sorry," Black Howard said to him. He was sloped back on the steps of the rostrum, resting on his elbows, his long legs stretched out and crossed at the ankles. His socks were bright red and pocked with holes. "Fellow with your abilities should never be sorry, Max. 'Bout nothin'."

He sat up and gestured to the new girl. "Now. I was about to tell you folks, this is Rosalie. She's our newest friend, along with Max here. Speak your truth, Ms. Rosalie."

The girl looked at the others with a deep gaze that made Max think of wild animals at rest; he felt her cool resolve ripple out, carrying a sense of great sacrifice, vast inner strengths that were somehow comforting and unnerving at the same time.

"My name is Rosalie Gilleaux," the girl said slowly, with a dense accent Max had never heard before. "I am from Avoyelles Parish, Louisiana, the land first settled by Henri Peyroux de la Coudreniere. Acadie country. Swamp country. I meet Mr. Howard when his magic show come to town. Well, not my town, because I ride two hours to meet him." She looked down at her feet, as if they were part of a special memory. "But my *pere* tell me always I was special. He know it, my brothers know it, and I know it, too. I am different and that's why we go."

Her eyes strayed toward Black Howard, and a slight, bashful smile crossed her face, like a girl with a crush. "Before the show my *pere* call out to him, and he come to us, and when Mr. Black meet me and look me into my eye, he call me right onstage and tell me in front of the people that I am the strongest he ever meet, 'cludin' him.

"We spend time together, talkin', visitin'. He come to my home. For hours asking questions. After two days he tell my *pere* he want me to come here and do some learnin'. I never been to no school before, but he want me to come. And so I am here."

Black Howard drew one knee up close to his chest, exposing the hairy shin above his red sock. "Good," he said and turned to the others. "I should mention that this is not a school. This is a *job*. This is a big job. You are here to master your roles as *They Who Long to Cross the Horizon*. But Rosalie is right. Moment I met her, there she was plain as the nose on my face. I could feel it right away. She got the *tamkarra* like nobody I never met." In the glow of Black Howard's praise, the girl breathed deep, nostrils flaring, chin tilting up with pride. Max caught a glimpse of what she would look like as a mother, as a middle-aged elder. Noble, defiant, serene, fearless.

Black Howard's gaze now took in the whole room: "All right, first. Essentials. After that, it's all you. So listen: *Indocilis privata loqui.* Who knows what that means?"

Durga glanced around, maybe to see if someone would volunteer, then back at Black Howard. "No secrets told."

"Yep. You better believe it, people. But what does it *mean?*"

Durga put his finger to his lips and said, "Sssshhhhhhhh..."

Max blinked. That gesture again. That ruined mouth again. It never failed to give him a cold needle-prick of alarm.

Black Howard grinned. "Ah, yes, the golden rule in our little oasis. Nobody tells nobody nothin'. 'When the pupil is ready, the teacher will appear,' and all that U Street jazz. You learn it for yourself, all of it, even here, even in class. Diviners like us, we don't *need* to talk about it. If you need to talk about it, you ain't got it. And if you ain't got it, no amount of gabbin' about it is gonna do you a lick of good." *Diviners.* Max had never heard that term before. It sounded mysterious and powerful and strange.

"Then why are you here?" Sage said. "Why have an instructor at all?"

Black Howard pointed at her. "Good, you're good. I'll tell you why I'm here. Even if you're ready, everybody needs a little push. Or a tug. Or a way in, somebody to pull up the back of the circus tent and say, '*Psst! Over here!*'"

He stood and stepped closer, and Max saw again how handsome he was—dark eyes set wide under thoughtful, knitted brows. "Now, listen. All this hush hush, you know there's more to it than just that. There's a great debate in our world about silence. Secretiveness. Restraint. Withholdin' information." With a wily eye he looked around the room, and his gaze settled on Max. "Why are you here, Scotty boy?"

"Me?" Max blurted. "I—I mean, I—"

"Be quiet." Startled, Max shut his mouth with an audible snap. Black Howard turned to Durga, and pointed at him. "So you. Bombay. You in the wrong place?"

Durga shrugged. "I would ask instead who is to say what is wrong or what is—"

"*Shht!*" Durga stopped, a look of irritation on his face. Black Howard loomed over them and raised his arms, like a revivalist preacher. "In fact, let's all of us be quiet. And just listen."

The five of them fell silent, motionless, ears cocked. Outside the tent, birds called as the whiff of a breeze came and went. The pavilion walls wafted in and out. Leaves whispered in the trees, branches groaned, the high whine of crickets. Black Howard looked expressively at each of them in turn. "Hear those birds?" he said finally. "What are they?"

Sage spoke up: "A grebe. Out in the trees."

"Anything else?"

"A hawk," said Rosalie. "A red-tailed hawk. High above."

"Do you know what they're sayin'?"

The four of them were quiet again. Durga said, "How are we supposed to know what they are saying?"

Black Howard lowered his hands and stuck them casually in his pockets. "I do."

"Well," Durga said after a pause, "what are they talking about?"

"The hawk is telling another where a fallen comrade lies. And a meal—a dead field mouse. The grebe is namin' her children. There are grouse, and ducks out on the lake. At the edge of the woods is a meadowlark, telling the others we're talkin' about them. They hear us. They know." The four young people sat up straight, listening in concentration, unnerved to hear so much around them of which they were unaware.

"They are telling secrets, yes? Things only they can understand, the hidden language of the birds, yes?" Black Howard shook his head. "No. *They hide nothin'.* They speak plainly, as plainly as I do to you now. But you do not hear because your ears are not trained to hear. This is what we mean by secrets. To those who would understand, there are no secrets. To those who cannot understand, the world is made up of nothing but."

Max glanced at the others. They were listening, intent; no one dared say a word. "In this way, I cannot give you my lessons. You must earn them. Just as you must first understand the letters of the alphabet before you can read, you must first understand the symbols, the clues, the signs of the universe, before you can make it do what you want."

Black Howard began pacing at the front of the semi-circle of young people. "Now, it's true that many of our great and lastin' texts have misleadin' information planted into them, to make them harder to understand. This is intentional. This is to hoodwink the insolent and the rude. The presumptuous who would swim out beyond their depths. They are purposely being led away from true knowledge. This is for their own good as much as anyone else's. By using tools they are not prepared for they could easily end up injured, or insane, or even dead. But make no mistake—secrecy is not the same thing as silence. The two are often confused with each other, just as information is often mistook for knowledge. Information can be found in a book. But knowledge, as with experience, must be earned. Through much work. Through talent, through time."

He squatted down to pick up the glass of water that had not been there a moment before. The four young people watched him as he took a long drink. When he finished, he put it away but stayed low, resting on his haunches.

"Of course, there are those who use secrecy as control. A source of power. A weapon. But usually this is to keep the neophyte from misusing the master's tools. Partial knowledge is a dangerous thing. If I gave you those tools right now—all that I have—could you recognize them? Would you be able to use them?" None of the young people answered. They exchanged uncertain glances, and for a moment Max felt better; plainly they were learning, too.

Black Howard, in his way, turned his head and looked at them aslant. "So it seems that, yes, we do speak in riddles. Their eyes do not see. Their ears do not hear. But if they could learn to listen in the right way, they would understand." He was quiet again, but his words hung thick in the air. "Now. The Avian language has long been known as the tongue of the angels. The Parliament of the Birds has been known to speak to many—Tiresias, Athena, Suleiman, Agrippa. Throughout time, the birds have given us their secrets. They have helped build cathedrals. They have advised kingdoms. They have altered the course of wars. The Sufi text *The Conference of the Birds*, by Attar the Chemist, speaks eloquently about this. But, okay, this is important—*the medium is the message*. There are hidden allusions within the very syllables of the text. Puns, wordplay, ambiguity, symbols, metaphors. A sort of Ur-language that has been taught throughout the ages. There are those that say the green language of the birds is derived from the one encoded into our very bodies."

Durga leaned forward, both elbows on his knees. "How is this?"

"Well. There was a discovery, a scientific discovery, a little over...what? Thirty years ago? A type of substance in our cells known as a protein, which makes up the language of our bodies. This protein is said to emit a form of light, essentially, a system of talkin' between our cells—coherent, that is, to that which can comprehend it. It may be the first language, the origin of all language. The language of initiation. This protein is made up of a dual chain—one link runnin' one way, the second runnin' the other—that looks strangely like the snakes that twine around Hermes' staff in the engravings of old. These days you will often see doctors and physicians—much like our own good Dr. Stout—using the caduceus as a symbol of medical knowledge. This is not a coincidence."

Black Howard's face was open, his eyes full of faraway things. "Now. This parlance, of course, has been known to the Gypsies for thousands of years. Egyptian hieroglyphics, known sometimes as the Divine Language, was often called the Alphabet of the Birds. It is the tongue of outsiders, of thieves and heretics at the fringes of society. So you see the correlation—there are secrets all around us. But to see them, you must have proper vision. You must have eyes. This is what we are here to do."

With a groan, he stood up; his knees popped, loud in the tent. "Damn, chillen, I'm gettin' old. But there are other uses for secrecy. We could get all theoretical and talk about Harpocrates, or Hermes himself, but in the real world, you gotta understand, another reason for secrecy is this: *People just don't fuckin' like us.* We get burned at the stake for witchcraft. Drowned in rivers. Shot. A Dominican monk from the 16th century, Giordano Bruno. Now *there* was a man who had a lot on his mind. He was trying to teach, to explain his profound ideas about man and his place in the universe. And what happened to him? Put to death, burned at the pyre, tongue staked so he couldn't even talk. Executed not for his knowledge but for the sin of trying to explain it. For the crime of merely trying to tell his side of the story."

He took a moment, as if in reverence for the fallen monk. "So. We been hung from our neck, we been crushed beneath rocks or buried while still alive. Even when we have good intentions. '*Specially* when we have good intentions. Now, why is that?"

Rosalie spoke up: "People are afraid of what they don't know."

"How 'bout that. Ignorance. Fear of the unknown. We been demonized. *That,* good people, is our inheritance. We are the Other. Now, do you think people woulda persecuted us if we'd been even more forthcoming?"

Durga, sitting forward with his chin in his hand, gave a half shrug. "Maybe."

"No maybe about it. The knowledge, and the fear of it, is the problem. Like Rosalie say, people fear what they don't understand, and a goddamn lotta people don't understand a goddamn lotta things. So that's the issue—under the threat of death, we learned not to talk about it. We *never* talk about it. Well, almost never. And then only if it's couched in symbols and arcane terminology that only a few can read and understand." Black Howard pointed to each of the young people in turn. "'*The teacher will appear when the student is ready.*' The world is our teacher, and until we're ready, the world looks just like the world. But to those who are prepared, the world is a very different place."

Max glanced at the other students, thinking of the Moorlander and her gruesome smile. The night he had seen her, the world had become a very different place, indeed. He had been deeply unprepared for her, and also for everything that followed.

Black Howard scratched his neck, a half-smile on his face. "All that said, I do want to speak on a few things. We have to, or the work will go unfinished. But know this—never discuss what we learn here outside of class. Not with your friend, not with your grandma, not with your brothers, not with Dr. Stout or that tall nurse, I forget what her name is. This is for you, and for me, and all us here, alone. Got it?"

The young people all nodded. Black Howard grinned, and even through his nerves Max felt the beginnings of a kind of wary and timid love for him.

"Now. I am your *fqih*. Your schoolmaster, enlisted to lead prayers and invocations. I just do it in my own weird way." He laughed a little and reached up, and from the air he produced a book—a very old book, bound in cracked leather, the pages choppy and uneven. He held it out with both hands for the group to get a closer view. "Now. This is *The Discoverie of Witchcraft*, by a man named Reginald Scot. One 'T.' Late 1500's."

He passed the book to Sage, who opened it gently and looked it over. "Treat her good, now, she's old. This is, in my opinion, the very first book—the first Western book, I should say, there are others, much older—that addresses the idea of conjury. It is partly a debunkin', the charlatan stuff at least, but in other places Scot was surprisingly on target. Most of the copies were burned by none other than King James—yes, he of the Bible. Believe it or not, Mistah Jimmy had a thing for demonology and witchcraft—but for purposes of torture, not enlightenment." He let that sink in. "As I say, folks like all us better watch out—we aren't well-liked unless we're on the stage doin' a soft shuffle with a painted-on smile and acting like we're grateful to the crowd for givin' us a penny." Black Howard smirked, but behind the humor, Max could see there was pain there, too. "If they only knew what we could really do."

He stepped back up on the dais, and fell into his big chair. His big brown knuckles gripped the lions' paws at the end of the chair's arms, and he looked, more than anything, Max thought, like a Nubian king on his throne.

"So this here ain't no schoolin'," Black Howard went on, "and this sure ain't no one-way ride. It's better to know one acre of land well than a thousand miles of easy travel. There are many, many subjects of study and practice, but in our time together I want us all to think of one particular discipline and explore that one thing. Right? From there you can look into the others, like spokes on a wheel."

His fingers did a *rat-a-tat-tat* on the wood of his chair. "So that's my shuffle. And this is where you show me what you got. Who goes first?"

The mood in the pavilion changed. Max, his insides suddenly heavy and dragging him down, tried to melt into his seat; he wished he could slop onto the floor and leak away. The ghastly visit last night had dulled his perceptions with fear and exhaustion, and he was beginning to wonder if maybe jail or hanging was better than this. He glanced at the others: Durga was relaxed and self-assured; Rosalie was quiet but seemed unbothered; Sage simply studied the hairs on the back of her hand.

Then her small voice piped up: "I'll go." She seemed to be addressing the group, though she never looked up. "I mean, if you want me to."

Black Howard crossed his legs beneath him in the leonine throne. "All right. Good. What're you gonna do for us?"

Sage looked up, eyes unfocused, at the roof of the pavilion. "I don't know. I could use the æther. Check the Akasha. The Akashic Records. I could bring something back."

"Well, okay, good, that's a start. Maybe you need to tell everybody what the Akashic Records are."

Sage's eyes were still fixed on the roof of the pavilion, as though she were too shy to acknowledge the others. "It's kinda like this thing, this, um, this place in the æther. Like everything that ever happened, and everything that will happen. It's all, it's all right there. It's different for everybody. Kinda like whatever you've done or are gonna do—you can touch it, see it. Grab hold of it. The future and the past together."

Black Howard spoke to all of them: "But you don't want to stay there too long. The human brain is not built to spend eternity in there. We're temporal creatures. And trust me—it can be an eternity. In the Akasha, time has no meaning. Five minutes can be five days, and the other way 'round, too. So you get in, you do what you gotta do, you get out." He nodded at Sage again. "You sure?"

Sage shrugged. "I do it a lot." She slid herself upright and folded her hands in her lap and closed her eyes. The group watched as she took in a lungful of air and became still. The wind in the trees outside picked up a bit; the tent walls billowed. Max could hear Black Howard's palms rasping back and forth on his thighs.

Then, almost imperceptibly, Sage became inert, lifeless, like a sewing mannequin or a dress-store dummy; Max couldn't tell if it was his imagination or not, but something, a slight gust of air, seemed to brush by him. Like the whiff in the room when Daniel Pepper was leading the séance, he felt a momentary chill, and then it was gone.

Black Howard tilted his head sideways and listened for a moment. He said, "Somebody go look out front."

The young people all got up and rushed to the door. Durga pulled back the curtained flap, and out in the broken sunshine of the forest, Max saw a faint presence moving among the trees. It was Sage, shimmering and soft, slipping away from the pavilion, further out into the wild.

Rosalie turned to Black Howard. "Where is she goin'? If everything is here, if everything is now, why do she leave?"

"Ah, yes," Black Howard said from his throne. "In the Akasha, time and temporal space are one. Sometimes they will overlap, and often they are swapped. And just as you leave your location to go somewhere else, the same can be true of time—we often need to unfasten ourselves from our specific whereabouts to slip into the past. Or into the future. I hope she knows which is which." Black Howard sat back, a restless thumbnail picking at a place on the armrest. "Might be a while now. Let's move on. I'm looking for somebody else this time. Who wants to show me what they can do?"

Durga cleared his throat and went back to his seat. "I will."

"You will...what?"

"I will read," Durga said and turned to Max and smiled wickedly, "Max's mind."

Another pulse of dread: Max tried not to let it show—the idea of someone rooting around in his mind, in his fears, in his past, in his plan, was the last thing he wanted right about now. But he knew there was nothing he could do about it—if he complained or refused to play along, it would only draw attention to his failures. Or maybe give the others the feeling he had something to hide.

Black Howard looked at him, eyebrows raised. "Max? You okay with that?"

Max went back to his own chair and sat down, feeling blood pulsing in his temple. "I mean, not really, but..." He blinked, feeling the class watching him with new fascination.

"Look," said Black Howard to Durga, "just don't go deep. Remember, our private matters are who we are. Let them be."

Durga smiled again, and stared hard at Max. Uneasy, Max met his gaze. After a moment he felt an itching somewhere inside his head, a stirring, someone rummaging around in the messy attic of his memories.

"He's frightened," Durga said, "he feels like he doesn't belong here. He is confused and wondering if he made the wrong choice."

Black Howard shook his head at Max, dismissing the idea. "Everybody feels that way."

"He is hungry. And tired."

"Who the hell ain't?" Black Howard said. "I could eat a pack mule, and that's just for breakfast. Now, let's see what Rosa—"

"But he is concealing something," Durga said dreamily. "A guest, a visitation." He leaned forward in eager focus, an archeologist on the cusp of discovery. "Someone...came to him last night, someone that he doesn't—ah!"

Durga stopped, and let out a little cough. He tilted his head back and closed his eyes. In a moment, a seep of blood shone darkly below his nostril. He wiped it away with the back of his hand.

"Durga?" Black Howard watched him closely.

When Durga opened his eyes, they were glassy and dazed. "He was visited in the night. By...by Mister Splitfoot."

Black Howard's mouth fell open, and Rosalie turned Max's way, her dark eyes squinting at him. "Max? Is this true?"

Max was trying not to feel guilty for something he didn't fully understand. He swallowed thickly. "It is."

A long silence. "Why didn't you tell us?"

"I—I don't really know who that is."

Black Howard leaned in. "What did he say?"

"I mean. Not much. Mostly he just laughed. This...this crazy giggle. Then he jumped into the mirror and was gone."

"The mirror." Black Howard frowned at him. His face was more serious than Max had ever seen it. "Did he mention me?"

"Well, uh..." *That coon?* The dread, swallowing him up again, crippling and oppressive. "I don't think so, no."

Durga stood and went across the room to dig into his pack. Rosalie chewed her fingernail, while Black Howard sat, lost in thought. "Why would he come visit you?" he said after a time. Max shook his head; he had heard about him, but that was all. He had no specifics. "You don't know who he is?" When Max hesitated, Black Howard said, "Mister Splitfoot is...he—or *it*, I should say—is...an essence. A malevolent, chaotic set of inclinations. A *thing*. Not a person, not by a long shot." He cupped his hands and breathed in them, as if he had taken a chill. "People first heard of him down in Kentuck', when there was a coal mine collapse. 'Bout forty years ago. Word came up there was a man, some young fella, tearing away the supports down there with his bare hands." Max watched as Black Howard's gaze turned inward. "Seventy-one miners lost their lives."

"That's what he was," Max said glumly. "A young fellow." *Seventy-one miners.*

Black Howard's eyes were still focused far away. "Dark hair? Filthy, like he'd been diggin' in the dirt?" Max nodded again. "Did you summon him?"

"*What?*" Max sat up straight. "No, no! He was just...there. He woke me up. Talked to me a little bit."

"What did he say?"

"Not hardly anything," Max said. *Thems ain't your friends,* he heard the gritty voice say. *Thems don't have your bestest prosperity in their hearts.* Max's head was pounding. "He said he would, um..."

I could just eat—you—UP!

THE OCCULTISTS

"He said that he was watching me and that I'd better be careful."

Black Howard's eyes were wide, which unnerved Max. He didn't like that look. "That's something else. He's...he's not a good spirit to talk to with, Max. He's uncontrollable. *Mean*. Got this crazy mountain accent, but they think that's just 'cause he heard the miners talking and mimicked them. Like a goddamn mindless parrot."

"*Mastah Splitfoot*," Rosalie said in an affected accent. Everyone turned to her. "That's what we call him in Avoyelles. But ain't he the Devil? I mean, we are talking cloven hooves and everything, right?"

"There ain't no Devil," Black Howard said. "Wish there was, because lots of things would be simpler. Close as we know, Splitfoot's some spirit got caught up in that mountain, some deep mineral vein, and the coal mines down deep dug him loose. Free and unfettered now. On his own terms, his own order o' business. Which nobody can get a handle on. Maybe not even him."

"Have you seen him?" Max asked.

Black Howard sat there for a long time, nostrils flaring, temples and jaw pulsing. Max wondered if he hadn't heard, but then the older man wiped a thumb across his lips and sat back, and Max could see that he was wondering whether to tell them something of consequence.

"One time I did, yes," Black Howard said slowly. "From a long way off. I was on a train, headin' through east Texas. Must've been fifteen, sixteen years ago. We were movin' through this lonely area—low hills and meadows and trees. Real nice. Must've been right noontime, cause it was hot and nothin' had a shadow. We passed this old broke-down water tower and there was this...this *boy*, this teenager. Out in the field. Just standin' there. No shirt, long hair flailin' in the wind, holding somethin' in his hand."

He let out a shuddery sigh; the day had taken on an unyielding strangeness. "Must'a been fifty people on that train, so how he saw me I don't know. But he looked right at me, and he grinned and pointed at me. Like this." He held out his arm and pointed across the room with his middle finger.

A cold drop of sweat slipped down the back of Max's neck. Mister Splitfoot had pointed at him the exact same way.

"And I knew knew knew that he knew me. Knew who I was, knew that I was Black Howard, even back then, before maybe even I knew it. Saw what I had in me before I did. I got chills—still feelin' them to this day. And it was only then that I realized what he held in his hand. He raised it up and I could see as we passed that it was a—" He stopped, and took a moment before he could start up again. "A human head. An ole white woman's ripped-off head." The woods outside were hushed, as if it too were listening to the story. "He raised it up, let me see what it was. Eyes like rotten spots on a peach. Mouth just a gash. And then. Then...he threw it at the train." He shook his head in blank, terrible awe, and rubbed at his temples. "Now, I knew he was too far off for anyone to really make that throw. But he threw it pretty damn good, way way up in the air, so far up I couldn't see it no more through the train window. Thought I was dreamin'. But then a crash came a few windows up, and the head burst through the glass and landed on the floor, and it rolled right down the aisle toward me. Toward us, I should say—there were others with me. Normal folk, don't you know. Coupla them were screamin'. And that woman's head tumbled right to my feet. Like it knew where to go. Its eyes were open, and its mouth was movin'. Like it wanted to talk, like it was cut off but the brain was still workin', the eyes lookin' at me." His gaze was turned inward again, one eyebrow raised higher than the other. "I got over my fear and I bent down. It was trying to talk to me and I leaned down and heard it whisper."

No one said anything; Durga stood off in the corner of the pavilion, holding a cloth to his bleeding nose. From out in the trees came the sudden, distant firecracker *pop! pop! pop!* of a woodpecker at work.

But Black Howard was lost in memory. "It said in this hoarse, bubbly voice, like a gurgle. *We will meet proper one day. And then I will sep'rate your head from your body.*" The pavilion seemed smaller somehow, seemed to vibrate with tension, poised for panic.

"Good lord," Durga said then, from the back of the room. "That's insane."

"And then the head went still. It died. I saw the light in its eyes go out. And I ain't never seen him nor heard from him again. 'Til now."

Black Howard looked over at Max, the fear plainly readable on his face. For the first time Max saw the magician was not some larger than life figure come to bestow unworldly wisdom. He was just a talented, charismatic man from Virginia who was as terrified of everything as anybody else. "You say that's all?"

That coon. "Yessir," Max said. "He told me, *I'm watching you, and you better watch for me, too.*"

Black Howard didn't answer. He was looking over at Sage, sitting there as still as a sculpture. But then she wasn't still anymore—her chest rose and fell, her eyelids fluttered. Durga came over and took his seat near Rosalie, and all of them, a little rattled now, watched as Sage came back to life.

Black Howard, seeming to try to dispel the darkness that had settled into the room, cleared his throat and sat back in his chair. "Hello, Sage. You back?"

The girl raised her head and looked vacantly around. A glaze covered her eyes, like a patina, and she twitched with odd, quick little birdlike movements. "I am here," she said, her voice weak.

"Where'd you go?"

Sage smiled, mostly to herself. "I travelled. I went places. It was a long time in there. Longer than you think."

"How long?"

"Most of a week." The group was silent as they all thought about this; an uncertainty was drifting though the room, like woodsmoke. Even innocent things had a new grim tinge to them.

"Well, what did you see?" Black Howard said finally.

That private smile again. "I think I went the wrong way."

Black Howard's eyebrows furrowed, and he fixed her with a look that seemed impatient, as if she'd done something he'd asked her not to. "The wrong way?"

"I tried to go back into the past, but I got lost. I think I ended up...somewhere else." Sage looked around the room, seeing the dour faces. "What's going on? Is everybody okay?"

Max looked back over at Black Howard, whose hands clung to the lapels of his jacket; his mouth was a thin slash, and he stared vacantly at the dirt floor, like he was trying to see something below it, beyond it, to dig it up and stomp it to death before it had a chance to do any harm.

TWELVE: THE LESSON

FOR THE REST OF the week they gathered in the Hall of the Woods, as someone—maybe it was Sage—had called the pavilion, and soon everyone was calling it that. It became clear that Black Howard was not really a teacher, but instead a combination of safari expedition guide and cheerful devil's advocate; he would slouch on the steps of the dais and speak at length about the astrologer John Dee and his search for "pure verities;" or the Enochian System; or Euclidean geometry and its relation to Newtonian mechanics; or maybe the four elemental weapons—"the wand for fire, the cup for water, the dagger for air, and the pentacle for earth." The young people were directed to explore their own unique talents in whatever way they saw fit. They spent most of their mornings in four separate corners of the pavilion—"*Fire, water, air, and earth, people, you'll hear these everywhere from now on!*"—quietly practicing their craft. Black Howard would crouch next to them, looking on, whispering and coaching.

At some point a small bookcase in the corner unceremoniously appeared, jammed with spine-cracked volumes without titles, many of them printed with strange leathery bindings that were unpleasantly familiar to the touch. Max found the books technical and arcane, intimidating and scary, often written in languages he didn't recognize, their brittle, hand-made pages full of bizarre drawings and upsetting sketches of things he didn't really want to look at anyway.

Later in the day, when the initiates were tired, their energies spent, Black Howard would sit on the leonine throne—Sage probably coined this, too—and entertain them with colorful and instructive tales about his life on the circuit.

Durga was expert at many disciplines, of course, but mind reading seemed to come most easily. He insisted he was careful not to use it unless he was asked. "It is a little unethical," he said to Max one night while they were eating in the empty mess hall. "It is also less interesting than one might think. If you know what someone is going to do before they do it, there is very little surprise in life. All becomes predictable, and the ease with which you can control people—to put thoughts in their minds, to make them think things—is quite distressing. There is no joy in using people like marionettes."

Sage was also good at more than one discipline—scrying and the reading of the tarot, mainly—but astral travel was clearly her favorite. But she became distant and distracted, even more so after her periodic escapades. "Time pulses in there," she told the group one faded, rainy morning, "surging and retreating like waves on a beach." Max thought she even began to look different—she'd always been willowy, but after several weeks, her face and body seemed to melt into a kind of haggard, almost skeletal look, all hard-angled shoulders and collarbones and elbows. Black Howard whispered warnings in her ear, but as far as Max could tell, she ignored them all.

Rosalie, of course, was Rosalie: an air of quiet and calm followed her around like her own personal climate, but she seemed to have a bit of trouble focusing her skills. Her gifts seemed as wild and primitive as her native swamps—one day they would be on full dazzling display while on others they sputtered and sparked and refused to catch fire. Her most consistent talent was for scrying; she told the initiates that she'd been able to do it since before she could remember. The first time was when she'd cast visions in a cup of water at only three years old; her two brothers, who were twins and two years older, screamed simultaneously when her cup appeared to predict their mother's early death by falling down a flight of stairs in the hotel where she was a maid.

Max laughed at her stories and was charmed by her accent, a slurry mix of the rural South and a French Creole patois. "It is quite simple," she told him one night about her scrying. "You only ask the instrument, whether it is a rain puddle in the road or a coffee with cream, to give you its secrets." Max asked her how she did it. "You must trust," she said. "If you think about it, it will not happen. You must fall into the trust as *sweefly* as diving into a pool of water."

He watched admiringly as the others presented their little miracles—their *tamkarra*—but mostly begged off when asked to perform something himself. It was a miserable, cowardly approach, but miles better than trying and failing and making a fool of himself. One day Black Howard insisted he at least give it a try. He suggested levitation—what the more technically-minded occultists called psychokinesis—and proposed that Max work with an old badger's tooth, which for some reason known only to the magician, he kept always in his pocket. For four days Max stared hard at the tooth, smooth and yellow and dull; willing, concentrating, trying anything he could. Depressingly, it stayed exactly where it was.

But there was one time, when Durga crept up behind him and spooked him, making him jump. The tooth shot across the tent and imbedded itself in the pavilion's heavy, patterned canvas.

"Well, *howdy*," Black Howard said, rising up to his full height with a look of cool satisfaction. He turned to the rest of the class. "Like I say, we all got a measure of talent, we just have to learn to nurture it. Think of a like hundred-car train creepin' out of the station. Sometimes the ones who start slow have a bigger load to get going." Max hardly heard him, his heart had seemed to pause; he went to the tent's canvas siding and pulled the tooth out, caressed the tiny rip in the fabric. He closed his hand around it: his *tamkarra*, his own shitty little miracle.

That night, in his room with candles burning—he had finally managed to find bedsheets and covers; the nights were consistently cold now—he sat cross-legged on the bed and tried for hours to lift the badger's tooth with his mind. It never budged, not even once. The light from the candles flickered on the wall, casting shadows of the things he couldn't do, and the tooth only sat there, mocking him. He got up and searched through the desk drawers. They were dusty and empty, except in the very back of the middle one there was a slim letter opener someone had left behind; maybe it was the girl's who lived here before—poor Florence, who had to leave so suddenly. Max took it out and put it on his desk and studied it—the rusted, reflective surface, the sleek, virile lines. It had one blunt side and one slightly sharper side, but it was nowhere near as sharp as a real knife. He picked it up, held it to the light, put it back down. In the candle's glow the shiny blade reflected the pocked ceiling. He slid his chair back, rolled the stiff joints of his shoulders, got comfortable. He stared hard at it. He wanted it to lift, to hover, to flip or spin, anything except simply lie there doing nothing. But it didn't move, it didn't shift, it didn't budge, not even a shudder or a leap across the room. He glared at it for five minutes. Ten. Twenty. Nothing. The chair creaked. Grouse prattled outside the window. A headache bloomed behind his eyes, like a cruel thunderhead gathering rain, but the letter opener never did anything but be still.

Max got up and went to the wash basin. He splashed his face and stared bitterly at his reflection in the water. In the time he'd been at Steppeland, he'd lost weight, and his skin was stretched across the bones of his forehead and his cheeks and chin. He looked older, but no wiser. "You fool," he said to the face in the water, "you stupid, fouled-up, idiot fool."

At the desk he wrote a brief, falsely optimistic letter to his mother and Ethie and went to bed, staring nervously at the mirror he'd turned to face the wall.

The next morning, Max went to the chilly creek to give his clothes a good old-fashioned creek thrashing. The previous night's nasty business still loomed over him. He'd never thought of himself as ambitious, but with a few notable exceptions, when he put his mind to things, they generally worked themselves out. But now the world around him was different; his life had taken a grave turn, more serious and solemn, full of genuine nightmares that seemed to spring on him out of nowhere. *This is not part of the plan*, the faraway voice whispered, *the plan is broken, there is no plan anymore.* Bitterly, he wrung water from his shirt and laid it to dry in the sun.

Something out on the rolling prairie caught his eye then, and he was surprised to see a small faraway figure wading out into the tallgrass—dark-haired Durga, sloshing through the grass. It wafted all around him in pockets of wind, like schools of fish or flocks of birds darting this way and that. Standing there, shivering and half-naked, Max felt a catch in his insides, a sudden need to talk to him, to consult with him, to ask his advice, to beg for help. Even though each student was on his own—*Indocilis Privata Loqui*, always and forever—maybe there was a way. Maybe the Breakaway Plan could still be fixed

For some reason then, Durga stopped and turned, and in the distance he saw Max watching him. Max raised a slow, tentative hand in greeting. When Durga did the same, Max took his damp shirt and went across the gravel drive and waded out into the weeds as he wrung it out and dragged it on. Durga waited for him to catch up.

"What are you doing out here?" Max called when he got a little closer. It was chilly. Annoying little burrs had already caught on his clothes here and there.

"Oh, nothing, nothing at all, really." Durga looked at Max expectantly, maybe wondering if he had come to give him some important news. His long fingers—surgeon's fingers, mortician's fingers—held a slender black book. "And you?"

Max came up to him, eyed the little book. "Are you studying?"

"I was planning to do some reading." There was a slight hesitation in his voice. "There is a little knoll I favor not far from here. With a gnarled old cottonwood. Quite lovely, really." The two of them stood there looking out at the morning. A slight breeze had picked up, and Max hugged himself in his wet shirt so he wouldn't shiver. Durga turned to him, hands clasped behind his back, plainly deliberating.

"Would you like to come with me?" he said. There was a note of resignation in his voice. When Max shrugged, trying not to seem too pathetic, Durga led him out into the weeds, the stalks and seedheads pocking at their legs. They trudged for a little while, the morning quiet except for the birds and the hissing of the tallgrass. "What are you thinking, Max?"

He was thinking that he still struggled to keep his head above everything that had gone wrong—Mister Splitfoot, his own failures, his mother and Ethie abandoned back home like so much unwanted junk.

Durga seemed to understand. "Don't worry so much, you have it, Max. Everybody does. It's innate, remember?"

"Maybe. For some people it seems to be a bit more innate than others." He wondered if Durga understood what he was getting at. It would be beyond pathetic to come right out and say it.

"You need only to pierce the veil, Max. It's simple. Once you get on the other side of it, you'll see what I mean."

"It's one thing to say that." *Easy to learn, but hard to know.* "But it's different to actually do it."

"But you moved the badger's tooth. I saw it myself."

"I have no idea how. I can't seem to make it happen again."

Durga gave him that wicked grin again. "Maybe I should come up behind you and shock you every time you practice divining." When Max didn't laugh, he said, more seriously, "Have you said anything about this to Black Howard? Or Dr. Stout?"

"I wouldn't know what to say. I can't risk going back to Selleford right now. I...I'm wanted back there. It's a long, horrible story. But if being out of place wasn't bad enough, now I've got this Splitfoot fellow showing up in my room, completely unannounced. Threatening me." He was trying to delicately lead Durga to a place without seeming to; he was afraid if he said any more it would be obvious.

Durga wiped his face with both hands and stared sullenly at the tallgrass waving all around. He seemed to take Max's point. "All right," he sighed. "I will help you."

Max kept his satisfaction from showing, but he felt the color rising in his cheeks anyway. "You will?"

"I don't know. I suppose I can introduce you to some elementary ideas and techniques that might get you started. But do not mention this to Black Howard, or to anyone. Do not speak of this. *Indocilis privata loqui*, always."

"Of course. Always. I won't mention a word, Durga, I promise. You have no idea how much this means to me."

The Indian boy slapped a bug on the back of his neck and studied it. "Oh, it is not for nothing," he said cheerlessly. "You will owe me, Max Grahame. You will owe me quite a bit."

"So what do we do?" The morning still had a drowsy quality, as if it was having trouble waking itself up. Clouds had moved in to cover the sun, and the light was scattered and dim.

"Do you have anything you like to use?" Durga said. "A tool, that...that animal tooth, some other thing?"

Max pulled the letter opener from his back pocket and presented it sheepishly. "I've been using this, but it hasn't happened."

"Goodness. Well. You keep it with you." Durga took it, held it lengthwise between his hands, point to point; it shone in the dull light. "Expecting and hoping for a result is not enough. Intention, Max. You need intentionality."

"But I did. I wanted it to lift, to spin, to fly across the room. It didn't do anything."

"And thus your problem. You had multiple objectives for it, rather than one single goal. In fact, if there is more than one objective, you will certainly fail, every time. Specificity is key."

Max remembered what Peter Sylvester had written in his ledger: *The will can and does kill.* "So what do I do?"

They had come to Durga's cottonwood tree. It stood alone, leaning slightly, its branches bursting out into a radiant, autumn-yellow crown. Though there was no shade, Durga stood under it and balanced the letter opener on the end of his index finger, and from his showy dexterity Max could see he'd done quite a bit of legerdemain; Max was beginning to wonder if there was anything at all Durga couldn't do.

"So this is our tool?" Durga asked. Max nodded. "Be careful. A neophyte messing around with this can quite easily lose an eye. But we will use it if you want." He turned to face the prairie, which rolled out before them like the open pages of a book, and put the letter opener flat on his open palm. "Watch."

He concentrated, staring at the blade for five or six seconds. It started to quiver, then more violently, and suddenly it stood on its sharp end, as if pulled up by an invisible string. It stayed there on its tip, balancing improbably on the heel of Durga's hand. His palm was so pale it seemed to glow.

"You see how it works. Focus: Intention: Result. Clear your mind, give it space, make this the one and only thing you have in your thoughts—the result that you want. You'd be amazed at what you can do."

The letter opener lifted itself about a foot or so above Durga's palm and began to twirl there like a spindle, picking up speed ever more quickly until it was only a blur. With his eyes half-closed, Durga made a kind of glottal cluck, and the letter opener dashed away, out over the weeds, and paused there for maybe five seconds. Then it spun around and bolted like a dragonfly between them—"*Shit!*" Max yelped, and dodged aside—to stab itself in the trunk of the cottonwood.

Durga was right, that thing was dangerous.

"Not recommended for novices," Durga chuckled. "So, Max, if I am to help you, if I am to temporarily break our code of silence, you must tell me about yourself. What trouble are you in?"

Max licked his dry lips, looked out over the prairie; the idea of getting back into it didn't appeal to him. He said, "Can't you just read my mind?" and the Indian gave a polite smile, but he didn't answer. So Max went through a quick version, leaving out many of the more depressing details. It didn't take long.

"*Baap re baap,*" Durga said emphatically when he was done. Max had no idea what that meant. "Very interesting. Much of this sounds familiar. The Hearst sisters, of course. And I am very glad to know you have the support of Peter. He is a strong ally in times of need." When Max looked at him strangely, he said, "Ah. You understand that I know Peter Sylvester. The Postmaster. Or rather, I have met him. On two separate occasions, in fact."

"How do you know him?"

"Why, Steppeland is his clinic." Max glared at him, amazed. He'd thought Dr. Stout was the head of the clinic. "Peter, yes. He even visits from time to time. Comes to make sure everything is going well."

Peter? "Dr. Stout works for *him?*"

"For him and the rest of the Aurora, yes."

"The Aurora," Max said. That name again. "I keep hearing about them, but I still don't know anything about them."

"This is as it should be, of course." After a long pause, Durga said, "The Aurora are the ones who are organizing and financing this Steppeland facility. And others. Surely you know that. They are very ambitious. Working with Peter and his society, I have found, has been a great learning experience. They are focused and very powerful. More much so than working with the others."

"The others?" He felt suddenly dim, sidelined, even more so than usual. "Others? What others?"

"The others, yes. Here we are. The Faqrs." Max had never heard this word before; in Durga's pronunciation it sounded like *fahkkers*. Durga laughed when he saw Max's bewildered expression. "I suppose I should not speak of this. They would be unhappy with me. But since we are fondly trading secrets, I will tell you what I know. It isn't much." Durga plucked a plume of barley, and looked over at the letter opener embedded in the trunk of the cottonwood; the blade had almost disappeared into the wood. "The Faqrs were the ones who first brought me here to America. Recruited me, you could say, from Dharwad. First to Tibet. And then to Morro Bay, in California, as I mentioned. And then to New York City. I lived with them for seven months until it became obvious it was time for me to leave."

"What happened?"

"They are an interesting organization, the Faqrs. Quite a bit different from what we have here. There are fewer of them, I think, than the Aurora. Rather poorly funded and organized. I can only hope that Mme. Z— has attempted to cultivate quite a few more wealthy benefactors before she took her dispute into the public realm."

The words rolled like thunder in Max's head: *Mme. Z—. The dispute.* This was what he had heard Peter and Addie Sylvester talking about all those weeks ago. Durga went on: "In the last several years the discord between the two groups has taken a turn for the worse. Since that Polish man killed your, your president—what was his name? Mac...Kenzie?"

"McKinley."

"Right. But before that, even, the two groups had drifted farther from each other than ever. Long ago they had tried to work together, and once were in fact one single entity. But their contradictions pulled them apart. Now they are quite different."

Max blinked at Durga. "How so?"

"Well. All of this is my opinion, as you understand. And if someone asks me about this conversation, I will of course tell them that you had imagined it." Durga put the end of the plume in his mouth, and it jutted out, making him look like a particularly handsome dark-skinned hayseed. "But the Aurora and the Faqrs are two distinct groups, and display two distinct philosophies, two very different approaches. Opposing, even."

"In what way?"

"Well. The Aurora is more—what is the word? *Hierarchical.* The Faqrs are more...er, I don't know the English. *Egalitaire.* More accepting to new people and new ideas. And to the spreading of ideas. It is hard for me to put in your terms."

"I heard someone talk about Mme. Z—. They said she was trying to bring in some kind of...Buddhist thinking?"

"Right. Yes, that's it. Tibet. Mme. Z— wants a more open society, less restricted. Whereas the Aurora are more...er, cautious. Confidentiality, discretion. A confined and controlled path to knowledge. Exactly what Black Howard was saying."

"But what's so bad about being open?"

"Well, in the abstract, not a thing. But if you think about it, when we talk about conjury we are in actuality talking about power. Influence. Mme. Z— is attempting boldly—many say foolishly—to spread knowledge. Dangerous knowledge. She has published books about it. The Aurora publishes also—no doubt you know that Peter Sylvester is the editor of some notable publications—but they tend to be more prudent, more concerned with investiture, with, um...reticence and the careful rationing and dissemination of wisdom. Rather than a crude belching onto a populace that lacks both the capability and the cultural maturity to handle it."

Max saw what he meant. The grim notion of someone like Sig skrying or reading minds—that was a sober thought, indeed.

"I do not think this country—or this world, for that matter—is ready for this kind of understanding," Durga went on. "What would our civilization be like if we all could travel astrally? Or speak to the dead? Society would collapse. And so these two groups—the Aurora and the Faqrs—they are at odds. And yet Mme. Z— continues to freely publish her work. Luckily for us, no one has read them much."

We will reciprocate, Max remembered Peter Sylvester saying. *She has no idea the power she will unleash.*

There was a scatter behind them, and they turned to see a host of sparrows—dozens of them, rising up from nowhere and taking flight—ribboning out toward the far horizon. Max took a deep breath, and let it out. The scent of barley wafted heavy in the cool air.

"I suppose we should get back to what we are here for," Durga said glumly. "Your talent. Or, rather, your lack of it." He dug in his pocket and pulled something out and presented it—an Indian Head penny, worn almost smooth. Max wondered if he kept it as some kind of weird joke. "Shall we try something a little less, er, lethal?" Durga said. He gave it to Max, who laid it face up in his own palm. "So. Let's try this. One intention—only one. Clear your head of everything. Deep breaths, calm heart. Now, your only desire in this moment is for this penny to raise up one inch above your hand."

Max stared at the penny, the feathered headdress flowing back from the Indian's featureless, almost girlish face—the curl of hair, the thrust of chin, the dull gleam of sunlight along the edge. "One inch," Durga said calmly, "that is all."

One inch, Max thought, one inch. Nothing else, just one inch *oneinchoneinch ONE INCH.*

Just then, the penny shuddered; the edge of it raised a bit, tilted upward.

"*Haan,*" Durga said. "Now. The other side." Max focused on that one particular side, the one still touching his hand, and it too shuddered and raised up. The penny floated—levitated—in the air above his palm.

"Good. Now make it rise. The entire thing."

Max stared at the hovering penny and sent his intention. Wobbly, falteringly, it rose and came to a place about ten inches above his hand.

"Holy Jesus," he said, stunned. He plucked it from the air and shifted excitedly from foot to foot. The penny—the whole world around it—had become a wondrous thing.

"Well," Durga said. His eyes were hard to read. The sky was darker now; the wind had picked up and the clouds were growing fatter. "This is what I have shown you. It is a start. Now you are on your own. But please practice with the penny, and not the letter opener. I want to see you with both of your eyes intact tomorrow." He sounded as if his thoughts were already far away. He let out a polite, distant chuckle, and brushed a grasshopper from the sleeve of his shirt.

Max went to his own cabin and sat cross-legged on the bed again, and for the rest of the day, as rain thundered outside his window, he levitated the penny at various distances over his outstretched fingers. "Not so hard," he whispered to himself, fierce now and feeling a surge of electricity throbbing within him, thrumming through his bones. "Not so hard at all."

In the morning he was exhausted and excited but also weirdly reluctant to show Black Howard and the rest of the class what he'd learned. The others would be mostly unimpressed, but for Max it was a colossal leap forward. Finally he had pierced the veil; the journey had begun in earnest. He came into the pavilion, and was surprised to see Black Howard talking to someone—a girl—her back to the door, with a body language that seemed immediately, alarmingly, familiar. When Black Howard glanced over her shoulder and nodded at his arrival, the girl turned also—and Max felt a silent percussive wave hit him, as though dynamite had gone off somewhere deep in his own catacombs.

It was Harriet.

She regarded him coolly, not smiling, not even a hint of recognition. She went back to what Black Howard was saying, the two of them oddly intimate, absent of that dreadful and awkwardly lumbering sense of self Max had felt the first time he met him.

Soon the others drifted in and took their places. Harriet never said a word or met anyone's eyes, and found a chair on the far side of the room. The others, particularly Durga, considered her with some curiosity.

Black Howard took his seat in the big chair. "Now, people, I want you to know we have a new student—Miss Harriet Blackwood." He gestured to her, and the others craned over for another look. She nodded at each person in turn—Durga, Rosalie, Sage—but ignored Max completely.

As if to cheer him up, Black Howard gave him an engaging smile. "Now, I believe that Max and Harriet know each other—crazy, but they're from the same small town. Proves that talent can happen anywhere, and that there's room here for everybody. Let's make sure we make her welcome." The others turned toward Max, searching his face, his posture, for any signs of sentiment or emotion. He tried to look as blandly indifferent as Harriet did.

"And also, I have it on good faith"—Black Howard drawled showily, like a stage performer warming up the audience—"that Max has had a breakthrough." Embarrassed, Max couldn't help but glance at Durga, who crossed his arms and leaned back, showing no signs of his involvement.

"Yessir," Max said, wondering how the magician knew. "I, um, came up with a few ideas." Across the room, Harriet's unreadable gaze studied him, but he tried to put it out of his mind. "I spent a couple of hours yesterday, learning to...to levitate, um, a...a penny."

The room was brutally quiet. Then Black Howard exclaimed, "A *penny!* Nice, Max! Hey, people, it's a start." He nodded grandly, honoring Max. "Now, who here can levitate a penny?" The others gave a variety of muted, non-verbal responses that amounted to the same thing—Max was the last one to be able to learn that particular parlor trick.

Black Howard clapped his hands. "Well now! Harriet? Would you like to tell the others who you are, and what you can do?"

"Not really," she said.

Black Howard looked blankly at her for a moment, not accustomed to having his requests ignored. Then, in thoughtful good humor, or maybe relishing the challenge, he straightened up. "Harriet, I get it. Your spirit and your grit. In fact, I *want* it. Both are fine qualities, for initiates and for the study of divinin' itself. But unless we see what you got, ain't nobody knows. It's a thing we do here."

"You want to see a trick?" Harriet said moodily. "Of mine?"

"I wouldn't phrase it quite like that, but yes. That would be a good place to start."

Harriet looked around the room, and her glance fell upon the glass of water at Black Howard's feet. She got up, all eyes upon her and her fetching yellow dress and her shiny, buckled shoes. She stepped up on the dais. "May I?" she said.

Black Howard gave her a bemused smile. "Of course."

She bent down and picked up the water, and brought it to her lips and tasted it. "That's good," she said. With everyone's eyes following her, she stepped down from the dais and stood among the loose circle of initiates, presenting the water with the air of a practiced stage illusionist; first to Sage, then to Rosalie and Durga, and finally to Max.

"My trick," she said, seeming to enjoy the sound of the word. "My ruse, my subterfuge, my *bamboozle*." The red light of the tent glinted through the glass, and her thumb was refracted to twice its normal size. Max could make out the wavy lines of her fingerprint.

Then she dashed the water in his face.

The splash was cold and sudden. Max sat back, shocked, dazed, mouth open, shirt drenched, his face dripping.

The other kids chuckled nervously. Water splatted into small puddles beneath him. An eerie, placid smile, almost unnoticeable, formed at the corners of Harriet's lips. She returned the empty glass on the dais next to the leonine throne, found her seat, and folded her hands demurely in her lap.

"There's my trick," she said.

THIRTEEN: BLOOD BOY

WHEN BLACK HOWARD CALLED the end of class, Harriet got up and went out the little back door into the clinic, as if she had known about it all along. Max called after her: "Harriet!"

In a moment she was gone. He followed her through the pavilion door and stepped out into the hospital corridor, looking to see which way she had headed. She was already a dozen steps down.

"Wait up, Harriet—please!" When he came alongside her, she gave him an impatient, sideways glance but didn't say a word. After everything that had happened, he was shocked at the bitterness in her eyes. It was still fresh, still ripe. "I know you're angry," he said, "but I had no choice, and you know it. The cops were looking for me." His voice had a frailty, a weakness, that he despised. "If I'd stayed, the whole thing would have been opened up. The Postmaster and Addie Sylvester and the Hearst sisters—and you, too. And I'd be in prison."

Harriet stopped. "You think that's what happened?"

Max stopped, too. "I'm—I mean. Yes. Am I wrong?"

Her response was a look of disgust so pure Max felt scalded. She started down the corridor again.

"Harriet!"

"Please leave me alone," she said over her shoulder. "I can't stand the idea of having anything to do with you." She skimmed silently down the empty hall, yellow skirt flipping, black shoes shining, and disappeared around the corner.

For the next three days Max secluded himself in his cabin, shirking the sessions in the Hall of the Woods and obsessively levitating Durga's Indian head penny. There were improvements. In less than a day he could twirl it, toss it, make it orbit his body at different speeds, put it in each of his pockets without using his hands. He flipped it, made it land heads up twenty times in a row, tails up fifty times.

With a tiny measure of hope, Max turned his attention to the letter opener. Manipulating that was very different; the letter opener's mass was heavier, but there was more to it than that. The shape, the load, the three dimensional mass, even the surface sleekness of the thing—all of this required a different approach. But he made inroads, and within four hours of practice, he was able to lift it, stab it, slice it in the air. He got to know its intimate contours and formed an intuitive awareness of the amount of energy it took to make it move. Psychokinesis, he was learning, was as much a proportional awareness, a control of the area surrounding the object, as it was a control of the object itself.

But when he tried to levitate the penny and the letter opener at the same time, his progress wobbled to a halt. Their differing qualities were hard to mesh—one was large and long, the other small and round and weighed maybe a tenth of the former. Maneuvering them together was like trying to swim in a quiet pond and a rapid river at the same time. For hours Max practiced at the desk, then moved to the bed. He paced the room, tossed the items in the air. Nothing worked; one would catch in mid-cast, while the other clattered to the floor.

He kept at it. Hours passed. Evening rolled into night, night spun into morning, morning wheeled into day and night again. His head pounded, his stomach growled. He was tired and depressed, but didn't allow himself to feel anything but the hollow, jittery drive to prevail. For the next thirty-one hours he had no food, no sleep, and no luck.

But then something happened. Sometime during his marathon session, maybe as the second night dissolved into the third morning—he wasn't sure what time it was, but it was dark outside—he was sitting on his bed facing the wall and still trying when he heard a tapping at the window.

He spun around, suddenly terrified, certain that Mister Splitfoot had come back. But he hadn't; it was only a bird. At the edge of the candle's parabola of light, a black-billed magpie was waiting there, on the sill outside the glass; in the darkness most of its body was lost among the shadows. Oddly, it held something in its beak.

Max got stiffly up from the bed, trying not to frighten it, but when he crept over it fluttered away into the night. The thing it carried, however, had been left behind on the weathered brick of the sill. Max rammed the window up—it was a struggle, it might have been decades since it was last opened—to find an Indian head penny, similar to the one Durga had given him. But this one was bright and new. He turned it over in his hand, inspected it, wondering what in the world would cause a wild bird to drop a new penny on a windowsill in the dead reaches of the night.

In his lectures, Black Howard had made much of the Parliament of the Birds, what he often called the *Green Language*. Learning to speak their tongue was one of the central rites of passage for many of the occultist luminaries throughout time. But Max had never been entirely sure if the language was figurative or literal—the birds didn't really speak to these people, did they? Or was it more probably an understanding, a secret code or method of communication among Gnostics? He couldn't say for sure, but the fact that a black-billed magpie had just provided him with a shiny new penny was certainly cause for wonder. On the mattress in the flickering light of the candle, the coins looked like button-eyes, or tiny dark holes into some other-world beyond.

And then he understood; because they were identically shaped and weighted, it would be only a small leap to manipulate both of them at once.

With a resolute lurch of faith—right now he wanted only to sleep, not flip pennies like a goddamn vaudeville clown—Max sat down on the bed and lifted Durga's penny using only his thoughts. As it floated and bobbled in the air before him...he lifted the other.

It was devastatingly easy. He turned back to the window and sent a silent prayer of gratitude out into the darkness.

For another two hours, he levitated the two pennies—spun them, rotated them, flipped them. Made them dance around each other, orbit each other, circle the bed, circle the room. It was another tiny victory, but it loomed absurdly large.

Woozy now, Max looked over at the desk and saw the letter opener there. A thought came to him, slow and sluggish: Once he'd learned to perform *tamkarra* with both pennies, it was yet only another tiny leap to performing *tamkarra* with a penny and an item of disparate size. *It's like crossing a river*, the little faraway voice said, sounding as depleted as Max himself. *You only hop from stone to stone.*

Easy to learn, but hard to know.

For another short time—at least he thought it was short; by now the hours were slopping together into one big watercolor smear of days—Max stared at the penny and the letter opener, concentrating, getting the feel of them. Slowly he was able to lift the two of them together. Clumsily at first, then deftly. In less than an hour, he was able to wield them both as easily as with his hands.

Finally: Intoxicated now, feeling light-headed and punchy, *stone to stone*, the voice kept repeating, *just go stone to stone*, the breakthrough of the third item came, which arrived as breakthroughs often do—in a frenzy of exhaustion, with a feeble sigh of relief. The three items drifted lazily over his bed, the letter opener in the middle, spinning like a drill, and the two pennies flipping lethargically over and over on either side. Tired as he was, he stood up, feeling the oxygen and the blood and the energy throbbing in him. He stalked drunkenly around the tiny bare cottage, furiously pumping his fists while the three objects hovered and tossed beautifully in the air. He had done it. Finally, finally, he did what he had set out to do.

There was a knock at the door. As if waking from a reverie, a three-day dream, Max glanced over to see blue light seeping through the uncurtained window. Morning. Morning had come.

He opened the door to see Tom Howland standing there, in his banker's suit and bowler. "Tom, good to see ya," Max slurred dully, not at all himself.

"Operating theater," Tom Howland said. "You're blood boy." Without waiting for an answer, he turned and high-stepped off into the tallgrass.

Max swayed in the doorway. "What?"

"Ten minutes," Tom said, and was gone.

The hallways just off the operating theater led to separate men's and women's changing rooms—cavernous, low-ceilinged, perpetually dank chambers with benches against the walls and cubbyholes for clothes. The rooms had apparently been built to accommodate an army of employees, many more than were using it now, and the area reminded Max of some spooky, clammy catacombs from a Gothic novel—*Dracula*, maybe, or something from Poe. From a folded stack of uniforms, he pulled a musty white smock that seemed closest to his size. They were as itchy as ever.

A young nurse in the dressing room antechamber told him blood boy was a crucial but unskilled role on the operating team. He would stand by with towels and rubber-edged squeegees to sop away the mess from under the doctor's feet. Max hoped that was as technical as it would get—with the exhaustion from his sleepless days of *tamkarra* sparkling like fireflies at the periphery of his vision, he was certainly in no shape to do much more. He ducked into the operating theater to find the tiny stern nurse, whose name he still didn't know, helping the younger nurse prep a twin pair of dull metal tables in the center of the room. Max's own station, a rusted chrome table loaded with folded towels and the rubber-edged squeegee, stood in the corner, dwarfed under the watchful gaze of the rows of empty theater seats. The young nurse waved him over and handed him a crumpled piece of white cloth. He gazed uncomprehendingly at it until she said, "Surgical mask. You put it across your face and over your ears." She showed him how.

Nurse Agnes led the patient into the room, a middle-aged man, balding, with a bird's nest of a beard and a pregnant paunch waddling inside a loose hospital gown. She helped him up on one of the tables. "This is Mr. Lawson Briggs," she announced, and stepped back to let the tiny nurse strap him to the table—wrists and ankles down, knees fixed, bent and open. "He is a coal miner from down in Cass County."

"Hello, Mr. Briggs," the two other nurses chimed in unison.

"Howyadoin'," the miner mumbled. He was plainly terrified. The tiny nurse placed a rubber mask over his mouth and nose and began pumping a little squeeze-bladder to administer the analgesic.

Then Dr. Stout bustled in, wearing his mask and trailing an air of brassy assurance, and went to a tray of instruments on the far side of the tables and began picking through them. The young nurse stepped back as Stout held up an alarming, theatrically large needle. He turned to Nurse Agnes. "We are prepped?" he asked. She nodded.

The young nurse smiled at Max through her own mask, and then pointed to a porcelain bowl holding some type of clear liquid. "Antiseptic," she whispered. She dipped her fingers and stood back, motioning for him to do the same. "Courtesy of Sir Lister." Max blinked blearily at her, having no idea what that meant.

Stout approached the dazed miner. "How we doin' there, Mr. Briggs?" he said loudly through his mask.

"*Nahsagood.*"

"No need to be scared, just a few tugs here and there and we'll be done before you know it. Your virility will be the delight of all the lady miners."

The man, his forehead pale and damp, tested his restraints. "There are no lady miners," he murmured.

"You comfortable? Shall we begin?" Dr. Stout took the huge needle and stabbed the man in the groin, once on one side, and again on the other. The miner grimaced, grinding his teeth and puffing out his cheeks. The young nurse swiped at his forehead with a towel, and Dr. Stout passed the needle to Nurse Agnes, who passed it to the tiny nurse.

The door in the corner opened and a young boy came in—astoundingly young; Max thought he couldn't have been more than nine or ten—leading a gangly black and white billy goat by a frayed rope. Still in his dirty stable clothes, the boy picked up the billy and hoisted him to the metal table next to the miner. Nurse Agnes grabbed a scalpel from a nearby tray, and nodded to Max, who was hovering, near-senseless, in the corner. "Mercurochrome," she said, and pointed to an orange bottle on the tray next to the goat. To Max, the world had taken on a kind of gauzy distance, as if a soft membrane lay between him and everything else. He came over and watched his arm pick up the bottle, and stood staring at the label. Someone had written "antiseptic" on it in tiny, precise letters.

Nurse Agnes leaned in. "Testicles, Max, wash the testicles."

The lid of the bottle was loose already, and it contained a little built-in brush. The stable boy held the goat while Max dabbed at its fuzzy gonads, which hung like figs from its hindquarters. He stepped back as Nurse Agnes took her scalpel, and the goat let out a ragged bray of protest as she deftly made a slit in each of its sacs. In seconds she had placed two bloody objects, like oysters swimming in a watery tomato stew, on a stainless-steel tray. She passed the tray to Stout, who took a close, savoring sniff of them—a fine diner relishing a fresh plate of escargot. The stern nurse handed Stout a second syringe, full of what looked like the mercurochrome, and he injected it into the drowsy man's gonads. Then he took the scalpel from Nurse Agnes, and leaned in to make two quick incisions in the strapped-down man's own scrotum. And that was when everything went wrong.

"YOOORK!" the man howled from under his mask, and jerked. The right-hand strap on his knee came loose and it knocked Stout's arm. "*Oooh,*" the miner complained. "Jesus Matthew, that goddamn *hurts!*" The tiny stern nurse rushed in to re-secure the man's knee, then furiously pumped his mask.

The miner hyperventilated, the goat wailed; Stout stood back, frowning.

"Nurse Agnes, please come here," he said with an odd, unsteady waver in his voice. Nurse Agnes turned from her work suturing the struggling goat. "Can you look at this?" She peeked over his shoulder, and Max heard the doctor whisper, "*He knocked my arm.*" Nurse Agnes' gaze grew grim. "All right, he's all right," Stout insisted, "he just knocked my arm."

"Meredith, we need gauze," Nurse Agnes said, "right away." Her voice was flat and contained, like it was coming from inside a box. "Hemorrhage. Right away, please."

The tiny nurse—*Meredith, that was her name,* Max thought from a thousand miles away, *Meredith*—hurried over, her little eyes wide. "I think the cremasteric artery has been severed," Stout whispered. He turned to Max. "Blood boy."

The goat brayed gratingly as Max stepped up and sopped the mess away from the miner's bloody groin. The bright liquid oozed back. "Again," said Stout. Max wiped the blood and the towel was instantly sodden, his hands slick and sticky. More blood slopped in at once.

"All right, this is not workin'," Stout said, his voice shaky, and stepped back. He pushed his glasses up his nose, leaving a tilde of red across the bottom of his lens.

"*Wha'appen?*" the miner said. He'd taken on a waxen, glassy-eyed look; he didn't seem to be in much pain, but he struggled feebly against his straps. "Lemme up." The goat bleated loudly again.

"*Get that fuckin' thing outta here!*" Stout yelled. Terrified, the stable boy came over and hefted it and whisked it away, his own clothes now smeared brick red and rust orange. On the floor a spattered trail of blood followed them out of the room.

"Scrub nurse!" Stout said. Max and the women all looked at each other, their nerves buzzing, but no one moved. Stout spun to Max: "*Scrub nurse! You, you, goddammit, blood boy, you!*" Max stepped in and swabbed again; in two seconds it was as if he had never wiped at all. Blood oozed thickly, like soup. A puddle clabbered on the floor under the table.

"I need a clamp, quick," Stout said. Nurse Agnes stepped up, a shiny, scissors-like forceps in her hand, and passed it over. Stout took it with slick and bloody fingers, and, face set and eyes staring blankly up at the ceiling as he used only touch to guide him, he felt down into the heart of the wound. By now the miner's eyes were closed and his breathing had slowed.

"It's there but I can't find it," Stout said to no one in particular. In the corner the young nurse licked her lips, her hands clasped helplessly at her breast. Max stepped in to wipe, but the doctor knocked his hand away. "Not now, you idiot! When I tell you!" The chamber went silent as Stout felt inside the miner's open wound. More blood spurted and pooled beside the man on the operating table and pattered on the floor. From the chest to the knees, his gown glistened with red. "I can't find it, I can't goddamn *find* it!" Stout hissed.

"Fit the edges together," Nurse Agnes offered.

"It's a laceration, it's not the kind I can just splice back up!"

"Then clamp it."

"I can't goddamn clamp it, I can't fuckin' *find it!*" Stout's voice was beginning to unravel. "Help me turn him up."

Nurse Agnes rushed to undo the miner's restraints, and she and Stout grabbed him by the shoulder and the hip and rolled him over so that the hemorrhaging wound in his groin was higher than the other. Stout dug in the incision for a moment, but then said, "No good, access blocked. Take him down."

They flopped him on his back again. By now, blood was everywhere—a slick scarlet swill on the table, on the miner, on Stout's hands. Beneath the table now a pond of gore was clotting. The man's skin now resembled a kind of spongy marble, and his chest rose in slow, shallow hitches. Max stood by, the rubber-edged swiper in his hands, but his feet felt numb and embedded in the floor.

The doctor stepped back, panting. "I need to think." He pulled off his mask and stretched his mouth and eyes wide in a sudden grimace, as if to loosen them up. When he adjusted his glasses he left another swipe of red. He looked over at the nurses, and in a calm, tired voice said, "Blood, blood—he needs blood, get some blood."

The young nurse stood flatfooted for a moment, frozen. Then something behind her petrified eyes fell into place, and she rushed out of the room.

Stout turned back to the miner. "Nurse," he said. Again, no one moved, though they were all jumpy and terrified. "Max—I mean, Max, *blood boy—clean, clean.*" Max dashed in and tried to wipe the blood, but there was too much of it now. He ended up only smearing it around.

"Okay," Max heard the doctor whisper to himself, "exsanguination, okay." Stout's breath was ragged, his hands twitchy. His goatee dripped red. He closed his eyes, stood motionless for a time, and opened them, blinking rapidly. Then, louder, to the people in the room: "We have maybe a minute before this man bleeds to death right here on this table."

He turned helplessly to Nurse Agnes, who stood as composed and imperturbable as ever. Then to the tiny nurse, who only mirrored his desperate glare. Finally, he looked at Max, his eyes as helpless as if he were dying himself.

"Max," Stout said, oddly polite, as if he were a dinner party guest who was changing the subject to something more pleasant, and cleared his throat. "You've been spendin' quite a bit of time in that—that *area* out in the woods." Max shifted his feet. What did that mean? He tried to think of something smart to say—he couldn't guess what Stout would want with him. "We don't have time to find Black Howard," Stout went on, "but maybe..."

Like a flurry of wind, it came to him—Max knew what the doctor wanted. Of course. He was one of the special students. Stout was asking if he could find a way. "What do you want me to do?" he said.

"We have maybe forty seconds," said Nurse Agnes, not sounding any different than she usually did.

Stout dabbed at his face with his spattered mask. "I can't find the artery in there to clamp it. Too much...um, fluid. What can you do?" He rolled his hand. "Your, your—your, you know."

My you know... My tamkarra.

Max thought back to his efforts in the cabin—the letter opener, the pennies. The way he'd kept a picture of them in his mind, a sense of the area displaced, a clairvoyant's feel for the mass and the space around them, how he could maneuver it all at the same time. It was clearer to him than the room around him now.

"Max," Stout implored. "*Max.*" But Max was wasted with exhaustion; the miner looked dead already.

"Twenty seconds now," said Nurse Agnes.

The boy pushed out a deep breath, and stepped up to the patient and opened his legs wide. The man's penis lay bent like a bloody slug. The wound itself was submerged beneath a sticky soup of blackish blood. But, as if time had slowed, as if he were in a weird fever dream, Max sent his thoughts down into it, down into the man's groin, into his wound; he imagined himself tiny, pictured himself swimming, paddling and kicking down into the blood, up into the flow, into the spurt and pulse of it. He resisted every thought, every sensation, but this one. He sent out his intention and he could feel it, he was there—all around him was a thick stew, he was pushing blindly, kicking upstream in a viscous river of scarlet darkness. The spurting pushed against him now, faint and weak, but he could feel the flow—by mere sensation he could understand that the burst of blood came from his left

—from there—

from that way, and he pushed into it until it seemed the very strongest. He came to the place where the flow pumped out of the artery. Each wave was weaker than the last.

From faraway, Nurse Agnes' voice: "Ten seconds, people."

And there it was—the laceration. It was a simple matter then, just pinch it closed. Max felt the cut, a jagged, sloppy gash on both sides, more like a rend. With his awareness of the space within the wound, he found the surge and went upstream just a bit more...found it—surrounded it—

—and clamped it. The flow stopped. Max held his breath, and waited. The pooling, as bad as it was, did not build. It was stable.

"And he's done," Nurse Agnes said evenly.

Back in the room, his feet on solid ground again, Max let the air out of his lungs and stepped away, swiping at his eyes with his forearm. "I think I got it," he said, and staggered. The opposite wall was a hundred yards away. The room was quiet except for the soft spatting of liquid; the empty seats in the theater above watched him. Nurse Agnes pursed her lips, her eyes cool. Stout, his hair hanging in sweaty, desperate coils, went over to put two fingers on the miner's

THE OCCULTISTS

neck.

The young nurse came back into the room then, a heavy black bottle of blood in her hands. She stood there, uncertain, until Nurse Agnes waved her over. "Quick, quick," the older nurse said, and took the jar from her and put it onto the table next to the miner.

Stout looked at Max. "Can you hold it until I stitch it back up?"

"It'll last," Max said, not sure how he knew this. "At least for a little while." His voice rattled in his head, making him dizzy. The pooled blood was slick as he stepped away and tread evenly through it, leaving red footprints across the room. He went and stood with his back to the wall. It was cool and solid, two things he needed just then. His brain felt scraped out; he'd never done anything like that before, and it occurred to him that if he'd had a moment to think about it, surely he would have failed. Only through working by instinct—quickly, hazily, blindly—did he have any chance of success at all.

He felt a pair of eyes blazing at him, and looked up to see the tiny stern nurse—*Meredith, that was her name, Meredith*—standing there with the black bottle of blood in her hands. Stout and Nurse Agnes and the young nurse had run a suction tube from it and into the miner, and were working calmly and deliberately, refilling the miner's tiny empty tunnels. But the stern nurse wasn't watching them; she was watching Max. The bloody mask across her face puffed in and out with her breath. Tendrils of hair had come loose and hung wild about her face and neck, and the plane of her chest rose and fell with her breath, and she was looking at him with something like fear.

FOURTEEN: EAVESDROPPING

WITH THE INCIDENT IN the operating theater, Max's *tamkarra* found an unlikely boost of momentum, and his work quickly moved beyond pennies and letter openers. Soon he was levitating clothes and pens, books and shoes, creek pebbles, birds' nests, coffee cups, and once—one late exhausted night after he'd been practicing all day and his mind had slipped into murky, unexplored places—his own bed. He'd been lying there on top of it, eyes glazed, needing to sleep but wanting one more victory. Drunk on his newfound abilities, obsessed with gaining new ground, he clenched his fists, stretched his legs, felt the oxygen burning in his lungs. Fatigue chewed at the edges of his perception, but he kept his focus—his *intention*, as Durga had said—on the task at hand. He closed his eyes and invoked in his mind a picture of his bed, hovering a foot above the floor, the four legs bobbing slightly as if floating on calm water. Once he had that image, he visualized the articles in his room—a drinking glass he'd swiped from the mess hall, the two Indian head pennies, his pants on the floor, a writing pen, his shirt draped over a footstool, the footstool itself—all of them rising and circling around him like satellites orbiting a star. He concentrated; with his eyes squeezed shut, he sensed movement. Physically, it felt as if nothing had changed, but in his intentionality he kept his blind focus for maybe a minute, until a single dribble of water splashed his forehead and ran down the scalp above his ear.

He opened his eyes. His bed was off the floor, the ceiling two feet above him, and the items he'd pictured spun in the space between: the tilted drinking glass, still holding a swallow of water, the wadded up pants, the stool, his shirt with its wrinkled empty arms splayed as if pleading with him to stop. All of them spinning, spinning, endlessly spinning.

Max's mind reeled. A new confidence rose inside him, a fragile emerald sprig breaking through into warm sunshine. His intention, his conjury, his *tamkarra*. Black Howard was right; he could do it, too.

He set the bed down, but left the other items up there, spinning, spinning, rolling and tumbling. He pulled up the covers and drifted into sleep.

He awoke in the cool, cloistered hush of early morning. Maybe it was still night. He looked toward the ceiling. In the shadows the items were still spinning, silent, almost frictionless and without resistance. A drowsy thought came to him: once set in motion, they would stay that way until he wanted them to stop. He put his head back down and slept deeper than he had in weeks.

September passed without incident—sessions in the Hall of the Woods; two more happily uneventful turns as blood boy; letters to Ethie and his mother; *tamkarra*.

Black Howard was delighted that Max had made inroads. The first morning back in the Hall of the Woods, he reached behind Max and from nowhere produced a ragged bouquet of elephant's foot blossoms, their stems squeezed down into a long-necked vase. Their spindly lavender petals practically demanded the boy be proud of himself. "They won't die," Black Howard whispered after their assembly, as Max carried them out the little door. "They'll never die." In his room Max watered them and put them by the window, in the sunlight, just in case. They brightened the place considerably.

Every week or so, castoff trinkets would appear on his windowsill—from the magpies, surely, though it happened mostly when Max was asleep. Dull cufflinks, rusted military medals, torn ribbons, jeweled hair combs with missing teeth, and, once, a broken glass bottleneck the very same medicinal green as a Uranithor bottle. It made Max think of his mother and Ethie again; he had tried to put them out of his mind as best he could and get on with things, but they were there, always there, lurking painfully at the edges of his thoughts.

By now it was the second week of October. The tallgrass had grown to its full height, sometimes as much as chest-high or even taller. Out on the prairie the gentle hills and swells seemed to rise and fall of their own accord, and more than once on a walk Max felt the world pitching like an ocean, swaying gently from side to side. The air was mild in the mornings and afternoons, but an hour after sunset temperatures would dive to near freezing. The night sky burned crystalline and cold, the stars flashed grandly, and Max spent more than a few evenings huddled outside his cabin, face craned skyward, studying the constellations. He learned of Aquila the eagle, Ursa the bear, and Perseus, the slayer of the gorgon Medusa. Afterimages of the twelve signs of the zodiac burned in his vision at night when he lay in bed.

The other apprentices were the same as ever: Sage, gaunt and dreamy; Rosalie, distant but proud; Durga, keen and vain. From time to time Max and Durga ate dinner together in the mess hall and attempted a real friendship, but for some reason their efforts sputtered and failed. Their dinners were polite affairs, full of cordial questions, respectful smiles, and even an occasional laugh, but soon they dropped their forced efforts and kept mostly to themselves.

Harriet, petulant and radiant as always, had taken up residence in one of the empty rooms in the clinic, seeming to prefer actual plumbing to scrubbing her clothes in the icy creek. In the Hall of the Woods she would either ignore Max or vaguely threaten him, depending on her mood on a given day. The one time he had gotten up his courage and approached her, she gave him a disgruntled, almost snarling glance, but didn't say anything. He had found her sitting in one of the rocking chairs in the sunny foyer and reading a book. "I know you're still angry," he said, sitting down and trying to respect her feelings by getting right to the point. "And I see why you're angry. And I'm sorry. But I didn't know what else to do." Without a word, she closed her book, stood up, and went out the front door into the bright pale sunshine. And thus he learned to keep his distance.

One afternoon when he was in the goat stables visiting the kids, Sage mentioned that she had heard Peter Sylvester himself would be visiting soon. Max's ears perked up, but when he asked her about it, she had few details. But the next morning when he came into the Hall of the Woods, he found the place was practically spare and empty, as if Black Howard were planning on moving out and moving on.

"Naw, just gettin' ready," the magician told them after Rosalie had asked about it. "When somebody like the Postmaster comes to pay you a visit, you scrub the outhouse and comb the tangles from the horse's tails." Max was surprised at this level of honor accorded his old friend; while Peter Sylvester always demanded a certain amount of respect and even admiration, the fuss seemed ill-suited for the daftly quaint old man.

And that afternoon Max saw Tom Howland's buckboard rattling into the circular drive, and there he was—the Postmaster, his swirl of white hair longer now, wearing a pinstriped Prince Albert frockcoat and string tie, making him look as if he had stepped out of some Victorian dandy's version of the Wild West. Max felt a warm cheer whirl through him, and he went wading through the tallgrass to meet the old man.

"Hello, boy, hello, mighty nice to see you," Peter Sylvester said. He grinned as he jumped down, and they hugged. Inside, the Postmaster paused and looked around, seeming to savor the mood of the place. He sniffed the air, shuffled his feet on the old carpet, shouldered off his coat and tossed it onto one of the rocking chairs. He said, "I've heard you have had a triumph of late, young man."

A sudden clammy humility fell over Max. "Uh, yessir. I...I'm getting better. I helped Dr. Stout in the operating room."

"Saved a man's life, no less."

"I wouldn't go that far. It was...terrible."

"You did something that very few people are able to do. Dr. Stout was enormously relieved. And grateful. I had told him that you were a very special boy, but I'm not sure he knew how special until that day." He rubbed his hands zestfully together. "How is Harriet?"

Max was staring at his feet, not sure how to get into it. "She's, uh..." He thought of her dashing the water into his face, the heartless jolt of it, how it had felt like a warning, or a threat. The darling flip of her skirt as she left him in the empty hallway. "She's—she's good."

"Well, yes, yes," Peter Sylvester was saying, in a tone that told Max he wasn't really listening. "This is as it should be, then." They heard footsteps approaching, and turned to see Nurse Agnes coming down the hallway. The old man leaned in to Max, and said, "I would like to have a talk with you later, young man. In private."

Max nodded, and then Nurse Agnes was there, and she and the Postmaster hugged warmly and stepped off together, chatting arm in arm, toward the infirmary.

Max waited in the foyer, sunning himself on the sprung couches in the light from the big windows. He was surprised by his own slightly improved mood at the old man's arrival; the Postmaster's quiet ease, his familiar gentle way, somehow made the bleak halls of Steppeland feel just a tiny bit more like home. After half an hour or so, the slap of bootsteps came from down the hallway, and Max looked over to see the old man rounding the corner. "Now. Max. Where can we talk?" he asked brightly. "In private."

"Um. One of the classrooms?"

"I would prefer somewhere more private." The old man tugged at his beard for a moment, and then said, "Right. I know where we can go." He led Max out the front doors and down the wide steps and off into the southern edges of the campus. Max hadn't explored this area much before, preferring the lake and the hills to the east and north. They found a narrow path through the tallgrass and went past a scattering of low trees, where the ground grew rocky and hard. The trail led into shoulder-high weeds, and then all at once they were in a clearing—an open glade larger than the classrooms. The ground was a bare floor of rock; with no trees to shade it, the sun-warmed stone invited them to bask like lizards in the afternoon.

The Postmaster sat, firm and quick. Max was surprised again by his resilience; he'd seen Peter Sylvester working at the post office many times, of course—loading mail bags, carrying boxes, briskly hitching a horse—but he had forgotten his physical, almost simian grace. The old man moved like someone half his age.

Peter Sylvester squinted up at him. "Have a seat."

Max did. The air felt good—fragrant and clean, balanced on the edge of winter. The sunlit rock beneath him slowly warmed away the chill, and they both gazed contentedly up into the sky as the distant bleating of goats came through the tallgrass.

"I hope I didn't worry you by asking for a private conversation," the old man said. "But I wanted to find out from you how things are going."

Max wasn't sure whether to tell the truth or paint the usual rosier picture. "Things here are...are good. I've had, you know. Successes. But it's been slow.

How is Addie?"

"Oh, fine, fine, fine as always." Peter Sylvester nodded sensibly. "As for you, this is as it should be. Sometimes we find ourselves taking a little longer than we would like, but it is a big job, indeed. For everyone."

"I'm learning that."

"How are you getting on with the others?"

"Okay. More or less."

"That boy Durga? He's a handful, I know. But bright."

"Yessir." Max's first impulse was to skip telling him about Durga's help with conjury, about their little agreement to skirt around *Indocilis Privata Loqui*, at least once. But then he thought better of it. The old man was his friend; maybe, he reasoned soberly, his only friend. "Durga is the one who—who... He helped me. Taught me. But just one time."

"Ah, good." The old man didn't seem too concerned about this. "I'm not familiar with the other two—Sage and that Rosie girl."

"Rosalie. I don't know them very well, but they've never been anything but nice to me." Max didn't mention Sage's self-destructive habit of wandering in the Akashic wilderness, or Rosalie's seeming lack of interest in anyone but Black Howard. Overhead, a gaggle of geese sailed by in a loose, triangular V, their cranky old man's honk briefly drowning out the distant braying goats. As they passed, Max wondered how much of the real truth, the ugly truth, he should tell the Postmaster. There had been victories, yes; his recent small successes had given him a timid new belief in himself, as fragile as a candle flame. But other things were deeply off-kilter. He felt lost, genuinely lost. The episode with Mister Splitfoot had cracked his brittle world wide open with terrifying ease. He still couldn't understand what the crazy hill spirit had wanted with him, and there wasn't a single thing he could think of to do about it.

He rubbed his eyes, trying to distract from how worried he was. "But it's...scary. I'm sure you've heard of my visit from Mister Splitfoot."

"I did. Very troubling. I'm sorry that happened, my boy." The old man's woolly brows knitted together with concern. "We have heard of isolated moments like this. Through the years—the decades, really—he has briefly appeared, and frightened people, and then usually moved on. He seems to particularly enjoy tormenting non-adepts—nescient folk, like the two terribly sad Burke girls. More capable and self-reliant individuals—people like us, people who can defend themselves—get a much lesser share of his attention."

Max thought of Black Howard's story: *We will meet proper one day. And then I will sep'rate your head from your body.*

"I don't think you will have to worry about him," the old man was saying. "He's...inexplicable. But despite what you may have thought, any actual consequences from his presence are quite rare."

The old man ran his hands vigorously through his hair. "But listen," he said, his tone brightening. "I want to talk about something a little more cheerful. I know you're worried about your family back home. I bring good tidings. Everyone is fine. Your mother is not completely mended, not yet, but she is much better. Addie looked in on her not long before I left. Improving every day. Happily taking her tonic. Addie has made sure to let them know what is happening here with you—they are concerned but relieved that you are safe." He shook his head in admiration of all that had happened. "The Hearst sisters have helped them somewhat with finances. I'm not sure your mother and Ethie know what to do with those three odd ladies, but the nuisance has been rather good for them, I think. Stirred things up a bit. And that Beckman fellow has finally stopped badgering the both of them, and they have resumed their normal—well, somewhat normal—lives."

"The police are still at my house?"

"Not anymore. Beckman believes the accident which took your stepfather was a random murder. Probably a vagabond or hobo. You have been deemed a witness that got spooked and ran. I don't think you are off the hook quite yet, but it shouldn't be long now."

Max looked up at the sky. The geese were gone. It was open and sapphire clear, ready for the coming winter.

"Your situation was not exactly good for your mother's state of mind, you understand that. But when she learned things had leveled out for you, she seemed to perk up. I wouldn't say she is healed—heavens no—but I would say she is much improved. And Ethie, of course, is Ethie. Solid and cranky as always."

That was good to hear. Ethie could always be counted on to supply some dry acerbicism to put things in perspective. Maybe he could go home soon and leave this crazy divining business to the people who wanted it.

"She's gonna be fine, Max. We all are. We have asked quite a bit from you, but would never do that without providing something of our own in return." Max smiled. "Things are changing, my boy. And for the better. We feel great possibility in the air. I've always said it. Your role in Dr. Stout's operating theater is no coincidence. We have asked him to work a bit closer with you than with the others. In this way you can learn and observe. Nurse Agnes, Tom Howland—we all agree that you stand apart from your peers. We want you to study as much as you can, to grow and become ascendant with our brethren."

The faraway voice echoed from out on the prairie: *Ascendant with our brethren. Our brethren. The Brotherhood of the Aurora.*

The old man put an arm around Max's shoulders and they sat wordless, feeling the lovely cool air drifting against their faces. Maybe for the first time since he'd come to Steppeland—certainly the first time since he'd told Black Howard his story—Max felt himself relaxing, sensed the tight clockwork coil of anxiety unwind and release a bit of its strain.

"Are you hungry?" the old man said. "I'm hungry."

"The food here is terrible. Everything is bland."

"Stout has the culinary sophistication of a snap turtle." The old man laughed and stood gracefully up. He dusted the seat of his pants, and held his hand out for Max to pull himself up. "Let's go eat."

That afternoon, Max had been asked to deliver several files from the infirmary to Dr. Stout's office. He did, taking the papers from the tiny nurse, who was not stern anymore, but terrified; she could hardly look him in the eye, which he supposed was a slight improvement. But something was digging at him now, a comment the Postmaster had tossed off in their conversation: the odd idea that his mother was "happily taking her tonic." It was a tiny thing, really. But Lora hated that stuff, had hated it from the moment Sig had pressed it upon her. Max suspected the Uranithor had more than a little to do with how unhealthy she became. She had never, not once, "happily taken her tonic."

He came into Stout's foyer, a tight little cell-like room, made smaller because every wall was lined with brick-like medical texts stuffed into dusty shelves. The books looked easily as cryptic and inexplicable as any of the ancient tomes in the Hall of the Woods' library. Max guessed they hadn't been touched, let alone opened, in years. From inside the office came the low drone of conversation. He was about to knock, but then paused, file in hand; he couldn't quite hear what they were saying, but it was clearly the Postmaster and Stout, having a tense conversation, from the sound of things. As the words volleyed back and forth, Max's curiosity got the better of him. There was an air vent about two feet from the door, and he crouched down close to it. The voices were clearer now but still not quite discernible, so he took a moment to calm himself and closed his eyes, and did what he had done only once before in his entire life: he sent his intention, his awareness, outside of himself, of his own body, down into the grated passage of the air vent.

For a moment he was wildly disoriented, and nothing made spatial sense. The ceiling was a mile above, the dirty carpet was a wild forest of fuzz, and the bookshelves towered above him like the walls of a canyon. But his perspective had merely shifted, relocated, resized itself, and he took a moment to breathe and get his bearings. The air gate, with its repellently grimy iron crosshatches, loomed like something from some immense industrial factory. He climbed past an old spiderweb littered not only with the husks of insects but the disarrayed corpse of the long-legged host herself, and into the open orifice of the vent. Against the far side there was a huge cabinet pushed up to the grate, so it was dark and he couldn't see the two men, but as he approached, their voices immediately became more clear.

"They've made it plain," Stout was saying in a tired voice. "These federal people have targeted me, they want me out of business." When Stout got nervous his voice took on a shrill, tinny quality, which it had now. Max pictured him at the window, red-faced and sweaty and swiping the lenses of his spectacles with the tail of his shirt.

"I can assure you that no one is targeting you, William." This was Peter Sylvester. "No one important, anyway. These people of yours, whatever they are called—"

"The AMA," Stout interrupted. "American. Medical. Association. In Chicago."

"This...A-M-A," said the Postmaster slowly and evenly, as if he were talking to a child, "whoever you believe is targeting you, they are not the ones you should be worried about. Trust me—these people are just a distraction. Forget about them."

"But why are they after *me? Us?*"

"I should think they don't like your billy gonads, William. It doesn't take a genius to figure that one out. But there are other people, other concerns, who are far more important. Our real worries are elsewhere."

A silence fell. A chair shifted, floorboards creaked. At first the Postmaster didn't say anything. Then, almost reluctantly: "This is not something we share openly, William. But these people—they are on a path of exterminating any rivals. All rivals. Extermination. We are at war. I am happy to say they seem to be close to collapse, but you never know. Until then the situation remains very serious. We need to ready our initiates and keep them that way."

"Ready them for what?" Stout must have been stung by the rebuke, because his voice now was as small as a child's. "Protection? Incursion?"

Protection? The words caught in Max's mind. *Incursion?*

"We aren't breeding goats, William. The young people are quite naive and inexperienced, most of them. They are chosen in part because of this. They are a particularly uneven bunch. Thus we need things hurried up a bit. We need them ready."

The word still buzzed in Max's brain. *Incursion? Incursion into where?*

The Brotherhood and the Faqrs, Durga had said. *They are at odds.*

"Do they know anything about this—this conflict?" Stout said. "Do they know what you're trainin' them for?"

"Well, no." Peter Sylvester sounded irritable and bored. "Too much disclosure is ill-advised. As you know."

For a long time the men were quiet; the silence was loud. Max pictured the Postmaster rubbing at his temples, Stout still at the window, maybe looking out at the lake.

There was another creak, and the old man's voice came and went now, as if he had started pacing the room: "Think of it like this. Anyone who gets in our way can be persuaded. The initiates can be very useful. And there are more of them, more than you know."

"Persuaded? That's a funny way to put it." When Peter Sylvester didn't answer, Stout said, "But your opposin'...the—the people...the who?"

"For God's sake, they're called the Faqrs, William. The Faqrs."

"Your...your fuckers. *Fakkers?* They're the only ones you're at war with?"

"At this point, yes. Everyone else is a distraction. Including your idiotic AMA."

More petulant silence. More creaking chairs. A drawer opened and shut and Stout said something Max couldn't hear. Then: "Durga's quite talented, and can—"

"—Durga is an Indian. He knows nothing of American protocol, of Midwestern politesse. Smart but far too arrogant for his own good. And the others—what's her name—Sage? What can we say about her? She won't look anyone in the goddamn eye. And I don't know this negro voodoo girl. That leaves Harriet, the one with the scowl. Talented but moody. Addie and I knew her previously and were quite impressed, but her impetuousness is an issue. And the Grahame boy is a bundle of nerves. Like he's seeing ghosts around every corner."

Max felt as if a knife had pricked him. Stout was quiet. The old man must have sat down, because a chair creaked and his voice was clearer. "But we'll need them soon. There is tremendous potential out there in the woods, William. Explosive potential. You literally have no idea what can be done. Any and all splinter organizations will be silenced, I can promise you that. Mme. Z— will be among the first."

Mme. Z—. Max's heart quickened; he hadn't heard her name in a while.

"And the AMA," Stout said.

"All right. Them, too. If we need to use our initiates to protect ourselves from these people of yours, or from anyone—well, that's not a tangent. That's *why we're here*, William. That's why *you're* here. Let us know what you need and we'll take care of it."

Another pause. Stout said in a small, scolded voice, "Well. We'll move faster. I'll let everyone know."

Max heard someone stand up again, and he just had time to pull his awareness from the vent and stand up when the door opened. Peter Sylvester stepped out, but he stopped when he saw Max. He grinned suddenly, which struck Max as odd; just a moment before, he sure didn't sound happy.

"Hello, Max."

Max held up the files. "I'm supposed to give these to Dr. Stout."

The old man turned to address Stout. "You have our blessings, William," he said. "We are truly grateful for all of your efforts." There was a leather portfolio in the old man's arm, and he took a moment to showily collect a few papers that were threatening to slip out of it. Then he left the office.

Max turned to give Stout a quick fake smile and hand him the files, but the door had already slammed in his face.

Back in his bungalow, Max sat at the battered desk. The overheard conversation buzzed in his mind like angry little insects. He knew he and the other initiates were being trained for some purpose—even at his young age he understood that nothing in this world was truly free—but the tense discussion in Stout's office had unraveled him a bit. *Mme. Z– and the Faqrs.* That darkly succinct use of the term "silenced." Even Stout had seemed alarmed by it. Max was reminded of McKinley's assassination; he certainly was "silenced," wasn't he? Was *Tchowgosh* part of the Aurora? Or the Faqrs? And who really were these Faqrs, anyway?

Ready them for what? Stout had said. *Protection? Incursion?*

There is tremendous potential out there in the woods, Peter Sylvester had said. *Explosive potential. You literally have no idea what can be done.* And then the talk of Max himself. *And the Grahame boy seems like a constant bundle of nerves. Like he's seeing ghosts around every corner.*

Explosive potential.

We are at war.

We need them ready.

It was too much. Max went outside in the dusk to stare at the Steppeland Mercy Hospital, black and hollow against the blue evening. The dread had returned, heavier than ever. He put a palm to his forehead and felt hot, feverish skin. He missed Selleford, he missed his home, he wanted to be back there sailing on his bicycle down wide, tree-shaded lanes in a world where none of this conjury stuff ever existed. Even Sig was better than this. Instead there was just this dismal clinic—dark and empty, the giant rotting husk of a molted insect.

He needed to talk to someone about this. What Nurse Agnes had told him—what Peter Sylvester himself had told him—had very little to do with what he had overheard in Dr. Stout's office. And the Postmaster himself—who really *was* that behind the closed door? Because it certainly didn't sound like the man he had come to admire.

Durga was the obvious person to talk to, but he'd made it clear more than once he was finished helping Max. "They are going to think that you and I are a connivance of two," he'd said one night while eating dinner, before asking Max to wait five minutes after letting him leave the dining hall unaccompanied. Max thought he was joking, but for a week after that Durga hardly said a word to him.

He went back inside and lay in the bed as the pale glow of afternoon shaded down into evening. He was cold and restless. He put on his shoes and went to the commissary, took a meager meal—a lump of meatloaf, bland mushroom gravy, a hard sourdough roll—from the old lady. The room was empty. He pulled a chair over close to the fire and ate alone, the plate perched on his hot, clasped knees.

He didn't really know Rosalie well enough to ask her about it all. Her quiet, sphinx-like self-assurance had always intimidated him, along with her shrewd gaze that was not altogether friendly. And Harriet, as always, was simply out of the question.

Then there was Black Howard. He was as real and pure as the icy creek outside the cabin. But Max had to admit didn't fully understand the nature of his commitment to Steppeland, and to the Aurora. If nothing else, he was certainly in their employ. At best, his loyalties would be torn. Max swallowed meatloaf and shook the hair from his eyes; it needed more parsley and less thyme. No. He doubted Black Howard would make anything of it, but he couldn't take that chance.

So, more from the lack of other options, rather than a sense of any real affection or friendship, it would have to be Sage. Sage, who had hardly said a nice to word to him, or anyone, in months. He would ask the barley-headed girl from New York for her help.

The moon was just a slash in the night sky, an opening into some far bright world beyond, as Max paused outside Sage's door. Could he trust her enough to tell her what he was thinking? It was only remotely possible that she would have an answer; most likely she would ask him to leave. Either way, he supposed, it would be some sort of resolution. He knocked lightly on her door.

It opened almost at once. "Max," Sage said, surprised. She wore what looked like a man's formal shirt, which buttoned up the back and draped down to her thighs, with no pants or skirt underneath. Her hair was tied up in a half-twist, and in her hand was a half-eaten apple. Max felt an impulsive flash of regret, and wondered if he could turn this sudden intrusion—*incursion? no, intrusion*—another way.

"Is something wrong?" she said thickly, her mouth full.

"Um. No. Why do you say that?"

"You look so stricken. What are you doing?"

"Nothing. Hi." His throat was suddenly dry; he swallowed self-consciously. "But can I talk to you? About something?"

Sage gave him a funny look but she opened the door further. "All right." He stepped in. The floor plans of all the outlying cottages were the same—one modest, nearly square room—but the interior of this one was uniquely, singularly, hers. Scatterings of clothes on every surface, drawers askew, jewelry draped everywhere. A heavy tapestry—men and ladies on horses, sculpted hedges, castles in the background—hung on one wall. A trio of antelope heads, their eyes dusty and cataracted with age, staring down on him from the others. Thick rugs on the floor, and a frayed Victorian couch, its embroidery stained, was tucked along the wall near the window. The bed was the messiest, with piles of clothes—skirts and scarves and blouses—strewn across it. Most of it pushed aside, with a reedy, human-shaped indentation on the very edge.

Sage went to the couch and sat down with one bare leg folded under. A spine-cracked book sat open-faced on the arm of the sofa. Several cigarette ends lay bent and stubbed in an ashtray on the floor.

"Please," she said politely. Max folded himself into the far end of the couch, aware of how cramped her cottage felt. Compared to hers, his own was barren and huge.

"I'm sorry to bother you..." he said, and let his eyes settle nervously on her face. "But I have something to tell you about, and see what you make of it."

She crunched loudly into her apple. "What is it?"

Feeling petty and ashamed of himself, Max told her about his eavesdropping of Dr. Stout's office—the air vent, the conversation between Stout and Peter Sylvester. He told her about that curious name he kept hearing, Mme. Z—. He told her about Czolgosz and President McKinley and the opposition between the Aurora and the Faqrs. *We are at war*, the Postmaster had said. *Any and all splinter organizations will be silenced.* Max still didn't have a firm grasp of what all that meant, but he had a pretty good guess.

Sage listened, the apple devoured, legs bent under a hair-strewn blanket. When he finished, she just shrugged skeptically. "I mean, of course we're to be useful. Why do you think they're teaching us? I'm not exactly swooning with shock, Max."

"But Nurse Agnes told me the ones who graduate from Steppeland go on to enjoy peaceful, happy, useful lives." *The mastery of the universe, for the benefit of all mankind*, she'd said. *There are more of them than you know. A vast network of initiates, all working quietly together for the betterment of the world.*

Sage's voice brought him back to the room. "That's what I was told, as well."

Max blinked at her. "So what do you think about this 'silencing' business?"

"I don't know anything about that. I can't believe that's true. But even if it were, I'm not 'silencing' anybody, if that means what I think it means. I don't care who it is."

"That's what I'm saying. It's making me very nervous." An image pushed itself into Max's brain: Sig's gruesome death by the Moorlander—it had come so suddenly, so horribly and irrevocably, that every foul word Sig had said, every hideous deed he had done, seemed to pale in comparison. The more he thought about it, the more Sig's fate felt drastically out of proportion. He almost felt sorry for the man.

"Well, we're not being educated and nurtured to do stage illusions, that's for sure. So yes, they do have an agenda. They want us to be useful."

"How? Séances?"

"Maybe. Other stuff. Divination. Astral travel."

"For what? Silencing? Incursion? Extermination?"

Sage pursed her lips. Her sandy hair fell in a long sheet along the slope of her neck, one bare collarbone asserting itself from under the folds of her shirt. The hollow above it was deep enough to hold water. "That sounds sort of drastic, Max. Maybe you're confused, maybe they meant just...I don't know, *scaring* them or something."

"'Silenced' is what they said. Persuaded. It didn't sound encouraging. This place has given me the willies ever since I got here, and now it's gotten worse." He looked at Sage's apple core, which sat on an old shipping case that she was using as a side table. The white flesh of it was turning brown. "Do you think I should talk to Black Howard?"

"I wouldn't. I don't really like him anyway. He creeps me out, the way he looks at me."

"Is there anything you can do? You know, the...the way you do it?"

"You mean the Akasha." Sage picked a long, listless strand of sandy hair from the blanket and held it up to the lamplight. "You want me to *spy* on them?"

"Why not? For our own good?" Sage didn't answer, she just looked at Max in a way that made him feel pitiful. She was right. He was paranoid, his sad little attempt at solving mysteries killed in its infancy, cut short before it had even really begun. He looked up at the tapestry. There were many details in it—hills, roads, a fantastical viaduct in the distance—but the one that caught his eye was a stag hunt in the lower corner. Men on horseback, with dogs racing breathlessly after a hart which leapt over colorful lakes and trees. Its breast was already pierced by half a dozen arrows.

Sage leaned over and touched his knee. "Look. Let me help you. Something to ease your mind."

"Like...what?"

"You're worried about your family. I'll go to them. Tell them you're okay. That you love them."

Max stared at her. "You can do that?"

"In a limited way, yes. Write in mirrors, notes in the dust, that kind of thing. The Akasha is every time and every place." She wiped her nose with the heel of her hand.

But notes in mirrors and that kind of thing would only scare the hell out of them. "I don't think so," Max said. "And anyway, for me it'll be minutes. For you it could be days." In the time he'd been at Steppeland, Sage was looking quite a bit older already. It had been the subject of many whispered discussions among the other initiates—she was healthy and clear-eyed, but visibly more mature than the others. It was disturbing, once Max thought about it.

She leaned over and affectionately pinched him. "I'll keep it quick. I promise." He looked back at the tapestry, let out a worried breath. "You look so sad, Max. Like a little boy who's lost his mommy. Anyway, I've never been to that part of the country. It may be, you know. Fun."

Max thought of Selleford: trees, Main Street, post office. Sig's big, dark house. It was November, but the afternoons would still be warm. "It's depressing down there," he said.

"I can look around." A smile had crept onto her face, and he could see she was pleased with herself, with her talents and how far they had come. Like him, she had made inroads. "Tell you how things are going. Put your mind at ease."

"I can't ask you to do that. It's too much."

"You didn't ask, I offered. I want to. For you."

"What happens if you...you know?" *If you get lost. If you don't come back.*

"I've been doing it here at night by myself, Max. I like it, it makes me feel good to be in there." She straightened up and turned to him. "So. Where am I going?"

Reluctantly, he told her about Selleford, about his family, about Sig's big house. When he was done, she sat up, cross-legged, and slid closer to him.

"Let me look at you, here, in the eyes." She took his hands. Her dark gaze met his own. "Like this. Yes, all right, hold it, *sssshhhhhhhh...*"

Max felt almost embarrassed, a dry cough tickling in his throat—which he forgot about when he felt the slight movement inside his head, down in his brainstem and then upwards, into his lobes, a fleet footstep roaming in his thoughts and memories. It was Sage, digging around in the attic of his mind. Rashly, before he could stop it, he wondered if she could tell that he found her too skinny.

She smiled. "I am *not*," she said. "You're too fat, you soft silly boy." But she grew suddenly serious, and flinched as something flashed by in her eyes. "Oooh. Your stepfather! Ah! I'm sorry for what happened, Max. That's terrible! And the police! Did they really think that you—?"

She jerked away, taking in a shaky hiss of air. "Wow," she said, blinking. "I had no idea. You've really had a time of it."

For a moment they sat there on her couch in silence. Then she said, "Okay. Okay," and wiped her nose again. "It'll be twenty minutes or so. Maybe an hour, I don't know. You don't look so good, Max, maybe you'll want to, I don't know, take a nap or something." She sat back and put her feet flat on the floor and her hands on her thighs. After a couple of deep, calming breaths, she became still again, like an oversized ventriloquist's dummy. In a moment she wasn't there anymore.

He got up and went to the window and pulled back the curtains. And there she was: in the night, a diaphanous, willowy form drifting away into the tallgrass, pushing out toward another time and space.

He went back to the couch and sat down next to her. Her body was there, just a shell. He looked idly around her place—battered books, wrinkled clothes, tacky costume jewelry. He knew he couldn't sleep, and it felt too weird with her right here, too much like eavesdropping again, which hadn't made him feel very proud at all. So he decided to step outside and get some fresh air.

Above the silhouette of the clinic hung the bright band of the Milky Way—a vast splendid tapestry all its own. The rustle of the tallgrass comforted him, a million voices all murmuring together at the same time, whispering to themselves in their unknowable tongue. Max's head hurt, but the air, as always, felt good; the sweet smell of oats and hay drifted on a slight breeze, over the sour and fecund but still slightly pleasurable scent wafting from the goat stables.

Just then a light threw itself across the grass, and his shadow appeared before him. "Hey," said a voice. He turned and saw Sage there at her opened door.

"You're back?" He felt suddenly worried again. "Already?"

"It's been hours." Her glance was agitated. "Yeah, very strange."

"Why?"

"There was nobody home."

"What?" Max felt his pulse quicken. Nobody home? His mother never left the house. She was practically an invalid. He went to Sage. "What does that mean?"

"There was no one there, Max. I went to your house. It was dark. Closed up. Smelled...moldy."

"Moldy?"

"Musty. That closed-in smell. Like it had been shut down for a while."

"No one? No—no maid?"

"I checked the rooms. It was all empty." Sage went inside the cabin, to the window and wrenched it open. "I hate that smell, that mildew smell. Like too many wet sickly moldy spores growing all at once."

"You sure you didn't get there in the...in the future or something? Or maybe the past?"

Sage looked at him sharply. "Max, I know. I'm good at this now. I went through the house. Your clothes were in your closet. Your stupid books in that bookcase. They had your name in them. It was hot in there. Two horses in the stables, but they were skinny. Starving, actually. They'd been cribbing away at the wood of their stalls. It was all chewed up. I looked for something to feed them, but there was nothing. Their water was dry. I went and brought them back some water." Her nostrils flared and her eyes were troubled. "I was there for hours, Max. For a good part of the whole day. Nobody else came around."

Max stood in the doorway, flatfooted, an ache spreading up the back of his shoulders and his neck. He put a palm to his forehead, and found it hot. Maybe he really was getting sick. The little faces in the tapestry on the wall all seemed to stare at him. Why was the house empty? Why were Jefferson and Pearl starving? Where was his mother? Where was Ethie? He crossed his arms and leaned his head against the doorjamb. Peter Sylvester had assured him that things were good, that Lora was being taken care of. But he never said she wasn't even in the house.

He turned around and looked out at the night sky; the stars were brighter than ever. "Moldy," he said to no one.

FIFTEEN: ABSCONDING

FOR SEVERAL HOURS MAX paced or sat at his desk as the loose contents of the bungalow whirred in a slowly spinning vortex up near the ceiling. He felt unbalanced, off-center, listing to starboard and unable to right himself. He peeled himself from his jacket and lay in his bed, wondering if maybe it was time for a little exploring of his own. But how? Confronting them directly wouldn't work. They were too smart, too easily immune to any pleas or threats he could make. He could flail and cry, but it wouldn't make a mouse shit's bit of difference. No, it would have to be stealth or nothing at all. He could sneak into Nurse Agnes' office near the infirmary, go through her desk when she wasn't there. But something told him that would be a waste of time; more likely than not, nothing was there. And he kept picturing himself being discovered by the tiny, stern nurse, the one who was afraid of him. The wild, terrified charges she would make. What a calamity that would be.

But Stout's office, now that was an interesting thought. Max had seen glimpses in there. Contracts and charts and cabinets and all kinds of paperwork.

He sat suddenly up in his bed. There were tons of files in there. He was sure of it. A person could learn a lot, looking at that stuff.

The next morning, Peter Sylvester said his goodbyes to everyone, and Max gave him a quick, falsely affectionate hug before he was taken by Tom Howland back down the circular drive and out of sight. They had wanted Max to go, but he pleaded sickness to throw off any errant mind reading. For the next several days he skipped Black Howard's sessions in the Hall of the Woods and quietly shadowed Dr. Stout as he moved about the clinic. Stout seemed always to have busy mornings, but was performing fewer glandular replacements lately, and he came and went from his office with frustrating irregularity. His afternoons were calmer, filled with administration, correspondence, meetings in his office; Nurse Agnes stopped by maybe half a dozen times a day, and others, too—orderlies, nurses, various assistants, many of whom Max had never seen before. There were times in the afternoons when Stout left for half an hour or so—quick meals in the commissary, conversations over cigars on the clinic's back balcony, which overlooked the goat stables, the booming grounds, and the undulant vastness of the Sand Hills beyond. In the evenings he often worked late, sometimes until 10 p.m. or so, and after that every door to the clinic would be locked except for the very far end of the north wing, the same one Durga and Sage and Max had gone through the night they had first shown him the bungalows.

When he wasn't roaming the halls, Max would sit in the sunlight in the big chairs in the foyer, pretending to read one of Black Howard's books or watching the delivery carriages come and go in the circular drive. Stout would stroll past in that shuffling, short-legged gait of his, down into his office, shutting the door behind him. The clanging echo would roll up the empty corridor like a bowling ball.

Finally, it was time: when the hour grew late, Max slipped through the north-wing door and returned to the chairs in the foyer, where he sat in the shadows for maybe half an hour. Anxious, needing to spin off some jittery energy, he set all the chairs around him gently rocking with his *tamkarra* and smirked to himself in the darkness, thinking the foyer must have looked as if it were possessed by a coterie of geriatric ghosts. After a time he heard Stout's door open; the chairs all stopped at once. Stout emerged, hat in hand, and headed toward the south wing, toward the operating arena. He didn't turn Max's way.

Max took a moment to let the footsteps die in the distance, then approached the doctor's suite. The hallway was silent and empty, the door firmly locked. He thought of all the items spinning above his bed—practically everything in his room that wasn't bolted down—and the vast negative space surrounding them. He'd literally wrapped his mind around them many times now. Now he did the same thing here: leaning casually in the darkness with his back against the wall, hands in his pockets as if he were waiting on someone, he sent his intention down into the keyhole.

Dust and grease covered everything around him, but in the shadows he sensed a row of spring-loaded pins. There was a worn circular brass housing and an easily discernible line that all the pins had to clear before the housing could rotate to open the lock. He felt for the pins keeping the lock in place and lifted them easily. The brass housing spun, and in a moment he heard a click. The door was unlocked. Easy as pie. Easier, in fact.

Inside the suite, the inner office door stood slightly ajar. Max went in the office, and glanced around in the darkness. On the opposite wall facing the desk was a huge portrait of Dr. Stout; in it, he was reading a book of some sort, looking handsome and young and significantly less doughy. That Stout sat and stared at an idealized painting of himself all day struck Max as grotesque, but somehow predictable. Max had never liked him, and liked him even less now.

Along the walls, multiple medical degrees were framed, and above them primitive childlike drawings and thank you letters had been tacked onto every available space: *Thank you for restoring my masculine essence*, one of the notes said in guileless handwriting. *I thank you and my wife also thanks you, hee hee hee hee hee!* The window behind the desk was open just a crack, and a faint antiseptic tang blew in from somewhere. Stout's desk was cluttered—accounting statements, correspondence, a poorly folded map, a letter opener surprisingly similar to the one that Max had used, a pair of binoculars, scattered shells for his gun, a box of cigars. A file cabinet stood in the corner, with various labelings on the drawers: *Patient History*, *Research*, *Accounting*, *Taxes*, and in a somewhat different script at the very bottom, *BA*.

Max went around the desk and opened the first drawer. It was stuffed with papers, which, upon close inspection—in the dim light from the window, his eyes comically close to the paper—were mostly bookkeeping reports, receipts for commissary food stuffs, hospital expenditures, medical supplies, custodial expenses. The second drawer proved just as fruitless. Patient records, the problematic ones, at least, including an astonishing amount of threats and retributive lawsuits. In the back were reference photographs, most of them bloody and distressing: severed penises, pools of blood, blank staring corpse eyes. The third drawer was the same.

As Max looked at the last one, the one labelled *BA*, a cold prickle of dread crawled up the back of his neck. Honestly, he preferred not to open it at all, thinking it would be better not to know. But he forced himself to pull it open, and immediately saw a stack of letters. His own letters.

His heart thundered in his ears as he took them out and inspected each one. They had been cleanly opened, meticulously sliced at the top—those goddamn letter openers again—and presumably read. They were all here. Every single one of his letters was here. Opened and read, but never sent. He looked in the drawer for others, maybe from the rest of the initiates, but his letters were alone. Otherwise, the drawer was empty.

They were singling him out. Him and no one else.

With cold hands, Max put the letters back and closed the drawer. For a long time he sat in Stout's chair and simply breathed, trying not to think. Surely there was some mistake. Surely other letters were kept somewhere.

This Grahame boy seems like a constant bundle of nerves. Like he's seeing ghosts around every corner.

His mind swung from possibility to possibility, hoping to find a reason why his letters were never sent. Maybe they were trying to test his paranoia. Or maybe they had been mailed, and then for some strange reason returned.

But that was stupid. His letters were here. He opened the drawer again: there they were, clean and smooth and stacked in the bottom drawer of a file cabinet. Read but never sent. A sudden growing unease overtook him, a sense that he was being watched. He turned toward the window. The circular drive was empty, the lake and the copse of trees beyond just a dark, shapeless stain, like smoke in the distance. The smear of clouds above was as still as an oil painting.

Every loose object in the room was spinning again.

Max lay in the bed, his dark thoughts whirling the items not only around in a circle, but this time rotating individually as well, at their own rate, like planets and moons in an orbit. Some twirled fast, some slow, clockwise and counterclockwise, a private Copernican galaxy made of household items.

Anger, it seemed, was good for *tamkarra*.

Max lay there, feeling drugged from frustration, his thoughts coming slow, as if his dark mood were mutating into some horrible brain disease. He was trapped between two unpleasant realities: staying at the school and denying his own needs—*his mother, for god's sake!*—or absconding for home and permanently damaging his relationship with Stout and Black Howard and most likely even with the Postmaster himself. If he left, there would be repercussions. Most likely he would be considered an antagonist, a rogue ex-ally. He carried their lessons. He carried their secrets. They would not easily let him go.

His thoughts went back to the young woman who lived in this cabin before him—Florence, her name was. *She left suddenly last year, some kind of personal emergency or something,* Durga had said. Max wondered if she had been removed, or if her family had been "silenced." There was no way to tell, but it didn't cheer him up that this had happened before.

The next morning, he left his cabin, sleepless and exhausted, and headed for his first session in the Hall of the Woods in days. On the way into the clinic he saw Tom Howland standing on the front steps, feet planted, head lowered, consulting his timepiece. He didn't look Max's way.

Black Howard's assembly was busy as usual, but Max didn't wait around after class. He took the long way back, through the old forest, along the muddy lake path and into the clinic. By now his stomach was hollow, so he headed for the commissary; he got his lunch, a brick of too-salty pork loin and a decent tomato and onion salad with lemon, oregano, and oil—hard to mess *that* one up—and wolfed it down. But when he went down the hall, Tom Howland was there in the foyer, sitting in the chairs. Rocking slowly, bowler on head and staring out the big windows at the lake. He didn't turn as Max passed; he looked like a well-to-do traveling salesman who had just been given some particularly bad news.

With a quiver in his gut, Max went back to his bungalow. Everything in the room was spinning now up near the ceiling. The thought of taking a carriage and one of the bays appealed to him, but he knew that would only signal Stout and the rest of the staff that he had fled. Fortunately, since he'd taken to moodily disappearing into his cabin for days at a time, no one would miss him, or even come looking for him, for the better part of a week.

That evening he packed his few things together, and with the menagerie still spinning up near the ceiling, he left the bungalow and made his way through the tallgrass down to the drive. He paused in the night breeze. The Nebraska weather—chilly and dry, but the cold wasn't too brutal, at least not yet—had grown on him. And he wanted to say goodbye to everyone—to Sage, to Durga, most of all to Black Howard—but it was too risky. Maybe he would see them all again under happier circumstances. He hefted his bag and started walking.

The hike to the train station took a little more than seven hours. Whenever the rumble of approaching delivery carriages and milk wagons and even a few motorcars rose up out from over the flat horizon, Max rushed off the road to crouch in the tallgrass until they clattered by. Soon the sun peeked over the edge of the world and the morning came rushing at him across the flatlands. By the time he reached the little town, a glorious day had opened up like a jewel box, the pearl of the sun cradled in morning clouds that were still in the process of burning off. He had yet to learn if the town had a name. He strode casually past the train station; he had no money and no way to buy a ticket, and he didn't want to be marked as someone expecting an arrival, or to be marked as anything at all, really. The cafe where he and Black Howard and Tom Howland had feasted was closed and empty. No Joe Miller Joe anywhere in sight.

A lonely dirt frontage road rolled past the tracks, and Max ambled down it as if there were business to be had that way. About a quarter of a mile beyond the station, scrubby thickets grew along the line, and once he was out of sight of the buildings, he cut through the brush until he found a good place to hide. Jittery, more impatient than he'd ever been in his life, he crouched down and settled in to wait. The sun rose higher, but the clouds moved in and the day grew oddly colder; it was that time of year. He slipped on his coat and squatted in the gravel.

Several hours later, he heard a train approaching, but from the east, from Lincoln or Omaha or even Iowa, which was the wrong way. He readjusted himself back into the weeds. After another interminable period, the hiss and chug of a coming train came bouncing across the fields—this time from the west to the east, from Cheyenne or Casper or maybe Denver, which meant this was the one. Max blew out a breath, and shook his trembling hands; he'd never jumped a boxcar before, but he had read about it plenty of times in his adventure books back home.

As the train approached the station, it slowed but never stopped, and with a stab of frustration he realized it wasn't a passenger transport, but a goods wagon—a freight express, with no stopping, no need to let anyone on or off. It blew right past, and as if in a bad dream Max watched most of the cars slide by, the wind ruffling his hair. Before he knew it, the last few cars were coming—a couple of boxcars, a granger, and a battered rust-red caboose.

It was time. In a sprint Max left his protective thicket and caught up with the train. He came alongside one of the last boxcars—the sliding door was open by about eight inches, with a pregnant, velvety darkness inside—and he elbowed it slightly open and pushed his bag inside. Then, in a wild awful leap, he pulled himself up.

For a desperate moment his feet dangled; the only thing keeping him from falling under the wheels were his two palms pressed against the rust-crumbled sill of the boxcar—but then somehow he managed to balance forward and tilt his center of gravity inside. From there he was able to wedge the door further open with his shoulder, get his knee up and swing his legs onto the platform.

For a time he lay there, his breath catching in his throat; he let out a raspy, lunatic chuckle that rang against the metal sides of the car. The floor was dirty hay-strewn hardwood, deeply scratched from a thousand loads. He struggled up onto his knees, half-euphoric and half-terrified, foolishly proud of himself now, and stood carefully, wide-legged and unsteady in the train's constant wobble; the ghost of someone's frenzied laughter echoed in his head.

That was when he noticed two dress shoes in the dark corner. Max blinked. Oddly, the shoes were on the wrong feet.

A dull realization dawned over him. Above the shoes were dress slacks, trim hips. Wrists jutting from cuffed sleeves. A chest, a vest, a suit coat. A timepiece. And in the shadows, a face: Tom Howland. From under his bowler, he looked at Max, serene and cool. His temple and his jaw clenched and unclenched.

Max's heart froze. He looked at the door, the bright world outside rushing innocently by; four steps and a maniac jump and he could be free. He would land and fall and maybe hurt himself, but he would be free. He glanced back at Tom, and for the first time ever—and also for the last time, though he didn't know it then—he saw Tom Howland smile. It was a tiny thing, but the glare of it was like a kerosene lamp held too close: bright, unwelcome, pernicious, and hot.

He didn't jump. There was no point in it. This whole charade of escape, of emancipation from the Brotherhood of the Aurora, was over before it had ever begun.

Tom pushed himself up from his leaning against the wall, and came over. With a loud shrieking bang he slid the door shut.

Sixteen: In the Basement

THE CHAMBER WAS IN the cellar below the clinic—a tight, rock-walled, damp and dusty catacomb right out of Poe. The smell of rot was sickening. Four chairs crowded a small wooden table in the center, with several burning candles that nudged the shadows into the corners. Max had never been down here before, nor heard anyone speak of it; when Tom Howland and he had left the freighter and made their way back to Steppeland, Tom had simply brought him down here and pushed him into one of the chairs. Now he wasn't even sure whether the door to the corridor outside was locked or not. He supposed it didn't matter either way.

After a couple of hours, Nurse Agnes and Dr. Stout filed inside and quietly sat down. Nurse Agnes smiled at Max, but it was the sad, pitying smile of someone with terrible news. Stout seemed stern and impatient, as if dealing with the insolent boy had pulled him from important work elsewhere. Maybe it had.

"So, Grahame, you want to tell us what's goin' on?" Stout asked, taking off his glasses and rubbing the twin red indentations on the bridge of his nose.

Max shrugged. He didn't have anything to say.

"You're worried about your mother, is that it?" He considered Max through pale, puffy eyes. "This is a private clinic, son, a highly specialized facility. Once you associate with us and take from our stores, there're no do-overs." His hands were fidgety as he folded and unfolded his eyeglasses. "Do you think Durga is worried about his mother? Or his family? He is chasing preeminence, Grahame. *Global merit.* Do you think Black Howard would walk away from his work, his legacy, because of his siblings? Rosalie? Sage? Whatever that other girl's name is? All of them—*all of us*—have agreed to put that aside in order to learn. To *work.* To develop skills that are wondrous and powerful beyond any rational person's imagination. And here you are, worried about your mommy like a petulant fuckin' child."

Max stayed silent. His tiny family was all he had. *Once they're gone, they're gone,* Sig had once warned him. He'd been scolding Max about how few practical skills he had learned. *You better get your head outta them storybooks and watch and take from me while you can, sonny boy, 'cause ain't none of us gonna be around forever.* Sig was right; in the weird, enchanted world in which Max now found himself, Lora and Ethie were his sole remaining lifeline to a familiar world of sense and reason. But even in this, even in matters as mundane as family, Max felt isolated: Harriet's parents were evidently still alive and still present in her world, as were Rosalie's and Durga's. He didn't know about Sage, but he couldn't imagine she had been ripped from her familial circumstances as violently as he had been ripped from his own. Impatient,

Stout slipped his glasses back on, carefully folding the curled temple tips over his ears. Nurse Agnes' dismal smile flickered out, but then came back. The silence grew long.

Then, before he could lose his nerve, Max blurted, "How did Tom know where I was going to be before I did?"

They looked at him blankly; it occurred to him that maybe they didn't know. But Stout turned to Nurse Agnes, and said, "Get Tom in here."

She stood and went to the door. "Tom? Would you come in?"

Tom Howland stepped inside the little room, still wearing his banker's coat and hat. "Have a seat," Stout said. Tom pulled out the last chair, almost clumsily fell into it, and pointed his blank stare at Max. "Tom," Stout said stagily, "how did you know where Max was going to be?"

Tom didn't reply, he just glared at Max. And then his eyes went black. The scleras and everything else, like a void; not a shiny, reflective black, but the black of a tomb.

Max's mouth fell open. He had known Tom Howland was a peculiar fellow, but this was unexpected. He stared, horrified, unable to look away.

"Grahame, this is a matter of mutual trust," Stout said. "We are tellin' you your family are fine. Why is it so hard to get through to—"

"He saw the letters," Tom Howland croaked suddenly. "He went into your office and saw the letters." Nurse Agnes' smile faltered again; Stout scratched his ear and cracked his knuckles; Tom's breathing was rough and irregular.

"This much is true, Grahame," Stout admitted with a tired sigh. "We never sent your letters. You had misgivings. It was a lack of trust. And so the letters were a form of scrutiny."

"What happened to the girl before me?" Max asked. "Florence?" Stout drew in a great, shuddering breath, and he and Nurse Agnes shot each other a hesitant glance, but no one said anything. "She was silenced, wasn't she? She didn't fit in and she was removed." Max glanced painfully at Tom Howland, who only maintained his dead glare. "She's not back at home living a normal life again, is she?"

"Sage," Tom said in his rusty fence-gate voice. He kept his hands loose on the table, not moving a muscle; the cuffs of his sleeves were the brightest things in the room. "Sage visited Max's house. She went there."

Stout stiffened. "Sage? Visited where?" Tom didn't answer. "What house? Max's house? You mean in her—her way?"

"Through the æther."

Stout turned to Max, color rising under the stubble on his cheeks. "So now you have brought others into your misdeeds."

The table in front of Max had many nicks and scrapes, but nothing he could pretend was his pyramid scar. He ran his fingers over the biggest of the scratches, a vicious curl scraped into the wood. It didn't help at all. "She offered," he said. "And I told her yes."

The mood in the room had changed; it was subtle, but Max could feel it—a quickening of the frustration around the table. Shadows pressed in. Nurse Agnes uncrossed her arms, her expression shocked, her sad smile forgotten. Stout frowned with a new frustration and rose slowly, as if resisting some great weight from above. He gestured for Nurse Agnes to come with him, and they left, and shut the door. This time the key turned in the lock. Max was officially a prisoner. Again.

Tom's black eyes had finally shifted away from him. He stared across the table at the mossy stone wall, as still as a stereograph.

"Who are you?" Max said. He clasped his hands to keep them from shaking. "I mean, really." Tom Howland didn't reply. Max couldn't imagine what was going on in the man's head—or even if he was a man at all. By now he'd learned not to take anything for granted.

"Can I stretch my legs?" His voice sounded out of place, dull and echoless in the room. Tom kept silent, his dark stare unwavering. Max stood up and walked around the table, circling the dim chamber on stiff legs. He paused by the door and listened: nothing out there. He kept walking, counterclockwise, turning in right angles every twelve steps or so.

An hour later, the key rattled in the lock, and the door opened. Nurse Agnes stood there, a tray in her hands. The tiny stern nurse, the one named Meredith, stood behind her, one hand anxiously clutching her collar; in the other she held a rusted tin bucket. Nurse Agnes' sad smile was back, and without a word she placed the tray on the table. It was food from the commissary—a wedge of bread, a broken chunk of cheese, a few pepperoni sausages, and an apple, mealy from the sad look of it. Beside the plate was a pitcher of water, a cloth napkin—weirdly tented just so, as if this were an elegant restaurant—and an empty upturned glass. She took the rusty bucket from Meredith's hand, and set it under the table. For a brief moment, Meredith's pained gaze met Max's own, and then the door closed and the key clicked in the lock.

The boy stood there, not sure what to do. He wiped his hands on his pants. But then his stomach gurgled and he remembered he hadn't had any food since yesterday afternoon. He took a seat at the table, and looked over at Tom Howland. He said, "Do you want any of this?" Tom didn't reply, not even a shake of his head—he only sat there, stoic, his shoulders pushed forward from the hollow of his chest. Max was impressed by how small and compact the man was. "Do you even eat?" Still no reply.

But Max was hungry, and in little more than five minutes he had wolfed down the entire meal. He drank half of the water, leaving the other half for Tom, just in case he wanted it. He didn't.

This pattern repeated itself for the next three days.

Max paced relentlessly: step after step, turning again, and again. Around the table, circling the silent and motionless Tom Howland. For hours he marched, and when he didn't march he sat on the floor in the dim cobwebbed corner, as far away from everything as he could get. In all that time, Tom never moved, never said a word; his black vacant eyes only stared at the opposite wall. When exhaustion set in, Max slept fitfully on the dirt floor, turning over a thousand times. Occasionally in the darkness the delicate tickle of insect legs and antennae grazed across him; if they were small and in a hurry on their way to somewhere else, he let them be. If they were big enough and not particularly quick about their business, he swatted them away. Every eight hours or so—at least, it felt like every eight hours; down here in this timeless, dank sepulcher he couldn't be sure—Nurse Agnes appeared at the door with more water, more food, more candles.

Left alone in the crawling darkness, Max's thoughts wheeled obsessively round and round, always toward what had happened—or was happening—to his family. Obviously things weren't right, or else had gone terribly wrong. These thoughts filled him with a morbid gloom—a maddening powerlessness that depressed him beyond all words, made him want to curl into a ball in the corner and will himself back to sleep. Sleep was an escape. Occasionally his thoughts went to the other initiates and what could have happened to them. No doubt they'd been questioned, interrogated, cross-examined. *This Grahame boy. Seems like a constant bundle of nerves. Like he's seeing ghosts around every corner.* They were right. Who wouldn't be high strung and nervous around here? Max thought back to Peter Sylvester and Addie, and a bitterness passed over him like a cloud shadow. If only they hadn't taken him in, none of this misery would have happened.

After Meredith brought in yet another cold meal, so soupy and bland it was like slurping creek mud, Max realized that in the back of his mind he'd been formulating a compromise. If they would let him go—if somehow he got himself out of this terrible situation—he would swear to abandon it all, renounce his *tamkarra*, walk away from his studies, leave this life and go find a new one. He would never say a word about any of it. Maybe he could become a cook; a new beginning. With his love of recipes he could create unique dishes for regular people, normal people, no magic at all, just taking familiar flavors into new places. It would be better than any stupid *tamkarra* anyway: it would be real. Maybe he would work in Chicago or Detroit or St. Louis, some elegant eatery full of black ties and white aprons, maitre d's, the smell of fennel, the pop of champagne corks, the snap of tablecloths. In the darkness he let out a choppy laugh. No. It was all gone—his silly childhood dreams, his family, his home, his *tamkarra*. They would never let him have any of that now. He would join poor, doomed Florence, whoever she was, a cautionary tale for initiates yet to come. They would whisper about him, tell horrible stories about him. He wiped tears with gritty shirtsleeves. Now they would just kill him. Silence him.

Or banish him to the æther. Whichever one it was, it would come as a relief.

And then, finally, the key clicked in the lock and the door opened. Nurse Agnes and Dr. Stout shuffled in. Their faces were grave and serious; Stout had gotten a haircut.

For the first time in seventy-two hours, Tom Howland moved, looked impassively up at them. At some point his pupils had returned to their usual slate grey, and he stood to give them room. Max watched, unnerved; Tom didn't seem to need to stretch, or shake the stiffness from his bones. He merely went to stand by the door, wrists crossed like a jail guard. Or an undertaker.

Stout and Nurse Agnes looked around at the dreary room. As if only to break the silence, Stout said, "Grahame, how are you?" He sat down, and squinted at Max as if he were far away. Max didn't answer. After three days of not talking, his tongue was thick and clumsy. "Eating well?" Max shrugged. Nurse Agnes also sat down, her face turned away. Max tried to read them both, every expression, every gesture, for clues. He caught a slight note of disaccord; Nurse Agnes wasn't happy about something.

"We've questioned the initiates," Stout said evenly, almost placidly, "as well as Black Howard. Most of them did nothing wrong. Sage will be disciplined, but will remain here with us at Steppeland." Stout lifted his shoulders and let them fall. "You, however, will not."

"That's...that's perfectly acceptable," Max said. "Let me get my things and—"

"But there are complications. You have knowledge of many things, Grahame. This is quite dangerous." Max looked nervously up at Tom Howland. He was standing in the corner, so motionless again it was as if he had been switched off. "Now," Stout went on, "Peter Sylvester is occupied with other business, as are many of his associates. As you know, he left mere days ago. Thus you will stay here for now, until he can find the time to deal with you."

"In here?" The rock-walled room was only twelve paces to a side. Max's breath caught; he felt hot panic and dread. "I'll die in here."

Stout's smirk was cruel. "It is tight," he agreed. "We know of your talent to access locked doors, Grahame, so we'll allow you to leave this room. The cellar outside is quite large, and should quell any claustrophobic or self-destructive impulses." He gestured beyond the open door of the room, to the dark, dirty corridor that paralleled the first floor of the clinic directly above it. "But the lock, and even the few windows, have been charmed. There is no way through, not even for you. We will bring you food. You can eat, you can sleep, you can beat your head silly against the wall. But you will not leave."

A miserable thought came to Max—imprisonment in this cell, this vast, moldering tomb, was surely a form of psychological torture. "For how long?"

"We don't know. My honest answer. Until Peter Sylvester can find the time to deal with you. And let it be said that you are not very high on his list of priorities." Stout stood heavily, and turned to go. Nurse Agnes joined him at the door. Tom Howland didn't move.

"What will I do?"

"Maybe, Grahame, you can think of why you did not do what was asked of you. Why you acted like an impertinent, ungrateful guest. Why, after we took you in and fed you and nurtured your talents, you deceived us and decided to play at deceit. Maybe by the time Peter Sylvester is here, you will have an answer."

Max's brain was dizzy and buzzing; nausea chucked in his stomach. "Is this what you did with Florence? Take her away? Torture her? *Silence her?*" Stout didn't answer. He stepped into the corridor, and Nurse Agnes and Tom Howland followed, this time allowing the door to stay open. Max watched them cross the dim hallway and slide back the scarred metal door on wheeled runners on the opposite side. "How many more students disappeared, Stout? It's not just me and Florence, is it?"

The three adults went through the door, and Tom Howland, his expression as dead as ever, slid it shut behind them. The cellar's irregular limestone walls muffled the clanging echo, as well as the clicking of the various locks into place. And then there was silence.

From what Max could see, the cellar roughly mirrored the immense, empty clinic above it, with subterranean chambers and wings that jutted out into long, dreary shadow. At the far ends of the main corridor were tiny slitted windows, high up on the wall, too small to climb through, but they let in just enough daylight to put edges to everything. Here and there jumbles of old discarded furniture huddled against the walls—chairs, desks, boxes, mirrors, medical equipment, old bookcases—some still with decayed books on their shelves, the mold crawling almost visibly across their spines. None of it looked as if it had been thought about, let alone touched, in decades.

In the corridor, the metal door was thick and meat-locker solid—heavy iron, latches and gears on a sliding track. When Max tried to work it with his intention, a counter-intention seemed immediately to push back, as though a heavy, invisible tide swept against him and thrust him back out of the keyhole. For a long time he stood there, feet planted in the dirt, palms against cold metal, concentrating hard, feeling his intention checkmated again and again; he prodded this way and that, looking for an opening, a mental foothold, a crevice or crack in the current that he could wedge himself into. But there was nothing—just a solid, blank resistance, many times stronger than his own. After twenty minutes or so he was drained and miserable, and he gave up. He was going nowhere, at least not through this door.

He made his way down the wing to the very end of the corridor. The single window was above his reach, maybe fourteen inches wide by seven inches tall. There were vertical metal bars and glass so smudged he could hardly see out. The window was for ventilation, he assumed, the bars to keep animals out...or maybe to keep prisoners like him in. Either way, they were clearly solid.

But then an idea struck him: not far from the window was the equivalent doorway, one floor down, where the initiates accessed Black Howard's Hall of the Woods. Max felt a thrill in the possibility—very remote, he knew it already—that if he went through it, he would be transported to the pavilion, or at least somewhere other than this terrible place. He went to it; there was a doorway here, too, though this one lacked an actual door. He stood in the threshold, facing a dark recess about the size of one of the empty classrooms. A scatter of split logs were piled just inside the door, near a bundle of disintegrating clay pipes used for plumbing. Several mildewed Victorian dresses slouched over an old sofa that had been shoved face-first up against the wall. Bizarrely, a full-sized carriage, a once-exquisitely detailed cabriolet, crippled now with only two wheels, leaned like an injured animal in the far corner. Max tried not to think about the fact that it was too big to fit through any door down here that he had seen.

He took a moment to focus his mind and gather his intention. He exhaled sharply, closed his eyes...and took three steps forward.

Nothing. No swirling of the air, no rustling canvas. He opened his eyes to find himself standing just inside the doorway. He had gone nowhere.

The huge, dreary space overwhelmed him, loomed above him like a giant exoskeleton—lonely corridors, empty storerooms. He stepped back into the hallway and extended his arms, imagining that by his movements he could control the entire structure. What a sight that would be—his eyes looking out through windows like eyeholes in a helmet, as he stomped over hillsides, demolishing everything in his path: trees, buildings, people.

Well. Only certain people, not the friendly ones.

The friendly ones. Were there any friendly ones left anymore? Were the other initiates worried about him? Were they bitter that his actions had brought a hostile, militant response from the school? What about Black Howard? Did he have any concern for his wayward disciple? Or was he already—one foot in and one foot out—slipping away to the next circuit?

Max took a calming breath and looked around. The windowless chambers, as numerous as the classrooms above, were packed with the forgotten debris of decades of medical practice. He wiped a dirty hand across his face. There was a ton of stuff down here; might as well see what it is.

In the nearest chamber was a pile of old furniture—a cast-iron fireside bench, broken chairs, a rotted roll-top desk with its drawers missing. Just inside the doorway, a pine armoire with a single hatch opened onto a tangled nest of rat skeletons, maybe a dozen in all, dried and embalmed in their private den.

Maybe they had gotten into some poison. Max closed the door with a shudder and moved on. The next chamber was similar: a broken painter's easel, an apothecary cabinet, a cracked and tarnished full-length mirror that swiveled up and down, his own gaunt reflection peering back at him, dirty and feral. Beyond that stood a broken file cabinet with documents folded inside—yellowed newspaper clippings, which in the gloom revealed themselves to be about the University of Nebraska and its growing dependency upon its various sports teams.

And so on. Many of the chambers were empty, nothing more than dark, hollow storerooms, but others were packed almost to the doorway. Searching through the mess, he quickly became even filthier—his fingers, his clothes, his hair. It was fine dirt, fusty dirt, an empire of forgotten dust down here that hadn't seen the sun in half a century or more. He kept looking.

By the afternoon of the fifth day, Max had explored everything in the cellar; peeked in every cabinet, searched every drawer. The only truly interesting thing he found was in one of the chambers of the northeast wing—an old oak desk, massive and heavy, with tarnished brass handles and a peeling leather top. It sat in almost complete darkness, behind a block of old medical furniture—parturition tables, dispensary cabinets, examination stools—that had been meticulously arranged, right angle to right angle, as if an entire sickroom suite had been relocated down here all at once. It took half an hour to shift the other fixtures enough to gain access to the desk.

Its drawers were empty, but as he pulled them out, one in particular drew his attention. It was thicker, slightly heavier than the others, and it sounded solid when he knocked on it. For several minutes he sat back and considered the desk itself; something about it gnawed at him. He knocked on the drawer again. Still solid. He was about to turn away when impulsively he felt with his hands up into the hollow below the first drawer-fitting: it was where his mother had hidden her own private stash of money from Sig in the dresser. Shuddering from the horror of what his fingers might find—stinging scorpions, millipede colonies, monstrous spiders—he groped up in there to find a stiff but yielding resistance, like cardboard or heavy paper. It was wedged solidly up there, and he scrabbled at it for a time before he could find an edge to grip and pull it out.

It was a wrinkled accordion file, still tied with frayed and rotted string. Inside was an irregular quire of used paper—handwritten correspondence. Letters someone had collected and kept together. A scatter of hollow, dismembered insect hulls littered the bottom of the file. Due to the pressure of how the paper had been stored, the papers were brittle but in relatively decent shape. Max took it outside into the light of the corridor, to the closest barred window, and found a seat on a wooden crate.

The first note was undated, from a man named Oliver Ainsley. Ainsley was a Yorkshireman, gauging by his many references to York, Staithes, Whitby, Robin Hood's Bay. His handwriting was precise and fussy; Max got the feeling Oliver was, too. The letter was concerned with the lustful nature of religion— *"All faiths are phallic, sir; ALL OF THEM"*—and the uses of scrying mirrors in consecration rites. It went on for four pages, objecting to the arrival of this *"new, nonsense-knowledge generation of so-called talent."* The next letter, also from Ainsley, angrily denounced somebody named *Chevalier Gustav de B—,* who had evidently been a child medium in Berlin, a neophyte of the Orphic Circle in London, and became an adept in something called the Fellowship of the Temple of Thebes. But it was the third letter that caught Max's attention.

"I am happy to attest that the Elloran Brotherhood has been extinguished, it read in a handwriting different from Ainsley's, much sloppier and harder to read. *As such, I am requested to bring under your notice the particulars relative to the destruction of rival cabals and confederacies, and the formation of a select colony of our western Brothers. There are many men who are apt to be an excellent choice for regional leader, but in my estimation one Peter Sylvester shall be supreme."*

Peter Sylvester; Max's skin prickled. The air in the cellar seemed to grow suddenly compressed and diamond clear. With a mixture of curiosity and dread, he kept reading.

"In this quarter alone there are many who possess a proper instruction, whose talents are laudable but whose motivations are quite incompatible to that state which is essential for the complete evolution of the sublime powers of their souls. Time after time have their simple but urgent requests for brotherly alliance been made, and at length it has been decided to place the scheme before those of our brothers who are in a position to aid us. For, make no mistake, there is a coming conflagration; maybe not for a few years or even decades, but it is necessary herein to observe that the whole plan has been met with the hearty approval of our revered brethren, whose valuable assistance has been kindly promised to us in the arrangement of all necessary laws, powers, studies, magickal explorations, etc., for the government of the Colony, and also their special guardianship over the training of those acolytes who belong to it."

Max settled against the wall. He could only guess that the accordion file must have been purposefully hidden, stored furtively in the desk, and then either forgotten about or lost. Maybe somebody died. Either way, when the desk was relocated down here to the cellar, the letters effectively disappeared. They went on to describe, in preparation for this *"coming conflagration,"* the need for a colony to be established somewhere in the United States, a situation which could assist the Brotherhood of the Aurora in preparing for *"the inevitable proelium."* Max had heard Black Howard use that term a time or two, and understood it to be Latin, meaning battle, or fight. Or maybe war. But against whom, the letter didn't say.

The next letter was from the same unknown person, in the same loose handwriting, and detailed plans for this new colony.

"Since 1839, Aurorans have devised a most practical scheme for the furthering of

our intentions. The best method for the fulfillment of this absolute plan would be to select a small municipality in the eastern United States of America, somewhere in either the coastal range, the Appalachian Mountains, or the foothills of the Adirondacks, such land to be selected within a reasonable distance from a thriving but modest and unexceptional market city.

"A position of some use in the town is preferable, such as shop keeper, postal man, or accountant or banker. Amongst this section of our worthy Brethren are many who are practically familiar with every branch of these duties, and who are ready and willing to form such a colony at perhaps a month's notice. But in all of these matters, Mr. Peter Sylvester is advised to be the chosen one, and when the position is filled, then the Temple, Grove, and School for the purposes of initiation or special Instruction, would be appointed free of charge.

"I shall be happy to give any further counsel upon this subject, if required—Yours Fraternally, R.J.W., Private Secy. of the Interior Circle of the Brotherhood of the Aurora."

Max looked at the top of the letters: the first was written on Dec. 11, 1846, the second, Feb. 6, 1847. It was now November, 1904. Between the letters and the present day, fifty-seven years had passed.

Fifty-seven years; the number burned hot in Max's mind. Peter Sylvester had been suggested—and chosen, apparently—as the Postmaster nearly six decades ago. At that time, the old man would surely have been an adolescent younger than he was now.

Max watched a dreadful caravan of long-legged crickets creep up the wall as he tried to piece together a rough chronology. So the Aurora had been in London—or somewhere in England, at any rate—and planned a colony here in the U.S. for the purposes of finding new initiates. That would be, Max knew, young people like Harriet and himself and the others. And they had chosen to put their colony in the foothills of the Appalachians, rather than New York or the coastal range. There was no mention of Steppeland, or even Nebraska, but it seemed only a short leap of logic from establishing a colony in the South to forming another one in the Midwest. And now, according to Peter Sylvester, there were even more.

Max read more letters until the light from the window had faded to dark. All the others were written by this R.J.W., whoever he was; plainly a person of high position in the Aurora, maybe higher than even Peter Sylvester, if there was such a thing. R.J.W. went on to describe how Peter Sylvester had been appointed, and in 1858, not long before the beginning of the American Civil War, had opted to become a Postmaster first in Milledgeville, Georgia. Then a Postmaster outside Spartanburg, South Carolina, and eventually a shopkeeper and Postmaster again in Palatka, Florida. Both East and South, not far from the coast, these towns were perfect positions from which to operate, simple and anonymous places to run the business of the eastern Brotherhood of the Aurora, to create occultist manuals to be distributed across the country, and to quietly till the local community for potential initiates.

Fifty-seven years ago. How was that possible?

Max looked up. He was tired; the light was fading. As he unrolled his bedding in the insect darkness, he wondered what it was they seemed to be after. The creation of various colonies in the new world; the observance of the rituals; the discovery, indoctrination, and training of initiates; the tactical elimination of rival sects. From that perspective it did seem very much like preparing for a war. An incursion, as Dr. Stout had said. A *proelium.*

He took a sip from his glass of water. In the thin candlelight he saw a millipede struggling in it. He fished it out and drank the rest. Then he put out the candle and lay down, wondering what the Aurora's true goal was—for him and for the other initiates. From all the talk of the Faqrs, it seemed both groups had been at odds for some time. More than six decades, in fact. He had an impression of immense planning, a massive intricate framework of design, over half a century—maybe more—of schemes and plotting, secrets and strategies. But their ultimate aims were still murky. The Postmaster's voice sounded in his head, distant and hollow, like someone shouting from down in a well: *Anyone who gets in our way can be persuaded. The initiates can be very useful. And there are more of them, more than you know. Any and all splinter organizations will be silenced, I can promise you that.*

Max tossed and turned, still seeing Tom Howland's dead black eyes in his head. Still mulling over the letters and Peter Sylvester and *silencing.* At some point he must have slept, because the next thing he knew a pale light had appeared from outside in the corridor, as quietly and softly as if someone had flipped an electric switch. It was just...there. Casting shadows and giving alarming light to things that hadn't had it in years. Movement caught his eye, and when he looked up he saw, on the ceiling above him, hundreds of subterranean crickets staring back at him; barnacles on a sea rock, all watching him with little black pinpoint eyes. Like Tom Howland's eyes. Startled, fifteen or twenty dropped down onto him and bounded away.

In the hall outside, the light—it was pale, with a jade hue, as if shining through an emerald—still glowed.

Max sat up. "Hello?" No one answered.

He stood and edged into the hallway. The light flared from a chamber about halfway down on the westward corridor. The greenish glow was wan and cold, without the warmth of a candle or a lantern, or even an electric bulb.

"Hello?" Still no answer, no movement. "Mr. Howland?"

After a moment, holding his breath, Max crept slowly down. It was a long walk. He eyed the doorway closely, waiting for someone to appear out of it, to peek around the corner, but no one did. His imagination saw all sorts of terrible things as he approached, but he kept going.

When he came to the chamber, for a tense, terrible minute he stood at the threshold, not wanting to look inside, his breath trying to flutter out of his chest. But he made himself do it—he pushed himself into the doorway for a better view.

The room was a crypt-like, windowless chamber, like all the others down here. He knew this place; he had been in this very room two days ago. A clutter of cabinets, hospital gurneys and a jumble of discarded dining chairs turned upside down were piled high in the center of the room. But the weird light radiated from some kind of globe on the far side, hovering unsupported in the air—like a scryer's ball, giving off a greenish, swirling glow: sunlight filtered through seawater. And there was a man on the far side of the tangle of chairs, facing the other way, facing the blank dirt wall. Wide shoulders, head bent, face out of view. He stood there, unmoving, just his back and shoulders rising and falling with breath.

"Hello?" Max said. The man turned. From across the crowded chamber, Mister Splitfoot grinned at him.

Max's mouth tasted suddenly of blood. He felt as if he were hurtling through dark, featureless space, a train rushing through a tunnel.

"Hello, Maximilian," Mister Splitfoot said, grinning through broken teeth. He didn't look good, but instead seemed unhealthy in some vague, indefinable way. Mottled skin, sallow bags under his eyes. His dark sheared hairline was apishly low on his forehead, and his close-cropped hair exposed the knobby, irregular bulges of his skull. Seeping sores dotted his scalp like leopard spots.

Max felt a blunt, mindless panic—it was all he could do not to run from the room. But down here, in this locked-in cellar, there was nowhere to go.

"How ya been?" *Bee-yun?* That weird, magnified Appalachian accent.

Max licked his lips. They were cracked and dry. "Not—not so good."

The man-spirit giggled, and Max was astounded by how insane it sounded. It was the glee of the asylum, the mirth of abandonment and night alleys and mold-rotted mountain hollers. "I got something for ya, ya know."

Max didn't want it, but Mister Splitfoot held it up anyway. A severed head dangling from his fist. It stared back at the boy through the legs of the upturned chairs with eyes that were amazed and alarmed, and it took Max a moment to recognize it. The head was Black Howard's. His mouth was turned down on one side, as if he'd had some kind of apoplexy. The wound was ragged and messy with black, clotted blood. It wasn't a cut, it was a rip.

"AH!" Max cried, and clapped his hands to his eyes. But it was too late—the ghastly sight was imprinted on his retinas. His stomach pitched and he felt a need to gag.

"Do you like it?"

Max couldn't answer. His mind was white hot, blistered into numbness. He felt his hair standing on end, his mouth gaping but unable to make a sound. Then, when he had found his breath again: "Leave me alone!" It came out like a sob.

Mister Splitfoot set the head upright on a table behind him—it tilted slightly on the torn, uneven flesh—and wiped his hands smoothly on the lapels of his jacket. He was bare chested beneath it. "I can help ya, ya know," he said, his voice bland.

It took a moment for Max to find more words. "I don't want it."

The tangled mound of furniture between them was like a buffer. But Mister Splitfoot's smile faded, and he stared at the boy for a long time. "You don' fancy me, do ya, Maximilian?" His eyes weren't dark, but Max wished they were. "You think I'm touched."

Max closed his eyes against this nightmare. His thoughts in a whirl, unable to decide the best course of action, he could only be helplessly honest: "I'm afraid of you."

"Whyever would ya be afraid? I'm on yer side."

"I'm not sure which side I'm on."

Something caught his attention across the room, movement or some type of change, and Max glanced over to a ruined dresser on the opposite side. In the faded light he saw a full meal, as nice as anything from Joe Miller Joe's— broiled chicken, French rolls, roasted sweet potatoes and buttered peas, and a pitcher of milk so cold that sweat ran down the sides. "You hungry?"

Max felt his hands ball themselves into tight, painful fists. "No, sir. I am not."

"You can eat, ya know. I ain't no faery king, this ain't no kiddie story where ya get witched by yer appetite. If I wanted to witch ya, Maximilian, I don't need no supper to do that."

"Thank you. I'm fine."

Mister Splitfoot giggled again, but Max heard a gusty loneliness in his voice, a desolate sense of self-loathing. A thought came to him: *He hates himself.* He tried to put it out of his head—he hoped Mister Splitfoot, whatever he was, couldn't read his mind.

From across the room, there came another repulsive laugh. "I kin get ya outta here, ya know. Safe. Back with yer famly. Happier 'n a dead pig in the sunshine." *Sunshahn.*

But Max's thoughts were still scorched, twisted, inexplicable; he couldn't unravel them, force them to make sense. He wanted out, but not with this fiend. "Thank you, but I'm fine," he said again, shakily, stupidly, as though he'd been invited to dinner.

"Yer mama's dead," Mister Splitfoot said.

Max closed his eyes again and leaned his head against the doorjamb, needing solid support. For a long time, it was quiet. Max silently counted to ten, and opened his eyes, hoping it would be over. But Mister Splitfoot was still there, still waiting. In his hand now was a bottle of Uranithor, flat on his palm, as if he were presenting it in an advert.

"But it ain't what ya think, Max. It warn't them 'Rora, no no no, *unh uh*! It was this! She took too much o' this! She was tellin' you all along it warn't no good, and you made her take it anyway!" He unscrewed the top of the bottle and sniffed it, then grimaced. In a showy effort, he reared back and pitched it at the far wall. The bottle shattered, causing Max to flinch, and it left a dark, dripping stain.

"Thangs didn't go well fer her," Mister Splitfoot said. "Thangs didn't go well for her at all."

Max was afraid to ask, but made himself do it anyway: "What—what are you talking about?"

"See fer yerself."

There was a shuffling in the corridor behind him. As Max spun around, in the pallid glow of the green sphere he saw a figure there. Draped in a damp, dirty nightgown.

It was his mother. It was Lora. The gown clung to her flabby breasts, to the curve of her distended belly. Mister Splitfoot was right, things hadn't gone well, not at all. The bottom half of her face was missing. Her lower jaw was gone. Her pulpy tongue lolled in the recess, and drool strung down from her upper palate to the scooped neck of her nightgown. She was wet; the ripe, balmy sweetness of saliva wafted around her. She groaned wordlessly and looked at Max with creek-pebble eyes. Her voice was horribly familiar. He backed into the room, and she took several shambling steps toward him and slowed in the doorway. Her shoulders and clavicles were angular and gaunt in the pale light from the sphere.

"Got herself dead," Mister Splitfoot said. *Da-yead.* "Too much tonic. Too much o' anythang's bad for ya, Maximilian."

Max turned back to the man-spirit. Maybe in his own lunatic way, Mister Splitfoot was trying to be helpful. "Let her go," Max said.

"If ya can't use mah help, I thought maybe then ya could at least use some comp'ny. Unless'n ya want to come with me right now." *Raght nay-ow.*

Max looked back at his mother. Was she really dead? He couldn't tell, because here she was, standing before her only child. Swaying and drooling, in a disfigured state, but upright. Her tortured gaze pleading with him.

When he turned back, Mister Splitfoot was smiling. His square mouth and broken teeth were grotesque. "I could just EAT YOU UP!" he said, leering.

Max felt himself wanting to shriek, felt himself caught between the insane spirit and the grotesque thing that was once his mother. "I DON'T HAVE ANYTHING FOR YOU! LEAVE ME ALONE!"

But Mister Splitfoot's smile widened. "Ya don't have anything for me—not yet, ya don't. But ya will, Maximilian. I promise ya—ya will!"

He plucked the green ball of light from the air and let it settle into the palm of his hand. Then with one last demented grin Max's way, he flung it hard at the wet stain of Uranithor on the wall. The ball burst, exploded like liquid, into bright glowing droplets which scattered and spilled onto the furniture. The light lingered, then faded slowly like the smashed guts of a firefly. In less than half a minute, darkness had reclaimed the chamber and the corridor outside.

Mister Splitfoot was gone. The cluttered room was empty. Max didn't know how he knew it, but he did: he was alone.

Well, not truly alone. From behind him in the pitch black, just inside the doorway, came a low moan. The thing that used to be Lora was still here.

"Mother?"

No moan then, just the scuffling of feet, a horrid rustle of wet sticky cloth.

"Mom?"

Silence and breathing. That sweet saliva smell. There was a dragging sound. A shuffle. Even without seeing her Max could tell her movements were different from the gait he had known his entire life—devastatingly wrong. In the darkness, she took a few steps toward him, a gritty, hobbling approach. Max stepped away, feeling like a ghost in his own body, unable to bear the thought of her touching him or hugging him or kissing him. With his hands out like a blind man, in the darkness he stumbled his way between the wall and the tangle of furniture, through and over the chairs and the medical equipment, over to where Mister Splitfoot had first been. His mother's steps followed. She was pursuing him.

He kept going, knocking over chairs, brushing by something that felt horribly like hair, like a black man's hair. A section of the pile of furniture collapsed with a tremendous clatter.

Max shuddered. He stopped, and listened: footsteps, shambling slowly around the jumble of chairs. Another low moan, like a sob.

Panicked, Max scuttled over the collapsed pile, around the other side, sliding across tabletops, crawling on all fours through upturned chair legs—one fiercely jabbing at his cheekbone and just barely missing his eye—feeling with desperate hands against the wall, corner to corner. Only once did he fall, his head slamming packed dirt; little green flares bloomed like fireworks in his vision. He was nearing—he thought with the shred of himself that could still have a rational notion—where the door was located.

He heard his mother stop at the heap of fallen furniture, over near Black Howard's head, and then reverse her path and shuffle back toward him. In a terror Max reached for the doorknob and couldn't find it. Her footsteps scuffled closer, one shoe slapping and one bare foot gritting on dirt, and he scrabbled for the door and then miraculously it was there. He felt her bare foot touch his own, and then a hand clawing at his hair, but he pulled himself free. As her fingers raked across his face and his shoulder he clambered through the open door and heaved it closed behind him.

For the second time in ten minutes, he felt the need to vomit. His guts were loose, like they had shit themselves outside of his body and lay unwound around him on the floor. He slid down and sat on the dirt in the dark corridor, holding the knob shut, shivering, queasy, cold and sweaty and sick. A clamor came from inside the closed room. She—it—was stumbling around in the darkness. His own mother. But how could he be sure?

It's her, the little faraway voice assured him. *You know it is. Speak it*, the voice said. *Say it. Say it out loud.*

"It's her," Max heard himself say. "It's really her."

The knob rattled. The door jerked against him. She was trying to get out. In the dim murk of the corridor, the far window showed nothing but a black square of night. On the other side, though, two battered headboards leaned against the corridor wall, just out of reach. With one hand on the knob, he desperately stretched over, and in an adrenaline frenzy he mightily pulled one, and then the other, under the knob in front of the door. They leaned in against it, their legs tight on the dirt floor. No matter how hard she pushed, she wasn't getting out.

Max collapsed onto the floor, debilitated with horror.

SEVENTEEN: THROUGH THE LOOKING GLASS

THE FACT THAT LORA was dead was less of a shock than Max expected. More than anything else, it came upon him as a surge of relief—her suffering was done, as well as his own on her behalf. Well, mostly; in its place was a gaping hollow, a cold furious ache that pulled at him and made him want to seek revenge. But against who? Peter Sylvester? Dr. Stout? Mister Splitfoot? Uranithor itself? Down in the center of his gut, Max somehow grasped that wasn't right. Why Mister Splitfoot had insisted it was the Uranithor, he couldn't say. But something—some insistent seed of instinct deep inside his core—told him that was wrong. His mother had been deliberately silenced. He knew it in his heart. But why? And by who? And what about Ethie—where was she? One thing, though, was certain—he couldn't bear to think of that creature trapped back in that windowless chamber as his mother. It was too grisly, too yielding to the vicious, heartless circumstances in which they both had found themselves. So he began to think of it as *the motherthing*.

He spent the day in his own windowless chamber, and after yet another fitful, mostly sleepless night, when pale light crept down the corridor and finally told him it was morning, he rose and blearily returned to the old accordion file full of forgotten letters. He found a good eastern window, far from the chamber in which the motherthing mindlessly paced and clawed and moaned, and from a stack of red bricks and old two-by-fours he made a comfortable place to sit and study them all.

There were twenty-six letters in total. Most of them were mundane and of relatively little interest—the Aurora's various business affairs, internal political maneuverings, nominations and appointments to top posts. But one made him put down the others and re-read it at least three times. It was different from the rest; set aside in an envelope of its own, sloppily folded, and written in an insistent, almost drunken scrawl.

my dear sir(s),

this latest round of chicanery beggars belief. the society to which you refer is only a simpleton's scheme, merely an effort on the part of mr. p—s— to empower himself by selling his books and magazines and caprine gonadal services by using the popularity and forum of the b.a. mr. p—s—, has nothing, has never had anything, and never will have anything more than you can read in any common brochure or farmer's almanack. their so-called "foot soldiers" are mere children being trained in the art of levitation and stage magic. by mysterious pretension and running down eastern sages they hope to gain adherents and followers. for what purpose other than to amass power and eliminate adversaries i do not see. there is little talent and no penitence. krishna does not belong to them, nor to anyone of us, nor approve of them, nor denigrate them. but if you or your friends join in this lowly objective of abolishing every sect in the world other than the b.a., by force or by coercion, it will not benefit you. i promise you this. they have no concern with anything but themselves, and their neophyte business is all bosh. please shew this to the others. Give my regards to mrs. c., and your brother, and believe me for now your ally,

mme. z–.

sept 20, 1901

After Max read it several times, he looked at the date again: September 20, 1901. Only three years ago, and less than a week after President McKinley finally succumbed to the gunshot wounds from the anarchist Leon Czolgosz. *This latest round of chicanery beggars belief.* Max examined the envelope itself—the return address was from Manhattan, New York City, from a place named Corlears Hook. No apostrophe.

He studied the letter—the impatient handwriting, the granular firmness of the paper. *p– s–* of course could only be Peter Sylvester. The *b.a* would be the Brotherhood of the Aurora. And *mme. z–*: Max kept hearing her name, mentioned always in fear or derision. According to her letter, the young initiates were being trained as "foot soldiers." That would be us, Max thought. Peter Sylvester's obedient, unknowing, mercenary foot soldiers. Trained for the "coming conflagration."

But how did the Aurora get one of Mme. Z–'s letters in the first place? Clearly it was meant for someone else. Then he remembered: *Thank the gods we intercepted that one,* the old man said that summer afternoon at the post office. Peter Sylvester was the Postmaster, after all.

There were three more letters from Mme. Z–, one of them even more recent—it was dated October 28, 1902—and from the events and arguments they detailed, a clearer picture formed. The Aurora and the Faqrs had evidently gone to war with each other, both psychically and in the material world. Other sects had already been targeted by the Aurora—targeted and destroyed. Recent assassinations by anarchists in Europe had made security around President McKinley a priority, but the Aurora's neophyte Leon Czolgosz had finally broken through. At a public meeting in Buffalo, New York, he had shot the president twice in the stomach, to advance the purposes of "anarchism," which Max understood to be a loose cover for the Aurora. It had taken a week for McKinley to die. Max wasn't quite sure why Mme. Z– would detail these inflammatory ideas in letters sent through the US Post Office. Maybe she expected them to be intercepted.

Other letters referenced a secretive sect in Serbia—the Black Hand, they were called—and their attempts to bring about anarchy in Europe. They were hoping to find someone there to repeat what Czolgosz had done in the United States. As recently as May of 1903, the notes explained, the Serbian military, which evidently contained members of the Black Hand, invaded the royal palace; after a violent battle, the attackers captured the head of the palace guard and forced him to reveal the whereabouts of his king, Alexander, and the king's wife, Queen Draga. The two royals had hidden in a large wardrobe, and when they were found the king was shot thirty times, the queen eighteen. Mme. Z— wrote that "*the royal corpses were stripped, beaten and mercilessly sabred,*" and then the anarchists threw their bodies out of a palace window, ending any threat that loyalists would mount a counterattack. The head of the palace guard was then silenced, as were Queen Draga's two brothers.

"*thus ended the rule of the house of obrenovic,*" Mme. Z— wrote, "*which had kept serbia steady since the middle of the previous century. at present the aurora are seeking another figure to dispatch, most likely someone in the austria/hungary regime, in the hopes of bringing about global destabilization. This colossal perturbation will of course offer conditions favorable only to the aurora, just as moisture and darkness nurtures a pestilent fungus.*"

Global destabilization. The term rattled inside Max's brain. How goddamn big did this conflagration go?

Just then, from down the other side of the huge cellar, there was a hideous moan and a vicious pounding, and one of the pieces of furniture placed against the motherthing's door—he had spent an hour sliding heavy furniture against it—fell with a terrific clatter. Max rubbed the heels of his hands into his eyes, trying to will himself out of this terrible situation. Presidential assassinations, anarchic conflagrations, royal and presidential executions, global destabilization. Peter Sylvester, Mme. Z—, Czolgosz, Tom Howland, Mister Splitfoot, his own deceased but reanimated mother. Max felt like he was going insane—his brain was a boiling stewpot of pain, loss, conspiracy, and fear. Maybe they wanted to drive him insane. If so, it was working. And now the Postmaster would most likely have him silenced, too. If Mister Splitfoot or the motherthing didn't get to him first.

Max let the accordion file drop to the floor. If he was to survive this ordeal, he would need to be deeply resourceful. But how? He was locked in down here, with insects and revenants and forgotten letters and no hope of escape. His thoughts circled around again to the other initiates. Were they safe? Or had they been silenced? Max doubted it. None of them—not Durga, not Harriet, not Rosalie, nor even Sage, not really—had done anything wrong. Most likely they were still considered innocent of any charges. The Aurora needed them, after all. But Max needed them, too; if they'd turned their backs on him, as Dr. Stout and—surely—Peter Sylvester had, his adventures at the Steppeland clinic, both above and below, would clearly be finished. And sooner rather than later.

He slumped in the glare from the window, thinking about what he'd witnessed and practiced in the Hall of the Woods. Tarot reading. Mind reading. Scrying. Divination. Astral projection. Invisibility. *Tamkarra.* Of them all, the Akasha seemed the most useful to him now. The problem was that, despite several humiliating attempts, he'd never been able to access the æther, not even once. But now, with so much time on his hands, he had a perfect opportunity to try it again.

It had taken weeks of steady practice for the other initiates to learn their individual techniques; Max had watched fascinated and dismayed as Sage mastered her skills and grew into quick expertise. Durga had performed it fairly well, and with scant practice, one foggy September morning, but Durga was depressingly good at everything. Despite his own failures, Max had closely studied their techniques, and had a general feeling for how to approach it. But with the motherthing rattling and moaning so loudly, there was no way he could concentrate. So he went wandering the farthest dark corridors until he found a distant dusty chamber; there was an old piano bench in there, but no piano, which was just fine—he didn't need one. He dragged the seat into a half-lit hallway, sat down, and allowed his exhausted eyes to close.

From what he'd learned, the key to success in both scrying and astral projection seemed to be an odd mix of intuition, phenomenology, and spatial/temporal orientation. Through the mingling of directed awareness, induction, architecture, and visual context, a system of impressions and mnemonic associations could be used to occupy the mind, creating an altered state of awareness that would then serve as a starting point to the world beyond appearances. Max remembered Black Howard going on at length about his hero Giordano Bruno and his *ars memoriae*; all of this worked together to allow a person to map and influence the material world from an immaterial place.

In his mind Max began cataloging the space in which he sat. The castoff debris near the door, the chamber, this particular wing, the entire cellar itself; the bricks and the dirt and the joisted ceiling above and the cobwebs drifting languidly from them. He felt the woodgrain of the furniture, the tumble of dusty light spilling along the wall from a far window, the faint thudding of the motherthing stumbling over chairs in the barricaded windowless chamber.

After some minutes his heart slowed, his body grew numb. He imagined himself standing, going down the long corridor, turning the corner and approaching the sliding metal door—

max

—going to the metal door and slowly turning the—

max

He opened his eyes. He was still on the piano bench. Someone had been calling his name.

It sounded close, but from where? The nearest window was barred and blank, and seventy yards away. The long hall, this whole wing, was entirely empty.

Then, from the corner of his eye, he saw it: movement. Just down the corridor, a mirror leaned against the wall, a tarnished, oval looking-glass with a once-ornate gilded frame. He squinted into the darkness. Movement again; someone was there—inside the mirror. Max stood and approached it warily, to see someone looking back at him.

It was Sage. "Max! You're here!" She stared out at him just as he stared in at her. He had forgotten the sound of her voice, and now every word she spoke was a tiny miracle.

"Sage?"

"I'm here."

Max crouched in front of the glass. *Scrying*, he thought, *we're scrying*. "Good God, how did you—how did you find me?"

"We've been trying to find you for nine days, Max. I think they blocked us somehow. Were you...trying to project?"

"I was trying to reach the Akasha." He felt suddenly, weirdly sheepish. "I've got nothing else to do down here."

"That must be it then. You didn't find the æther, but you did open a channel. We've been blocked, but when you and I tried to connect at the same time, I found you and pried open a passage. In this mirror, at least."

"Where are you?"

"My cabin. I've been quarantined. You're in the cellar?"

"Until Peter Sylvester comes to get me." In the mirror Sage was pale, her hair mussed. Lines had grown at the corners of her mouth, and veiny hollows drew shadows under her eyes. All at once Max realized that she looked— alarmingly—much older. "Sage, are you okay?"

"We're all worried. We've been looking for you. Black Howard's not even here. We think he's moved on."

Max ground his teeth. He thought about telling her the awful truth—Black Howard's severed head in the hands of Mister Splitfoot. The head was still in the closed-off chamber with the motherthing. But he wasn't sure if sharing that now would serve anyone. He changed the subject.

"I'm losing my mind down here, Sage. Mister Splitfoot showed up again." Sage gave him a dismayed look, but didn't say anything. "He conjured my mother. Or...or something that looks like my mother. She's still here, banging around. I think they're trying to drive me crazy."

"Your mother?" Sage's dismay became sadness. "You finally found her."

"I've found other things, too. There are letters down here, messages back and forth. They've been silencing rival sects and are planning some kind of...I don't know. Occultist or...anarchist domination or something. Global instability. They hope to use it for their advantage."

"What are you talking about?"

"Are you alone? Are the others also in quarantine?"

Sage shook her head. "I'm the only one here now. Why?"

"How...how do they think of me?" It was a weird question to ask right now, but it mattered to him. "Am I hero or villain?"

"You're neither. They seem worried about you. About the both of us."

"Is there any way you can get me out? The door's charmed."

"The entire facility is charmed. We can't even approach the windows to the cellar. But I can talk to Durga, see if he has any ideas. Or Harriet."

"Harriet hates me."

Sage let out a little humorless scoff. "Harriet hates everybody." She went quiet, suddenly pensive, and chewed on a yank of hair. "Occultist domination?" she said, puzzled.

When Max heard it said aloud, by someone else, it struck him as strange and paranoid and wildly unbelievable. But it was true. "If I get a chance, I'll show you the letters."

"So what do we do?"

"I don't know. Can we...set another time to talk? That way we can be ready to re-open the channels. But I need to think." Max stood up, breathing deep. He was still fighting a wave of despair. Tom Howland. Peter Sylvester. Even if he got out of here, he would still have to contend with them. They would never let him go. Not now.

Sage must have seen his worry. "Have faith. Let's meet here again. Sundown tomorrow night. By then I'll have talked to the others and we'll see about getting you out of there. And me, too."

Max managed a tired smile. "Sage, you have no idea what this means to me."

She didn't answer, only stared flatly back at him, and then the mirror turned back into a mirror. Max was presented with his own disheartened gaze. In the reflection his hair hung in his face, his eyes were dark and rutted, and suddenly he knew what he would look like as an old man.

The next morning was spent reading the last of the letters. Several were by a Frenchman who signed his name M. *Ardant*, one of which stood out as a disturbingly unemotional register of the sects the Brotherhood of the Aurora had already silenced. It read like a certificate of extermination. Among them were *Hinter der Rose*, an order based in Munich, and the Freemen, from Inverness, Scotland—ironically not far, Max supposed, from Peter Sylvester's own native territory. There was the Fraternity of Saturn Which Is Hidden; the Paracelsans; a cabal based in northern China known as the Sons of Heaven. Each of them apparently proud traditions, factions with their own rituals, their own ambitions, their own initiates. And according to Ardant's letter, they had now been eliminated, or were scattered in disarray. All except for the Faqrs.

In several of his other letters, Ardant alluded to the skirmishes and bitter power plays between all of these sects throughout the centuries. The Crusades were only one example, he claimed, as was the crucifixion of Jesus the Christ himself—moments when the battles between the orders boiled up into such magnificent violence as to gain the notice of the general population. But mostly the war was held behind the scenes, in back rooms and boardrooms, in border wars and skirmishes in lonely mountain passes and scorching deserts. The conflict was still alive, still fresh. And Max and his fellow initiates were the ones being trained to create the havoc, assassinate the leaders, do the dirty work. To be the foot soldiers in the Aurora's war against everyone else. *We are no better*, he thought, *than Tchowgosh himself.* Max felt strange, feverishly tuned, as if his mind were sensing deep thrumming vibrations in the air. These were centuries Ardant was talking about—millennia. Occultist cabals, sometimes cooperating, mostly warring, with the spoils of the Earth as their bounty. And now the conflagration had been reduced to two: the Brotherhood of the Aurora and the Faqrs, who were headed as of late by the infamous Mme. Z—. Last seen in Corlears Hook, no apostrophe, Manhattan, New York, USA.

Max put his head in his hands. His thoughts ached. He was unprepared for the immensity of what he was trying to understand. Even as a child he'd known there were groups and organizations with hidden agendas, ulterior motives, covert allegiances; war was nothing new. But this made him sick. It was as if the puppet masters were controlling governments, nations, civilization itself, stringing it this way and that based upon nothing more than—

A crash came then from the other side of the cellar, followed by a raving, wordless moan. The motherthing. Max rocked and panted through splayed fingers, in and out, in and out, back and forth, trying to center himself. He was almost grateful for the distraction.

The day passed, agonizing and slow. In the afternoon he dragged the mirror down the corridor, closer into the light from the western windows. Far away in the primary wing, the sliding metal door opened and then closed: someone bringing food. Max ignored them. By now even the motherthing was quiet, as if it knew something was about to happen. Max was anxious, watchful, uneasy as he paced in front of the mirror. He cleaned it with his shirt, tucked sweaty hair behind his ears, rolled up the cuffs of his pants and retied his shoes. When the light outside the window changed, slipping from bright haze to deeper blue, he sat down on the dirt floor and closed his eyes and concentrated on finding unseen depths in the air around him.

After several minutes, it happened: he heard his name called as if from around the corner.

max

He opened his eyes. The person looking back at him was not Sage, but Durga.

"What?" Max heard the fear and uncertainty in his voice.

"Hello, Max," Durga said stiffly, and held up a hand in a typical American greeting. He was alone, his purple tunic bright against the wall behind him. "I am sorry for the unexpected. It is good to see you. Sage has told me what happened, do not worry. Her power by itself is not sufficient to pull you through. So we are all of us working together."

"I—I don't understand."

"We are going to get you out of the cellar, Max."

Max stared dumbly, until his brain came around—they were working as a team to get him free. His spirits lifted, just a little. If Durga was willing to get involved, they would have a much better chance of success.

"The clinic is charmed, Max. The entire facility. But we are thinking we have a way."

Down the hall, the echoes of the motherthing started up again. "How?"

Durga smiled faintly, condescendingly; his initial shyness had already dissipated. "Through the looking glass, Max. We're going to pull you through the mirror." There were a few moments of painful silence. Max's mind felt weak, atrophied, a calf kept too long in the stalls. "Sage is in her cabin," Durga went on. "She and you and I. Three vertices. With all of us working together, I should be able to reach through and pull you to me. Do you understand?"

"What do I do?"

"This is not unlike travel in the Akasha. We will need your eyes open, but centered. Sage and I will do most of the work." A focus came into Durga's gaze, an increase of energy and intention. "Are you ready?"

Max was ready. He pushed out his breath, let his shoulders drop, tried to still his frantic heartbeat.

"Look at me," Durga said evenly, almost dreamily, like a student of Mesmer. "Look into the mirror, into my eyes, but the middle distance. Lose focus. Go quiet. Relax but fixate."

Max sank into himself, felt his thoughts wading out into the shallows of a trance...and then an itch, a tugging, a soft, painless rooting deep inside his mind. Durga was reaching out.

But then—another distant crash from the far wing. The motherthing again. Max blinked, resurfaced. He rubbed his temples, trying to make the stress go away.

There was unfinished business.

"Wait, wait, Durga," he said. "I'm sorry." He wasn't ready yet to leave. He had one more task.

"What? What is it?"

"One moment, please—Durga, please, I'll be back."

Before Durga could object, Max jumped up and ran down the dark corridor, to the wing where the motherthing clamored in her windowless chamber. Soft, sobbing moans came from behind the door. Occasionally a piece of furniture inside was knocked and fell, or maybe was kicked across the floor. With a terrific heave Max wrenched away one of the desks and slid across another to get closer to the closed door. He put his hand flat on the wood, and leaned in to touch it with his cheek. It was splintery and strong and cool.

He cleared his mind again and sent in his intention, mentally surveying the contents of the room. Stale chilly air. The stink of saliva. A clutter of upturned chairs, decayed, crumbling tables and medicinal cabinets. With his *tamkarra* he probed one of the chairs and lifted it, and then another. He couldn't see them but he could feel them, and that was all he needed. He raised a desk, and then another, and then another chair. In less than a minute the whole snarled entanglement, like a decayed wooden rat king, hovered above the floor.

The motherthing went quiet. Her confusion was palpable, heavy, tactile.

Slowly, Max started the huge scatter of furniture rotating around the room.

The racket began right away. Wood slamming wood, edge banging edge, metal on metal. The pile of furniture tumbled against itself, floating, spinning, twirling. Max closed his eyes, envisioned it all circling faster, rotating quicker and quicker, a vortex of objects in the room. He felt the blank, ravenous presence of the motherthing, felt its uncertainty, but he made the cyclone move faster, and faster, and faster; it became a whirlpool, generating its own energy, the knocking of piece into piece was thunderous, and with his intention Max could tell from the sheer number of objects in the room the pieces were breaking apart, smaller bits now—segments, projectiles, ballistics, darts, and bolts. The sounds changed, became variegated, more delicate, more layered and intricate; he spun them faster, faster, faster. Scrap against scrap, slamming stone walls, splintering, a cacophony, segments crashing, fragmenting ever smaller, and in his mind he felt the number of items in the room increasing exponentially—fifty objects had become a hundred, two hundred, five hundred, then more, finer and faster, debris into dust. The sheer immensity of it all, the dizzying myriad of wreckage, testing his intention, but he spun it faster and faster, more and more, a microcosmic galaxy whirling at enormous speeds; harder and harder, ever increasing, the splinters had splinters now, and then splintered again. Powder, shreds and shards were all that was left—a maelstrom of ruin and wreckage and rubble. The cacophony in the room was deafening. With his cheek against the door, for another full minute he kept it going, as fast as he could. The violence was devastating.

Until finally he let it fall...and settle. A puff of sawdust came from under the door.

After a terrible pause, Max put his ear to the door and listened for any movement. There was none. For a moment he thought about opening it, to see what lay inside, but told himself no. He didn't need to see. Whatever wretched thing he was looking for would be gone. With mild surprise, he realized he was crying. He wiped it away and made his way back to the mirror, hoping everything would be better now.

But it wasn't.

When he got back, Durga was edgy and upset. "Max, what is the issue?" he snapped from inside the mirror. "Sage is ready for us!"

"Sorry, sorry, I'm ready now." Max fell to his knees in front of the mirror and did again what Durga had said—he let his eyes and his mind go loose and drifting, centered on the middle distance. In the range of Max's unfocused gaze, Durga's image became soft, hazy, then divided itself into two. In less than a minute, Max felt the Indian boy rooting again inside his brain; the blurry rightward Durga remained staring at him, but the blurry leftward Durga reached out through the mirror, the upper half of his body stretching into the dim light of the basement like a man leaning out a window. He grabbed Max around the ribs, and as Max grabbed him back his attention snapped into clarity.

"Watch your head!" Durga hissed, and Max ducked so he wouldn't thump himself on the frame. Durga lifted and Max pushed, and he felt a flush of chill, a bubble of cool—

—and then he was through. As dazed and disoriented and yanked from his world as a newborn. Durga let him go and fell back panting. It had been a terrific exertion for them both.

Max found himself on his hands and knees on a tiled floor, the ceramic cold and wonderfully smooth under his palms. Durga broke into a troubled grin. Max blinked back at him, feeling a surge of relief like he never had before; behind him, the mirror lay shattered now by his own extraction. Beyond it, the tiny nurse, the one who didn't like him—Meredith—stood staring at him with her back against the far wall.

Puzzled, Max looked up: it was the operating theatre. Above, in the auditorium seats, ten or so young men lounged. Some of them smoking, some with crewcuts, their rough faces lean and sun-weathered and unfamiliar to Max, their arms and legs splayed about as if they had been there for some time. They looked like farmhands. Several rows above them, leaning near the low door at the top and dour as a bank manager, was Tom Howland.

"What?" Max turned blankly to Durga. "What is this?"

"You wanted out," Durga said simply. His voice had an odd tone. "Now you're out."

The door slammed open. Dr. Stout and Nurse Agnes came in from the changing room, the sweat-darkened wooden handle of a pistol sticking out from the waist belt of Stout's trousers. Stunned, Max followed Nurse Agnes' gaze to where a gurney had been prepared: restraining straps, a loaded hypodermic syringe—comically large, as if it was meant for an elephant, or a prop for a vaudeville act—on a nearby tray. A cold, distraught thought came to him—this was a theater, and it was all a performance. There was even a proscenium to frame it all.

Max opened his mouth to speak, but Stout stopped him with a rigid, raised hand. He smiled bitterly. "Max, you've been a bit of a bother lately, haven't you? If you would've given us more time, we may have been able to salvage somethin'. But time and again you created a situation that has squirmed itself out of control." He pushed his glasses up his nose. "Now you're trying to run again. And this is how we'll deal with that."

Max crouched back against the wall. "Where's Sage?"

That bitter smile again. "Sage has been dealt with." Stout took the syringe and, looking over his glasses, held it up before him and thumped a bubble out of the barrel. "Unfortunately she chose to rebel in her own way, which has caused us all a great deal of difficulty. Black Howard has departed, to where we have no idea. Evidently he did not appreciate bein' put in this dicey situation. Our school is all in a muddle, thanks to you." He pressed the plunger slightly and clear liquid arced out from the needle. "Durga here has had to make some hard choices of his own. Happily, Sage came to him with her problems, and happily he has cooperated with us to remedy the situation."

Durga watched Max, his half-lidded gaze a mixture of remorse and conceit.

"Boys," Stout called, "it's time."

The young men in the seats above—farmhands, Nebraska farmhands, Max was sure of it now—rose casually and tossed down their cigarettes, and started making their way down. Several vaulted over the railing and landed with a solid TOOM! on the theater floor.

Max pushed himself up, and backed toward the corner where the blood boy supplies were kept. One of the boys—a red-faced, thick-looking yokel with a plug of chewing tobacco tucked in his cheek—came and grabbed him by the wrist, but he yanked it away.

From somewhere, then: a bell rang. The people in the operating theater paused momentarily to listen.

"Wait a second," Nurse Agnes said, frowning, her raised face into the air. Her nostrils flared. She turned to Stout, her features knotted. "What is that smell?"

The red-faced boy lurched after Max's wrist again, and caught it in a tight hold.

And then another bell, this one slightly closer. Nurse Agnes looked over at the tiny nurse. And again, from far off, maybe in a distant wing—a third bell. Jangling and shrill.

"It's a fire alarm," Nurse Agnes said coolly. Everyone listened, trying to make sense of it.

Then, even farther away, a fourth bell, another wing. The farmhands shifted uneasily—they seemed to have an instinctive flatland respect for flame. Nurse Agnes wrinkled her nose and looked at them. "It's a fire," she said with a mild sigh, sounding almost resigned.

Stout glanced at her as if he had never seen her before. "Where?"

She sniffed again, licked her lips. Up near Tom Howland, at the little door at the top of the room, whitish-blue smoke with an odd, glossy consistency like flowing porcelain drifted from a crack in the doorframe. Tom was staring indifferently at it; he could have been one of the farmhands wearing a Tom Howland mask.

Finally, Nurse Agnes spoke: "In the south wing." She listened, her head cocked, her nose working. "And in the west wing." She listened again; the room was strangely silent. "And also here."

There was a sudden, frantic scramble. Durga backed towards the door, but Tom Howland sprang into action and leapt down the steps. Max turned to see the changing room door slam shut on its own accord. Feeling as if some sudden nightmare had dropped upon him like a bizarre stage setting, he watched as Tom Howland leaned against the upper rail and fixed Durga with a stare—not angry, but searingly intense; his face lowered, his brows scrunched, and he glared at Durga with thin lips pressed tightly together.

Durga stopped, and turned oddly to stand with his fists stiff at his sides, face cocked up to the ceiling in a choirboy's pose, ready to sing. His eyes weren't half-lidded anymore, but fixed in a helpless mask of surprise and fear; he seemed to struggle from within, furiously and futilely rattling the bars inside in a locked cell.

The farm boys rushed the door and pried it open again. They crammed their way out, pushing down and trampling over the tiny nurse. Max made a scramble for the door, too.

"You!" Tom Howland yelled. "Stop!" And Max felt a sudden chih! like a hiccupping in his head, his thoughts skidding into somewhere startling and strange, and he instantly felt the most peculiar need to stand rigid with his arms at his sides, like scratching an itch—

it would feel yes feel so good and comforting and so good right now

—but then several fleeing farmhands came between he and Tom Howland as they charged for the changing room door, and the sensation, not yet fully achieved, popped around him like a bubble. Max dropped instantly, mostly from instinct, and scuttled low on his knees—under, around, and through the farmhands' legs, skittering past the edge of the doorway into the changing room just behind Stout and Nurse Agnes and over the tiny nurse who lay bloody by the work boots stepping on her. From the corner of his eye Max saw Tom Howland vault over the rail and down into the bowl—Durga still stupefied and frozen among the shards of the shattered mirror—but then the door swung closed and he was into the changing room and pushing through hectic people looking for a way out, and down the hallway and in a heartbeat veering with others out into the clinic corridor.

Max stopped. Smoke hung in slick Spanish moss-like drifts, already up near the ceiling. The fire was undeniably of supernatural origin—it had spread too quickly, and there was a strange polished quality to the smoke, like liquid marble.

He raced down the wing, calling, "Sage! Sage!" but there was no answer.

Around the corner, bluish-white flames, like shards of fine china, leapt at the walls and the curtains in the classrooms. As he ran down the hallway he saw the rocking chairs in the foyer were flickering, and the front ceiling sagged, already in danger of collapse. *How had it moved so fast?* The huge windows bulged inward from the heat, groaning in weird, almost humanlike voices, and ready to explode. There would be no exit from the front steps, that was for sure. Max didn't sprint past it so much as escape from it in a forward direction, face shielded, thinking the glass would shatter in at any moment.

With the smoke and vile sulfurous fumes clogging his breath, he sprinted down the hall and around another corner to the southernmost wing, toward where he had first slept at Steppeland, where shards of fire click-clacked like broken glass in the stairwell near the ceiling. The heat curled the tiles from the floor. Astounded, he stopped and listened as, with a great crash, a piece of the far northern wing of the clinic came down. *How could it have moved so goddamn fast?*

"*Sage!*" he called again. No answer. He dashed back among several skittering orderlies and cooks and around again through the foyer, which was hotter now and even more ready to shatter, the groans louder and the curtains and chairs blazing like some bizarre plantation tall-tale, and he darted down the hall, back around to the changing room. The knob was yanked from his hand and slammed against the wall by the pulling gusts of flame. Hoping against hope he wouldn't run into Tom Howland coming through the doorway, Max headed in.

The rooms were filled with smoke, and crackling fire had already taken over the operating theater. No one was there now except two singed and writhing bodies in the doorway. They were still alive, their seared black and red limbs curled in terrible broken displays of agony. One of them was the tiny nurse; she looked up at Max in a moaning plea of wordless despair.

Instead of helping her, he scrambled back out the hall and around the corner, going for the western exit, only to see another inferno there, a huge amoebic monstrosity of delicate porcelain shards snapping and lurching like storm-waves at the far wing—advancing in surges, the heat sweeping at his feet and pulling him down the hall in a powerful undertow of burning oxygen. The living fire came on like a riptide torrent, a hurricane flood of conjured flame, the floor and walls charring before its advance.

He couldn't reach the commissary. There was no way out. Near the ceiling the bluish smoke was heavy, descending in viscous filaments that reached down and snatched at his hair. In a panic, Max realized there was one hope left—in the wing behind him, a door he'd passed unthinkingly several times. He sprang around the corner and sprinted back to it, and by some miracle the door was unlocked, and as the smooth chalky smoke choked his breath and swiped at his collar, he fell through it and the rush of air slammed the door shut behind him.

The cool air slapped him like water. Dazed, he went down on his knees, chest aching and catching, his breath coming in ragged gulps. The dirt beneath him was reassuringly normal. He looked up, dreading what he might see, but the Hall of the Woods was empty; everything was in its place, as if Black Howard had just left it moments ago. Dust motes wafted drowsily as early evening seeped in through the bright canvas.

Someone was sitting on Black Howard's leonine throne. Blue dress, knobby knees, sandy hair. Harriet.

She looked at Max with unhappy eyes. A new worry unfurled itself suddenly in his mind: Was this salvation, or another terrible ruse? Was Harriet part of their terrible plan? He started to talk, but was cut short by a fit of coughing.

When he could talk again, he croaked, "Where's Sage?"

The corners of Harriet's mouth twitched involuntarily; she was struggling not to cry. "They put her down," she said. "They put Rosalie down, too. Like dogs, like bad dogs." Max stared at her, eyes bleary from the fire. His thoughts were listless and addled; what she said made no sense, it was as if the smoke had gotten inside of his head. The only thing he knew for sure was that he felt simultaneously like he was going to pass out and throw up. "They were going to put you down, too, Max," she said. When he looked up, Harriet's face was twisted, but her eyes glimmered with a terrible, blistered pride. "So I started a fire."

"That was you?"

"I couldn't think of any other way to get you out. Black Howard's gone. Everybody's gone. Except Durga."

"Durga's—" Max stopped. What had happened to Durga? He was just— *paused.* Weirdly halted by Tom Howland. Max thought of his own momentary paralysis, that terrifying moment when he had been overtaken by a powerful urge to simply...what? *Obey.* It had been intense and inexplicable. He felt the hair on his neck rise. "I think...I think Durga may be in trouble."

"He deserves it. He told them everything he knew and was part of their—their—" Harriet's face was a snarl, but her eyes went glassy, as if she were surprised at how terrible things had gotten. "They wanted to punish you, too."

Max glanced over at the tent wall, looking for the pock mark left by his very first *tamkarra,* his little miracle. It was gone. It had been gone for a long time. "What happened to Rosalie?" he heard himself say.

"They wanted her to band along, but she wouldn't. Not with Black Howard gone. It—it wasn't some big courageous refusal or anything, she just...didn't cooperate. So that man, that—" A strange look stirred in her face again, and Max saw fear churning behind her eyes. What had she seen? "Tom Howland silenced her."

A sharp blade of sorrow and regret cut him then, a slash to the ribs. He hadn't been close to Rosalie, not at all. They weren't friends in any sense of the word, but she had never been unkind to him, either. Whatever had happened to her, she didn't deserve it. "What about you?"

"They...thought I was with them. I'm sure this was on orders from Peter Sylvester. He always liked me, he must have thought our common history kept my loyalty. But he was wrong."

Painfully, tenderly, Max pushed himself up and went over and pulled back the pavilion threshold to peek out into the dark woods. The smell of smoke hung faintly in the air, sour and pungent.

Harriet came and looked over his shoulder. "We should go," she said. "It won't be long until they—Tom Howland or those cornfed thugs—find us here."

Max turned to her. "I thought you hated me."

"I *dislike* you. I never said I hated you. Nobody deserves this."

"What do we do now?"

"The fire will keep them busy. We can make our way to town and catch a—"

Max shook his head. "I tried that already. They knew what I was doing before even I did."

Harriet's mouth closed; fear rushed across her face. "Well," she said after a moment. "Let's just...I don't know. Do something they won't...think we're doing."

"Like what?" Max tried to think. "North? South? They already know what I'll do, Harriet. As much as I hate it, they've got me catalogued somehow. Figured out. I think it has to be you. You decide."

Harriet's hair had fallen in her face, and she was quiet, lost in thought, seeming to shuffle various options in her mind. The fear was gone, replaced by the vast strategic card game of choices—both rational and intuitive, planning, weighing, reasoning, many steps ahead. She shook her hair away from her face and spoke up: "West. The Sand Hills. They'll never find us out there."

The booming ground. Max gave her a bleak look, but he understood. She was right.

The sun was gone, but the edges of the sky were still pink and pale. Reluctantly they left the Hall of the Woods, and scurried through the high trees from cover to cover, until they rounded the evening lake and moved closer to the clinic's main building. The entire facility was completely ablaze now, all of the wings either sprouting dazzling milky blue flame or gushing so much marble smoke from the windows it was plain they were close to complete immolation. It was an inferno.

"Durga is in there," Max said heavily.

"Everyone's in there."

They dodged around to the north. The heat from the fire seemed to have a monstrous sentience. In the weird ivory glow of the blaze they pushed through the tallgrass and saw the goat stables up on the rise were free of flame—at least for now; the barley seed heads all around were worryingly dry. There were no orderlies or farm boys or anyone else. They'd either been charred in the flame or fled already for their lives.

Max and Harriet trudged up the slope and into the stables, where several agitated goats and kids stamped about in the stalls. Harriet took a moment to open all the doors and free the goats, shooing them away to the west, toward the vast prairie, while Max went to the front to watch the spectacular display of the clinic's immolation. By now the blaze had lost its pale tinge; it was mutating finally into a more traditional fire, and the flames above the burning clinic rose in red and orange sheets thirty or forty feet in the air. In the dark distance, Max saw the shimmer of the night lake, and the copse of trees beyond.

A cold dread touched his heart. "We should have stayed in the water."

"They would have found us if we had stayed in the water. Or in the Hall of the Woods. Or, like you said, on the road. That's exactly where they're looking. They'll have a harder time finding us out in the plains." Harriet came and stood next to him in the doorway, and both of them watched as massive cinders rose in the air, drifted slothfully, and then settled out of sight below the soft crest of the hill. Harriet glanced up at the roof, at the dry rafters overhead. "This barn's gonna go up fast."

"But you made the fire," Max said. "Can't you put it out?"

Harriet bit her lip and shook her head. "It's not mine anymore." Below, just over the hill, smoke was smoldering; in a moment the tendrils of the blooms burned visibly, candles in the new darkness, and in less than ten seconds the surrounding tallgrass was ablaze. It had spread now to the boundless tallgrass. It was coming their way.

Max tried to think of a strategy, of a decent plan or a way out, but came up with nothing. "Can we outflank it?"

"There's nothing but grassland. It's miles in every direction."

"Why didn't you think of this before?"

She scowled at him, her irritation always so ready, so easily at hand. "You wanted me to spend time thinking of the best way to get you out? You're right, Max—maybe I should have taken my time before I did it, considered it from every possible angle. Really dug into every feasible outcome."

Ominously, a breeze was picking up—the scorched, rising air had created a vacuum which the colder air rushed to fill, creating its own sucking wind. The air was literally pulling the fire their way.

"So what do we do?"

Harriet looked at him with a terrible clarity. Despite the bright flames, her face was white. "We run."

They left the barn in a sprint. Following and sometimes leading the goats through the tallgrass, Max and Harriet raced as fast as they could out toward the booming grounds. The animals bleated in panic, and in a minute the fire roared behind them, loud as a coming train. They all dashed through splintering darkness, down brambled hollows, and up over the hills, faster than Max thought possible; rabbits darted and cowered, grouse scattered and took to clumsy flight, and for a moment he felt a breath of elation—he thought maybe they could outrun the damn thing. But when he turned to look the massive swell of orange fire was speeding toward them like a great wave. He and Harriet ran harder, if that was possible, but pushing through the tallgrass was like splashing through water, and ahead of them and all around was nothing but dark rolling tundra and waist-high, autumn-dry weeds. There was no way to outrun it.

Max staggered to a stop, panting, holding a palm to his burning ribs. "Harriet! We gotta think!" he yelled. "We'll kill ourselves before that thing gets a chance to kill us."

Harriet caught up to him, chest heaving, and paced in frantic circles. Her sweaty face glittered in the wicked orange light. They looked at each other, and for the first time since the ceremony room when he chose to take her place here at Steppeland, he saw true helplessness in her eyes. His heart tumbled; Harriet was always so sure of herself, so fluidly in charge, that the idea she didn't know what to do troubled him almost as much as the fire. The grass all around was already brittle and withering even more in the intense heat, ready to catch fire in mere sympathy with the coming blaze.

"What can we do?"

"Max, I don't know."

"Can you—can you form a shield around us?"

"What? I don't—what are you—?"

"*Tamkarra.* A protective barrier! I can't do it but maybe you can!"

Puzzled, Harriet looked back at the coming inferno. It flooded toward them in a bright torrent, black smoke boiling furiously from the flames, hiding the dark sky and turning the night into a terrifyingly gorgeous gloaming. It would be upon them in less than a minute.

Max ran up several steps ahead, to a hollow in the grass, and fell to his knees. "Come here!" he yelled, and furiously he raked and pulled away the grass until there was a patch of bare ground—nothing but sand and dirt. Harriet crouched low next to him. "Now, take my hands." They knelt together and clasped fingers, looking desperately into each other's eyes. Sweat streamed down their faces and matted their hair. "We need an airtight covering between us and the fire," Max said. "It'll pass quick."

From nearby came a sound, a bleat—the terrified call of a kid. Harriet whipped around, searching, and impulsively she yanked her hand away from Max's. For a breathless moment she turned her wild gaze to his. "Harriet—" he pleaded, "*don't.*"

She dashed out into the tallgrass. Out here it was almost as high as her shoulders, and Max lost sight of her immediately. He leaned back on his knees, shivering with fear and stress in the intense heat. The approaching flames were three stories high.

Harriet was just...gone.

But then he caught sight of her, in the radiance at the top of a rise, pushing through the thicket. "*Harriet!*" The torrent was almost upon them. Already some of the blooms around him had caught fire and were spreading.

Then she reappeared, closer, shouldering her way through, cradling a brown and white kid that squirmed furiously against her grasp. A weird emotion caromed through Max, too quickly to recognize—the closest feeling felt like gratitude, or relief. He blinked tears again.

"Okay," she said when she got back and squatted down next to him. The little goat struggled as the firestorm came on furiously, and they clasped hands and stared terrified into the depths of each other's gaze.

"Do it!" Max yelled, and he shuddered as he felt something stir around them—a solidity, a clear chitinous thing that went up behind Harriet, and he sensed the same thing behind him—a crystalline shimmer in the air, not unlike the heat wavering all around—and the clear solid thing rose and crested over them and met at the top and then bonded and sealed. They were surrounded, enveloped, and now he worried if their oxygen would hold out. The flames came, charged upon them, above and all around, and as they huddled low their gossamer shield did the same. The roar was deafening.

"Put your mouth to the ground!" he yelled, and they both lay there prone, panting into the dirt as the fire burst everywhere. They were in it now and the sky was unbearable: white fire and impossible rage. The goat struggled in Harriet's arms, and when she tried to make it lie down it panicked and forced its way back up. The roar thundered and clapped and the fine edges of the scorching singed Max and even within their small shelter the fronds started to burn. The air was hot in their throats and around them the flames black and orange and white and tallgrass thickets exploding into flame like bombs.

"Down!" he yelled again, and pushed her face into the hot soil. The air was charred now and he could feel the oxygen roiling inside, trying to surge from the shelter, the world aflame, a boiling tempest of bright terror and thick smoke, and the moisture in the soil had evaporated and in the dirt Harriet's eyes were rolling back—*We're losing our oxygen*, Max thought and the radiant heat roasted his skin but he dug down, down, and pushed Harriet down too, he held his breath and scrunched his eyes and dug down, his mouth full of dirt, the ground hot and dry and the grass and dirt around them withered and black. Tendrils of Harriet's hair had started to smolder, and also his shirt, and he beat it out but she gave no reaction. Above them was chaos in its purest form—raging, roaring, crackling with the beauty of real terror, a maelstrom no living thing could withstand, the flames whipping in waves, never still, a pandemonium of bright power, the hair on his arms withered and his eyebrows and nostril hairs and he put his face into the hole and covered Harriet and the goat with him and all was heat and light and light and heat until—

Slowly. Painfully. Like a tired old man ascending stairs, he came into awareness.

He realized he'd been laying there for some time, idly watching the dry puffs of soil that rose every time he took an acrid breath. After several moments—*minutes?*—Max raised his head. The surging roar was off and away. Outside their little bubble the ground was nothing but scattered ash. The firestorm had passed over them and moved beyond.

The skin of his forearms was beef red and peeling and tender. The sound of the fire receded even more, like a train beyond the hills, and he got painfully up on his elbows. Harriet lay oblivious in the scorched dirt.

With a *pah!* the field above them popped casually, like a soapy bubble. Max took a deeper, exploratory breath. It was hot, caustic, but cool enough to sustain. He gagged, spat black phlegm. Harriet opened her eyes, blinked several times, and gazed dreamily at the burnt soil next to her. Her hair had been singed also. She started to sob, but no tears came. Her face was dry. In her arms, the little scorched kid had folded onto itself. Its milky eyes were open, but plainly it was dead.

BOOK THREE

THE FAQRS

EIGHTEEN: EXILES AND HORSE THIEVES

IN THE MOONLIGHT, THE charred, blasted landscape could have been a scene from Max's copy of *The War of the Worlds*: smudges of soot and ash layered the smoldering ground, and each step they took sent up dry little clouds of black dust. Every so often they stumbled across the seared remains of some poor, contorted animal or bird—rabbits, goats, grouse, deer, even the occasional coyote. Max's hands and arms were as raw as a roasted hen; Harriet's hair was singed, but otherwise she seemed all right. But they were parched and looking for a road, or a farmhouse, or a town, or anything, because now the Nebraska cold, forever harsh, always bitter, was starting to settle in.

After two hours or so, they came to a shallow, rocky river slicing its way through the darkness. The grass and the brush on the other side were mostly still intact. "This is where the fire choked," Max said as Harriet huddled to herself in the gloom. She didn't answer. They drank sparingly, and worried some about getting sick—what the folks back in Georgia would call "ground itch"—but they made sure to wash their faces and hands. The water was freezing but welcome, and felt particularly good on their raw places. But with the chill, they needed shelter, and most of all, some decent dry clothing.

For about a mile they followed the low, reedy banks of the stream, and came eventually to a modest bridge and a small road. From the looks of things, the road was rarely travelled, but it led west: that was something. By now Harriet was shivering, so Max gave her his singed shirt and walked beside her, hugging his bare torso, the tender skin of his arms prickling in gooseflesh.

After another half-hour they topped a small rise to see several man-made structures dim and flat in the moonlit distance. As they approached, they saw it was a farm—low and spread-out, a ramshackle accretion of homemade dwellings, with a boxy, two-story, tarpaper farmhouse standing lookout over it all. Everything was dark and huddled down for sleep.

Harriet waited out by the road while Max crept toward to the barn. It was decently maintained, and as he entered, the farm animals turned to look at him with their sad, glossy eyes, all at the exact same time, as if it had been rehearsed: five cows and three small, underfed cowponies. Max tried not to think of Jefferson and Pearl as he bridled the two mares in the quiet darkness, keeping the saddle blankets for the humans. As he sneaked the horses out to the road he found a jacket thrown atop a fence post, which turned out to be too small even for Harriet—it must have been a little boy's—but she squirmed into it anyway, and gave him back his shirt. In the moonlight he showed her how to mount and ride, and tossed the blanket around her shoulders. They were hungry and tired, but at least now they weren't freezing. And they could move a little faster.

But Harriet seemed to have taken a chill, and couldn't stop shivering, even with the jacket and the blanket. She pulled into herself and grew very quiet, which worried Max; after a time, they rode together on one horse and led the other. He sat behind her, preserving her body heat, both of them huddled under the filthy blanket and trying to keep her fever from getting worse.

Sometime in the early morning they came upon another cluster of cabins. Most of these were empty and abandoned—prairie boomtowns, even tiny ones, had a way of going up quickly and then, for obscure and often tragic reasons, falling apart just as fast. But the lone occupied home looked fully awake; almost every window was bright, even at that dismal hour, and they cautiously approached. Max knocked shyly, with great worry, and in a moment a man came to the door. Middle-aged, slump-shouldered, flat-faced, a folded newspaper in his hand. Despite the odd hour and the isolated circumstances, he looked at them without fear.

It wasn't hard to get his sympathy; two scared and dirty teens, one of them taking a chill, tired and thirsty horses, a devastating tale of firestorm in the prairie—it was practically an automatic invitation to *Come own in, siddown here, have a cup o' hot milk, are ya hungry?*

The teens were hungry, and after warming up in front of the fire, they ate as much milky smashed potatoes, buttered peas and salty smoked ham as their swollen bellies would allow. Harriet was already asleep by the time she was carried to a creaky, weirdly high feather bed in a back bedroom, while Max stayed up with the man. His name was Arthur Manderson, from back east, he said. Farmer, retired milkman, widower and veteran insomniac.

When Manderson asked why they were alone and scorched and in such a hurry to get west, Max's impromptu patchwork of truth and fiction was vague and purposefully dull. They were Jack and Hettie Beasley, younger brother and elder sister; hairdresser mother in Lincoln, tonic distributor father in Cheyenne. He and Hettie had gotten lost and separated in a flash fire while running horses around an uncle's goat farm. This satisfied Manderson, or at least seemed to.

After a washcloth bath, Max climbed into bed next to Harriet as the flat line of the eastern horizon began to glow. Harriet woke, said sleepily that she was feeling better. With muted voices they wondered what they should do now: Harriet wanted to make her way back to Selleford; her parents were there, she said, her whole world, really. But Max told her there was no way he would surrender that easily into the hands of the Postmaster and the Aurora. The group would be looking for them, and both Harriet and Max knew without saying it that Tom Howland, whoever or whatever he was, had somehow survived the fire. Max didn't know if the Aurora could track them if he and Harriet used conjury—he thought they probably could, they could feel it somehow, or smell it. Either way, he didn't want to find out. So, as the room emerged around them in the growing dawn, Max offered a somewhat different proposition. "What about Manhattan?" he said. "What about New York City?"

Harriet was silent for a time, her breathing soft, the gleam of her stare pointed up at the ceiling. From the next room, Manderson's snores surged and ebbed like a tide.

"You're talking about Mme. Z–," she said. She turned toward him, propped herself on an elbow, and he could tell that though she was fighting it, the idea had sparked in her imagination. New York City was maybe the largest, and certainly the greatest, city in the world. It was a swarming, crowded metropolis, always moving, always growing, with thousands of hopeful and quixotic immigrants shipping in every day. Max had only seen pictures of it in books, but if someone wanted to get lost, the squirming bowels of New York City seemed like a good place to do it.

"If Tom Howland gets anywhere close to us," he reminded her, "it's over. Maybe Mme. Z– can give us protection."

"But you don't even know her, Max. She's evil and deceitful and breaking with everyone and going rogue."

"But that's what they *want* you to think." Max tried to sound more convinced than he felt. "Don't you see—they're no friends of hers. From what I know, they've gotten rid of pretty much everyone *but* her. We're out of allies." Briefly he told Harriet what he'd read in the letters he found in the cellar, including the one from Mme. Z– herself.

When he was done, Harriet became quiet again. Max could tell she was struggling with a wave of emotion—regret, anger, frustration, fear. She'd always been one of the Aurora, born into it, ready to rise into the discreet ranks of true disciples. They'd trained her, nurtured her, given her young life its shape and meaning. And she was genuinely fond of the three Hearst sisters. Years of séances and rituals and holidays spent at their woodland home, helping and being coddled and promised a bright golden future among the Brethren. But now her actions had positioned her against them, had forever branded her as an outcast. An enemy. Max knew firsthand it was not a good place to be. He waited for her to break into tears, but she never did; the gleam of dawnlight in her eye merely became a little glassier, a little more damp, and she rolled away from him.

Soon her breathing slowed, and for several hours she was quiet.

By midmorning, Max was up and feeding the cowponies. Their presence calmed him. When he was almost finished, Manderson came out of his house, the screen door clacking behind him, and offered to take them into town.

Guardedly, Max looked at him over the horse's mane. "South Platte?"

"Hyannis." Manderson spat chewing tobacco and wiped his mouth with his shirtsleeve. "From there you catch a train. Omaha, Lincoln, wherever ya wanna light out for."

If Hyannis was as far as Manderson could take them, then that's where they would go. But they had no money, and no clothes other than the filthy things they'd been wearing for more days than he wanted to count. Manderson said he would have bought the horses from them, except for the fact that they were obviously poached. "I ain't gonna turn ya in or nothin'," he said, "but I can't use me no crowbait."

Max asked him if he knew of anyone to whom they could sell the horses—even at a steep discount. "I could might help ya out there," Manderson said. The sun was just beginning to break over the run-in shed's corrugated tin roof, and his face was sunlit, and he squinted down at his boots. "But these boys I'm thinkin' of can be right rough. Bunch o' scofflaws. Been known to pull one out on folks from time to time."

Harriet came out of the house onto the porch, and Max caught her eye. She gave him a testy look that said, *We can make these people do whatever the hell we want.* Max shook his head: *No tamkarra.* Harriet shielded her eyes and turned to stare down the dusty road.

Max smiled back at Manderson's bright face. "Yeah, we're not really worried about that sorta thing."

They tied the cowponies to the back of Manderson's milk cart, and with a massive Morgan leading the way, the three of them set out south, toward an area called Bucktail. The sky was flat and hard above, the land still rolling, with gullies and ditches scoring the great leveled plains. Short, stubborn Hawthorn trees fought for survival here and there. Max found it desolate but weirdly beautiful—a perfectly ideal landscape for exiles and horse thieves.

When they came to what Manderson called "the compound"—down a sandy road hidden in a low area between eroded sandstone formations—they didn't announce themselves as Max expected they would, but simply rode up through broken fencing toward a weathered clump of half-finished buildings. Before they could get too close, two men—one short, one tall, both as perfectly ragged as if they had been cast as Wild West bandits in some community theatre production—came out of the house to meet their approach. The short one had a sawed-off shotgun slanting off one shoulder.

"Whatcha doin'?" he called out mildly.

Manderson stopped the cart and looked evenly at the men. "Otto here?"

"Otto?" The ragged men looked askew at the visitors, both of them with the same lazy, wandering eye, and Max saw that despite their differing sizes, they were brothers. Maybe even twins. The tall man gawped at Harriet, and Max reached over and showily took her hand.

"Why the hell would Otto wanna speak to you?" the short man said.

"I'm the dairyman. 'Member? Me and Otto's got friendly. These kids here's got these ponies they wanna lose. Right now, on the spot. Cheap as dirt."

The short man's face stretched into a grin. "Oh, milkman! Thass right!

How ya doin? Ain't seen you since you retired." It sounded like *retarred*. The man nodded to his taller brother. "Go git Otto."

The big guy ducked his head and went inside the shack, and in a moment a third man—heavy set, with wild brown hair and a tumbleweed beard—came out. This, evidently, was Otto. He wore spotted but once elegant tuxedo trousers over bare feet, but inexplicably they were so large even on his fat frame they dragged the ground. He limped, as though every step pained him. Maybe he had the gout, Max thought; Sig had had it for a time and could hardly get out bed.

"Milkman! How you been, boy?" Otto said, tottering gingerly down the porch steps and into the yard. Manderson climbed down from the cart and went over. For a moment the two regarded each other without expression, then clutched one another in an impressive, rib-cracking bear hug. With his arm slung around Otto's big shoulder, Manderson brought him closer to the two teens. The big man seemed to grin at them, but Max couldn't really tell; his mouth was just a slight hollow in the nest of his beard.

"Otto, this here is Jack and, uh..."

"Hettie," Harriet said.

"Jack and Hettie. They's got caught in that prairie fire over near Johnstown. Now they's lookin' to buy a train home, but they ain't gots no money. But they do gots these bobtails right here."

"Howdy, kids," Otto said. He looked at Harriet's scratchy hair, at Max's pink, blistered skin. "Prairie fire, huh? Everybody good?"

Harriet nodded uncertainly. Max couldn't get a handle on the man; he seemed curiously polite for a rogue. "Yessir," he said. "We're just trying to get home."

"Well, goddamn, lemme look see," Otto said, and limped over to the horses. He inspected their eyes, their mouths, their ears. He lifted their feet and raised their tails to look into their asses. "Good lookin'. Not well-fed, but not marked, neither. Good for som'body." Manderson turned, gave the teens a raised eyebrow and a doubtful twitch of beard. "Snitched, though."

"These are good horses," Max said. "Working horses."

"That may be," Otto said, "but they ain't nothin' but snitched." He paused for a second. "Let me get a look at you, boy."

Max stood awkwardly as the big man limped closer. With a wily eye, Otto looked him over, from his melted shoes to his tousled hair. He spent a long time staring into Max's eyes. "Where you from?" the big man said. "You ain't from here. And you ain't no horse thief, neither."

Max opened his mouth to reply, but then shut it again. He leaned back against the cart, and for another moment the two of them stared at each other. Max felt as probed as any diviner's mind-reading—his empty places, the shadowy crevices that kept his sorrows and fears. And now a new place, a place of expulsion and exile. The fraught and fugitive sense of being lost with no way to get home.

Otto must have found whatever he was looking for, because he laughed and spit in the dirt. "Boy, I don't know what the hell you done did, but it was somethin', I know that. You ain't never gonna be right again. You an outcast, whether you like it or not. You one of us now."

He went and put his arm under one of the mares and squeezed its barrel chest, then straightened up and licked his lips. "Ten dollars."

"Ten dollars," Max said, "*each*. These horses should get at least ninety apiece."

"Ten dollars for *both*. These is lifted, meanin' I cain't git but a quarter what they're worth for none o' em. Anythin' beyond that and I cain't make my money."

Manderson scratched his hairy neck. "Ten dollars on the train'll git ya pretty much wherever ya want to go, Jack," he said. "Shit, here to Baltimore if ya want to."

"With nothing left over," Max specified. "We have to eat."

"But if you's just goin' to Lincoln, like you said, that'll be mor'n plenty."

Max kept quiet. Harriet watched Otto, her eyes clear.

The big man sighed thoughtfully. "Lemme tell you what," he said. "I like you. You two seen somethin'—I don't know what it is and I don't want to know what it is." He nodded over at his half-finished house. "Fifteen. And you take me up on my offer and come in there, I'll have my momma make you the best goddamn buffalo chili you ever had. On the house. You nice't enough, she might even be wonned over to send you a little somethin' along the way. That and fifteen bucks'll get you a good start."

Max wiped dust from his face. They were in a hurry. And worn out. This was as sure a deal as they were going to get. He glanced at Harriet again, and she gave him an almost imperceptible nod. He looked at the two men and said, "All right."

And that was that. Otto took them inside, and they gathered around a table in the long, narrow cabin with only three rooms, all in a row. They met Marta, the boys' mother, a leather-skinned older woman who did indeed make an amazing buffalo chili. They were properly introduced to Emil, Otto's short and scruffy younger brother, and Calvin, Otto's taller and even scruffier younger brother. They laughed and listened to the family's wild stories as they ate—horse poaching, farm equipment theft, the occasional act of flatland generosity—and departed that evening, their bellies full, with several wedges of cornbread wrapped in a greasy cloth napkin and fifteen dollars folded in Max's right front pocket.

The three of them returned to Manderson's, and that night Harriet and Max slept for nearly twelve hours. In the morning, after breakfast, Harriet went into the parlor and stood before the mirror with a pair of scissors. She came back ten minutes later with her singed hair all hacked off and looking like a disheveled pre-teen boy.

Max's heart fluttered, but he glanced away and stepped out onto the porch.

They rode with Manderson in his milk cart to the little crossroads town of Hyannis, which was set along a low hill as if slung there. Max thanked him, and Harriet gave him a tight hug and pressed two dollars into Manderson's beefy hand. Then they caught the four o'clock train east. To New Jersey.

NINETEEN: THE MYSTERIOUS MARTIN PAINE

FOUR DAYS LATER, THE train arrived in Jersey City. The trip passed without incident. Max and Harriet ate sparingly, slept in their seats, and tried to blend in as well as they could. Harriet was slowly acting more like her old self again, but this only meant her capriciousness had returned, with long stretches of levity plunging suddenly into sullen gloom. Sometimes she went wandering the aisles and didn't come back, and Max would find her in the dining car having a glass of cold milk and a day-old blueberry scone, or runny eggs and overcooked bacon. When he would gently, warily, remind her of their tight budget, she would only smile and stubbornly nibble her food, and together they would look out the window at a bleak world where most of the people they knew were dead.

The train line terminated at the Hudson. With nearly the last of their money they bought two tickets for a ferry crossing into Manhattan, the cold water slapping the hull as they stood against the rails feeling the sharp, salty wind and staggered spray. Gulls hovered lazily above them. As they looked out over the reach, Harriet seemed all at once to molt from herself, to cast off the slim boyishness of the adolescent and move toward the soft lines of young womanhood; the curve of her cheek, the slip of her jawbone, the calligraphy of her neck. As the battered Chelsea Piers approached, she seemed even to stand differently, taking on a kind of effortless, feminine grace.

They stepped off the ferry and looked around; noisy crowded scuttling New York City rose to greet them. Max felt like he'd wandered into a gigantic bog, with all manner of creatures coming and going—carriages, motorcars, cable cars, streetcars, horse carts pulling loads of rotting produce. The smells, the noises, the creaking, the cracking, the yelling and pushing; men in mustaches and bowlers, women in tight-waisted dresses and enormous, neck-straining hats. Watches and ties and vests. Wicker boxes and cobblestones. Gas lamps and awnings, water dripping from high gutters. Cabbages and garlic, rice, potatoes, raw steak and mutton. Bare-chested boys in loose suspenders and ripped sweaters, toddlers with dirty bowls on their heads, sunburnt immigrants on balconies. Shops, cafes, bistros and brasseries and taverns. The slam of humanity, and everywhere right angles—plane against plane, straight up or slanted over, towers overhead and shoals of low streets below, hard fixed lines determining the lives of millions of people.

Of course it thrilled Harriet. Her features came alive as they walked up Chambers Street, her gaze skipping down the avenues and up the side of buildings. Max was bewildered by the way she came into any new environment and made herself feel right at home, like a new bride sweeping into a room. The city was instantly hers. For him, the oppression of detail was assaulting—he felt attacked and ready to scurry back to the train, to the prairie, to the hills. Back to any place that wasn't defined by simple geometry and dank human need.

They had one dollar left—that and twelve cents. "Where do we go?" he said.

They'd never even seen a photo of Mme. Z—, and so had no idea what she looked like. Max pictured her as a thin, grandmotherly type, but odd—head wraps and spectacles and ribboned collars she would pluck at with reedy fingers. It didn't matter. The only thing that did was whether she could help them get away from the Aurora.

Harriet stared up Broadway, with all its receding angles and parallelograms. The blush of possibility had bloomed on her cheeks. "I think we just keep, I don't know," she said, seeming to sense Max's consternation. "Looking. She'll turn up."

"Should we find a place for the night? We need money."

Harriet turned to Max, eyebrows raised in her usual way, but he shook his head: *No tamkarra*. The only thing to do was to keep their profiles low, to meld into the crowd. To find Mme. Z—.

They spent the rest of the afternoon exploring the lower blocks of the city, soaking in its excesses—the hoof-clatter of the calashes and shays across the flagstones, the gear-ratchet of the cars, the parks, the trees, the tenements, the churches and theaters, the armada of clouds crawling across the November sky.

"I'm starving," Harriet complained as late afternoon began its slide into evening. "I'm hungry." She wandered over to an outdoor cafe and fell into a flimsy folding chair that looked like it might break under her weight. Max sat, too. He hadn't realized how tired he was; his feet hurt and his face burned from the wind that constantly whipped though the cement gorges. The idea of warm food seemed wonderful, but with so little money he didn't think they could afford it. "I don't care, I'm famished, I'm gonna eat," Harriet said, as if she had read his mind. For all he knew, she had.

A waiter came over, tall and narrow, his apron pulled tight around him. He peered at them over his *pince-nez*. "No, no, children—sorry, no, these seats are only for customers."

"*Children?*" Harriet's eyes shined in a familiar, worrying way, and she leaned forward over the table, claiming it as her own. "We want a menu, and both of us a cup of tea. Steaming hot. With lemon."

The waiter paused. "Show me your money." Max leaned over and rooted in his pocket for the very last bill that they had, and flashed it at him. "Okay, yes, yes," the waiter said, and then, in some form of apology, "We've had a bit of trouble with hedgehogs and urchins and..." He rolled his hand, as if to suggest more, many more, and left to fetch the menus.

Max sat silent and looked out at the ever-shifting mosaic of the city. He felt dazed and burnt out, even after the four-day train ride spent mostly on his ass.

They'd had food, they'd had warmth and clothes, they'd had rest, such as it was, but he couldn't rid himself of the jangly gnawing in his gut that things could turn terrible around them at any moment. After the fires at Steppeland, he didn't think the Aurora could track them right away—they would need at least a little while, he hoped, to get themselves together—but you never knew. And so, the panic of the flight, the endless dread of the prey.

The waiter came back, and with the last dollar to their name they ordered boiled new potatoes, roast beef, dilled string beans. They guzzled water and sipped hot tea with lemon, as much as they could take. Harriet even insisted on leaving a generous tip. By the time night had risen, they'd spent every penny they had. The street grew quiet, the air grew cool. Lights came on; frail gas lamps and electric bulbs here and there gave out a weak, lonely clarity. The hours ahead loomed like a giant unsolved problem. They had no money and nowhere to go.

Then Harriet, her profile bright from the yellow glow of the cafe, raised up and hugged herself against the chill. "I have an idea."

"No conjury."

"But a good idea." She nodded to the heavy, scarred door of a beer joint across the street. "Let's wait a while."

That went without saying—where else would they go? "And then what?"

She smiled brightly, feeding off the fresh energy of her notion. "We'll wait for money to show up and then we'll just..." Harriet snapped her fingers. She glanced over her shoulder at the waiter and raised an arm; he came and pulled at the thighs of his trousers through his apron and crouched next to her. "Excuse me, I'm sorry," she said. "We're supposed to meet somebody here but they haven't shown up yet. Is it okay if we...?"

"You...need some time?"

Harriet let out an airy, demonstrative breath; Max marveled at how she could always make her point so easily. The waiter looked around. Most of the tables were empty.

"The owner gets a little crazy at all the jossers and punks hanging around," he said, standing up and putting his hands at the base of his spine, as if he had a backache. "But I'll vouch for you." She turned to Max and gave him a self-satisfied shrug, and pulled the neck of her blouse close around her. They settled in as the night's cold came on.

Two hours later the cafe had closed, the waiter had long departed, and their breath fogged out in the chilly air. Harriet, eyes still bright, watched the door of the beer joint while Max put his head down and tried to doze on the table. Finally, he felt her hand on his elbow, and looked up; the door to the bar had banged open, and a man stumbled out and wove down the sett-stone street.

"That's us," she said, not even whispering. She bolted up as if she'd been ready all this time, and took off after the drunken man. Max rose also, blurry, doing his best to follow.

The man staggered down off the sidewalk and lurched leftward up Church Street. The way led thankfully into darkness, and Max hung back as Harriet surged forward. "Mister! Hey, mister!" she said, and the man turned to look at her. His spectacles exaggerated the drunken droop of his eyes, but his face was a knot of scarred wood. He kept walking, and she did too. "Hey, you dropped something."

"Get away," the man growled, and raised an elbow at her as he shrugged his coat tighter around himself.

"Wait, wait. I could help you look for it."

"I ain't got nothing, ya skunk." The slur of his words was plain, and also the scent of bourbon trailing behind him like a boat's wake. As they walked, a mounting fear put its clammy hands around Max's neck. He had never punched a man in his life, had never attacked anyone beyond the occasional rowdy childhood wrestling. He wiped his palms on his pants, sweaty despite the cold. Up ahead was a knobby board, a bed slat someone had leaned against the rail of a tenement stairway, and he snatched it as they passed.

"It's right in here," Harriet told the man, and she took his elbow and guided him firmly into an alley.

"What the hell?" the man mumbled, but he allowed himself to be steered into the gridwork shadows. Harriet turned to Max with fierce eyes, and suddenly he knew what to do. Before he could blink—before the nasty impulse clarified itself even to him—the faraway voice in his head said, *Sorry sorry I'm sorry,* and he rushed the man from behind with his piece of wood and slammed him on the back of the skull.

"Hoooooorrrrrssshhh!" the man said, and went down on his knees. But he still grappled, still fought; heavy arms pinwheeled out and grabbed Harriet's skirt, and then her legs, and she fell, too. In the darkness an inky mess spread across the man's scalp, and Max watched it, suddenly shocked and unsure.

"*Do it!*" Harriet hissed from the ground, but Max only knelt down and put his knee on the drunk's back. The man fought to get up, but couldn't, and Max snagged both of his wrists and held them as he wriggled there like a dying beetle. Harriet scrambled out of his grasp and went digging through his pockets.

There was a noise above. Max glanced up to see, framed against the pale night sky, a young woman on a tenement balcony staring down at them. A skinny baby pushed at her in her arms. For a second, she and Max locked eyes, and suddenly it was as if they knew each other—she saw the depth of his need just as he witnessed her own grim poverty. For her this type of violence was common; he and Harriet were just another pair of savage, predatory ruffians in a city full of them. She pulled her baby tighter. After everything that had happened, Max didn't think anything could make him feel worse. He was wrong.

Harriet held up a wadded mass of bills. "Cheeky," she said, as if no one could expect anything different. With a single easy motion that surprised even him, Max got off the struggling man and stood up, and after one quick reluctant glance back at the woman on the balcony, he followed Harriet out of the alley and dashed up Church Street.

They slept that night in a red-brick hotel in Chelsea. Harriet wanted separate rooms, but Max insisted they stay together—that way they could keep an eye on each other, and he could, perhaps more importantly, keep an eye on her. The walls of the hotel were thick, but in the hallway outside their door and out in the street people banged, laughter flickered, and women squealed until early in the morning. Finally Max slid into an exhausted sleep.

He woke to a bright clamor outside. In the other bed Harriet was still a lump in the sheets, so he got up and raised the widow and put his head out. Frantic activity to the left and to the right: the endless hurry of the city, the relentless clang and commotion. His muddled brain felt stretched and tangled, and he was startled by the seemingly bottomless depths of his anxiety; he was, after all, a small-town boy, and depended upon the silence more than he realized.

When Harriet got up, they went down and found breakfast in a tight little place on the corner. Over a plate of fried ham and toast, they discussed how they could go about finding Mme. Z—.

"I'm sure she's giving talks or readings somewhere, speeches to some group or other," Max said. "She can't be that hard to find. I mean, one of the reasons the Aurora's at odds with her is that she's going public. The fact that she *won't* hide."

Harriet's sleeves had slipped down over her knuckles, and her fingers cradled her cup like twin little hermit crabs had taken up residence inside her sweater. Max's heart squirmed warmly, and he picked at his half-eaten food, hoping to distract himself. "Maybe," she said, "we could send out smoke signals."

"Smoke signals?"

She just blew into her cup, her face full of indecipherable things. Then he smiled, *Aha*. He was always among the last to catch her sarcasm. He put his fork down and swiped his mouth with the cloth napkin. "Harriet," he said, quiet and even, hoping it gave his voice more gravitas, "you don't seem to understand. We're diviners, yes. But if we do it now, I'm pretty sure they'll find us. We have to stay—"

"Civilians?" A smirk.

"You maybe haven't seen them like I've seen them. They're awful. And terrifying. And smart. You know that. They know what you're gonna do before you do. And if we bring *tamkarra* into it, they'll find out. It's like a beacon, or—or a lighthouse. They'll just follow the signal."

"Quit using that stupid word. *Tamkarra.*"

"It's a Berber word. It means—"

"I know what it means." She slurped noisily at her coffee. "It's a stupid word. What do you suggest, then?"

"That we stay quiet. Hide in the crowd. Approach Mme. Z— only when the time is right." Weirdly, this idea was new to him, too—he realized he felt this way just as he was saying it. But it felt true, so he tried to sound like he had come up with it days ago. "She has no idea who we are, and if we move too fast, who knows, we could spook her and end up scaring her off." Harriet drew her eyes away and shrugged, a gesture of agreement, or disregard. "It's gonna take time. There's millions of people here. Maybe we settle in, get a job. Stability. I could work as a postal boy here in—"

"Not a postal boy. *Shit* no. Not that. If you're gonna work, you gotta do something else."

"I'll do something else. A market, a kitchen, a cleaners, whatever it is. But no conjury. And no more jossing, or whatever it is. The last thing we need is to get put in jail. We'd be sitting ducks for the Aurora then." He looked out the window to see a fat woman teetering by. A sad little boy followed her, struggling on stumpy legs to keep up; his socks were pulled so high that they went almost to his knees.

"No prison can hold me," he heard Harriet say softly, almost in a whisper.

Prison. Max tried not to think of the Steppeland basement, the barred windows and charmed doors. There was no way he was going back there.

Impulsively, he pushed his plate away. "We need money, Harriet, we need work. Because I don't know about you, but I'm not gonna let them get me. If they do, it's gonna be—" He stopped, unable to finish the terrible thought.

Harriet didn't turn from the window. Her face was bright from the reflected light, and her poise—dark, shrewd, without an ounce of pity—struck him again. Somehow she was a woman now, and he was just a stupid little boy.

She said, "I know."

They thought it best to explore their immediate surroundings, to learn where they were and what their options had become. From there they could widen their search wherever it needed to go. But they found the nearby tenements were nightmares of overcrowding, dark, airless closets not much cleaner or brighter than the one from which Max had recently escaped, full of tired-eyed immigrant families and wretched, snot-smeared children. The streets were soft with horse and pig shit. Wood and coal stoves gave heat but produced smoke that never fully wafted away; dark hallways, water pipes frozen in November, colorless laundry slung from lines, kitchen aromas from half a dozen different countries—curries and roasts, borschts and dumplings, sour pickled things. Germans, Scandinavians, Irish men, Italian women; rickety push carts clogging the sidewalks with vendors shouting miserable wares. Stairways and porches crowded with children, peeling floral wallpaper, and vermin—every kind of mouse, rat, and roach Max could imagine. There was so much activity quivering around Max, in fact—the people, the animals, the shouting, the drunks, the beggars, the police—that even after several days the dark memories of Selleford and Steppeland still rolled around in his head; his thoughts skittered across his brain like a pebble kicked across an icy lake. Back at the hotel he would go into the bathroom and sit on the toilet and try to keep his hands from trembling; in the evenings he lay in his bed, immobilized by the pressing weight of the sorrows from the past and his fears of the future.

It was Harriet who got him up and got him moving. She pushed the beds to the corner of the room, gouging deep, careless grooves in the scarred floor, and made him do exercises—stretches and lunges and windmills, and slow trunk-raisings with the tips of his toes tucked underneath the bathroom door. "That's it," she said, doing toe-touches herself. Her sandy hair flipped fetchingly up and down. "When you get the blood flowing and keep the windows open even in the cold, the mind will follow the body." And Max did feel better. Not clear-headed, maybe, but better.

They focused their efforts on 23rd Street. Three cafes, two hotels, two speakeasies, a laundry, a cobbler, a fruit stand, and so on. A week at their hotel would cost as much cash as they presently had, so they needed to find work soon, if not right away. So they split up—Harriet heading east, toward Sixth Avenue, while Max went west, toward the piers. But after a few days they both found no one was hiring. Harriet, being an attractive and confident teenage girl, had a little better luck than he did; she wasn't cursed at and run out with a broom-swat to the ass, as he was. A few days into his search, an idea presented itself. Nine blocks north of their hotel, Max found a decent-sized theatre where a local illusionist was holding an extended engagement. The poster outside the theatre showed a dapper man, maybe in his early thirties, with a high hairline, a thick dimpled chin, and a generous skull, as if the entire back of his head were being pushed out by his oversized thoughts. The man sat on a dark stage, in a chair that had been levitated off the floor, staring cock-eyed at the viewer as a pack of puckish red devils flitted all around him. The set of his features seemed capable and shrewd and, most of all, friendly. At the bottom it said, "The Mysterious Martin Paine."

So. Instead of trying to find a job at any place that would have him—his edgy-eyed, shaky-voiced desperation, Max was sure, was part of the problem—he wondered if this was a better opportunity, one where he was maybe more qualified. Not real conjury—that was off-limits, of course—but illusion. Stage magic. It made sense. He'd never performed for a crowd, but he did feel like he had some small insight into the craft. At Steppeland he'd studied the history and practice of spiritualism and the occult with Black Howard, who was surely one of the best circuit performers in America. Maybe he could offer something of use to this man. The more he thought about it, the more excited he got. This was their chance. If he could acquire some security for him and Harriet, they could use their free time to find Mme. Z–. Even better, this Paine fellow might know her personally; it would be so much easier to gain his confidence, and then he could help them to gain hers. Spiritualists and illusionists didn't have much common ground, but surely the metaphysical societies in *fin-de-siecle* Manhattan weren't so mutually exclusive that two occultist experts wouldn't at least have heard of each other.

Stone to stone, the little faraway voice said. *Stone to stone.*

Max hurried back to Harriet. "You've gotta come see this guy," he said as he shut the hotel room door. She was sitting in the window, a leaflet in her lap, airing her legs on the sill. The muffled hiss of the heater and constant throb of street noise reached up at them through the open glass. "He's a magician—a stage magician."

Harriet didn't look up from her booklet. "Stage magic?" She licked her thumb and turned the page. "Why do we want to see him?"

Her question caught Max off guard. He thought she'd be happy, or at least interested, to hear about this new plan, and he tried not to let it flatten his new rush of good spirit. "He can help us find Mme. Z–," he said. "Maybe they know of each other. Or at the very least he can maybe give us work—we can avoid being sweepers and millers for the time being and focus on finding her."

Harriet lowered the magazine and scissored her legs together and studied them. "You've got two things wrong, Max. First, forget the sweepers and millers. We don't have to do that, and we never will again." Her legs were pale and woolly from the Nebraska autumn. A long, discolored scrape, healing nicely now, ran down the inside of her right calf, and faint blue veins traced down the tops of her thighs, like water plants just beneath the surface of a pond. "Second, he's an illusionist. He's a fraud. He can't even do your silly *tamkarra.* You're already his superior, in every way."

She had a point. "Just come with me," Max pleaded. "Just try. Let's have some fun. It's only a little money. It'll be worth it."

She raised a newly reshaped eyebrow. "Okay. All right. And when we run out of cash, you'll help me get more?"

"I mean. I don't really want to do that."

"But let's make a deal—let's cooperate. I say yes to you, you say yes to me."

She had a point—money was a constant worry. But he had a feeling about this Paine fellow. Finding him had been a good idea, and he was determined to go after it with everything he had. He licked his chapped lips, and nodded.

Harriet sat up straight, shook out her short, choppy hair, and stared at herself in the mirror across the room. Max had been worried about the mirror and had wanted to turn it around to the wall, but she wouldn't let him. "Well," she said, and scrunched a face at herself. "We certainly don't have anything else to do."

That afternoon Harriet splurged on a cheap burgundy jacket to cover her faded dress and a flat-brimmed cycling hat to hide her unfashionably choppy hair. Max tucked his shirt in and ran a wet comb through his own messy mop, which was almost as long as hers, and that night they hiked up to the theatre. A low tent of bright clouds sagged just above the tops of the buildings. As they walked, the rumble of motor cars and cabs and the martial drumming of hooves clattered up and down the streets and all around them; Max felt his anxiety rising again, a tight, painful clutching which climbed the nape of his neck, but he did his best to push it away. Outside the theatre, elegantly dressed people crowded the sidewalk, all of them bathed in the marquee's cheerful electric glow. Harriet paused at the box office to look at Martin Paine's poster, reviewing it appraisingly, her chin jutting out as she took his measure in that way only women can do. Max waited, studying the cracks in the sidewalks. Then she said, "All right." She opened her purse and paid for them both, and they slipped inside.

The lobby of the theatre had once been grand, but had fallen now into a kind of elegant disrepair. It was bigger than it looked from out on the sidewalk, with carpeted stairs on either side leading up to the balconies that swallowed the guests like a maw. Max and Harriet were swept into the general procession of people headed to the floor of the main hall, step by step, and they passed through a murky vestibule lit by electric sconces, the walls lined with other posters from past performances—vaudevilles, burlesques, melodramas, operas, sermons, music hall productions, and tonight, The Mysterious Martin Paine.

The passage spilled out into the auditorium, which was already more than half-full with people yelping and tittering all around. The boxy room rose as high as it spread wide, with balconies full of frantic, bouncing children and tormented, badgered adults. Harriet and Max took a pair of seats about midway down, to the left side of the aisle, and sat silent and fidgety and waited for the curtains to part.

About ten minutes later, without fanfare, they did. A man dressed in formal wear strolled out onstage. It was Paine, older than in his poster, and slightly thicker, but his narrow chin and wide-set but still-small eyes were the only thing keeping him from being truly handsome. Wearing a top hat on his head, with white gloves and a cane, he went to a bare wooden table placed center stage, nodded demurely to the audience, and rapped his cane hard on the tabletop; it made a loud crack that sent an expectant giggle rippling through the audience. Then he lifted his face to the rafters, put the tip of his cane in his mouth...and pushed it down his throat until it disappeared.

The audience gasped. The Mysterious Martin Paine smiled and pulled the cane from the left pocket of his trousers.

Harriet leaned in to Max. "A retractable stick," she whispered. "He compresses it and then allows it to extend to its full length."

Paine bowed to the applause. He took off a white glove and with an extravagant gesture tossed it in the air. Instantly it transformed into a dove, which fluttered off toward the balconies. The audience hooted and clapped.

"He palmed the glove in his other hand," Harriet muttered, unimpressed, "and when he bent down for the throw he took the dove from a secret pocket."

And so it went. To his relief, Max found the show terrific and funny, and the Mysterious Martin Paine was charming and baffling and suave. His cane stuck like a magnet to the wooden table, then balanced on its end. He performed card tricks and legerdemain; he called for volunteers to come onstage, pulled billiard balls from nowhere, juggled six at a time, then eight, then ten; he produced a ferret from his hat, and later a bantam rooster, all to boisterous applause. Soon it was over: Paine bowed deeply, blew a kiss to the audience, and left the stage. Max and Harriet waited for a moment, then stood and swam upstream against the tide of exiting people to the side of the chamber. There, a dim hallway led from the floor to a half-flight of stairs up into the back area. The crowd's babble was loud with giddy bursts of laughter and after-show zeal. Max took a deep breath and started working up his nerve to go back there uninvited, but then a broad bull of a man, with a smushed face and a broad, flat boxer's nose—he lacked only a large ring in his nose to finish the full taurine essence—stepped in front of them to block their way.

"Yes, yes, we're just trying to say hello," Harriet assured the man, and smiled in her usual charming way.

It didn't work. The man, who wore a dirty white shirt and a raddled brown jacket and had flecks of food in his mustache, only shook his head and stood his ground. Max shuffled his feet; the heat in the room suddenly came at him, and the chatter of two hundred people exiting the theater rattled in his head. He felt that if he could just put the man's hand on his chest and let him feel his booming heart, he would change his mind. "We do magic, too," he said weakly. "We're like him, we're like Martin Paine."

With a forefinger and a thumb, the bullish man wiped the greasy, glistening corners of his mouth; for a puzzling moment he stared at the two young people...then smudged his fingers clean across the front of Max's shirt.

Harriet inhaled sharply; Max knew what she was thinking. He put his arm around her and pulled her to him in a silent plea for restraint.

She shrugged herself out of his grasp. "Look," she said sharply, "we just want to talk to the fellow. Pay him our respects."

"Go along," the man said. "Before we gets crude and grouchy."

"Grouchy," Harriet repeated in a flat voice. Her cheeks were turning red, her exhale hissed loudly through her nose. Max held his breath—he knew what she was capable of. But then he felt Harriet relax, felt her wilt under the man's gaze, or maybe her own dearth of options, and she took a half-step back. Max let his eyelids fall in silent relief. Reluctantly, he pulled Harriet after him, and they joined the slow march of the others, leaving through the long, dim hallway.

Outside, the night was clean and raw. It had rained, and then stopped; in the damp, the smear of gas and electric lights doubled themselves in the gauzy air. People fanned out from the entrance and went their way into the wet darkness. The fog of everyone's breath had started to collect into tufts of mist that hung in the air.

"I could have made that man kiss your balls," Harriet said.

Max felt defeated. "I'm glad you didn't."

"And what a sham! A farce! A phony! Anyone could do what that fellow did."

Harriet was right—it was all sleight of hand, not anything close to what they had learned back at Steppeland. Still, Paine seemed a brilliant stage illusionist. "He was good at it, though," Max said, not that he would know. "They loved him."

"Of course they did. These people wouldn't know real magic if it crawled up their asses and bit them on the inside."

Max gave a bitter laugh. They strolled back to the hotel, looking up at the clouds, around at the people. On the street most of the buildings were closed and dark, their lobbies lonely and haunted. Empty desks waited, stairways led to nowhere, elevators slept. Max felt like a stranger—the city was foreign and frightening, an animal too wild to tame, a wilderness too big to fully explore. It seemed a person could only know one edge of it, and then only for a little while, because it changed all the time.

Back in the room, Harriet was asleep in minutes. Max lay in his bed for a long while, thinking, worrying, listening to the sobs of a drunk woman wailing hoarsely down the street. "*Clifton!*" the echoes moaned. "*I'm sorry! I'm soooorrrrrry, Clifton!*"

The next morning, Max went back to the theatre. It was closed and locked. Despite his insistent banging on the door, no one came. He looked around, not sure what to do; people passing by, ignoring him, men in fedoras, women with parasols and satchels tucked in their elbows. A cart carrying a load of bright and gaudy American flags. Depressingly, Max's entire plan had consisted of merely getting an audience with Paine, and then convincing him with sheer bluster to help. There was nothing else he could think of except to wait for the man. The morning sun was warm and good on his skin, so he sat down on the theater's front steps and made himself comfortable, leaning back on his elbows in the manner of Black Howard, and watched the city open itself. This urban life moved so differently than the one from which he had come; here, anything of occult or esoteric origin felt distant and faraway—too many storefronts, too many lightposts, too many clanging streetcars and crowded crosswalks. Every passerby seemed to carry their mundanity around with them like an umbrella— a cheerful, arrogant ignorance they used to shield themselves from the elements. They had never seen the world crack wide open, never had to doubt their own sanity or worry that their private affairs could result in tragedy of unimaginable scale.

But then he noticed a policeman strolling by, and the policeman noticed him, too. Max was sure he was being taken for an urchin—his scruffy appearance, his worn clothes and his tatty shoes made the connection almost inevitable. The haunted look on his face surely gave the impression he was up to no good. On the cop's third time around, he approached.

"Good morning to you, young man." The man tipped his hat.

Max was in no mood. "I'm waiting for someone."

"You know this is private property?"

"I thought it might be, yessir."

The sun shone from behind the cop, and he studied Max through shaded eyes that were hard to see. "Who are you waiting for?"

Max had no reason to lie—he wasn't breaking any laws in trying to arrange a meeting. "Martin Paine, sir. The Mysterious Martin Paine."

"The magician?" The cop seemed stymied for a moment. He hadn't expected that answer. "Well. He's not here."

"Yessir. That's why I'm waiting for him."

The policeman scanned him again, then pointed up the avenue to a small park, where the sun broke through the trees and spotlighted the buildings on the opposite side of the street. "Park's up there, young sir," he announced in a loud voice intended to shame, letting other people on the street know that Max wasn't welcome here anymore. "Quite public. Move along."

The cop watched as Max stood—reluctantly, stiffly; he'd been on the step for an almost an hour—and shuffled the half-block or so to the little park. Max found an empty bench for himself, keeping the theater still in eyesight, including the little side entrance around the corner that he'd stupidly forgotten to include in his perch from the front stairs. The cop, he thought with an annoyed sense of gratitude, might actually have done him a favor.

After a half-hour or so his stomach was rumbling, but he didn't dare leave to find food—the moment he did, Paine's carriage would roll up and he'd be inside in less than a heartbeat. Oddly, as though the world had been reading his thoughts, at that very moment a horse and black hansom did clatter up and pause at the side entrance. Max leaned forward; on the far side of the cab a figure hopped down—a man of exactly Paine's size and bearing.

He sprang into action. "Mr. Paine!" he shouted, and sprinted across the street and down the block toward him. "Martin Paine!" It was Paine all right, carrying a briefcase and wearing rumpled street clothes. Puzzled, he turned and watched the boy hurry over.

"Sorry to bother you, sir," Max said as he came breathlessly up, "but I have a question."

Paine glanced around, as if to make sure he wasn't being buttonholed by a pack of scruffy teenagers; in a city this large and this wild, roving gangs of orphans accosting and even attacking people was a common affair.

"All right," he said warily, deciding it was just the one boy. His chin was blue-black with whiskers, but his dapper hair was parted crisply and two generous laugh lines framed his lips, as if everything he said was somehow parenthetically funny.

Max took a moment to collect himself. "I'm...I—I watched your performance, and it's...it's terrific."

Paine nodded faintly, eyes doubtful again and already drifting away. Maybe he was hoping for a more interesting exchange. "Thank you, young sir," he said and turned to go.

"But—I'm also an illusionist, and—" Max took a deep breath, ran his fingers through his hair. This was it—the time had come. "My name is Max. I want to learn from you." Instead of answering, Paine went up the side stairs to the stage door. Max felt a mad rush to add one more thing: "I'm the best I've ever seen. Besides you, I mean."

Paine turned and met him with a slight smile of appreciation and gentle rebuff. He'd heard this sort of thing many times before. "I never use assistants, and I don't tutor. But please, Mack—" and he waggled his long, delicate fingers in the air—"keep practicing. It's all in the hands, you know." He pulled a coin from his pocket, what looked like a ten-cent piece. With a flick of his thumb he sent it spinning high toward the boy. Max reached out to catch it, but lost it among the refraction of the sunlit buildings and the bright clouds. It never came down.

Paine winked and turned showily, making a point of his exit, and slipped inside the building. The door shut solid behind him. Several loud clicks came as a lock was fastened; no entrance.

The hansom's coachman, an older, solemn-faced black fellow, gave the boy a wordless rebuke from under salt and pepper brows, and the carriage noisily took off. Max found himself alone again, ashamed of what had gone wrong and not sure how to fix it. He stood there for another ten minutes, hoping that Paine would somehow come to his senses and take pity, would come back out and apologize and admit that a terrible mistake had been made. But he never did.

Shit. Slinking back to the hotel and admitting to Harriet that she had been right wouldn't work. He would regret it. Times like these reward perseverance, he told himself; if he had to wait it out again, by God he would. His stomach rumbled, so he thought this would be a good time to find some food. He had a little less than twenty-five cents in his pocket—Paine's evaporated dime would have come in handy right about now—but he found a fruit stand nearby and bought two apples and a donut, and went back to his bench in the park.

He sat there and waited all day. Aside from a few sessions of standing and pacing, and some of Harriet's squatting exercises to get the blood back into his legs, he kept an obsessive watch on the theater. His neck hurt from the constant twist; the rough dry wood of the bench chafed at his hands, and more than once he had a quick, cruel fantasy of sending hundreds of shards of splinters out into the crowded streets, wrathful little javelins to punish an unsuspecting public.

Instead, as the afternoon wheeled slowly into evening, Max came up with a new speech for Paine, this one full of confidence and brash, undeniable talent. Paine would be a fool to pass him up; as an employee, Max would be tantalizing and wondrous and seething with possibility. After several hours, after the shadows had steadily wandered across the street and began crawling up the buildings, an elegantly dressed crowd slowly assembled at the theater across the street, chattering and smoking and laughing; the doors were unlocked, and slowly the crowd drifted inside. Before long the theater steps were empty again.

By now Max had been away from the hotel for more than nine hours. Watching the cabs and the cars and the people coming and going all day had numbed his brain as much as his buttocks. His stomach rumbled again, and, since he stupidly hadn't thought to bring a jacket, he was shivering now in the evening chill. But finally the post-show doors opened and, like bats leaving a cave, the crowd came swarming from the theatre. The show was over.

Max got up and, shaking the stiffness out, went across to the theater, to the corner. He ignored the crowd and looked down the block to the side entrance, and sure enough, a black hansom led by an enormous gelding was clopping up right in front of it. Max waded through the people and went down the sidewalk to stand uneasily near the gelding. It was a fine animal—evening grey, its coat damp with sweat. Steam from its muscles wafted up in the cool night air.

Then the door opened and there he was again—Martin Paine, dashing now in his tuxedo, clean-shaven, coming down the steps where he and Max had spoken earlier. A woman beside him, her arm folded into his, laughing at something he said. Under her jacket she wore a shell-colored dress with a long, lacy skirt. It dragged on the dirty stairs.

Max took a deep breath, and boldly stepped up one more time. "Hello, Mr. Paine. My name is Max Grahame. I'm an illusionist. I want to work for you."

Paine stopped. He seemed at a loss, at first not placing the youngster, then wondering at the chances of being dragooned by street urchins looking for work more than once in a single day. Next, his expression changed, moved through a string of emotions: recognition, uncertainty, a type of raw bemusement at the crazy notion of a foolish desperate teenager waiting here for hours—all day, really—just to talk to him. Or maybe the kid was a dope fiend or degenerate.

"Are you kidding me?" he said. The woman, black-haired, with a fine sharp face, assessed Max through eyes he couldn't read.

"Yessir, I'm as good as I said." He was trying to look like an adult, trying to find the same cool assurance he had seen in Peter Sylvester and Black Howard. "I mean, no sir, I'm not kidding. But I'm good. Very, very good. Better than anyone you've ever met."

Paine sized him up, his shoes, his ill-fitting pants, the haunted look in his eyes. "Thank you very much, young man, but I don't use assistants. And if I did, I certainly wouldn't start with someone using no better judgment than soliciting me from the sidewalk."

And that was that. Max's hours of waiting and planning and rehearsing were tossed away in less than a moment. The black-haired woman whispered something in Paine's ear, and he snorted in sympathy, or derision, and they climbed into the carriage.

A breeze had picked up, rippling dresses and nudging up collars; men on the sidewalk clutched their hats. Max wished suddenly that he was someone else, that he had never heard of all of this. That was the only possible solution, the only thing that would make it better—just be somebody different. Across the street a stray cat, orange in the glow from the lamps, was slinking down the cobblestones. Max stuffed his fists in his pockets. There was nothing to be done now but grovel his way back to the hotel. He stepped away, down toward the main entrance.

That was when a voice called out: "Hey you! Venture boy! Mack!"

Max looked around. The illusionist was looking at him from over the Dutch door of the cab. "All right, all right, show me what you got," Paine said. "I mean, if you're the best you've ever seen and everything."

Max stopped. *Show me what you got.* He had nothing prepared—the speech was everything, he was empty-handed and had no idea what to do. But Paine pulled a deck of cards from the breast pocket of his coat, and lobbed them across. "What's your name again?"

Max caught the cards. "Max Grahame."

"Well, Max Grahame. Show me, gimme something. Something very very good, like you said."

Max went over and slowly unpacked the deck. It was used but in good shape. On the back of each one was a silhouette of a fairy with dragonfly wings perched on the cap of a mushroom. Max turned them over and saw the top card was a Four of Clubs.

"Good card, that's a solid good card," Paine encouraged. The woman, bored, picked at a thread from the arm of her jacket.

Max's heart thrummed with mild panic. Cards. He couldn't palm cards, he didn't have a hidden pocket to slip one of them into, and the few simple things he did know how to do he had forbidden himself. *No tamkarra,* he'd said a hundred times; maybe more than that. The days of looking for work came back to him, the rejections, the failures, the wasted hours and days; the need to find stability, and also Mme. Z—. He needed this man more than anything.

With no choice—with Paine and his icy girlfriend both watching him—Max put the cards in his palm and closed his eyes and told them he wanted them to raise up. Individually, just slightly separate from one another, and spin. He took a breath and said a wordless prayer that this would not attract the Aurora, and sent his intention. The cards shuddered, as if the cool wind had wedged in, and all fifty-two of them raised within a sixteenth of an inch of each other, lifting in a tight ordered stack above his palm, and began to twirl. Some of them he sent clockwise, some counterclockwise, at various speeds on their own unique, tiny trajectories. The effect was of a very complex clockwork, or a pile of leaves whirling in an autumn yard.

There was a confounded little noise from Paine, like a cough. "Good God, man," Max heard him say.

The boy opened his eyes and let the cards drop back into themselves and made a fist around them. *Please please please don't let that get us into trouble.*

"What did you do?" There was a new tone in Paine's voice. "That was no illusion."

"No," Max said miserably. "I guess it wasn't."

Paine sat back, and stared astonished into the night street. "Good God," he said again. His nostrils flared as he took a few heavy breaths. Max looked down the block; nothing but shadows and dwindling geometry, vague dark shapes passing in the intersection.

"Look, okay," Paine said then, and sat up and turned back to Max. "Fiona and I, we're headed somewhere. We have plans. But why don't you come to my place tomorrow and we'll talk. I want you to tell me about yourself."

"I don't—I don't know where your place is."

"Bowery." Paine told Max the address, making sure he repeated it back to him.

"Do you want to know how I did it?" Max said when Paine was done.

Paine snorted again, and Max saw that it wasn't scorn or contempt, it was simply his own unique version of a chuckle. "No, no, no way, Max—never tell, never tell." He put his finger to his lips and went, "Sssshhhhhhhh..."

Max glanced over to the woman, Fiona, who regarded him coolly, as though he were only an inconvenience. He knew that he was.

"Let's make it ten AM tomorrow," Paine said. "How does that sound?" Max nodded, and stepped back from the cab. Paine opened the Dutch door and slammed it shut again. "See you in the morning, venture boy," he said. And then as the carriage lurched off, his face craned back at Max: "Good God."

The cab clopped up the block and disappeared around the corner. Max lingered on the sidewalk, unsure what to make of what just happened; the only things he did know for sure was that he was cold and his stomach rumbled, and a blunt hollow hole was burrowing itself right behind his eyes.

TWENTY: TELLING THE TALE

"YOU DID WHAT?" HARRIET said, gaping at him.

"I had to," Max told her. "He put me on the spot. If I didn't do something for him right then, he would've left. And then we would have had nothing."

"But you wouldn't let me conjure," she said, "like, a thousand *goddamn* times!" He had come back to the hotel room; her lips were tight and curled into her teeth now, which made Max more than slightly nervous.

"I know, I know, I'm sorry, but it was the tiniest thing I could think of. Now he's letting me talk to him! Don't you see, it worked! It was part of my, my—the plan!" Harriet fell onto her unmade bed and chewed furiously at a fingernail. "Look, I'm not saying what I did was smart," he said. He felt as if his nerves were all buzzing and singing and coming alive at once. "But it was all I had. I don't plan on doing it again, I promise. Not for a long time, not until it's safe."

"I don't know what you want out of this guy. He's a fraud, Max."

"He's an illusionist, that's all. He's not pretending to know conjury, he never claimed that. But he can help us."

"With what? Cigarette tricks?"

"Help us find Mme. Z—."

Harriet didn't reply. Max sat on his bed, and they were both silent, each of them untangling their feelings among the matted sheets. It was easy to see how quickly the plan fell apart. And even if they did find her, who knows if Mme. Z— would take them in, or help them in any way? A strange and terrible idea came creeping in—the possibility that she could return the two of them, maybe in some kind of grand conciliatory gesture, an attempt to make amends, back to the vindictive whims of the Aurora.

She would never do that. Would she?

"Well." Harriet's voice was loud in the room. "Then I'm coming with you."

Suddenly Max felt a new bloom of distress, as warm and unwelcome as if he had pissed himself. This was *his* scheme, risky and foolish under any circumstances. But who knew what would happen if Harriet came along. She was careless and moody and plainly ungovernable. "No," he insisted. "I'm sorry. I need to go alone. I need to talk to him myself."

That look again. Miffed, but edged with a faint, pitying smile. "Why?"

"You want me to be honest?"

"Of course."

"I don't know what you're gonna do, Harriet. You're kind of..." He trailed off, not sure how to make his point without vexing her even more.

"What?"

He searched carefully for the word. "*Rash.*"

Harriet folded over with sudden giggles. "Is this some joke to you?" she said into the mattress. Through her blouse the bones of her spine pushed up, and she spread her shoulders and arms across the bed in a way that made Max think of the humerus bones of a bird's wing. "We have a group of very powerful people who are very angry at us, wanting to punish us—*wanting to kill us*, Max, not silence, not that stupid word, they're wanting to *kill us*—and you're worried about me being *rash*? *I saved you, boy.* But maybe I shouldn't have—maybe I shouldn't have been so fucking *rash*."

He said nothing; only stayed silent in his shame. After a time, her giggles faded, and she got up and went to the window. With a mighty effort she opened it, and immediately the street was louder, coming inside with the night air. She sniffed at it like a dog, her eyes surveying something down the block.

"All right," she said then, not looking at him. He was already an afterthought. "Do what you need to do. It's your plan, tough guy." Then she ducked her head back in and glared at him. "But if you screw this up, I'm gonna be very angry."

The next morning, after searching the same block half a dozen times, Max stood on the sidewalk and realized Paine's warehouse lacked a sign or an address or even an actual door. Instead it was just a metal roll-up security screen in front of a grimy building. For a few minutes he worked up his nerve, fighting a cowardly impulse to go back to the hotel and climb back into bed; it would be so easy to move on, to not risk failure, to find another way. Before he could change his mind, he knocked.

Prompt footsteps approached from the other side, and with a roar the gate pulled up. Paine stood there, dressed in street clothes—worn jacket buttoned once over a tan collarless shirt, a cigarette poking from the corner of his mouth. The part in his hair was as crisp as it was the night before. "Venture boy!" he said, and put his arm around Max, and led him into the gloom of his repository.

It was dark but spacious in there, crowded with cabinets and antique furniture. Farm tools, old maps, a longhorn steer's skull; bookshelves, rolls of fabric, stage curtains, birdcages, paper wasps' nests, coiled ammonite fossils, ornate mirrors, broken wagon wheels. A man-sized replica of the Leaning Tower of Pisa sloped against a far wall. And mannequins in dusty, exotic costumes—richly colored Persian and African turbans and robes—congregating in a corner. A tight corridor had been carved out for passage, and they moved through it like spelunkers exploring a cave. The only light was that which came streaming over the jumble from the open front gate, and Max wondered how Paine got anything done in here when the door was closed. The passageway widened out to a cluttered, pool-like workspace near the back, with a drafting table and a couple of stools. Paine gestured at one of the stools for Max, and took a seat himself.

"So, how ya doin'?" he said warmly, and pushed some blueprints aside, clearing the table. "And no, I haven't changed my mind about not learning your trick. But it did make me sit up and take notice. You made your point splendidly."

Max gave him what he hoped was a look of self-assurance, or at least one free of desperation. "I—I shouldn't have done that. It was a mistake. But I didn't know what else to do, I didn't know how to ask for your help."

Paine frowned. "I don't follow."

And so Max came to that choice, that precipice, which he had been dreading: to reveal or not to reveal? A tumble of paranoid thoughts snared him up like jungle vines—had Paine heard of the Brotherhood of the Aurora? Did he know who they were? By nature they were stealthy and secretive, and it was not unrealistic to think they had operatives here in Manhattan; Paine could easily be one of them. If he denied it, how would Max know for sure? But somehow, instinctively, he felt Paine was worth his trust—the magician's manner was relaxed and his gaze was pure. It was delicate ground. He decided to tell as little as possible, to make known only what he had to.

"I'm—I'm not looking for a job," he confessed. "Not really." Hearing it out loud made him feel like he was talking about somebody else. "I'm looking for a person."

"A person? Who?"

"Ah..." He could hardly speak her name out loud. "It's..." He cleared his throat, his tongue was thick and dry, and he had to will the words out. "It's Mme. Z—."

Paine frowned. "Mme. Z—?"

"You know her?"

Paine took a drag from his cigarette and put it in a teacup on the worktable, where it made a quick hiss. "The madame? I know of her. Not really my crowd." He stood up, brushed ashes from the folds of his shirt, and sat back down. "Illusionists and spiritualists—they don't, you know, they don't really see eye to eye."

"I...I know how spiritualists see illusionists. Clever craftsmen. Practiced artisans. But how is it the other way around?"

"Well, they, they're—they're frauds. Illusionists, people like me, we let the audience in on the fact that it's not real. It's show business. Sleight of hand. *Illusion*. But spiritualists and mediums and occultists like your friend are just...well. They don't talk to the dead, they don't levitate tables. They're just liars."

"What would you say if I told you that they're not? That I've seen it myself?"

Paine grinned irritably. A fresh doubt passed between them, as if Paine were wondering if he'd made a mistake in talking to the kid at all. "Look, Max," he said. "What may seem like magic is all in the fingers. Legerdemain. But angels and ghosts and séances and spirits—it's fabricated, man. It's a sham."

"But can you help me? Can you introduce me to her?"

"She may have a slight idea who I am. Why do you want her?"

That question again: Why. *Why?* He had to be careful. "It's a private matter. Between she and I. And a friend of mine."

Paine examined him in the half-light, sizing him up. Max felt the urge to explain himself, to make it right, to tell him what had happened. But Paine would never believe it; he hardly believed it himself. It would only make things worse. They stared at each other; the moment grew long, the doubt stretching between them.

But then Paine laughed. "You're a funny boy, Max. I like you. I won't have you for an assistant, but I will help you. This brilliant and mysterious Mme. Z— of yours."

A wash of relief lifted the boy, as if a little gust had blown up out on the sidewalk and a part of it had made it back here. Max took a moment just to breathe.

Paine looked in his teacup and put it back down. "I thought you were looking for a job, man. Or lessons, or something."

After a pause, Max said, "How do we do it?"

"Well. Presumably she's got some kind of lecture or assembly in the coming weeks. Or sooner, something like that. She keeps sorta to herself, I think. But she's, you know, a public figure in some ways, so..." Paine sat and tapped his toes on the straw-strewn floor, thinking. "How about this. Why don't you come back later this week and, I don't know. Maybe I'll have more for you."

Max didn't answer because tears were brimming now in his eyes. Relief had walloped him so heavily he'd gone numb—as if something large and terrible had passed him over, some great black bird of failure had decided to feast on, or shit on, someone else. He sat there for a moment, eyes wet, and then he got off his stool and went to Paine. And hugged him.

"Hey," Paine said awkwardly. "I'm with you, kid. Whoa, hey."

Max went back to the hotel to give Harriet the good news. But when he came up the street he saw her sitting on the front curb. The look on her face was full of trouble. "What is it?" he said, not sure he wanted to know the answer.

"Next week's rent. Manager wants his money, but we don't have it."

"I met with Martin Paine," Max offered hopefully. "It...it went well. He's a nice fellow. He doesn't know Mme. Z—, but he can maybe get us to her." Max didn't tell her of his sudden rush of emotion; he still felt a little raw and embarrassed.

"Did he offer you a job?"

"No. But he said he would help us."

"When?"

"Maybe in a couple of days?"

Harriet squinted up at him. "So what're we gonna do? They want their money first thing in the morning." Max looked up the sidewalk. A noisy little motor car, like a horseless carriage, was purring by, with the words DON'T WORRY WE HURRY painted on the back panel. He didn't have an answer. Harriet smoothed her skirt and hugged her knees and propped her chin on them.

But even with the dread, part of him was new and clean and clear now. Things were looking up. Paine said he would help. It meant a lot—a fragile little shiny gleam of hope inside this terrible, inexplicable mess that had somehow become his life. He took a seat on the curb next to Harriet and looked out at the street. The low din of the city rumbled on as always—the constant clatter and hiss of merchants and migrants, church bells and doors and windows opening and closing and workers and families and children chattering like birds. Maybe he was starting to get used to it. Max and Harriet's empty stomachs squinched at the exact same time, and they looked at each other and broke out laughing.

That night the two of them went out casing the drunks. Max came home with bloody knuckles, and Harriet with slightly less than eight dollars tucked into the top of her left woolen stocking.

They slept deliciously late. Harriet went downstairs to pay the manager while Max sprawled in the bed and stared up at the cracked ceiling. The broken dreams from the night still sifted through his thoughts, but they were only images, really; half-glimpsed, half-remembered. The worst one was back at Steppeland; Max stood waist deep in the sea of tallgrass, the wind rippling the bluestem spikelets all around. No road, no ingress or egress, just rolling hills like a moody ocean. Not far away, out on a gentle rise, farmhands sat around a table, eating. The men—thick-necked, laughing oblivious faces—talked and jeered through their meal. Every once in a while they looked over at Max as though he were their next assignment, their next job, their next casual kill. Their voices were loud even from far away, and Max had nowhere to go, just miles and miles of tallgrass all around. After a short time they tossed down their napkins, pushed over their chairs and, still chewing, started wading down the slope toward him—

Now, in his undershirt and briefs, Max got out of bed. He was instantly cold. In the mirror his tired, familiar face stared back, neglected and visibly scarred by the events of the last six months. He turned the mirror around and put its dusty face to the wall. On the back someone had scrawled in sloped handwriting: *Elizabeth Mackie was here but you wasnt. 1891.*

The door rattled, and Harriet came in. She beamed at him, her step lighter than Max had seen it in a while. "Two weeks," she said.

"That's good."

She paused and smirked at Max, who looked like a skinny, hairless rat in his t-shirt and underwear. "There was a note from your fella." She passed it to him. *Can you come by my warehouse tomorrow 2PM? Yrs, M. Paine.*

"Tomorrow," Max said, looking up.

"Today."

"What?"

Harriet went to her bed and sat with her back to the wall. "The front desk guy told me. Paine sent it last night. So tomorrow...is today." Her eyes studied him. "I thought you did great last night."

Last night. With her words came precipitous flashing visions of a heavy-haired immigrant, his skin a walnut brown. Coarse chin and mustaches, a sky-blue coat messy with spilled drink. Dead end alley, wooden baskets and empty boxes scattered in a far corner. Max had reluctantly hit the man with his stick, but the drunk just leered back; maybe the drink made him invincible, who could say, but he came on with an alcoholic rictus of spite and the stumbling pleasure of the fray. Harriet dropped him with a rusty bucket she found in the trash pile. Max thought the bucket's heavy edge had surely cracked the man's skull, but his pulse had been strong, his reeking breath still coming and going in a drunkard's rhythm.

"That's the last time," Max told her now, trying to sound more determined than he felt.

She shrugged. "Let's make today count."

They got up and got dressed and went down the tight, twisting staircase to the street. Max stood blinking in the colorless light. Harriet stepped up beside him, looking fresh and smart in her jacket and hat. He would have done anything for her right then.

After wandering for a few hours, they sat near the fountain in Washington Square, killing time and watching the electric streetcars come and go. They stood under the huge arch, which Max recognized from his cyclopedia back home, and he could feel all that enormous weight and power stacked high above. With her hands upraised Harriet mimed grabbing the square crest of the thing and bringing it down upon the crowds of people there. She laughed wickedly. Max didn't.

They went early to Paine's warehouse, and waited for him on the sidewalk. After a quarter of an hour or so he suddenly appeared, once again in street clothes that made him look like a gentleman farmer.

"This is Harriet," Max told him, feeling a strange burst of pride in bringing his friends together. Paine smiled and bowed and kissed her hand; this time Max could tell he really had charmed her.

Paine insisted on taking them to a nearby diner. "This month's favorite," he said. And when they'd all been seated and ordered their food, the illusionist leaned his chair back on two legs and gave them both a satisfied grin. "I've found her," he said, holding on to the table. "Already. She's here. First I sent someone looking for her residence, but what a waste. No luck. But then I remembered reading that Mme. Z— had given a presentation. Two weeks ago. A group called LPR—the League of Psychical Research." He took his fork and vigorously scratched his thigh through the fabric of his trousers. "She's doing it again. Tomorrow night. She's here."

Harriet sipped water. "LPR? What is that?"

"Spiritualist claptrap. Second-rate séances and nonsense and..." He waved it all away. Harriet turned to Max with mild alarm, but he ignored her. "They've got this thing," Paine went on, "she and this fellow, her partner, a military guy of some kind. Telling people they're communicating with the dead."

"You don't believe them?" Harriet said. Paine shrugged, seeming to not want to get into it. "What do you not believe?" Paine shot a wary glance at Max. *What is this?* his expression said. But Harriet wasn't done. "Mr. Paine, I've spoken with the dead myself." People in the cafe turned their heads, and she glared defiantly back at them, bugging her eyes out in a mocking grimace of disdain. She didn't care if New York was full of polite society or not; she didn't seem to care about anything.

Paine smiled in that same vaguely distracted, patronizing way. He let his chair drop with a thump and dug in his jacket pocket, speaking only to Max now. "At any rate, you wanted me to find her. I couldn't catch where she lives, but I know for a fact that she's in town. She's here."

"Thank you," Max said. He thought for a moment. "Is it possible you can get an introduction for us?"

"Well...seeing as how her line of work and mine put us essentially at odds with one another, it won't be easy. But for better or worse I have a bit of a reputation, too. Like I said, she might know who I am."

Max's hands were nervous and needed to fidget with something. He reached for the sugar bowl and started messing with the spoon, scooping and pouring and re-scooping, thousands and thousands of grains, a universe of them, right here in this bowl. "Anything you could do would be helpful."

Harriet broke in. "This opposition you're speaking of. It's that pronounced?"

Paine looked at her as if he had never seen her before. "Like I told Max—illusionists like me, we have no pretensions about ghosts, or magic, or reincarnation. We do stage tricks. Contraptions, cards, hidden pockets." He paused to strike a match off the sole of his shoe and light the cigarette he had pulled out. "Mediums, on the other hand, are tricksters. They take peoples' money and convince them they're speaking to deceased relatives. So, yes, there is animosity. They employ deception and untruths where we claim only technique and diversion." He nodded admiringly at Max. "Your own trick was one of the best I've seen. I'm still mulling that one over."

Max felt Harriet's hot gaze turn his way again. It was like sitting next to a fire. "Anyway," Paine went on, "I'm guessing I can at least get you in the room."

"Will you come with us?" Max said.

Before he could answer, the waitress brought their plates on a tray, and collectively they all leaned back, allowing her room to set the food down. Paine smiled at her as he stubbed out his cigarette. Max's own plate—the eggs like eyes, a crooked, woeful frown made of sausage—glowered up at him. He was not the least bit hungry.

"So what's next?"

Paine speared a pepper with his fork. "Well. I don't know. I suppose you should let me reach out to them. I'll give you the news. After that, you're on your own." He took a bite and said, "Tell me, Harriet, can you do tricks as well as Max?"

Harriet's eyes fell to her plate. She drew herself in until her head sat almost lower than her shoulders. "Tricks, hm, yes." She was struggling to stay polite. "Max will never be as good as I am. He wasn't born into it. But me, I'm—"

"We're learning, though," Max broke in, seeing how the conversation could easily go wrong. "Still learning."

"Learning...what?" Paine said.

"Conjury," Harriet said, her eyes still fixed on her food. "Divining, summoning. Real magic, the kind you think doesn't exist."

"Well," Paine said agreeably, reaching over with his knife to cut a pat of butter, "if you know real magic, why do you need me? Why do you need anyone? I get the feeling I'm still missing a big part of the picture."

"We've learned that silence is a virtue," Max said. "Magician's discretion and all that." Before he could stop himself, he blurted out, "*Indocilis privata loqui.*"

Paine stopped and looked at the boy, astonished. Then he smiled. "The magician's creed. Never tell, indeed," he said, and put down his silverware. He took a moment to think, his face serene, the bright little square of the opposite window reflected in his eyes. "But listen," he said, "there is silence, and then there is ignorance. And since you're asking for my help, I feel it's my right that I inquire about your motivations. I like you, Max. And I like you as well, Harriet. But I don't understand what it is you're doing. Or claiming to do."

Harriet shot Max another sharp glare, this one loaded with contradictory intentions. *Tell him*, it said.

Paine picked up his toast and bit into it with a crunch. "Look," he said, chewing, "I don't want to know your secrets. I certainly won't tell you mine. But I do want to know what it is you're trying to accomplish. I have to say, I'm a little skeptical of your assertions. And though I don't claim to know this

Mme. Z—, or frankly hold her in very high regard, I must admit to feeling a bit uneasy in clearing a path to her without knowing why you feel it's so important."

Harriet and Max held each other's eye—there was a silent battle of implications between them. And then suddenly, she'd decided. "You want us to tell you why we need her?"

"Well, yes. I do, yes."

"What do you want to know? I'll tell you anything."

Paine was about to answer when Max sat suddenly up in his chair. His reluctance bordered on revulsion. He felt Harriet watching him, felt the air between them crawling with doubt and reluctance and need. He took a nervous sip of coffee, and glanced at Paine, who stared patiently back. Max pushed his untouched food away so he could put his elbows on the table. There was no other way. They needed Paine, and Paine needed to hear their story. Witnessing was a powerful act in its own right, a balm in the mere sharing and knowing; maybe it would be a good thing to share the story, let someone else carry it for a while. He thought of that miserable young mother on the balcony with her baby. It was as if she had been looking into his soul. He forced himself to speak. "All right. We'll tell you."

Harriet leaned across the table and put her hand over Max's. Her eyes were gleaming, as if she'd been crying, or was about to. Paine was silent, looking back and forth from Harriet to him, confused.

Max dreaded telling it all, reliving it all, but he turned and caught the eye of a passing server. "Miss, can we have another round of coffee, please?" he said.

The telling took most of the afternoon and evening. The three of them moved from cafe to coffeehouse to bistro, strolling occasionally to stretch their legs around the dirty sidewalks of lower Manhattan. Max and Harriet spoke over the rattle of trolleys and carriages, busboys and paperboys, giving Paine the entire story—every wrinkle, every detail. For most of it the illusionist was quiet, smoking infrequently, listening with only an occasional comment or question. In cafes and diners, waitresses and waiters brought them more food, more coffee, more juice and water and hot tea, their faces sour, giving the trio increasingly annoyed service at their rudeness for lingering at the tables. Max and Harriet ignored it and kept on with their story.

"And so that's when we found you," Max told Paine after they had wrapped up their account with the train ride into Jersey City. They were in a cramped, subterranean coffeehouse in Greenwich Village; an electric light outside strobed off and on from the legs of the passersby moving across the high window. "We didn't know what else to do."

"No, no, good, that's good, I'm glad you did, I asked for it," Paine said faintly, sitting forward with a tired smile. He blinked hard a couple of times and rubbed at his eyes. He hadn't said a word for a time and seemed lost in a mad, mystic haze of clinics and séances and prairie fires. He took out his pocket watch and glanced at it. "Hookay," he said, sounding tired. "This has been...illuminating. But I've got to go. I'm sorry."

"Will you help us?" Harriet asked.

Paine turned to her. There was a reluctance in his face, a well of uncertainty in his eyes. Max could see he was wrestling internally with the whole thing, and mainly whether to believe their tale, which sounded plausible only in its careful particulars. He looked like he needed a hug.

"Of course," he sighed finally. "Anyone with more sense would stay the hell away from all of this. But I guess I'm one of those sad saps who tries to do the right thing."

Harriet stared hard at him. "You believe us?"

"I do. Crazy, but I guess I do." Paine glanced over his shoulder at the cafe door, as if the teens were holding him prisoner and he was ready to make a break for it. Before either of them could answer, he turned and looked them over. "If you're going to approach Mme. Z— you'll need better clothes. You look like two skint ragamuffins." Harriet self-consciously clasped the buttons at her neck and smoothed out her lap. "You need money?" Paine asked.

Max started to let him know that, yes, actually, they did need money. Despite the danger, they had become reluctant robbers and thieves. For all their wondrous unusable talents, they were only days away from being as poor as the urchins begging out on the street. The four dollars Harriet had tucked in her stocking wouldn't last them very long. He looked across the table now, seeing her insecure and absent-mindedly tucking a strand of hair behind her ear. Her frailty hit him like a slap: She was innocent of all she had been charged with, save helping him, rescuing him. He closed his eyes, and in the darkness the electric light against his eyelids came and went, broken by the people shuffling outside. They needed money, yes. But even more than that they needed help.

"Thank you," he heard himself say. "But no."

The next morning they went out and bought new clothes. Max's shoes had been in terrible shape even before the fire, and his shirts and pants might have been suitable for Selleford and Steppeland—at least when they were new—but not the biting, brick-funneled gusts of wintertime Manhattan. He bought a pair of boots, two pants, two shirts, and a warm black jacket. Harriet found several dresses in discount fabrics and modeled them for him, twisting in the mirror as her skirts swirled around her scandalously bare calves. She was graceful, an effortless *danseuse* in blue and watermelon pink, and her momentary happiness made his heart lurch and tilt all over again. They went back to the hotel, to rest up and wait for the evening. As they came in the lobby, the chinless little man behind the desk looked up and waved a note. "For Mr. Grahame," he said. Harriet went past him to the stairs, but Max hurried over to the counter and took it.

m,h–good news change of plans, it said. *come tonight how does ten pm sound? mp-*

In the room, the gas was on and the place was almost stuffy. Max came in to see Harriet at the window, heaving it open. "He wants us to come tonight," he told her. Happy for the free hours, Max lay down and spread out on the bed and closed his eyes, feeling good for the miracle of still being alive, of a soft mattress and clean sheets and the strong, hot shower that was waiting for him. Whatever else its faults, this hotel had terrific showers.

"Hey, Max," he heard Harriet say with a playful tone. He opened his eyes and looked over. She was by the window, face flushed with mischief. The top of her dress was unbuttoned and peeled back, and she presented herself to him, naked from the waist up. Her breasts were shockingly lovely, exquisite proof of her beauty and her youth; even with the sun behind her, reflected in bright windows from across the street, her eyes shone with a devilish light. "What do you think?" she said.

He tried to hide his true feelings, but couldn't. "I–I think you're...splendid."

Harriet came over. She put one knee on the bed. "I know," she said. Max was skittish and afraid. Where was she going with this?

She climbed onto the bed, unfolded herself alongside him, and, with the bodice of her dress bunched all around her waist, propped herself up with an elbow. It was like they were back in Manderson's all over again, only now Harriet was partially naked. "Do you ever think of me?" she teased. "In that way?"

"What? No!" Max searched himself for feelings, romantic or erotic or whatever young people in their situations felt; he couldn't find any he wanted to share. "I thought you didn't like me."

"Oh, please. Grow up, Max." With her fingers Harriet scrubbed her boyishly choppy hair. "I think of you," she said in a playful tone, as though talking to someone else. "Sometimes. After the fire."

Max didn't answer. He felt strapped to the bed. She bent a little closer and put her hand in the hollow of his sternum, rolling the pearly buttons of his new shirt back and forth. "This is a crazy world, Max. I'm glad you're here to see it with me." She was being honest, he saw suddenly, being herself, a true part of herself. A new swell of emotion lapped over him, and instead of feeling aroused he found himself suddenly resisting the urge to break into tears.

"You saved me," he said. His voice cracked, caught on the edge of a whisper. "Without you, I wouldn't be here."

"Twice. I saved you twice." Those lips. "But then you saved me, too."

It was too much. The alien closeness of her bare torso, her perfect delicious breasts, their ghastly history together. Max wanted to cling to her as much in fear as in gratitude. With the weight of their adventures, their mutual calamities, he started crying, feeling sorrows that came from some other part of him, a part that hadn't forgotten the terrible things suffered by people he'd cared for. Black Howard, Sage, Rosalie, his mother. Even Sig and Durga and Nurse Agnes. Their tragedies were bigger than he was—massive, gargantuan. He felt helpless against them.

Harriet pulled him into her and they lay together, a feral Madonna and Child. She held him bare-chested as he cried, and his tears fell between her breasts and disappeared around the ivory slope of her ribs.

TWENTY-ONE: MME. Z—

THAT EVENING THEY WALKED the twelve blocks over to Paine's warehouse to find the illusionist and his dark-haired lady friend, both of them in elegant evening wear, waiting on the sidewalk next to a gleaming, black cabriolet. The coachman, the stern black man with the greying eyebrows, sat stoic up on the settee. The gelding's breath blew fog.

"Max, Harriet, this is Fiona," Paine said, as though they should be honored to meet her. "My fiancé, my accountant, my patron, and my best friend." Fiona, her eyes as unreadable as ever, smiled faintly at them and looked away. She smelled of soap. The teens barely had time to climb in and take their seats before the carriage jerked into motion.

They bumped along the cobblestones, and Harriet pulled at her stiff jacket, which had bunched up inelegantly around her shoulders and neck. "Where're we going?" she asked. She'd pinched the apples of her cheeks so that bright spots stood out on her pale skin, and now, in the ruddy glow of the gas and electric lamps outside, it looked as if someone had slapped her.

"Your madame is here, she's in town," Paine said with smug satisfaction. "It's quite hard to know where and when these meetings take place. They're kept confidential for good reason. But we got lucky. Fiona comes from a well-placed family. Her father knows a man who knows a man and—well, we secured entry."

Fiona looked Harriet over, her eyes aloof and seemingly interested only in the younger girl's flaws. She caught Max looking at her and turned to the window.

They rode for half an hour, into an immigrant area of the city which jutted out into the East River. Paine told them it was a neighborhood called Corlears Hook—*no apostrophe*, Max was thinking with a mixture of apprehension and excitement. When they got there they stepped down from the carriage, the ladies holding their skirts, outside a tired building with hungry little hedges lining the sidewalk. Tenements crowded the street around them and hid the moon; the doorman, big and bald, with a red rage of eczema spread across the dome of his head, waved them through the double doors.

Inside, a dozen candles flickered from niches in the lobby walls—no electric light in this building, apparently—and in the shabbiness of the foyer everyone seemed overdressed. A man stood off to the side of the room, blocking a stairwell, clutching at his cuff links and looking them over; Max's worry kicked up a few notches but Paine and Fiona went over to the man at the stairs and said something he couldn't hear. The man leaned forward and listened with concentration. More hush-hush, more whispers and secrets; lately in Max's world secrets seemed to be inexorably—sickeningly—everywhere. *Don't worry, we hurry*, the little voice chimed in Max's ear. The man shook his head, *no*, but stood aside. "Here we go," Paine called.

They went up the stairs, around the balustrade to another dark stairway, and up finally to a landing which opened into a larger, brighter chamber. This room was arranged with chairs in loose rows, with coffeepots and half-full pitchers of water on card tables opposite the door. It seemed to be a meeting hall, a public room where various local groups gathered from time to time; despite the stealthy nature of the event, Max got the feeling the place was for hire on a simple nightly basis. Over by the windows, twelve or fifteen people clustered—men in beards and heavy winter coats, women in necklaces and earrings, clasping elegant furs around their necks. Max was relieved it wasn't just his group whose clothing clashed with the building's shabby state.

At the front of the chamber, a thin older man with a mossy thatch of beard stood shuffling papers at a lectern. Behind him was a heavy-set woman in a dark tunic and a blanket of velvet wraps and a fur collar, moping and pacing with the imperturbable dignity of a retired army general. But then a clap of recognition stopped Max's heart: this was her, the infamous Mme. Z—, in the flesh. No one else in the room had such confidence, such certitude, such curious and arrogant wisdom written right on their face for everyone to see. Max instantly understood why she was feared and admired at the same time: mannish, full-bodied and asexual but impossibly captivating, she didn't overstep the traditional approach to female decorum so much as ignore it entirely. She was a society unto herself; he couldn't take his eyes off her. He watched as she took a seat beside the tall man, stared at the floor between her scuffed men's shoes, and waited for the meeting to begin.

Paine ushered the four of them to a line of folding chairs near the wall. Soon the bearded man stepped up to the dais and cleared his throat.

"Good evening, everyone, thank you for coming," he said as people found their seats. His voice was reedy and sounded like it needed oiling. "My name is Colonel Edward Prescott, and I welcome you to the seventh meeting of the New York Society for Spiritual Edification. In the event that this is your first time here, let me welcome you and state the obvious. We are a loose but democratic society of men and noblewomen who are interested in occult research, in matters of esoteric spirituality and Hermetic scholarship. Whether it be from Cairo or Lhasa, St. Petersburg or the New World, the collection, preservation, and dissemination of the principles which govern the universe is our only true objective."

The old man gestured to a man even older than him, slumped in the front row with a notebook in his lap. He was corpselike and frail, and the notebook seemed to be the only thing keeping him from sliding onto the floor. "First, I am pleased to present to you tonight a lecture by Mr. J.G. Prest, on 'The Lost Principles of Proportion in the Kingdom of Mansa Musa.' Mr. Prest, of course, has travelled the world, and was a neutral observer in the first Boer War. In his subsequent explorations in the Sahara, he found himself fascinated by the arcana and wisdom that had been hidden for centuries, emerging from the sand in places like Timbuktu and Hausaland, and from Western and Northern Africa. No doubt he can tell it better than I. He is a fine speaker, and a generous man for allowing us to have a glimpse inside his research. Welcome him, please."

The scattered crowd clapped politely as the older man levered himself from his chair and took the podium. In a wan, halting monotone, he went into a long and very dull lecture circling around references to a lost mathematical formula used by ancient civilizations in the study of astronomy and the planning of cities and buildings, including, apparently, the pyramids of Cheops and Giza; the formula, the old man claimed, had been known only by chosen acolytes, and was the basis of several civilizations' advanced capabilities. But still he hoped before his death to discover it and use it for the benefit of all mankind.

"He'd better goddamn hurry," Harriet whispered, leaning into Max. Despite his travels, the old man's lecture was academic and vague, more speculation than actual practice; it was the kind of thing Black Howard could have tossed off in a minute, with more charm and twice as many particulars.

But Max was only half-listening. His eyes were glued to Mme. Z—. She was the only person he'd ever seen with the ability to dominate a room while doing nothing but sitting in it. She glanced listlessly around at the attendants, once even settling on Paine's face, and Max thought he detected a moment's recognition there. Maybe she'd seen his posters on the street and knew who he was. Then her gaze moved on.

After the speech, chairs were scattered and the people rearranged themselves in clusters of conversation, lighting cigarettes in long ivory holders and hypothesizing about antediluvian cultures lost to shifting desert sands. Mme. Z— was immediately waylaid by a pack of younger men as one of them tried out a pet theory. Not even pretending to be interested, she pulled a pinch of tobacco out of an odd little purse she had slung around her neck—it seemed fashioned out of some kind of unidentifiable but essentially intact dead animal—and hand-rolled a cigarette. One of the men fawningly lit it for her as he tried to persuade her of some mundane fantastical idea or other. When he realized she wouldn't be convinced, or even engage with his banalities, he drifted meekly away.

This left a brief opening. Paine grabbed the two teens. "Come," he said, and pulled them through the scattered chairs up to the front of the room.

Mme. Z— watched them approach, and squinted through her smoke up at Paine.

"Hello, Madame," he said, his hand extended, "I am pleased to make your acquaintance." Max was amused to see that Paine was quite nervous; he was practically a citywide celebrity, and here he was, frightened to meet this sloppy, overweight older woman. "My name is Martin Paine and—"

She said, "I know who you are." Her voice was deep, and her accent thick—Russian maybe, or Polish. She didn't take his hand. "You are the illusionist. Downtown."

Paine nodded, skittish as a schoolboy. "I am."

Mme. Z—'s eyes, green beads of malachite, like the watchful eyes of an exotic carved figurine, took in Harriet and Max, then went back to Paine. "And what does an illusionist make of a spiritualist's assembly, even one as dull as this?" she said. "I assumed we were nothing more than frauds and fakes to be discounted and exposed."

This made Paine even more nervous. "Ah. Yes, there has been a bit of that." He coughed bashfully into his fist. "But please, this is not my business tonight. Instead, I want to present to you these remarkable young people—Harriet and Max. They have come to me in great need. They've been looking for you, and asked me to help find you. In good faith I present them to you now."

The big woman shifted her green eyes again to the boy and the girl. Her chill gaze was like the wind at the edge of a cliff. "And what should I do with you?" she said, smoking.

Max opened his mouth, but found he couldn't speak; all at once, standing next to her with so much to say, so many worries to utter, he was frozen with fear.

Harriet did it for him. "We've come from the Aurora, from Steppeland," she said calmly. "I am Harriet Blackwood, this is Max Grahame. We are being pursued and hunted by Mr. Peter Sylvester, Mr. Tom Howland, and the rest of the Brotherhood of the Aurora."

Everything got quiet then, as if the air had left the room; time dragged; the people across the chamber seemed to speak in slow motion. Max's glance darted anxiously here and there, and he caught a glimpse of Fiona standing alone at the window, staring cheerlessly through parted curtains at the street below.

When he turned back, Mme. Z—'s expression had changed. Her air of jaded superiority was gone. Now there was only astonished recognition and mild shock. "My good lord," she said. She let her cigarette drop to the floor and stepped on it. "That was you? The prairie fire? The two acolytes?" Harriet nodded, and the older woman didn't answer immediately; she only stood there, a renewed consternation on her face. "This is risky," she said then, pursing her lips, "bold but very risky. We must get you out of here at once."

She turned and called to the old man, the Colonel, who was talking with several others. "We need to leave this place, now," she told him, quiet but urgent, when he came over.

The Colonel begged apologies from the others and left the room. Harriet and Max stepped back and stood along the wall, feeling dazed but oddly important as people turned to stare at them, wondering who they were and what the commotion was about. Fiona joined Paine, and they waited while Mme. Z— smoked nervously and watched the doorway for the Colonel.

In five minutes he returned, and the six of them—Max and Harriet, Paine and Fiona, the Colonel and Mme. Z— herself, were herded downstairs and outside, into a waiting coach, and rushed away.

Fiona wasn't happy. In the haste of leaving she had sat opposite Paine and the two teens and crammed in between the Colonel and Mme. Z—. Next to the big woman, she twisted an expensive ring around her fingers as the coach jarred along the cobblestones and stared irritably at the newly scuffed toes of her pearl satin shoes.

"The prairie fire was you two," Mme. Z— marveled again. Her gaze flitted from Harriet to Max and back, eyes bulging in wonder or dread or some kind of mad respect.

"I will take the blame for that one, actually," Harriet said. "They were tormenting poor Max. Maybe to death."

"*Blame?*" The woman cackled, then the humor wisped away just as quick. "If anyone is to be *blamed*, it should be Peter. That old goat always had a mind for misery. Hides it well, but he likes to make it hurt." There was a pause as they all thought about this. It was weird to hear the Postmaster mentioned like that, as if he were a normal person, or a colleague, or a feeble old man out doddering in his garden, rather than the leader of a secretive and vengeful organization. Max's head was starting to pound again.

Paine turned from staring out the window. "Forgive me, madame, but I don't understand. Why are we so frightened all of a sudden? Why the hurry?"

She gave him a withering stare. "Sir, do you not recognize the nature of the people pursuing these young ones?"

"I know the story," he said defensively. "But they got away."

"Then you know the Aurora are vast and they are powerful. Ancient and hostile and deadly as an adder. They will never let anyone just 'get away.'"

Max watched the Colonel, sitting next to poor Fiona and staring at nothing and absently smoothing his beard. He felt lost in the strangeness of this new situation—these people, their bizarre worlds and their bizarre lives. "How do you know about us?" he said. "How do you know about the fire?"

"News travels quickly in our circles. Echoes, ripples. Carrier pigeons. Indian drumbeats." Mme. Z— sat with her hands in the pockets of her trousers. Her thick knees were spread as wide as any man's. "But mostly the birds. The magpies. It's not hard to hear when you're really listening."

For another few minutes they rode in silence, the clockwork *clomp* of the horses' hooves loud in the cab. Then it was done; the Colonel was first out the door, and held it open for everyone else. They were herded into an aging row-house—for some reason Max imagined Mme. Z—'s home would be much grander, much higher in the sky—and up a narrow stairway like a culvert. Onto the second floor, through a paint-chipped threshold, and into a modest apartment. The Colonel went around the room lighting candles. The flat was messy but comfortable. A high ceiling sloped toward a bay window framed by once-pretty curtains; couches and chairs draped with afghans, their arms stained with use. Minimalist Japanese prints tacked to the walls, incense burners and dusty effigies of the Buddha, Ganesh, and Vishnu atop congested bookshelves. Overflowing ashtrays, gazelle's and baboon's heads watching the room from up near the ceiling.

"Can I get anyone anything?" the Colonel said in his creaky old man's voice. For the first time Max noticed how tall he was, and how slender. With his wool greatcoat and shoulder cape he looked like a time traveler from the 1840s.

"Tea, please," Paine said, and made a circling motion that included them all, as if the Colonel was a waiter. "For everyone."

The old man went to a small kitchenette in the corner of the room, while Mme. Z— collapsed into the low couch and slung her elbow across a threadbare patch of the couch's arm. It was clear this was her customary perch. She looked up at Fiona, standing there lost in the center of the room. "Come, my dear." She patted the seat next to her.

With a glance at Paine, who seemed unconcerned, Fiona went over and sat slowly and gracefully, smoothing the skirt of her dress underneath her. Mme. Z— put her arm around the young woman's shoulders. "Aren't you a lovely thing," she said, and her other hand went across Fiona's eyes and closed them. "I'm sorry. And...*down*." Fiona fell back onto the couch, unconscious. She looked serene at last, her chest rising and falling. Paine licked his lips, but said nothing.

"Sit, please, sit, everybody sit," the older woman said, waggling nicotine fingers toward the other chairs. "I know much, but I do not know everything. Tell me everything."

Harriet and Max took the two mismatched chairs on either end, and Paine sat opposite Mme. Z—, giving her an uneasy glance; he seemed reluctant to get back into the long story. But as the Colonel handed her some hot tea with lemon, Harriet began. Trading back and forth, for the next two hours the teens told their tale yet again, leaving out a good deal of the particulars. Mme. Z— somehow knew many of them already anyway. Not sure if she would appreciate the fact that he had handled and read her stolen personal correspondence, Max skipped the part about the letters in the basement.

But on the subject of the prairie fire, the old woman's eyebrows knitted in concern—the storm had evidently raged beyond even what Max and Harriet knew. And the details where the two young teens practically forced themselves on the Mysterious Martin Paine—the illusionist just smiled distantly, scratched his ear, and stared up at the baboon's head. The Colonel, sitting as still as a wicker man at the table near the kitchenette, said nothing.

When the two teens were done, they sat back, quiet with the dread of it all. Max's teacup was empty, his hands cold. But part of him felt good; a piece of a great weight—the burden of unshared experience—had been lifted from his shoulders. Outside the window, the night was peculiarly quiet, as if someone had dropped an enormous glass bowl over the building.

Paine broke the silence. "Can someone please tell me what this is all about? I mean, really?" He straightened up in his chair. "I appreciate all these adventures and real-life tall tales, but I feel like something is missing."

Mme. Z— leaned forward and drained the last dregs of her own cold tea. "With the Brotherhood of the Aurora, Mr. Paine, something is always missing. This is precisely the point." She exhaled heavily, and in her sigh Max sensed the weight of decades of opposition and failed amity between the two groups. "There have been times of cooperation—centuries even, of uneasy complicity. We have all tried to fit together—many distinct organizations, many tribes. But no more. Most of them now have fallen. Of the ones that are left, they can all be said to gather in the shadow of two primary septs. The Aurora and the Faqrs."

"Who—what—are these...tribes?"

The dead animal purse still lay across Mme. Z—'s sizable bosom, and she opened it and began rolling a cigarette. "Ancient knowledge—lost knowledge— has a pull, you see. The power it gives is almost irresistible. But poisonous in the wrong hands. It is an old story, sadly familiar." She looked over at Paine's sleeping fiancé. "Human nature has been depressingly consistent throughout the millennia."

"What is the nature of the disagreement?"

Mme. Z— struck a match and lit her cigarette, the flame intense and clarifying her surprisingly delicate features in the dark. "There are those who would withhold knowledge and power for private gain," she said, blowing out the match. "The darkness immediately flowed back in. "And there are some, like myself, who would share it prudently with the world, for the betterment of all."

"Prudently," Max said. Mme. Z—turned to him sharply, but said nothing.

"That's terrific," Paine broke in. "But I'm still lost. Who in the hell are all you people?"

"For the Faqrs, their principles begin in the East," the older woman said. "Tibet and India. Peter Sylvester and the Brotherhood of the Aurora, on the other hand, go back to Egypt and Northern Africa. Luxor, Cairo, and eventually Athens, Rome, and London." She pondered her cigarette, tapped it into her teacup, took a long drag. "And so you see. East versus West. Similar in kind, but quite different when you get into the details. Through all of civilization, there have been accounts of rare cooperation. But mostly it has been war."

The room was quiet. Max glanced at Harriet, who sat still and thoughtful, chin in hand. The shadows in the apartment had almost unnoticeably taken on a sinister feel; the Persian rug under Max's feet, peacocks and lotuses and lions and curlicue ivy, seemed oddly far away.

He said, "There was talk of a man named Czolgosz. The Postmaster spoke of him a time or two."

Mme. Z— raised her eyebrows. "They mentioned Czolgosz? In front of you? They had bigger plans for you than I realized."

"I read the newspapers everyday," Paine said. "I know who Czolgosz is. But what does one man have to do with all of this?"

"The murder of your President McKinley comes on the heels of the murder of your President Garfield two decades ago. You see, it is all of one piece. Czolgosz himself was thought to be a part of the action taken by the recent murder of the Italian, King Umberto. Not to mention the murder of the Serbian royals. So you see, the Aurora have been going at it for quite a long time. They find advantage in anarchy, in chaos and turmoil. They work to create it." Mme. Z—'s eyes drifted across all of them. "Their ideas were found first in a Taoist philosopher—a kind of pre-Faqr himself, ironically—named Laozi. Even Jesus Christ may once have considered himself an anarchist before he moved against it. And so now you have two vast, warring armies." Here she held up both of her hands—one open, fingers spread wide, the other made into a tight fist. "The desires of the collectivists, and the desires of the elite. Centralization of power. Consolidation of wealth."

She took another drag on her cigarette, and dabbed a bit of her saliva along one edge which had burned unevenly. "In Russia now, they have some very interesting events taking place, much talk of socialism and the destruction of the Tsarist autocracy. Worker strikes, unrest from the peasants in the fields, mutinies from the military. There is a powerful man, some call him Rasputin, who is said to be working to discredit the Tsar all the while claiming to be an ally. No doubt the Aurora have trained him and given him resources. So you see, great wars are built upon these ideas, generational combustions that never cease, using the bodies of young men and women as fodder in a quest for wealth and power."

Paine slumped back into his seat. He seemed deflated, overwhelmed at the obscure immensity of it all. "This is so fucking vague! Can we talk about what is in front of us? Can we discuss matters at hand?"

"Such as?"

"Such as... Do you actually know these people? This Sylvester fellow? Tom...whatever, whatshisname. Tom Harland?"

"I do know them, certainly I do. Or, rather, I did. Peter—he and I have shared many an excellent bottle of dry Claret together. It wasn't always this way. And Tom Howland—he is not a man named Tom Howland any more than

Max's Moorlander was an actual woman."

"What is he?" Max said. Uneasy, he looked over at the Colonel. It had been more than an hour since he had last seen him move; the old man's eyes were open, but he looked now as if he'd been stuffed by a taxidermist.

"Only Peter Sylvester knows for sure. But I estimate he—it—is a *pisacha* of some type of another."

Harriet leaned forward, her round face suddenly interested. "A—a what?"

"*Pisacha*. Not unlike Max's Moorlander—the succubus. A Hindu demon who can take the form of a man, or a woman. Incubus, succubus. A haunted, vindictive soul with access to great power. They live in a far, alien expanse of the Akasha. I've only heard reports, and from what I'm told it is a terrifying place, dry and dead, full of crawling things. We don't know how Peter Sylvester gained access to it or what its own motivations are. Obviously it is aligned with the Aurora, at least for now. Most probably they have subordinated it in some way, made it their servant."

Max closed his eyes; blood pounded in his eyelids. When he opened them, he saw Harriet's own gaze was vacant and tired. She had had enough.

In the gloom, Paine was studying his hands. "My next question, now that I know all of this, is whether I am in danger, too."

"I am afraid that you are," Mme. Z— sighed. "When you asked Max and Harriet to tell you their story, you became part of their tale." She smiled sadly. "I am sorry."

"Can you make me forget?" Paine nodded at the sleeping Fiona. "Like her?"

"It wouldn't make any difference to them, not at this point. You would still be a target. You are better off with your wits about you." Paine was silent, but in the half-light from the window, Max saw the color drain from his face.

"What do we do now?" Max asked.

"We will hide you. Protect you. If we spread ourselves out a bit, disperse the locus of energy, we may yet delay their attempts at finding you. The question now becomes the best way to do that." She turned and stared at the darkness outside the window, the spatial arrangement of the late night tenements across the street. She turned suddenly to Paine. "We will split them up. One of the wards will come with me, and one with you. Can you arrange that?"

"Split them up? In what way?"

"These young people can be helpful. An asset, if used wisely. A talented assistant, maybe. Max can go with you, Harriet will stay with me. And in the coming days we will be in close communication."

Paine scoffed. "I went through this with them. I don't use an assistant. If I did, it would be Fiona." They all turned to her, Paine's sleeping girlfriend, and watched her peaceful oblivious expression, her chest rising and falling, with some jealousy.

"But now you do have an assistant," Mme. Z— asserted. "His name is Max."

"But—young men aren't assistants. It's only females. Young women."

Mme. Z— smiled, and Max saw a familiar smirk on Harriet's face, too. "Fine," the old woman said. "Max will stay here with the Colonel and me. Harriet will go with you and be your assistant. No doubt she will look fetching in her stage outfit."

Paine took a ragged breath, but said nothing. The older woman made sure no one had anything else to add, then reached over and touched Fiona's forehead. The young woman's eyes fluttered, and she raised her head and looked over at them with a dreamy, somnolent gaze.

"You fell asleep, dearie," Mme. Z— said. "And without taking even a sip of your tea."

When everyone was gone, Max and Mme. Z— slept together in her high bed—atop soft mattresses piled with afghans and under rough quilts patched together from indeterminate fabrics. Max slept poorly due to her harsh rasp of a snore and incessant fidgeting in the night. More than once she bolted upright, coughing or gasping, which would wake him, too—terrified they were being raided by Tom Howland and his allies. But then she would lay back and slip into deep oblivious sleep, leaving Max to stare wide-eyed at the stuffed impala head glaring back in the dusty moonlight from the opposite wall.

Early the next morning he woke exhausted, and got up and went out into the main room to find the Colonel had already prepared coffee, a strong, sweet variety flavored with cardamom, which he explained was Turkish. On the kitchenette table he'd set out a saucer of freshly cut kumquats and Asian pears. The sugar and caffeine helped a bit; in less than half an hour Max was feeling more like himself. He and the old man sat wordless at the table, warming their hands from the heat of their cups as the buzz and rattle of hooves and automobiles rose outside in the street. It felt like this was a typical morning ritual—the Colonel's private moment of solitude before the cyclone known as Mme. Z— came roaring out from her bedroom to start the day in earnest. Ten minutes later, the bedroom door swung open and there she was, dressed already in extravagant furs and a thick hat, as if she were planning on sledding the forests of Siberia rather than strolling the sidewalks of early-winter Manhattan. She fixed the boy with a lucid glance. "Feel like a walk, Max?"

He did.

For a long time they rode in a cab up many blocks. "To the park," Mme. Z— had told the coachman, and she smoked and chattered the whole way about the city and how she loved it—the grandeur of it, the delirious energy of it, the boldness of the architecture, the immigrant avenues and the sunset streets.

But when they got to the park, with its paths and its heavy trees, she fell suddenly, curiously, silent; she started walking with a chuff of breath that looked like smoke, and Max followed. He had a million questions, but weirdly now his own thoughts came sluggish and slow. But she seemed to be waiting for him, for some kind of interrogation, so he obliged.

"Your accent makes me think of Russia," he said, hoping it was as good a place to start as any.

A smile found its way to Mme. Z—'s face, and there was a momentary glimpse of the lovely young woman she used to be. "You want to know who I am, before you decide to trust me." Max shrugged. Maybe there was a little of that. Not that he had any choice at this point. "You are close. Not from Russia, but from the Ukraine. A village, a long time ago. Another epoch. Since then I have become a citizen of the world." She walked with hands clasped behind her. "I married a man at a very early age—too young; it wasn't my preference, you see—and I was unhappy. So I ran away. And because I had no place to go, I travelled. Alone, and extensively, for decades. Egypt, Sudan, Ethiopia. Europe, the Far East. For a time, I was the only Western woman in all of Tibet. There I met people many would consider to be the most sacred, most venerable on this planet. And I learned a great deal from them."

She stopped at a frozen puddle. They both looked into it, and in the cracked milky depths their reflections caught each other's eye. "I came to your country, Max—to learn, to teach, to disseminate. It has become my life's work. Unfortunately, as you know, others would prefer to keep this knowledge to themselves."

The park was huge, the bare branches overhead cutting the sunlight into lacy designs on the sidewalks. Ladies in long coats and hats strolled past cabs and horses waiting at the edge in the street. But Mme. Z— took Max by the elbow and guided him inward, under stone bridges toward the center of the park, where they could talk in confidence.

"The knowledge comes of its own accord, you know," she said. "Whether it is a Buddhist monk meditating in a monastery, a sadhu, a Dervish, or a pious Quaker on his knees in a pine church—a master will come only when the apprentice is ready. Usually the master who finds you is yourself. But I am a populist at heart—I want to make sure everyone receives their share. I think the Bolsheviks may be onto something."

Max was quiet as Mme. Z— stopped and huddled against the wind to roll and light another cigarette with expert skill. She blew smoke and the wind took it immediately.

"But let me be clear," she said. "What Peter and his Aurora are doing is not mere restraint, nor mere caution. It is a vile hoarding of power, of knowledge and privilege. More than anything, they desire control. All of which is to say, do not be fooled by Peter's seeming modesty. The Aurora are exceedingly wealthy, very organized, and highly patrician in nature. They desire power and dominion."

Max thought back to the elegant guests that evening in the post office's upstairs ceremony room: the women's bright, gaudy jewelry, the men's expensive coats and shiny silk gloves. They weren't farmers, that much was for sure. And the Hearst sisters—that big, dark house alone in the woods like a country estate, all that gleaming oak and brass.

"The letters I read talked about others," he said. "Other groups. Other approaches."

"Yes. Sadly, they are all but gone. Targeted, and silenced. Perhaps the only one left of any note who is not affiliated with either is Theodosius. So it has come down to him, and the Faqrs, and the Aurora."

Max hadn't heard this name before before. "Theodosius?"

"Theodosius the Sorrowed. You don't know of him?" Max shook his head. "Well then, some things at least are as they should be. Theodosius is, ah...unique. He feels that it is best to let events unfold as they may, without interference. He stands apart, preferring the oblivion of solitude. The company of stones and stars."

"Stands apart?"

"Yes." Mme. Z— took a moment to gather her thoughts, sifting through past exploits and undertakings. "Theodosius is a man—well. Most people say he is a man, in this world you never know anymore. But he is old, perhaps the oldest man alive. Certainly the most stubborn. He is blind. He lives—or rather, is thought to live—in a compound he devised himself. Most likely by only his imagination. He spends his days practicing a complex ritual, a living design, if you will, said to be so arduous that to perform it is in and of itself a cause of great awakening. The rigor, you see, is entirely the point."

"Have you met him?"

"We travelled together for a time along the Silk Road. For many months, until in disagreement his path diverged from mine. Since then we are not in communication at all."

Mme. Z— paused then, became quiet and withdrawn; maybe she was thinking of those lost years. She and Max walked on in silence—around lakes, through fields humped with smooth, sun-thawed boulders, through winter arbors as tall as the buildings off in the distance. They didn't talk, and Max didn't feel the need to; her presence was so lulling that he felt like a child again, a swaddled baby. She wasn't a warm woman, but instead a superbly confident one. If she said something, it was to be believed.

It started to snow. The ground faded first to gray, and then to white. They hailed a cab and made their way back to Corlears Hook as Mme. Z— puffed silently on a cigarette, the flurries outside the carriage only slightly more dense than the roiling smoke inside the compartment. When they came to her block and got out, she stopped Max on the slick sidewalk.

"Let me tell you one more thing, Max, and this is important for you to understand. I am a populist. Do you understand? A populist—to the bone, my boy, to the bone and nothing more." She glared with one squinting eye. "Now, let me ask you a question. What are you? Are you a populist? Because if you are not, we have nothing further to say."

Max was caught off-guard. He'd never considered this question before. He took a moment to think it through, remembering Steppeland, the workers there. Selleford, his little mining town in the toenails of the foothills of the Appalachians. He thought of his connection with his maid, Ethie, and his pride at landing his very first job, at the post office. Cabal or no cabal, that pride had been real. Affluence had never suited him. Sig's big dark house felt ill-fitting and just...*wrong*. Stuffy. Unhappy. Mme. Z—'s question had been complicated, but it demanded a simple response. He already knew the answer to it. "Yes, ma'am, I think I am. I think I am a populist."

The big woman grinned against the smoke from her cigarette. The snow made everything black and white, and Mme. Z— turned and went *clomp clomp clomp* in her bulky men's Oxfords up the stairs.

TWENTY-TWO: THE LIBRARY

IN THE NEXT SEVERAL weeks, Max's life leveled out into a simple, steady routine, one like he hadn't experienced since before he left Selleford. He and Mme. Z— met briefly with Harriet and Paine back at the hotel in Chelsea, to collect their few belongings and share a warm, nearly wordless moment before heading their separate ways again. Harriet looked terrific—well-slept and well-fed—and she wore a green dress and a fringed silk shawl Max hadn't seen before. Her hair had been cut again and looked more proper now.

But the most surprising thing was how she and Paine had grown visibly closer. Max noticed their candid glances and the easy warmth they had, standing shoulder to shoulder or slipping tightly past each other through a doorway. Out in the hall Paine and Mme. Z— exchanged a few whispers, then the four of them parted again, Harriet heading off with the illusionist and Max and the madame going back to the crowded flat they shared with the tall, asthmatic Colonel.

After that, Mme. Z— didn't let Max leave the apartment. "There's been enough of that," she said, "and then only very early in your stay."

Early in your stay. The thought bounced off the walls. How long would he be here, anyway? He felt less like a guest and more like an inmate, though he knew it was for his own protection. In his tedium he found himself exploring the apartment inch by inch. It was larger than it first appeared. Aside from the parlor and kitchenette and two separate bedchambers, there was yet another room, a tight, windowless boudoir off Mme. Z—'s own, not much larger than a walk-in closet, converted now into a kind of tiny library, with shelves crowded with mementos from her travels: prayer wheels, Tibetan singing bowls, ritual swords still sharp in their jeweled scabbards. And there were books—volumes of old, cracked, unraveling books of the sort Black Howard had kept in his own library. As the days marched on, Max began to gravitate toward these. No one said it aloud, but it was understood that he would sit at the lamplit desk there in the cramped corner and take a good look at them. A good long look.

More than a few of the books were written by Mme. Z— herself. Histories of Buddhism, Theosophy, Neoplatonism, Hermeticism; chronologies of alchemy, astrology, philosophy. The lives and teachings of Robert Fludd, Nicholas Flamel, John Dee, and others. At first Max was reluctant, thinking of Black Howard and his ancient books with their curious bindings you didn't want to touch or think too hard about. But soon with the boredom closing in, he found himself devouring them all.

Mme. Z— kept busy herself. From the tattered couch in the main room she was focused on something she called "astral dictation." One of the Faqrs in some far-flung eastern territory was evidently writing a book through her, and she dictated to the Colonel in a spectral, boomy voice, her graying hair sometimes shading to a glossy black and her skin darkening slightly, as if she were slowly melding with a Hindu Master. Max watched mesmerized while she and the Colonel worked; the air filled with the scent of cassia bark and saffron, and distant pungi music floated eerily in the apartment like some aromatic open-air market in Bengaluru. Max couldn't help but think of Durga; a low rumble of mixed regret and hollow grief would roll through him, booming and echoing in his brain.

In the weeks he spent with Mme. Z— and the Colonel, Max had a chance to learn a good deal about their lives. To his surprise he found they were practically penniless. Though she had descended from Ukrainian royalty and had at one point enjoyed a generous inheritance, all of that was in the past. She was supported now only by benefactors—wealthy patrons who lingered quiet and wraithlike in the shadows of various occultist societies. Mme. Z— was a woman of many passions and sometimes threw fits in the small apartment, which Max and the Colonel did their best to escape—the old man in his bedroom, the boy cowering in the library as crashings and shatterings came thundering in from the other side of the closed doors. More than once Max worried about her using conjury against him, like some bizarre folktale wicked witch, a Baba Yaga terrorizing her own Lower East Side flat. Thankfully, it never happened.

Aside from her work with the Faqrs, Mme. Z—'s most ardent passion was a nascent political movement, the campaign for women's suffrage. Sometimes the apartment crowded with middle-aged women zealously planning until all hours of the morning, organizing and maneuvering with others to gain themselves and women around the world the right to vote. Personally, Max agreed with this—he saw no reason why women, who were the superior to men in so many ways, couldn't have a say in how their country was run. But several times he was awakened from Mme. Z—'s bed by heated voices in the other room, and got up and peeked through the crack of the bedroom door to see cadres of women, the air clouded with cigarette smoke, chattering furiously over Turkish coffee or amaretto. The Colonel advised him to keep hidden during these meetings, unless he wished to find himself backed into an argument with a red-faced suffragette who may or may not have realized he was actually taking her side. There were also long discussions and quarrels between the women about cosmology or chemistry or physics; or the science of atomic structure; or the separation between Swedenborg's levels of meaning in the natural, the spiritual, and the divine; arguments about the theory of correspondence—*As above, so below*, Max heard more times than he cared to count—and clairvoyance, phrenology, and psychology; as well as Mesmer's trances based upon animal magnetism and electro-biology.

But otherwise, Max had the madame mostly to himself. Over late night dinners of *budaatai huurga* (delicious, Max thought; the rice nutty and perfectly steamed), she entertained him with tales of her days as a concert pianist in Serbia, as a Polish circus horseback rider, as a Parisian importer of ostrich feathers. She'd prevented a German Baron's assassination in Turkey, fought in Hindustani armies, survived shipwrecks, ran an ink factory in Romania, studied the Cabal in Cairo, learned voodoo in Haiti, traded weapons with Mexican bandits. Mme. Z— knew everything and everyone. Late in the evening she and the Colonel would dreamily reminisce about the various prominent Faqrs that had lived throughout time—the Buddha, Roger Bacon, Serapis, Solomon, Abraham, Moses, and, most recently, an obscure Hungarian prince named Rakoczi, whom she had actually met and lived with for a time.

Max continued his studies. The books were endlessly fascinating, but with an entire history of gnostic metaphysics at his fingertips, he was reminded that research and study were not the same as exercise and experience. It was not enough to contemplate; one must also *do*. And so, after the better part of a month in the apartment, as ashen November edged into damp December, he found himself pacing restlessly, eating too much, trying to nap; he was peevish, claustrophobic, feeling the yank to get back to the true task at hand—developing his *tamkarra*. His little miracles.

One night he sat at the table as Mme. Z— and the Colonel came in from wherever they had gone. He watched them nervously, restless, knees bouncing, hands fidgety, as they stood at the sink, both of them looking down into the drain for some strange, annoying reason. Then he blurted, "When can I restart my practice?"

Mme. Z— lifted herself, turned his way. "What's that?"

"Practice. My practice. I need to practice."

"What about it?"

"My conjury. I need to get back to it. To work at it. Not just hide in that...book closet."

For a long time her eyes peered at him over the top of the silvery reflections in the lenses of her glasses. The Colonel turned to Max and lifted the peat of his beard away from his chest. "What would you have us do?" he wheezed. "You are learning, are you not? Observation and witnessing are key. More important perhaps than anything."

"Yes, I mean—I know. I want to learn. But I also want to *do*. Not to just read about it." Max looked at his hands on the table. With their soft, uncalloused fingers, they seemed impotent, incapable of controlling anything. "It's been weeks now."

Mme. Z— came around the table and sat heavily in the opposite chair. "It's too dangerous, Max." Her voice was deliberate; this was something she'd considered. "We can't take a chance on anyone locating you."

"What would happen if I did?"

"If you practiced conjury?" She spread across the table, arms splayed, palms down. Her bulky breasts propped themselves on the rough edge. "First off," she said, "the Aurora would notice. Peter Sylvester would notice. Tom Howland would notice. As surely as if you're shining a spotlight into the sky and yelling, 'I am here.'"

"But how?"

"There are ways. Many, actually. Your initial instincts were quite correct, I assure you. Most likely they have set up a system, like a beacon or an alarm. They're looking for you, Max. If you practice, they will certainly come."

"But I've done it already. When I first met Martin Paine."

"Yes. And I understand in that moment it was a necessity. Perhaps they missed it, perhaps they did not. We don't know. But the more you do it, the more certainty of them finding you."

"So what's our plan? To keep me in hiding forever?"

The woman raised up and looked vaguely at him, lost in thought. She dug into her pouch for a rolled cigarette, struck a match, taking a long while as she lit it, and chuffed smoke. Then, through the fog: "What would you have us do?"

Max fidgeted. The pair of eyes on him were hot and clammy; he felt claustrophobic, bricked-in, out of air. Then the Colonel's rheumatic voice spoke up: "What about a zone of refusal?"

Mme. Z— didn't turn, but her head tilted and her eyes cut sideways. "What's that?"

"A *dharani*. A zone of refusal." The word seemed to come from some faraway place. "Create a space. For experimentation."

Mme. Z— leaned back. "A...*dharani*." She seemed to sample the thought, bit by bit. "You are saying we should open a sphere...and then contain the sphere within this apartment."

"If we work together, we can craft a hidden shield around this place. A demesne of security, if you will."

"A goddamned *mnemonic?*" Mme. Z— leaned forward again, her eyes focused on Max, but her gaze looked beyond him. "But yes, yes! Sanskrit: *To hold or maintain.* Like a bubble." She lumbered up and, smoking furiously, started pacing the room with the bravado of a lion tamer—when a problem presented itself, she stared it down, subdued it with sheer defiance.

"What is a—a *dharani?*" Max said, certain he was mispronouncing the word.

"It is a safeguard," the Colonel explained. "A way to isolate something— segregate it, contain it. The precise meaning is 'to hold, to bear or support.' Usually rafters, of a small house, or hut. It is meant more for keeping something in, rather than keeping all else out."

"Why did she call it a...a...?" The word escaped him.

"A mnemonic. It is part of a ritual, a mantra that is chanted to protect. What it refers to contextually has been lost. But now it encapsulates the thing itself. It has become a proxy, if you will—a surrogate for a much larger, much more powerful ritual."

"But it would work," Mme. Z— said in amazement, "it would." Her eyes were red and bugging out; she rubbed at her cheek with the hand that held the cigarette and for a second Max worried she would put out her eye. She stopped pacing and glared at him, her gaze as fierce as if she were contemplating his death. "But you couldn't charm anywhere but here—the zone wouldn't be on the city, or even *you*—it would be around the apartment." She stabbed at the floor with her cigarette. "Only upon *you here*."

That sounded reasonable. Max shrugged. "Better than what I have now."

"But let me be clear. We will be making two *dharani*. One to contain you, the other to contain the first *dharani* in this location. Don't you see? The combined effect will work only in this space."

"But if I stayed here could I learn conjury? Practice it?"

"As long as you remain within these walls?" She smoked. "Oh, yes."

"Look. I want to continue my practice. It's my right and I want it."

"It won't last for forever." Mme. Z— turned to the Colonel. "Do you want to start now, or should we get a night's rest first?"

The Colonel leaned against the sink, thin as a broom, and nodded vaguely.

And so, relieved but nervous, Max watched as the big woman wrenched the kitchen table into the center of the room. She had him sit there while she and the Colonel warbled and chanted over him for the next hour. From what he'd learned in the library, their words seemed to be some form of Sikkimese, or maybe Qiangic, he couldn't be sure. They paced and waved hands and spun a Tibetan prayer wheel; the sunlight from the window bloomed oddly brighter and then dimmed, as if storm clouds were crowding a sunny day. At one point, Mme. Z— went into the library and came back with a stone from one of the shelves, a river-smooth rock that fit neatly in the palm of her hand. She told Max to smear a bit of his saliva across it, and with an ice pick from the sink she carved some runes onto the stone and spun it on the table directly in front of him; he kept waiting for something to change, some odd sensation to slide around inside of him, but nothing did.

Eventually the chanting tapered off, and the Colonel and Mme. Z— went to collapse onto the couch, both of them sweating, their faces feverish. Max sat there, thinking maybe the ritual had been a failure. But the older woman leaned forward in her seat and watched him with furious satisfaction. "How do you feel?" she said. She looked beautiful then—no trace of the inner young woman now, but a bright middle-aged handsomeness, a hale happy presence. It was plain that even with all of her politicking and speeches and astral dictation, she missed the physical rigor of performing spells.

Max said, "Did it work?"

"Of course, it worked." She swabbed sweat from her chin with her knuckles. "Everything I do works." She stood up from the couch—lightly, lighter than he had seen in weeks—and came over to him. She put her hand on his shoulder, and at that moment, just like everyone else, he realized he had fallen in love with her. She could be blunt, and her presence wasn't a maternal energy—it transcended male or female—but he loved her all the same. She bent down and kissed his cheek. Her breath was hot and sweet and smelled of tobacco.

"You are free, Max. For a time, at least. You can do what you want, smart boy. You can't leave, but you can practice."

Max didn't say anything. He was quiet, out of ideas. The faucet dripped. "What should I do now?"

"No one can find you, at least for a little while. Not even Peter Sylvester. My advice is to use this time to acquire as much information as you can."

"Acquire information? I'm sick to death of just...*reading*."

"Let me show you something." She waved him through her bedroom and into the dim, cramped library, where she spent a few moments pulling out various tracts and booklets. Not the bold, glittery volumes that caught the eye, but the smaller, duller books he had overlooked, the ones he hadn't noticed—insignificant, handwritten, unlovely, loosely bound. She pulled fifty or so of them together and lowered herself to the edge of the desk, taking a quiet minute to arrange them in a particular order. When she was finished she put them in four stacks and tapped the first one with a yellowed nail.

"These, Max. These are your teachers now. Your lyceum. For the next few weeks, study only these. When you are done, come to me and your schooling will begin again."

"But I told you. I don't want to read anymore."

She looked at him as if he had unbelted his trousers and urinated on the floor. "These are *different*, Max," she said sharply. "These are not unique, individual works, but in fact one single sovereign volume. It is known, rather informally, as the *Quarto*. When studied in a particular order, they contain a powerful, mystical experience. They are not easy to understand—on the contrary, they are challenging and quite rigorous—but the increase of effort and attention required to understand them is part and parcel of the design. As always."

The bland stacks of books on the desk didn't look very important; they looked boring and beyond tedious, worse even than the blocky medical volumes on Dr. Stout's shelves. But Max knew that appearances in this strange world were usually, unnervingly, deceiving.

"These particular works, Max, in this particular order, were first compiled by Theodosius the Sorrowed himself. Without the zone of refusal, the mere act of you arranging them in this way would have been enough to alert anyone paying attention. Like a signal."

Max looked at her, alarmed. "But I've been rooting around in here for weeks."

"You must have eyes to see, my dear. And there was virtually no chance that you would have assembled them in the correct order. It would have been impossible."

"But why not just...put them away? If they're that powerful?"

Mme. Z— almost smiled, but beneath it she was hard as iron. "The books do not wish to be put away, dear boy. The *Quarto* does not walk in shadow. Deception is Peter Sylvester's legacy, not our own. To those who can properly see and hear, these volumes stand tall among the work of all time. They reflect the sunlight of eternal honor and universal glory."

"What's in them?" Max heard fear in his voice. The books on the desk seemed so harmless, so slender and modest and unassuming. But that was their power.

"Everything is in them. All that exists, or has existed. All that will be. The end and the beginning. Every mystery. But you must have proper understanding. The *Quarto* will not surrender its secrets easily. In here is how to amass an army, and how to destroy one. How to scale a mountain, though there is not a single mention of mountaineering. How to bed a queen. How to build a fire, how to build a boat, how to build an empire." Mme. Z— looked at him, her nostrils flaring, the red patches on her face and neck just beginning to pale, and she wrapped him in a quick, strong hug. Without a word she left and shut the door behind her.

Max looked at the books, slightly afraid now. He brushed his hand lightly along the one on top, half-expecting it to burn him. It didn't.

In the parlor outside there was a muted exchange of words, and a shuffle, as if she and the Colonel were putting on their winter coats. The front door opened and closed, and then everything was silent.

He was alone again.

He sat down and thumbed through the stack. Hand-scrawled volumes of incantation that had been transcribed by someone, some meticulous monk maybe, long ago, but never properly printed. He paged through the few on top: tarot, astrology, microcosm, macrocosm, divination, alchemy, invisibility, transformation, clairvoyance, scrying, astral projection, forecasting, geomancy, the cure of diseases—all of it, all forms of knowledge, but seen slightly more aslant than the Western approach of the teachings at Steppeland. Even at first glance these ideas felt stronger than any conjury he knew; they seemed oblique, a flowing, liquid magic, a magic of ideas and perceptions, creativity and flux, rather than pure, headlong intent.

Max put the books in a neat stack, settled into his chair, took up the one on top. With a nervous puff of his cheeks, he started reading.

TWENTY-THREE: DIVINERS

FOR THE NEXT THREE weeks, Max sat at the desk day and night—studying, absorbing, steeping in the quiet wonders of the *Quarto*. Names appeared and receded and resurfaced like the tangled banks of telephone wires crossing over the city: Agrippa, Cagliostro, Bruno, Levi. Arduous and dense, the language was rhythmic and musical; portmanteau, neologism, cadences ushering him into daydreams, phrases that made no sense; similarities, echoes, cross-cultural correspondences, structures behind the words, underlying patterns below the ideas like joists beneath a floor. Some of the tomes were composed in words as guileless as children's books; drawings and pictograms, texts and diagrams often contradicting each other. With Latin, German, Italian, and Tibetan dictionaries close at hand, Max felt the words gouging into him, realigning him, sorting his mental rigging into echoes of the *Quarto* itself; he studied until his back ached, then stood and studied as he paced. When Mme. Z— and the Colonel were gone, he would go into the parlor and nap on the dirty couch and dream of Bukharan streets and high Thimphun monasteries. The Vedas, the Lords of the Dark Face; Cavalieri's Principle, the Mahatmas, the Adepts, Trithemius and Rosencreutz and his coterie of mystics. Manifestos weaving Turkish, Arab, Persian, and Sufi influences into a single mystical Gordian knot. Pythagorus, the Chaldean Brotherhood, the magicians of Babylon and the guardians of the Orphic mysteries. The Knights Templar. Neo-Platonism. The secret unnamed doctrine to unite all occult and religious systems and finally bridge the gap between science and magic. Max felt infirm, feverish, reading a book a day, a magical system a day, all of it working to lift him from his mental terrain as carefully as a gardener repotting an orchid. When he finished each one, he placed it in reverse order at the foot of the desk.

Late one night he was studying in the library, with the voices of some suffragette or occultist meeting droning softly in the parlor—at least he thought there were people in the apartment, but he couldn't say if they were real or if he only imagined they were—when there was a rush of blood and a whirl of air across his brain, as though he were about to faint; his skin flushed and his thoughts lurched, and he felt suddenly inside out, confused as to whether he was reading the books or the books were reading him. A vision came—it seemed like a vision, whether it was or not—that his thoughts were located not within the confines of his own brain but rather inside a silent, infinite space contained within the lamplit spaces of the library, and with the library itself deep within. Instead of a small, cramped room, this one was much larger, a vast array of books about any subject he could care to learn, so many their numbers had become measureless; they contained such a multitude that their contents were indistinguishable from the universe around him—the books had become the world and the world had become the books, and the distinction between the two meant nothing.

Max groaned and put his head in his hands. His breath hissed in his ears; he couldn't tell anymore whether it was noon or the middle of the night. After a long, quiet pause there was a slight cracking on the far side of the room. Dreading what he might see, he forced himself to open his eyes. For a heart-stopping second, he knew Mister Splitfoot had come back, to taunt him, to torture him or kill him. But the room was empty. The library was silent. Everything was still except for the lamp flicker. Quiet voices in the parlor buzzing on—discussing a recipe for *datshi*, maybe, or some rare strain of Afghani tobacco. Somehow though the chamber felt different.

Then with a gasp Max saw that it really *was* different—instead of a smallish square room he was now in a slightly larger hexagonal one. Somehow two additional walls had been made, the room absorbed, digested into a new one. The bookshelves, dark in the dim curve of lamplight, were smooth as always, their corners met as ever, but the room was physically larger now. Containing even more of the *Quarto*.

He made a faint noise, not knowing if he should feel happy, or feel dread. Maybe a bit of both. He looked down at the book on the desk, a musty, anonymously authored volume bound with reeds of dogbane; he took a few minutes to finish the last couple of pages, but instead of placing it on the stack with the others, he raised it with his intention, sent it spinning into the higher, newly recessed ceiling. The book fluttered, wheeling above him; it was good to flex muscles he hadn't used for months.

From the stack of books at his feet, the ones he'd already read, he sent two, three, then five. Then all of them—fifteen, twenty—up into the air, every one of them orbiting overhead in a drowsy whirl. Watching them made Max feel dizzy. He pressed his knuckles in his eyes until he saw lattices and stars.

And so it went. In the next few days, after finishing a book, he would raise it swirling aloft, and spend the evening musing on what he had learned. Clairvoyance, levitation, divination, transformation. A slow and slightly dreary gratitude crept over him; after all this time and all this work, many of the feats he'd seen the other initiates perform were now within his own reach. Mme. Z— didn't say anything, but she didn't have to. She only leaned in the doorway, smoking and smiling at the whirlpool of books eddying overhead.

Sometime in mid-January, it came to Max with a mild belated surprise that the Christmas and New Year's holidays had come and gone completely unnoticed. Neither the Madame nor the Colonel was a Christian, so the day had passed with no fanfare—not a tree, not a wreath, no presents, nor even a mention of Jesus the Christ, though he was referenced occasionally in Max's reading. It was just as well. Finishing as much of the *Quarto* as he could was his only goal.

Then, in the fifth week after he'd started his studies, the Colonel came to him and put a hand on his shoulder. Max looked up from his reading. "Someone to see you," the old man said. Puzzled, Max stood and stretched and followed him out into the parlor.

Harriet was sitting on the couch near the window.

She was beyond lovely. Her hair had grown out, and she wore a dark blue dress and a black peacoat, her slender ankles sloping into leather half-boots. Surprisingly, she had put some sort of cosmetics on her face—her eyes were darker and more dramatic, and she looked older. Max thought maybe he looked older, too.

"Hi," he said, feeling strangely out of breath.

"Hello, Max." Her voice, though, was exactly the same—a sandy, surprisingly boyish rasp that still carried traces of the Georgia woods. "How are you?"

"I'm...learning," he said, his words coming thick.

"I've heard. I'm jealous. But I've been learning, too." He wasn't clear on her meaning—whatever library Paine had was surely no match for Mme. Z—'s. But then she stood and snapped into a pose—hips cocked, legs spread just so, her hands playfully pretending to display something astonishing.

A smile broke across Max's face. She'd become a stage assistant to the Mysterious Martin Paine. They laughed, and caught each other in a marvelous hug.

"Fancy a stroll?" Harriet said. "Mme. Z— told me it would be okay to go out together. It's been a good while." She was right. Months had passed since Max had left the apartment. But right then there was nothing he wanted more than to escort this young lady for a proper stroll out among the wintry streets of the city. Through the door into the bedroom, they saw Mme. Z— sitting on the side of the bed with her back turned, thumbing through a journal or a daybook. Without even a glance their way, she nodded slightly. That was their permission. Max had been cooped up long enough. So he found his shoes and slipped into one of the Madame's massive Siberian fur coats, and they went out into the chilly Manhattan afternoon.

Max was surprised to find the city had been replaced by a grainy old photograph of itself. The buildings, the ferries, the trains, the massive bridges reaching over icy rivers, even the people—it all seemed so monochromatic, as if Old Man Winter had drained the color from the city like a blood-let corpse. Max's time in the library had changed him, but it had also seemed to change Manhattan—the geometry of the skyline, the defiant gallantry of the architecture, the tight crowds and dappled languages—all of it was different now. As he walked along, the streets whispered secrets to him; the aromas of the cafes and bistros and restaurants—the curries, the chowders, the feijoadas, the tavas, the borschts. With wide eyes he looked around, and for the first time he understood; rather than a chaotic tangle of places and smells and streets and noises, the city was in fact orderly, gentle, strangely sympathetic and curiously sane. It was perfect: the surly shopkeeper was only a worried father; the brougham clattering past was a pair of underfed Shires and a harried driver hurrying to make it back before the stables closed. Nothing intimidated, nothing alarmed; everything was a pleasant pull, a gracious invitation to dance. The warmth of a smaller world, even in the cold.

"You okay?" Harriet said. "You look flushed."

"I'm a bit overwhelmed, I think." He turned to her and admired her hair lashing in the wind. That too was perfect. "What about you?"

"Well, like I was just telling you, Marty—Mr. Paine—has been helping me to learn to be his assistant. It's kind of neat. It's not conjury, but it's, you know. It's fun. And I've learned that I like the, uh...the attention."

"Have you been practicing your *tamkarra?*"

She shook her head. "Mme. Z— spent a few evenings with us at our place, and forbid anyone—well, forbid *me*—from practicing. So Marty and I work on illusions. It's a big job—card tricks, disappearing acts. He saws me in half." She giggled, and Max could see she really was having a good time. "We have a performance coming up, actually. I was hoping you could make it. My outfit's cute. Sequins and stockings and purple ostrich feathers."

Max's heart tumbled and rolled. "Well, yes, of course I'll come."

Harriet looked over her shoulder, and like a lifelong resident of the city she hailed an approaching cab. "What are we doing?" she said. "Where do you want to go?"

Max said, "I know a place."

They got in, and he called to the coachman, "Central Park." As the cab made its way up the avenue, a light, drifting flurry began. A few stray snowflakes wafted in through the cracked window, and Harriet must have begun to feel a chill because she lay against him, pulling her coat tight against the cold. Max still felt dazed by the city, and it was nice to be out of that library, away from those heady books. And being with Harriet again was a special kind of magic—not the magic of books, but the magic of her flushed red cheeks and nose, her bright blue mittens, the playful tassels on her hat. "Tell me about your illusions," he said.

For the rest of the ride, she told him how she and Marty had been practicing in a small rented theatre somewhere down in the Bowery, not far from his warehouse. He'd shown her many things—sleight of hand, cups and balls, handcuff release, card tricks, egg tricks, vanishing tricks. She said Paine's bride-to-be Fiona had been hauling the illusionist away from their rehearsals earlier and earlier in fits of paranoia, worried the girl would somehow steal him away. Harriet snorted with contempt. "Here I am, only just now seventeen, while he's practically thirty!"

At Vanderbilt Gate they paid the cab and entered the park on foot. The ground was dusted with snow as they strolled beneath the high trees. Harriet asked him about his own work, and as he told her guardedly about Mme. Z—'s library, it occurred to him though Harriet hadn't read much of the *Quarto*—maybe hadn't even heard of it—she apparently didn't need to; she'd already innately mastered most of the ideas and approaches he was just now coming to understand. As with everything else, he saw her differently now; for the first time she seemed less a fickle princess of divination and more a very smart, determined and lonely girl from the hills of Georgia. Her talent was the very thing which had kept her so isolated; she'd had no one even close to her own age who could teach her, keep up with her, challenge her.

Her voice wavered as she told Max she hadn't heard from her parents, not even once. She was worried that her family, like his, had been silenced. For now, there was no way to know for sure. "If I ever find out what happened," she hissed, "Peter Sylvester should be afraid. I'll rip his cock off quicker than any Moorlander!" Her eyes were glassy and her nose was runny and she was shivering. Max pulled her closer. The temperature was dropping. He saw a distant wrought-iron gazebo half-hidden under a screen of trees, which maybe offered at least a little shelter from the wind, and he nudged her toward it.

The gazebo was leaf-strewn, and hadn't seemed to have been visited in weeks. They huddled on the cold iron bench in the back. Mme. Z—'s fur coat was enormous—Max remembered her telling him it was made from Khakassian beaver, of all things—so he was able to drape it around them both, and they nestled together in the womb of it, giggling and warming their hands. Their breath fogged out as the snow turned heavy.

Max felt a strange flurry in his stomach, caught between the cold air and the warmth of their bodies. They looked at each other, both of them wondering if the other felt the same thing—a thawing, an ascending tug that had started in their guts and flowed up into their fluttering hearts. Max reached out and cupped her breast. It was warm, the knob of her nipple through her brassiere hard and firm. He felt himself breathing, heavy and full of need. Harriet's own breath was sweet and warm and stale as she leaned into him and kissed his lips. The curved planes of their bodies came together; she pushed herself deliciously against him, her hands fighting at the layers of his clothes. Suddenly her hand was inside—cold fingers against warm ribs and he heard himself gasp, and she laughed as they kissed, her lips stretching away from his in a smile that made him smile too. He leaned into her. She took a moment to unhook most of her buttons, and pulled them apart to expose her bodice, which she parted to free her perfect breasts, more perfect than perfect, with lively blue veins pulsing with life. Hungry, he put his hand on one, and felt its purity, just as she reached down between his thighs and touched the growing heat there. Her fingers raked across his skin and he felt himself tighten against the chill, felt the warmth they produced together, and he wondered if he would ever be cold again.

The snow fell now in fat, wet flakes, and jittery grey squirrels did acrobatics above them along the branches of the old trees. Arm in arm, Max and Harriet came to the perimeter of the park. She stopped when she saw the streets leading to Columbus Circle up ahead. "You hungry?" she said. "I could eat a horse turd."

Max didn't have any money, but supposed that Harriet might; Marty, no doubt, was doing pretty well for himself.

"I haven't eaten anything since last night," she said. "Yesterday afternoon, really. I want a full course. Roast beef. Dilled potatoes. Creamed spinach. Buttery rolls steaming from the oven. And some kind of pie, a sugary fruit tart so sweet it makes my teeth ache."

They cleared the trees and Max spotted a restaurant beyond the statue of Columbus, under a forest green awning. *Steakhaus Vogel*, the sign said. Watching for traffic, they crossed the street and went inside. The interior was dark polished wood and leather, and it smelled of seared meat and caraway and cabbage, and underneath, a sour, oozing smell of too many people working and sweating and drinking in too small a space. But it was warm and had an unhurried mood. As they found a table in the back corner, a waiter in a jacket and bow tie hurried over, a frown across his wide catfish face. "All right, you two, what gives," he said.

This was depressingly familiar. "We're here to eat," Max said.

"You meeting somebody, yes? Mom and dad?"

"Just us."

"Yes, yes." He wiped his hands on the rag tucked in his belt. "No. I'm so sorry, I need to see some cash. We've had too many hedgehogs in here, grubbing and then stealing away."

Harriet smiled, a little nervously, but she dug in her purse, in an envelope, and pulled out a ten-dollar bill. Max caught a glimpse of more in there—quite a bit more, actually. She spread it flat on the table. It was the freshest, most unwrinkled bill he had ever seen. They all quietly contemplated it for a moment; then she turned to the waiter. "Let us eat," she said, "and leave us the hell alone."

The man took a step back, as if Harriet had slapped him. He said, "I'll get the menus."

Max felt dreamy and drugged, as if something strange was happening, but it was a good kind of strange. The gazebo was already like a dream, a reverie, like he had imagined it or it had happened to somebody else. For a moment he reflected on how good things like that rarely happened to him; his life so far had been hard and meager and fraught with dread. *But it doesn't have to be that way,* he thought; *maybe everything doesn't have to be so goddamn grim all the time.*

Harriet broke his mood by pulling herself into a half-standing position over the table, and kissed him on the lips—a warm, wet smack that tunneled his vision, that made the entire room fade, and for an instant her face was all that there was. She sank back down and giggled.

The waiter came with the menus and presented them formally, as if the two teens had become suddenly important. Max supposed that they had. *We are diviners,* he thought. It was a curious word. Black Howard had used it several times, but Max had always hesitated to apply it to himself. It had seemed to point to everyone but him. But now, with all the work he'd been doing in the library, and Harriet sitting across from him, the taste of her lips still on his own, it felt more fitting. Across the room there was a window, and beyond it the snow was heavier than before. It was magical, this feeling, but a different kind of magic from what he'd felt before. This was a magic that felt real, that much of the world had already known—every couple in love, every handsome boy, every rosy-cheeked girl. *We're diviners,* he thought again, *all of us, everyone, we're all diviners.*

"Forget the steak," Harriet said, her face turned down into the menu. "They've got red-head duck with currant jelly. How does that sound?" She raised her eyebrows at him.

Max nodded. "It sounds divine."

Twenty-four: The Performance

FOR THE NEXT TWO weeks the library jutted bigger and bigger as Max immersed himself in the *Quarto*, until it was many-sided—the size of a more proper library, even larger than the one in Selleford he had visited many times with Ethie. Fifty or so books spiraled lazily now up near the ceiling, tumbling and spinning like asteroids in a belt. When he finally looked from his work it was early February, a Thursday, the day Harriet would make her debut with the Mysterious Martin Paine.

That afternoon he came out from the library, neck stiff, feeling like his brains had been inflated to the size of one of Ferdinand von Zeppelin's rigid airships. But there was something new draped over the arm of the couch—two classy, crow-black tuxedos. Max went to them, marveled at the fine fabric; the only dress clothes he'd ever worn was his roomy sackcoat, and he'd never dreamed he'd wear anything like this. He could tell from a glance that the one for him fit perfectly. How Mme. Z— knew his measurements, he couldn't say; she'd hardly ever touched him except to hug him or brush hair from his shoulder. But there it was, right next to the long and slender outfit for the Colonel.

They spent the evening getting ready. Mme. Z— trimmed Max's hair, and combed what was left of the Colonel's. For her part, she wore what she usually wore—loose-fitting men's pants, frayed cuffs dragging on the ground, and a caftan draped over the sycamore log of her upper body. A viny twist of bangles and necklaces around her neck; her dead animal bag, a shapeless jacket and a scarf, which she could alternately wrap around her neck or around her head in the manner of a gitana's shawl. She smelled, as she had since the first day Max met her, of jasmine ittar and tobacco.

The three of them rode wordless to the theatre in a closed-topped old landau. Despite a dirty snow and the cold, the streets were crowded and people were out. Whatever else you could say about Manhattaners, Max thought, they were hardy folk, and didn't let a little damp or cool temperatures scare them indoors. Outside the theatre, the snow flurries gave the marquee lights a milky, radiant quality. The crowd practically bubbled, heady with anticipation, but it was significantly smaller than when Max had been here before. This was Paine's first public performance in three months; most likely he had lost some of his following in the public retreat imposed by Mme. Z—. Max was quietly ashamed to know this was mainly because of him.

They filed inside, and down the long passage with framed posters lining each wall—The Mysterious Martin Paine in Barcelona, in Nice and Marseilles, in Lisbon, Chicago and St. Louis. Just like the first one Max had seen, in most of them Paine was assisted by some type of little red goblins or spirits as he studied in a chair, or inspected a skull, or worked in an alchemist's lab. It all seemed so simple, so childishly charming. Max wondered what people would have thought if the posters featured the Moorlander or Mister Splitfoot ghoulishly grinning over Paine's shoulder, their wounds and festerings crusted and seeping. He doubted it would have had the same appeal.

The theater's seats on either side were partially cordoned off tonight by velvet ropes and thick brass stanchions, to accommodate the smaller crowd. Max felt another pinprick of guilt, but didn't say anything.

"Over here," Mme. Z— said, and pressed herself stoutly sideways down a row about halfway from the front of the stage. The three of them took their seats and sat staring—silent, expectant, restless—at the curtained stage. The seats quickly filled as the buzz of conversation rose gradually in the room. The air above them became hazy with smoke; Max glanced up at the immense canopy overhead, and saw through the tobacco fog the ceiling had been decorated with the celestial stations of the zodiac—angels flying among the stars, little cherubs with bows, rams and lions and crabs. He could see in the particulars the details the painter had gotten wrong—the way Castor and Pollux were depicted wearing Mercury's winged helmet, or how Scorpio was drawn opposite Virgo, rather than Taurus—but this didn't give him much satisfaction at all.

Without fanfare then, the proscenium curtains pulled back, and there stood Paine, square-jawed in his tux, his face fresh under a rim of pomaded hair. Next to him was a small table covered with a blood red tablecloth. The audience broke into applause—more than a few of them actually roared—and he bowed from the waist, wearing an expression of fierce satisfaction. Max had forgotten how handsome Paine was, how at ease he was on stage, how it seemed as if he took nourishment from the applause itself.

Paine flashed a grin at the crowd and gestured offstage, and Max's breath hitched as Harriet pranced out from the wings. There was no half-tuxedo as he had expected, no long, visible thigh; instead she was dressed in white gloves and a lavender gown that evoked the Orient, or at least that obscure part of the world beyond Constantinople. Her tawny hair had been braided and pinned back onto her head. The little bands of anticipation that had clenched Max's heart all day snapped suddenly, and he realized he was clapping, the audience was clapping, even Mme. Z— was clapping. Harriet moved like a dancer, stepping lightly on her toes as she circled Paine, smiling broadly, and curtsied. The audience roared approval.

"This...is Hettie," Paine announced above the noise, and took her hand. Max grinned blissfully. *Hettie.*

Maybe it was the risk of live performance, but under her usual air of confidence he could see she was plainly more than a little nervous. Paine reached behind him and produced a bouquet of some type of white flowers—lilies, or gardenias, it was hard to tell from where Max sat—and passed them to her. She admired and sniffed at them, and with a coy smile she tossed them out over the crowd. The pale petals burst into doves and a scattered gasp rose as they flew off for the high, smoky corners of the room. Even the Colonel had a dazed smile on his face.

Harriet: those ruddy cheeks, the vernal tilt of her chin, the way tufts of hair had come loose and hung in her face. Somehow Max knew this moment would stick with him for the rest of his life. More than any other, this image would sum up their time in New York—Harriet's lips parted slightly in proficiency and pleasure, looking wicked and proud in her elbow gloves and lavender dress on a stage before hundreds of admirers. As if she'd belonged there always.

The performers parted to opposite sides of the stage, and Paine pulled a walking cane from his pocket, which he rapped on the table to prove its rigidity. Then, with a great swing, he shattered it against the wooden stage with a loud crack. Pieces flew; some bounced across the worn floor and some went into the audience, who fought over them. Paine bent to collect most of the bigger bits, and with a great two-handed toss he flung them over to Harriet, who somehow caught an intact cane, straight and still gleaming.

Paine pulled a top hat from somewhere, then produced a fidgety white dove. Harriet swiped the tablecloth from the table and they came together to wrap the bird carefully and delicately inside. The crowd watched, as purely mystified as children, as Harriet took the folded fabric and unfurled it with a dramatic flourish. Hundreds of white flower petals scattered out, showering the first few rows of the audience. Paine pulled the walking stick from his pocket again—Max glanced over and saw it was no longer leaning on the table, though he hadn't seen anyone take it—and with his palms and fingers spread, the illusionist transferred it from hand to hand, moving with such speed that the audience could hardly keep up; abruptly he sliced the stick at Harriet—one, two, three times—making a wicked hiss in the air. Harriet never flinched, but Max did; the girl stood firm, a calm smile on her face, and somehow the cane had passed right through her. Paine turned and lofted the stick into the air out over the crowd, where half a dozen hands reached up to catch it. But it had vanished somewhere overhead, and never came down.

The crowd hooted and clapped. Some stood in guileless admiration.

For most of the next hour, Paine and Harriet went through their routine, stepping and prancing, gesturing and smiling. Rabbit tricks, rooster tricks, billiard ball tricks, lightbulb tricks, sword routines. Harriet levitating, in a box, impaled with swords. Cabinet routines—Harriet placed inside and then disappearing, and so on. Every one performed without a single flaw.

All was perfect until the second half of the show. At one point, Paine shook out his right hand, as if it had fallen asleep; his concentration broke for a moment, then he stretched his fingers, annoyed, but kept on. Max knew illusionists depended upon near-miraculous dexterity, so a lurch of alarm rose in his throat when Paine dropped a deck of loose cards from his right hand. A brief flash of worry crossed the illusionist's face as he bent to pick them up—or, more accurately, to nudge them around, scattering them even more, because evidently the fingers of his right hand weren't working so well anymore.

Max shot a glance at Mme. Z–. She was staring asquint, head thrown back, through the lower lenses of her spectacles.

The crowd murmured, confused. They thought maybe that Paine had made a rare mistake, or, more likely, it was a setup, a part of the act. But Max saw Harriet's face, and the distress there—because now she was rubbing her limbs too, as if they'd gone numb or fallen asleep. He craned forward, confused, disturbed, fighting a desperate urge to dash up on stage.

Paine stood there, limbs now stiffly extending, the expression on his face close to terrified. Mme. Z– turned to Max, brows furrowed, and shook her head—*Don't do it.* She put her arm across his lap, forbidding him from going anywhere.

"What's happening?" Max said, barely able to keep from exploding.

But now Harriet too was having trouble moving, and before ten seconds had passed the two of them were standing slack as marionettes, blinking down at their bodies as if they'd become something foreign and horrific.

Max broke past Mme. Z–'s arm and bolted up from his seat—but was yanked back by a strong hand. The Colonel grabbed his shoulder and the collar of his jacket and wrapped his ribs in a sturdy bear hug to hold him down. The commotion in the room was loud, half of the crowd cheering this odd turn of events, the other half grumbling and confused. Paine looked out into the gallery, his face sweaty and drawn. He was looking for them, Max knew with terrible panic, for Mme. Z– and the Colonel and him. He tried to pry the Colonel's hands away, but they were strong; stronger than any normal man's.

"NO!" Mme. Z– hissed at him. "*Not now!*"

"What is this?" Paine yelled from the stage, his voice sounding pinched and squeezed. "What is this? Help us! Help meeeeeee-*eeee-iii-iii!*"

His voice slipped, took on the high inhuman rattle of a cicada, then the light in his eyes whiffed out like a candle flame. They went black. His face centered and turned upward, a counter-tenor singing to the rafters, but out of him came an alien shriek: "*riiii-iii-iiii-iii-iiii-iii!*" It was a terrifying sound, the wail of a storm whistling through the open doors of a derelict house. There was nobody home.

The crowd tossed like stormwater. Max fought to free himself from the Colonel's iron grip, but couldn't. Up on stage next to Paine, Harriet was struggling, her beautiful face straining terribly, and then—

And then she was gone. Her eyes went black too, her skin slack and shiny with sweat. Calmly, looking insensibly upward into the middle distance, her thin soprano joined Paine's: "*riiii-iii-iiii-iii-iiii-iii!*" The two of them stood together like toy soldiers, rasping out a pitted, gruesome sound.

Max went limp, stunned. Then, from behind, a little boy's voice said matter-of-factly, "Fire." Then, after a charged moment, louder: "*FIRE!*"

The crowd exploded in confusion. Max realized he'd been smelling smoke for some time but it hadn't come to his conscious attention. A rush of people pushed suddenly for the exit, and Max—the Colonel still restraining him—looked around for the cause of the trouble, at the room, the stage, the audience.

What he saw made the bottom of his soul drop away: through the throngs of people pointing to the stage or fumbling to get out, Tom Howland stood—ahead of him and to the right, in the front third of the room. His face impassive as ever. Someone had knocked off his hat, which revealed him as he stood there in three-quarters profile. By now everyone in the room was clambering down their row or hopping seats for the exit, and Max had a moment to bizarrely think, *My God, he's losing his hair,* before the crush of the crowd hid him again in their scrambling.

"There!" he yelled to Mme. Z— and the Colonel, and pointed to Tom. The strange man seemed to be in a trance—fists firm at his sides, his gaze and mental energy directed up onstage. Mme. Z—'s jaw fell open and her face went white. In the horror of their distraction, Max broke the Colonel's grip and vaulted over chairs and rushed across the seats and into the aisle. Onstage, Harriet and Paine continued their reedy insect-rattle, but their voices, the air constricted now, had taken on a clammy, guttural whine, a viscid quality, as if their throats were pressed together. The blistering thought of what was going on in Harriet's mind—if she was still capable of thinking—terrified Max; he couldn't win in a struggle with Tom Howland, there was no way, so he looked around for something, anything, to stop him, he had to stop him now *right now*—and his gaze settled on a tipped-over stanchion. The commotion around Tom cleared, leaving him alone in an aisle of empty seats, and Max grabbed the heavy brass pole and dragged it over.

The odd noises onstage changed again, and he looked up to see the nightmare of Paine and Harriet deflating somehow, crumpling like air leaving a punctured rubber raft, the molted husk of their bodies sucked dry. The whistles faltered and gurgled, became horribly more guttural, throats folded in on themselves.

Max came up behind Tom Howland, whose attention was focused entirely on the stage, and braced himself to lift the heavy stanchion, which must have weighed fifty pounds, and with the wide, flagged base being the heaviest part, he spread his legs and found a leveraged stance and raised the heavy post into the air. Beyond Tom Howland, the crushed and crumpled forms of Paine and Harriet had squeezed themselves into irregular, wadded shapes, like rinds or husks or snakeskins or cicada exuviae, and with a horrifying severity their clotted voices suddenly cut out, the sound left now with nowhere to go.

Max swung the stanchion as hard as he could at the back of Tom Howland's head.

It hit him on the right upper quadrant of the skull, the flange of the base crunching into the globe of his cranium. There was a crack as bone and skin—or something similar to bone and skin—gave way, and the force of the blow carried through and Tom Howland and Max both tumbled with it. They went sprawling across several rows of chairs, Tom's legs and torso stretching over them, his crushed head dipped out of sight, Max toppling over the seats and onto the floor. The post fell with a *clang!* and Max caught himself and rose up to look to the stage: two collapsed forms, wrinkled now like half-filled misshapen knapsacks—Paine's black and a marbled yellowish pink, Harriet's a horrible lavender and pinkish cream. Still and quiet as stones, no sound at all now. Instead, the screams of the crowd shot up as they tried to get out of the auditorium. But the exit was blocked; people had fallen, causing others to scramble over them and further clog the way. Ribbons of smoke explored the room and Max caught a glimpse of bright scattered flames near the exit. This was no accident; someone had caused this. With a *chiff!* the curtains caught, and a great radiant blaze burst upwards toward the ceiling.

He looked back at Mme. Z— and the Colonel, but they were gone.

Tom Howland's body was still. Max crawled over two rows of seats to get a better look. Tom's head was down in the shadows, near the feet of the chairs. The back of his skull was crushed, with no seeping blood, just a rind of ruptured skin and a hint of thin, yellowish bone underneath, like an eggshell. A dark, dry hollow cavity lay within. He didn't move.

Max leaned against a chair, dumbfounded. It took a moment in the wild, terrified crush of things to realize he had just silenced Tom Howland.

Through the crowds of panicked people, the two misshapen spheres onstage were still there, still motionless. If they were alive now, it would be a miracle.

The air was malignant. A *ploom!* sounded above, and Max looked up to see the extravagant moldings on the ceiling catch fire, charring the Astrological angels and the crabs and the goats, and ash and flame began to drift down like lazy autumn leaves onto the crowd still scrabbling to get out. The plush seats near Max started to catch, and in several heartbeats flame flared all around. The long hallway out was a catastrophe with no egress—a crawling horror of wailing people, sobbing and struggling and kicking to get through. Smoke hung low now, and Max pulled his collar over his mouth to filter the air, but it didn't much help.

There was a cry in the aisle, and he turned to see a little dark-headed girl, maybe five or six, panicked but alone, no doubt separated from her parents. Flame had sprung up on the seats nearby. She was rooted with fright, her eyes fixed on the two cruel forms up onstage. There was no way she would get through all the panicked people—the exit was choked.

Max scrambled over and put his arm around her, and she turned fearfully to him, tears cutting the grime on her face. He knelt and hugged her and closed his eyes and, despite her struggling, he concentrated. Trying to calm his thinking and bargaining within himself to find what he needed, he took a breath, and with a moment's plash of impulse and intention—

—the air suddenly became cool.

Cold, actually. The shriek and thrash of the crowd was immediately gone.

Max opened his eyes. They were huddled in the center of a street in the darkness. The little girl stood next to him, eyes fixed in a stunned daze. For a second they crouched there, both of them in a shock, and then he heard a voice behind him roar, "*OUT OF THE WAY!*"

He spun around to see a fire-wagon—six Bays pulling a large coach filled with firefighters and barrels of water—galloping directly at them. He grabbed the girl and dove to the side of the road and landed hard, his face scrubbing gravel as the firetruck burst by, and then it was gone.

Painfully, Max rolled over. The night glowed bright above the tops of the buildings and a block away, a single orange spire of flame leapt up at the night sky. The screams and cries of the people still inside the theater were muted but still audible, not unlike like the gurgled, chuffing sounds Harriet and Paine had made before they were wadded into empty casings of flesh and cloth and bone.

The little girl sobbed then, her panic dream broken, and Max scrabbled himself against the wall of a building among a pile of trash and pulled her close and tried not to listen to the screams. "*Mammina, mammina,*" the girl cried, and Max knew she couldn't speak English. The sharp edge of her shoulder poked hard into his chest. "*Sssshhhhhhhh...*" he told her. "*Sssshhhhhhhh...*"

For a long time he lay there, only half-aware, unable to stand up, or even move. The shock had clubbed his body numb. Warmth seemed to drain from the open spouts of his palms and the soles of his feet. The girl was gone. He was face up, something digging at his back, his feet wet with sewage and slush. He didn't care. With the faded cries and the sobbings from a block or two over, he didn't care about much of anything right then.

A small astounded thought came to him—a spark of disbelief in some interior place to which he only had partial access. He had silenced Tom Howland. It was something he didn't think possible. That awful cracked-egg cranium, that weird blank hollow within.

He kept seeing Harriet, standing there motionless, *riii-iii-ing*, and then crumpling...collapsing into a sphere no larger than an old woman's washing basket. He tried to imagine the sensation, but his brain cut out—just went blank, unable to consider it. Instead, a strange echo came to him, clanged around in his mind: *Don't worry we hurry, don't worry we hurry, don't worry we we we...*

He lay back amid the rancid food and the rubbish and stared up at the night clouds splatted over the city. Snow was breezing again. The flakes wafted down over him like approaching stars and gave him the sensation of vast movement, crossing time and distance. He was flying among the heavens, passing constellations as they formed and fell apart in an instant—

TWENTY-FIVE: ALMS FOR THE BIRDS

SOME TIME LATER, A dim pale glow bloomed in the east. Morning was coming. There were no more cries, no orange nimbus flowering over the roofs a block to the west. The smell of ash and sweet, charred flesh wafted in the air, not unlike the kitchens at Steppeland—pork and buffalo and kid roasting in an oversized oven. Max wondered vacantly what had happened to the old cook he had seen working back there. What was her name? Dollie? He never got a chance to talk to her, to ask her what secrets she held. Probably she died in the prairie fire like everyone else.

The prairie fire. He laughed out loud, his voice a thin, crazy bark in the cold air: *Which fire? That fire? No, this fire.*

Too many fucking fires.

He sat up slowly, feet numb, silk shirt clinging wet and cold to his back, and realized that a coat—a woman's heavy long-wool coat, pink and sooty and smelling of smoke—covered him like a quilt. Someone must have thrown it over him in the night. His tuxedo jacket was gone, and his shoulders ached, probably from the horrendous effort of lifting the stanchion and slamming it into the back of Tom Howland's eggshell skull.

Max shivered. He didn't know what to do or where to go. Mme. Z—'s apartment was perhaps being surveilled by Peter Sylvester and his Aurora. But maybe the silencing of Tom Howland had been a setback for them. Maybe they were reeling just like he was. It didn't matter. He had no other options.

The walk was twenty-one blocks. He limped, huddled into himself the whole way, drawing scowls from the jobbers opening their shops for the morning. For all the world he looked like a wasted dope fiend, who'd spent a coarse long night in a fog of wagtails and morphine. One angry vendor even went so far as to try to box him with his broom, but Max caught it and gave him such a searing look the man took a petrified step back. Max carried it unthinkingly, until he dropped it in a gutter ten blocks further down.

By the time he came to Mme. Z—'s flat, it was full light. He squinted up at the apartment. The front window was open, the curtains fluttering outside in the chilly air, but he had no way of knowing whether they made it home. He plodded up the several flights and knocked wearily on the door. Immediately he heard footsteps. "Who is it?" A cautious whisper. High and reedy. The Colonel.

Max leaned against the wall, laid his temple against solid plaster. His feet wouldn't hold him anymore. "Please let me in."

The door opened, and there they were—Mme. Z— and the Colonel, their faces masks of shock and ruddy distress. They seemed smaller, looking lonely and frail and terrified. Max was surprised that even the mighty Madame could be rattled. He'd doubted it was possible.

"Come in, come in," she said, and with a force of will he unpeeled himself from the wall and went inside. He dropped the heavy pink coat and stripped off his wet shirt, and fell hunkered onto the couch. The room and the world around him tilted and receded.

Then the Colonel was there with a long nightshirt and a heavy blanket, and the two adults wrapped his shivering body and let him put his head down. The last thing he knew was Mme. Z— leaning over him, whispering into his ear.

"Sleep, child." Her grey eyes gazing into his, glassy as the stuffed animals on the walls. "But not for long."

Max woke to the smell of coriander and butter tea. He opened his eyes. The two older people sat at the table, surrounded by a timid clank of forks and knives. They were eating, but Mme. Z—, her hair even more mussed than usual, had a cigarette going. She saw that Max was alert, so she stood up and came over.

"How do you feel?" she said, her mouth full.

For a time he wasn't able to find his words. His brain was only at half-mast. Then: "Not great."

"Hungry?" He shook his head, hoping she wouldn't ask him anything else. Mme. Z— went back to the table and stood there, taking quick nervous drags on her cigarette. The Colonel kept eating as if nothing was amiss. They watched the boy, smoking and chewing. Max sat up slowly and the room pitched and then righted itself; nausea advanced and retreated. He searched himself for feelings and found that he had none. He was an empty vessel, a hollowed gourd scraped down to the rind.

But then, like a tide, like approaching thunderheads raging above the flatlands—he could see it coming before it hit him—the flood of emotions swallowed him up. Sorrow, shame, regret, a sickly mottled grief that pushed up from somewhere and belched out of him, and he retched and vomited on the floor between his feet.

When the heaves had emptied themselves, he tilted back down onto the couch and sobbed, swallowed up by the loss of Harriet, of Martin Paine, of his own blamelessness. Weak with shame and sorrow he lay back, half under the blanket with his arm over his eyes, reminding himself to breathe. *Harriet, Harriet, Harriet.* He kept seeing her on that stage, those white gloves, that lavender dress draped just so over her exquisitely developing body. That vulgar gleam in her eyes.

She didn't deserve what she had gotten, she didn't deserve any of it. She should be holding séances back in Selleford for the next sixty years, taking money from wealthy dowagers to consult with dull, dead relatives. She should have become a choleric old woman threatening to turn young ruffians into frogs—and she would have done it, too. The only reason she was part of this catastrophe was because she had lowered herself to help him. She had taken pity on him.

And the same with Paine—a decent man. A kind man. Brilliant, tender, full of promise. His career had been cut short due to Max's own wretched, pathetic need.

And also the Aurora's cruelty.

On that notion, his grief took a wild turn, careened into something new: rage. *The Aurora.* They were the ones who would be silenced now. Max would do it himself; just as he silenced Tom Howland, he would crush all of their skulls like eggshells. This thought helped. He pushed himself up again. Mme. Z— and the Colonel sat wordless at the table, watching him. The Madame shot him a hopeful smile, and the Colonel took his cloth napkin, wet it deeply inside his glass of water, and then lobbed it across the room to him. Max caught it, bent between his legs and began sopping up the mess on the Persian carpet.

"What are you thinking?" Mme. Z— said, chuffing smoke.

"What am I thinking?" Max scrubbed hard. "I'm thinking I'm going to destroy them, that's all. Assassinate them. Silence them."

From outside came a clatter of passing carriages. Men's voices, cursing at each other, a single discernible word: "*Meat?*" Then it passed.

"We have to leave," Mme. Z— said.

Max knew that they did.

"They know where we are. If you hadn't silenced Tom Howland, we would the three of us be dead already. Dead, or whatever happened to Harriet and Paine."

Whatever happened to Harriet and Paine.

Max shivered again. He finished his scrubbing and stood up and crossed the room and dropped the messy rag in the sink. He splashed his face with the water in the washbasin—pale, soggy particles of food floating there, it hadn't been changed in days—and stood leaning on it with both hands.

"We are separating," Mme. Z— said. "The Colonel and I are heading in one direction. You, my dear, are heading in another."

This came as a kind of relief. Max was silent, his face close to the wall. His breath bounced back at him, warm and cloyingly sweet.

"There's no way we can resist them, Max. We can't fight Peter Sylvester. They're too strong. Too capable. We'll—" She broke off, but Max knew what she was going to say. *We'll end up like Harriet and Paine.*

He splashed his face again, and, still dripping, came to sit between them at the table. Runnels of damp slipped down the neck of his shirt. It felt good. He wondered if he was getting sick. "Where are you going?"

Mme. Z— and the Colonel traded solemn glances. They'd been partners for a long time. "India. Near Uttar Pradesh. Best if we don't say more than that. Suffice that it is hidden—protected, secure. Not of this realm."

The only sound then was the racket coming from outside. Max's stomach was a twist of hot metal, warped by rage, sorrow, hate, fear, regret. He wasn't afraid for himself, not yet. But he knew that would come.

"We can't tell you what to do," Mme. Z— said delicately. "But I can give you my thoughts." Max waited, listening to the pull of his breath rasping in his ears. "Max. Look at me." He lifted his face and considered her; she was an old woman, a frumpy, snory old woman. A brilliant middle-aged matron who had an unusual but by no means unshakable amount of scholarship. She was merely a genius, and that was all.

"Theodosius," Max said, cutting her off. "He can help us. I'll go to Theodosius the Sorrowed."

For a long time again they were quiet, trying to appreciate what he had said. It was a loaded thought, full of odd, layered implications. Oblivion was so close he could taste it, feel the hot wheeze of it on his face. "Easy to learn," Max said. "But hard to know." Mme. Z— looked at him. "Theodosius," Max whispered again, mostly to himself. The street outside creaked and groaned.

Mme. Z— rolled another cigarette and struck a match. "You don't know who he is." The rasp of flame, the inhale, the exhale. "But we do. We can tell you where to find him. The manner in which to ask him to take you in."

"But he'll be...unconnected."

She shrugged. "He may not do what you ask. But he doesn't like the Aurora any more than you do. He, ah..." She paused, and Max could hear her thinking, the gears turning. This was new territory, terrifying even for her. Normally, this would have made him nervous and worried with the dizzy uncertainty of it all. But now there was nothing left. "He's no friend of theirs," she said finally.

"He's in Europe?"

"Near the Black Sea."

A noise came then, scratchy and grating and odd: the Colonel chuckled. Max had never heard him do that. He wanted to punch the old man, to launch himself across the table and take him by the collar. Surely the old man was like Tom Howland, like the Moorlander—some nameless visitor from some nameless place, from some grotesque realm Max had never been nor would ever want to go. Surely his skull was hollow, too.

"I don't think you want to find Theodosius," the Colonel said in his high wheezy voice. It was like a woodwind instrument. "He certainly doesn't want you to find him. At any rate, it will take months. A transatlantic voyage. Trains across the continent and into Eurasia. This will be far too long. By then we will all of us be dead."

Part of Max—a wild, feral part of him—didn't want to go anywhere. It wanted to face anyone and everyone head on, like a boxer, like a gunfighter from the Old West, like those two-fisted, square-jawed heroes he'd read about in his adventure books. But a quieter, sharper voice said, *If you do, they will get you. You will end up like Harriet and Paine.* He had to be smart—to act, and not simply react. To react would only mean his death. His silencing.

Mme. Z— seemed to understand. "This is the beginning of their final assault," she said. "A razing. Which is why we"—she nodded at her thatch-bearded partner—"are headed away. To the Faqrs. To regroup. To let them know what is happening. What to expect. There is a chance we can survive."

Max spread his hands flat out on the table. The skin was red and creased. A dried-blood wound slashed across the knuckles of his right hand. "I silenced Tom Howland," he said.

"Yes. A glorious triumph. But Tom Howland was not the head of the organism."

Max looked up, caught a glimpse of himself in one of Mme. Z—'s mirrors across the room. His face was scabbed, his hair askew. He watched as a scraped hand ran across his forehead, trying vainly to wipe the pain away. His sixteenth birthday was less than two months away. *The master,* he thought; *the leader, the chief, the Postmaster.* Peter Sylvester was the head, the one to silence. If the head was cut off, the organism would die.

Brash, prickly Harriet came to him again—that chubby face, those hazel eyes. Her hair snapping in the wind. They hadn't always been on the best terms, but without her he wouldn't be here. Simple as that. He marveled at the bizarre, inexplicable turn of events. Maybe only an augur could have foreseen that of all of Steppeland's initiates, he would be the survivor, the widower, the one left to grieve for all the others. And he thought again of Martin Paine—a gentleman's gentleman. A brilliant young man at the height of his talents and career. Cut short only because a sad, desperate boy asked him for help and he had said yes. Max had caused Paine's death as surely as if he had killed the man himself.

Without a word, he got painfully up from the table and limped through the bedroom to the library door. He pushed it open. The room was bigger than ever now. The swarm of books wheeled lazily overhead. The far wall was seventy feet away.

That night Mme. Z— destroyed her library. Or maybe she put it temporarily somewhere else. All Max knew is that when he poked his head in there for one last look, there were no overstuffed bookshelves, no ancient weathered volumes circling lazily near the recessed ceiling. Instead it was a simple small boudoir again, and a dingy one at that; the faint ghosts of the few original bookshelves stood against the wall, and wicked scratches cut through the hardwood floors, as if heavy furniture had been recently removed. On the far wall, a little dormer door—there had been no door before—hung on one hinge. Someone had scribbled *Bertie likes boys!* on it in a pestering, childlike scrawl.

They went back to the red-bricked hotel in Chelsea, and after checking in to a room on the second floor—for some reason with Mme. Z— it was always the second floor—they sat across from each other on their beds and discussed their plans. All day he'd been thinking of an idea, a crazy stupid terrifying idea: If the voyage to Theodosius would take too long, maybe he could shorten it. When he told them his plan, they rejected it immediately.

"Mister Splitfoot!" Mme. Z— sputtered, the bed sagging under her weight. "We will *not*! I have never transacted with him, or it, or whatever he is, and I never will! He is to be avoided at all costs!"

This room was different from the one he and Harriet had stayed in. There was a fireplace, for one thing, but the walls were peeling, the wainscoting was grey in places with mold, and the whole effect was shabbier. Max picked at the bedclothes; tattered, with rips at the corners, they had seen better days. So had he. "Is there another way?" he asked. "I mean, if my own trip will take so long..."

"He'll ruin everything, Max. We can't control him."

"But we can reason with him. I can. I mean, he practically begged me to."

"Absolutely not. Our situation will deteriorate even quicker than it has now." Mme. Z— laid herself down onto the bed, horizontal, with the scuffed toes of her oxfords pointing up at the ceiling. "Of all the—*idiot*—" she blurted, then she put her hands across her stomach and didn't say another word the rest of the night.

Max hardly slept. Instead, he lay next to her, listening to her snuffle and gasp; he kept seeing visions of Harriet and Paine in the dark, their faces bewildered and horrified. A great weight pressed down on him, made it hard to breathe, as if gravity itself sought to punish him.

He was coming to understand what he must do.

When pale light pushed its way through the curtains, the other two slowly roused. Mme. Z— sat up, her hair crazy, and she rooted in her purse on the floor and struck a match on the rough plaster and lit a cigarette. She looked exhausted. Her own sleep was no doubt as terrible and full of bad dreams as his own.

"There is no other way," Max said, getting off the bed, as if last night's conversation had been minutes ago. "If you won't help me call him, call Mister Splitfoot, then I'll do it alone." A thin wooden chair stood in the corner across the room, and he went to sit in it. If there was an ideological opposition between them, better to embrace it physically as well. "The moment you're gone, I'll call him to me. I swear I will."

They sat in their lopsided triangle, a strange, padded silence between them.

It was the Colonel who spoke first. "If you do, Max, there is no guarantee he will come. You would have to persuade him to come, and persuade him to help. And there is no way to make him do this. He—it—is famously unpersuadable. Of anything."

"What if I, I don't know, did something drastic? To get his attention?"

"There is nothing drastic enough."

"There must be something." Max looked around him, as though the implements of conjury were in this bare, bleak hotel room.

"I confess we do not completely understand the nature of your relationship with him. I doubt anyone does, even you. Best forget about him."

Mme. Z— took in a great inward, shuddering sigh of a breath, and Max glanced over to see her fighting tears. This situation was too terrible even for her. She blew her nose into her blouse, and smeared it away.

"Well," he said. "What if...what if something happened? I mean, what if I was dying? And he needed to help me? That would get his attention right away. He likes me. He said so himself."

"*Dying!*" Mme. Z— blurted, and stood up. "I won't listen to this!" She went across the room and unlocked the door and peeked quietly out, both ways down the corridor, looking for...what? Max was afraid to ask. The Colonel only scratched at his beard. But she had nowhere to go, and she came back inside and sat stiffly down again. The bed creaked under her weight.

The Colonel had an odd look on his face, one that Max had never seen before. He said, "Go on."

Max's face felt hot. He looked around: two beds, an empty fireplace, a simple chair where the Colonel had thrown his coat. With a new sadness, he realized he didn't want to leave this place, this city. He'd gotten comfortable here. The life of a scholar attracted him—studying, learning, reflecting. The life of a warrior tempted him not in the least. But for now, he had no choice. "I don't know. I'm...grasping at things. Trying them out, that's all."

"It is not a useless idea. If your relationship with him is as you say, it might get his attention. He might...intervene. He could partake in the Bardo."

Mme. Z—'s round head swiveled toward her partner. "The *Bardo*? Mister Splitfoot in a *Bardo*? Please!"

Max felt left out. He'd heard of a Bardo before, but not in this context. "How so?"

"The state between two worlds," Mme. Z— explained, digging sleep from her eyes. "A Tibetan concept, of course. A kind of threshold between life and death. It is not a state from which you come back."

"But it is not, shall we say, a solitary one," the Colonel said. "There are often hallucinations, karmic restitutions. How is your karma, Max?"

Max stared at him, his brain razed from the lunatic realization they were talking about his death. "I...I don't know. I mean, good, I suppose." *If you don't count all the deaths you caused,* said the faraway voice. He slid down in his seat, trying to hide from his own doubts. "We don't have time. If there's no other way, I'm doing it. You can help if you want."

Mme. Z— only sat on the bed, looking worried, but the Colonel, in his gaseous wheeze of a voice, spoke up. "I agree with you, Max. We need this fellow's assistance. I will help you get it."

Max's brain was filled with the terrible implications of this. "Is there no better idea?" He waited for someone to say something. No one did; a new calm had descended upon the room, and Max knew they felt it too. "So what do we do?"

The old man didn't answer; he had gone back to thoughtfully petting his beard, as if it were a living thing.

"A *jhator*." It was Mme. Z—. "You will do a *jhator*." She was staring across at the far wall, unable not to be at the center of things. She looked a hundred years old.

Max was afraid to ask. "What is...a *jhator*?"

"A sky burial. Alms for the birds."

This didn't sound too bad. Max liked birds. Birds had helped him many times in the past. He trusted them, he owed them, he would give them alms, no worries at all. "How will it happen?"

"Hm," the Colonel said, and paused, seeming not to want to get into the details. His eyes were unreadable, sitting motionless and dark in their sockets. This unnerved the boy, and a deep part of himself was wanting to say, *No, no, I take it all back*, but he made himself stay silent. *For Harriet*, he was thinking. *For Paine*.

"The birds, hm, yes," the old man said. He thoughtfully scratched the side of his nose. "The birds will eat you alive."

"Are you ready?" Mme. Z— asked. Max didn't reply, avoiding her gaze.

The roof of the hotel was not as he had anticipated—a flat, empty, picturesque plane, open to the sky and the elements, with bricked edges jilted lovers could leap from. This roof was indeed open to the sky and the elements, but only after one made their way through a labyrinth of chimneys and stairwell doors and exhaust pipes and ducts. Vegetation grew everywhere— weeds sprouting between cracks in the bricks, but also some rooftop gardener's potted plants—lavender, honeysuckle, Virginia creeper. They were draped across the doorways and parapets and trellises like beaded curtains. The uppermost crest of the hotel, the very top, was a triangular structure with windows looking out only onto another thick chimney.

Max was swathed in torn and knotted bedsheets from the room downstairs, looking not unlike an Egyptian mummy. He lay on a cleared wooden table, and was letting Mme. Z— and the Colonel fasten him down to it, his arms and legs bound open, spread-limbed to the sky; it was a beautiful winter day and the sun was in his eyes. Unanswered questions jabbed at him, but he swallowed thickly and tried to let them go. Except for one. Mme. Z— wouldn't be able to answer to any satisfaction, but he asked her anyway: "Where is this...this other realm you're off to?"

"What?" She tightened a restraining strip of bedsheet. "We will assemble. And organize."

"If this works, Peter Sylvester will have to choose one of us over the other," Max said, realizing it as he said it. "This guarantees the survival of at least one party. At least in the short term."

Around her cigarette, Mme. Z— let out a dour cloud of smoke. "You are the decoy."

"My hope," Max said, talkative now for some reason; maybe it was the jitters, "is that the Aurora will follow me, attempt to stop me, while you and the Colonel prepare the Faqrs for the coming storm. Maybe if you gain some time there's a chance."

The old woman reacted as if the notion stung her. "We may win the battle, but we will never win the war." When Max only squinted at her, digesting this, she said, "The war will always be." She watched the Colonel finish with Max's bonds on the other side of the table. "But can we tip it in the short term? If we are smart. And lucky. Yes."

"What happened to the library?" Max said, testing his tethers. They were tight, tighter than he'd expected. He wouldn't be getting up from this on his own, that was for sure.

"It's still there, but in the Akasha. If we manage to survive this next chapter, I will access it from the knee-wall door on the other side, and reclaim my collection." Mme. Z— took a long last drag from her cigarette, and dropped it and stamped it out on the roof with the toe of her shoe. "Now hush, we need to concentrate."

"Are we going to sever him up?" the Colonel asked.

"*What?*" Max struggled to sit up, but couldn't.

"Hush, I said. No, we are not going to sever anyone up. And we have no lamas or adepts or even a dakhma, so we will advantageously forego that part of the ritual. Now here." She lifted Max's head and began to wrap his face and neck with more strips of bedsheet.

The sun was hot, though the air was quite cool; he closed his eyes as the white fabric enveloped him, blinding him to everything except the sun's ivory glow. He relaxed against his bindings and tried to get comfortable. His dread was a physical thing now; heavy, ponderous, tactile, more felt than thought. In a moment, they were done securing him, and he sensed blindly that they had stepped back to survey their work.

"Are you ready?" he heard Mme. Z— ask, but it wasn't to him; the Colonel's wordless assent came hesitant, almost silent, and a low chanting began, not unlike the dharani, but this time the language sounded different, a far mountain strain of Ladakhi, maybe. He had no idea what they were saying; minor words and phrases he understood seemed to leap out at him from strings of jumbled nonsense. He could hear as they slowly began to circle the table, their soft chanting and the crunching of their feet competing with the sounds of the street twelve stories below. A breeze wandered through, and a cloud maybe crossed the sun—the whiteness grew a bit darker, then returned for a moment, and then dimmed again, this time for good. The droning voices continued, circling him, circling him, and the city hissed and hummed to itself a world away. Max drifted, thinking of Mister Splitfoot.

There was a sound to his left then, a scuffle or a flutter which brought him quickly back, he couldn't quite make it out with the chanting voices; but then another one, this one down at his feet, and now another near his head. It unnerved him not being able to see anything. "Hey, wait a second," he said, but no one reacted; the voices and incantations continued, circling, circling, a cycle unto itself apart from him. Did it have anything to do with him at all?

A burning started in his groin, and he realized he needed to urinate. Badly, too. As in right now. "Hey," he said, "let me up, I need to piss." No response, no sign they had heard. "Let me take a piss, all right? I gotta pee." The droning chants continued, the slip of shoe leather on brick, automobile bleats and yelling voices from a world away. Another flutter now, to his right. And another, and another. More flutters now, from what kind of bird he couldn't say; not too big, surely—*Were there magpies in New York City?*—but there came even more flutters, and more, and now tiny sensations settling on him, stepping and hopping across his legs and his torso, little tiny dancing chorus line impressions. And now his arms. The burning in his groin continued, and he knew that if he didn't get relief he would piss himself right now, soak it into all the stupid bedsheet rags. Would pissing mess up the Bardo?

On his left calf now there came a tiny sensation like a weak pinch. One of the birds. The jumble of voices and droning continued, but oddly now they seemed echoed and farther away; with the sun behind the clouds he couldn't even see the ghost of the light anymore, and his bonds had seemed to retract, tighter now than ever. Another weak pinch, this time at his forearm, and another at his ankle. The birds were pecking at him. He wondered abstractly for a moment how they would negotiate the wrapped bedsheets, and then— "Ow! Dammit!"—one of them pinched his skin. That one hurt, like a malicious real pinch.

The droning continued, male and the female voices becoming indistinct and blurred, and it really was a chorus now, several people chanting, some hill language Max didn't know or care to at this point in time, he had to piss. And he remembered with a jump of his heart that he was supposed to call upon Mister Splitfoot, but just then came another peck, and another—a stab really— and another. More fluttering around him now, *Birds of a feather*, he thought, stupid and paranoid, there were more around him, and more. The pecking was at his feet, and his legs, and now his arms and torso, too; he pulled at his bonds but couldn't move, couldn't shoo them away, and they pecked at his ribs, digging into his flesh, stabbing at him with their sharp tiny knives.

"Okay," he said, "this isn't what I wanted, let's—Ow!" But then came more stabs, and more, and it was really starting to goddamn hurt now. They weren't gentle little pinches, these were hard and very sharp and intending harm to his body. The birds were heavy on him now, they had heft, and more flutters and more flutters as other birds arrived. "Look," he said, "I'm not sure this is— OW!" A bird got him in gut, the near the navel, and he felt a wet trickle of blood. Then the bird dug and dug in the wound, and then others stabbed him and dug in him too, and the pain quickly sandpapered his throat and he heard himself rasping out wordlessly now as the droning voices kept on. The stabbing continued, and wraps damp with cool blood were soaking his legs now and his ribs and the bandages were growing wet and heavy. There was an iron smell in the air. His hands and feet were still secured, and even as he pulled and struggled they let him go nowhere. The birds were heavier, more fluttering, they covered him on all sides, hundreds of them by the sound, all parts of his body, pecking and pinching and stabbing, and the pain was becoming a living thing shuddering from a thousand different points along himself; he screamed, a hoarse rasp made of gravel and pain, and he felt his bladder go as the droning kept on and he was poked and stabbed and torn away and then devoured. Devoured: He felt himself disappearing, down the gullet, piece by piece, peeled away and digested, less and less of himself every moment; the pain was itself a drone now, a solid undulating audible thing, and a wild thought came to him— *Shock, it's shock, will I be in shock?*—and then the pain droned and whipped again and drowned it out. They were disassembling him, granulating him, tearing him away bit by bit, *don't worry we hurry*, he was white hot and the air couldn't touch him anyway, he was covered with birds, he was made up of birds, birds and pain, and they tore at him and made him scream, all over his body and on top of his head and into his scalp. Wet cool smelly blood soaked his forehead as one, two, three of the birds danced up and began digging at the bandages over his eyes. *No no no,* a terrible desperate thought shivered by as he tried to shake his head and couldn't, *no no,* blinking and bright blood red, *please please, Mister Splitfoot, please my eyes not my eyes not my—*

Book Four

Lucky Ghost

TWENTY-SIX: MISTER SPLITFOOT

FROM SOFT, BLISSFUL NOTHING, he woke.

He was on his side, lying on moss. On the bank of a wide, shallow river. In the shade of a willow that dragged its fronds in the currents like a lovestruck adolescent. For a time he lay there, lethargic, merely breathing, surprised to feel blood pulsing in his veins.

His eyes were okay. Or were they? How could he be sure? He couldn't, but he could watch as a tiny ant made its long journey up a blade of grass near his face. Max reached out and let the ant climb onto the back of his hand—his wrists clear and free from the pressure of the straps—and wander around in confusion. Max should be blind. He should be dead. If he was in fact still among the living at all. Is this the Bardo? With weak hands he pushed himself up. His thoughts were sluggish and dense, but in those timeless moments, being eaten alive by dozens—no, hundreds—of birds, he'd never expected to wake up to anywhere ever again.

There was a noise—a soft, tuneless whistling.

Behind him on the bank stood a thin copse of sugar maples. A colony of tulip poplars on the far side of the river. Beyond them, pillowy green mountains bunched up into a ridge. And someone—a man—was sitting thirty or so feet away, hidden behind an ancient, knobby elm. His bare feet jutted out from pinstriped trousers that were ripped and frayed, like a marooned sailor. Dirty, wounded toes—it looked as if the big toenail had been ripped clean off—poked up toward the sky. Max couldn't see his face, but a cane pole right out of Mark Twain was propped in his hands, and a scatter of several fish—little white crappies, by the look of them—flipped and gasped on the moss next to his thigh.

Max didn't yet feel like he could stand, so he gave a hoarse, tentative call: "Hello?"

The man shifted, stabbed the end of the cane pole into the soft earth so that it stuck there. He leaned forward to let Max see his face. From the far side of the elm, Mister Splitfoot leered back at him.

His black hair was longer now, matted and stringing in his eyes. New sores blotched his face. Runnels of dried black blood cracked down along his cheeks.

"Hey there, Maximilian," he said, and grinned his insane, gaggle-toothed smile.

Max shut his eyes. Silence rose from the ground like mist, the absence of noise now, and even the insects had paused their blissful song. It occurred to him he may have been better off blind and dead after all. He lay back down, felt the hard ridge of his ribs falling away into the soft rising and falling plain of his belly.

"I needed you" he said after a time, not believing it himself. "And you came."

Mister Splitfoot laughed his loping, crazy laugh. "Ain't nobody gonna care fer you like me, Max." He stood up and spastically came over. His ripped dress pants were too short and left his sore-mottled ankles bare; skin peeled away, exposing red, raw patches that looked inflamed and itchy. They were the ankles of a corpse. "You should know that by now," he said. *Bah nay-ow.* He squatted next to Max and went suddenly quiet, looking pensively into the water, as if he had forgotten what he had wanted to say.

"Why?" was all Max could ask. "Why do you...?"

"Oh, I kin put you back with the birds, don't you worry none. I kin and I will, 'less we can come to one o' them 'greements."

Beyond the trees, the mountains were soft and green. Their peace taunted him, just out of reach; the trees were the bars of a prison. "Where are we?"

"Sweet Kentuck'!" Mister Splitfoot exclaimed. "Where I's borned and...well, you can prob'ly guess the rest."

Borned. Was a being like Mister Splitfoot ever really *borned?* Or just willed into squalid existence? "How old are you?" Max wondered aloud.

The man-spirit only turned and looked at him. One green eye had drifted and was staring downriver. Max shifted himself slowly up and waited for Mister Splitfoot to tell him how to proceed. A swarm of tiny lavender butterflies stormed a muddy area of the bank.

"Now, lissen," Mister Splitfoot said, rasping his dirty palms together. "We got ourselfs a mutual *goal* here. You wanna live, and I wants you to live. That's what we calls a *purpose.* But there's somethins in the way. Somethins we gotta talk about."

The only thing Max wanted to hear less than a "mutual goal" was the sound of more birds. So he pulled his knees to his chest and waited for it to continue.

"See, you got yer 'Rora"—Max took that to mean Peter Sylvester and his friends—"and then you got yer who-the-hell-ever else. I ain't worried about them, no I *ain't,* don't worry none, *nuh unh.* But I'm worried about YOU." Mister Splitfoot leaned over Max's shoulder, and his breath stank like nothing the boy had ever smelled: pus and horse shit and rotted apples and drowned pigs and mold in the walls. Max pulled away but tried to keep the revulsion from showing on his face.

"I like you, boy. I think yer somethin' else. Me and you, we gotta stay ourselfs *close!*" Mister Splitfoot thumped his chest once—hard, like an ape—and jumped up, excited now at this thought, and started pacing on the bank. His fingers were black, not with dirt, but charred, like the carcass of a man who had burned in a fire.

"I called you," Max said miserably. "And you came."

The man-spirit stopped pacing. He stood directly behind Max, who didn't see any use in craning around; he hugged his knees and stared out at the water.

"I came because *you*, Max Grahame, you got somethin' I's wantin'."

Ever since he had first met Mister Splitfoot, Max understood him to be a creature of ravenous, malevolent need. There was no way of avoiding it, so it was better to get it out in the open. Max craned around. "You want my soul," he said bleakly.

Mister Splitfoot considered him a moment, one skewed eye astonished and belonging in another face altogether. Then he doubled over in sudden, sharp laughter. It was that same manic, looping giggle Max had heard several times, but now there was something else—genuine surprise. The man-spirit's greasy hair flopped with his convulsions, and Max thought he could see something—a nest of spiders, or maybe a few of those awful subterranean cave crickets—stirring up there on his mottled scalp.

"*Ahahahaha!*" Mister Splitfoot roared as Max sat there, his face burning, feeling ashamed and numb and terrified. Finally the maniacal laughing dwindled away. With tears in his eyes—were they real tears, or just an approximation of what he thought an actual human might have?—Mister Splitfoot said, "Who do you think I am, boy?"

Another tense silence. Then, "Well, you're not the devil, I know that."

Mister Splitfoot fell to his knees in front of the terrified boy, like a dramatic revival preacher. "There ain't no devil, Max. Didn't that coon tell you that?"

"But just because you're not Satan doesn't mean you don't want my soul."

Mister Splitfoot wiped his eyes and seemed to take a moment to think through Max's logic. It was sound enough. "Naw," he said then. "*Hell naw.* I just want you to do something fer me, thass all."

"What is it?"

"We will talk about that. First, I want to know, will you do it?" *We-ull ewe dew it?*

"I...I don't know. I mean, I don't know what it is."

"Look. You got yerself two choices." The young man-spirit was deadly serious now, as if he had never laughed in his life. "You kin either say *yes*, or you go back with them birds."

"How can I say yes when I don't know what I'm saying yes to?"

Mister Splitfoot's one normal eye squinted at him. "It ain't that hard. You got yerself some unfinished business. I will let you finish it, if'n you say yes." The other eye stared off somewhere else, seeing other landscapes. "I ain't sayin' my request, but it will come. If'n you live to be an old man—*providin'* you live that long—I will find you and I will ask."

Max's fingers brushed along the tops of the moss. It felt good. Cool and alive. He sensed it striving for the sun above, for the rich soil below and cool moisture, fighting for survival. Respiration, transpiration, expiration. It was the normal, universal state of things: *stay alive as long as you can, until you can't.*

And just like that he knew then he would never go back to those birds, to that rooftop, not if he could help it. He would do anything—almost anything—to stay here, to stay alive, to have a chance to reach Theodosius. To find and silence Peter Sylvester. "Will you help me?" Max said. "Stop the Aurora, I mean?"

Mister Splitfoot shook his head and picked at a sore on the side of one of his toenails. "I don't get involved in alla that. That ain't none o' mah business."

"But you can."

"I mean, I *could*... But I don' know why I would. I mean, I been *tol'* before not to git too close to things like that." *Lack thay-ut.*

"Told? Told by who?" Something puzzled Max about that question, and it took him a moment before he could put his finger on it. He'd always assumed Mister Splitfoot was a kind of lunatic lone operative, a unique entity following his own defiled needs and impulses. But the idea that he was doing what he was told—following orders, from someone, from some*thing*—brought him a kind of demented pleasure, a weird, nihilistic satisfaction. Now he knew why the young man-spirit giggled so much: the idea that a puppet master acted behind him suggested an entire line of puppet masters—puppet master behind puppet master, and so on into a kind of recursive infinity, a notion that scrambled and pounded into Max's brain. It was like Mme. Z—'s ever-expanding library, or the endless Akashic realms of the unconscious. How far down did it go? At what point did the myriad representations of the thing twist like a Möbius strip into the thing itself?

It was too much. Max scrubbed his scalp with his knuckles, trying to get rid of these thoughts. He was thirsty and his head hurt and his stomach rumbled. But there was something he still needed. "I will," he said slowly, as though he couldn't believe it himself. "All right. I will do as you say. But there's one thing. Or no agreement."

Mister Splitfoot wiped his mouth with the back of his hand, studied whatever he had taken from it, then licked it with a long tongue.

"I *do* have unfinished business," Max went on. "I was on my way to find Theodosius the Sorrowed. But he's a long way off. You help me get there, and I'll do as you say. You let me finish my business, if I can, and I'll cooperate."

The man-spirit fell forward onto his palms, and like a crippled man he crawled closer, his legs dead-hauled behind him. He put his face close to Max's. "You'll do what I say?"

Max held his breath and fought an impulse to turn away. "Only if you let me continue on my journey. Then I'll do as you ask. I swear it."

Mister Splitfoot stared at the boy, his one good eye so close it was hard for Max to focus. The irises were pointillist flecks of ashy green and olive; bloodshot scleras that weren't white so much as a slate, sickbed grey. "Oh, you will do as I say, Maximilian Grahame, I assure you, *you will*."

And he reached out quick, and with a cold dirty hand that covered Max's mouth and chin, pushed him down—

—and a cool wheeze of air passed over his chest.

Max bolted up, gasping. Darkness. Noises from somewhere, from outside—shuffling, bleating. For the second time in less than an hour, he glanced around, not knowing where he was. A straw bed. A dirty folded blanket for a pillow. Thatched roof above, tiny spears of dust-mote light stabbing through the gaps. He looked down at himself, saw in the gloom he was clothed in what looked like a heavy wool jacket and roughly woven pants. Odd shoes—more like wraps, really—were tied around his feet.

It worked. Mister Splitfoot had helped him.

He laid his head back. It was daytime. He was in a thatched hut and he was alive. There were goats nearby. Goats, goats. Always with the goddam goats.

Max sat up, swung his legs over the side and stood; but it was too much too soon, and with white spots dancing and popping in his vision he let gravity take him back down to the bed. He stayed there for a time, blood pounding, breath wheezing; when he felt like he could try again, he stood back up. This time his legs held. He took an exploratory step toward the ill-fitting thatched door on the far side of the hut, and felt already that he was better, clearer-headed and more sure of foot. He pulled the door open, and stepped into the most majestic landscape he had ever seen.

It was a wide, grassy ridge, scattered here and there with scrawny, one-sided fir trees that all seemed to lean only uphill. Above him, rugged snow-capped mountains rose harshly in the distance. The largest of them loomed over the others with a curious double peak that curled inward, like devil's horns. Below him, the hill rounded down into downy clusters of stratocumulus clouds. It was the first time Max had ever been above the cloud line, and he stared at it in awe.

The bleating grew louder. He turned to see the herd of goats approaching from the steep side of the hill, coming up toward the rickety thatched hut. On the far side of the hut was the base of a primitive stone tower, maybe thirty or forty feet tall, with several high, narrow windows and a simple stone ingress going up and inside. It was like a fortress, but scaled down to fit a single household.

An oppressive, persistent wind rose up from the valley, the constant hard push of air, and all at once Max knew why all the trees leaned in one direction.

The goats came on, flowing like water, and then streamed around him as he stood there, too dazed to react. Following the last of them, a human figure trundled up the path, clad in furs much like his own, with a massive fleecy hood drawn about its face that obscured any features. Somehow, beneath all of that shapeless mass of animal pelts and leather—maybe it was the way the figure moved, a certain slope of the shoulder, a tilt of the head—Max could tell it was a female. A woman.

The shepherdess must have seen him, too, because she changed her course and headed his way. The goats were mostly beyond him now, and Max watched, slightly worried, as the woman came on and pulled back her hood. He wasn't sure what to expect—he wasn't taking anything for granted anymore—but he was relieved to see that she was reassuringly human; older but hardy, a weathered face with eroded Caucasian features and deeply sunken eyes that had obviously seen a great deal. Despite her feminine status, there was a coarse, sexless quality to her, like one of those leaning trees. A body shaped more by wind and hard work than anything else. But her smile was kind.

"*Hallo*," he called, not sure why he was adopting a silly accent. It seemed like a logical thing to do in a place like this. He hoped against hope she'd be able to understand him, but she answered with something—maybe it was Turkish, or Turkestani, or Baluchistani, or some type of Eurasian language—that sounded to him like gibberish. Ah well.

The old woman gave him a quick inspection. In his ragged furs Max looked like a goat-farming peasant from some far corner of the world, which was appropriate, he supposed. The woman said something else, and pointed up the mountain.

Max said, "Where am I?"

The woman kept pointing toward the mountain. Above them, a path snaked up slanted fields of stone-strewn grass, to a distant forested hillside which curved up miles away and very steeply to treeless, flinty highlands. The granite slopes raked and grew and eventually separated into the two twin towering peaks, sinister looking devil's horns that guarded the entire lonely panorama.

"Theodosius," Max told her. "I am looking for Theodosius the Sorrowed."

She gave him a toothy grin. "*Thee-o, Thee-o*," she said, nodding vigorously. "*Thee-o*." The woman said something else. And pointed a dirty, stubby finger again: *Up there.*

"Okay," Max said. He considered his oddly wrapped feet. Were they tough enough for walking? Would they keep his feet warm?

"*Diakh, modis*," said the woman, and motioned for him to follow. She went around the hut, to the stairs that led inside the tower, and steadily took them up. The stone steps were solid and worn away in the middle; at the top the threshold into the tower was low—even with his slight frame, Max had to duck his head to go inside.

The room was dark, and ten degrees cooler. A small, tidy sleeping area lay against the circular wall, with a fireplace opposite, and a thickly hewn table filled with leather work of all kinds. Jerkins, breeches, hats and hoods and gloves. Max was feeling as if he had gone back in time, rather than just across the world; maybe he had. The woman went to a small table near the bed and uncovered a saucer with several servings of assembled food, a charred hunk of lean meat—goat most likely, Max somehow knew, more goddamn goat—all wrapped in a flour-type pancake. "*Kababi*," the woman said. "*Thee-o*."

She motioned for Max to hold the plate, which he did, and she took the items and enveloped them in a dirty kerchief she pulled from her pocket. She placed the food in a small leather backpack she found on the floor, and pushed it at him.

"*Diakh*," she said, "*Thee-o*," and pointed outside, back up the mountain.

Max nodded. Evidently he was going on a long trek, up there, to look for Theodosius. He followed the shepherdess back downstairs and outside. By the way the light fell it seemed to be late afternoon. The air was chilly but not yet cold.

His legs were still unsteady, so he sat on the lowermost step and pulled the food from the pack. The woman watched as he unwrapped one of the *kababi* and took a bite. It was gamey but good—charred kid for sure, roasted over the fire, with onions and some sort of unfamiliar spices, all doused in a briny, almost citrusy juice and wrapped in a simple flour crepe. The flavors clanged in his mouth, but deliciously so. The woman's eyes never left his face; she seemed to relish his every bite. A strange mix of doubt and excitement had taken hold of him, and also gratitude for this last little bit of kindness. With every gnash of his teeth he wanted to tell her he loved her, that her beautiful face might be the last face he would ever see. In a weird way, he was glad they didn't speak the same language. He had no idea what silly, intoxicated things he might say to her if they did.

In a minute he was done, and he wiped his face with his sleeve. He smiled and rubbed his belly. "*Kababi*," he said, and spread his grin as wide as he could without making a mockery.

"*Kababi! Kababi!*" the shepherdess shouted, almost bouncing with joy.

Max turned to the twin summits at the top of the mountain. They looked like the very last place he should go, but he didn't suppose now he had a choice. With hands on his knees he pushed himself up, like an old man. "*Thee-o*," he said in that ridiculous accent.

"*Diakh, Thee-o*," the woman repeated, and pointed toward the two peaks.

Max gave her a quick, awkward hug, and shouldered his backpack. Then, on shaky legs, he started making his way up.

The path crawled faintly through the meadows and into the forest above, seeming to be headed, in its unhurried way, toward the two peaks. The fairy tale woods looked as charming and quaint as an illustration from a children's book. From what he could tell, the trees were mostly coniferous—odd variations of fir, yew, and boxwood, with some other kinds he didn't recognize. In a short time he pierced their curtain and entered the sanctuary; everything was silent, not an insect or animal of any kind in sight.

He kept going. As the afternoon faded into evening, several times the forest broke open and Max found himself in yet another upper meadow, with ever-changing views of the clouds below and the horn-peaked slopes above. His progress could be tracked by how quickly the paired summits grew above him—looming higher, ever more dreadful as the sun's fire crawled up along their crests, cooling and dimming until finally it surrendered and was gone.

But even down here, in the hush and the solace of the forests, the trees were twisted and grotesque, sparse and sporadic. He was nearing the timberline.

For hours he climbed through darkness. The thin altitude burned his lungs, and the wind was quite cold now. He kept moving, trudging along hunched into himself, sometimes stumbling over rocks in the darkness, into ever-thinner copses of trees and out again, the path before him ever steeper. Step by step the dark hulking contour of the two peaks rose higher and higher, finally blotting out even the stars themselves.

Sometime in the night he stopped and hunkered below a sheltering boulder and ate his second *kababi*. This one was nearly frozen, tough and near-tasteless. He chewed grimly, then made himself get back up and—leaving his empty pack in the path for some other traveler to find—started climbing again.

After several more hours, when his mind had been a mass of squirming, contrary fears and then settled into a numb exhausted throb, he finally broke through the last of the trees. The light was just beginning to turn in the east; a pink flush was rising now, and above him was a last steep walkable ridge before the final terrifying tilt upward to the two highest peaks. These were forbidding mountains—wrathful, dour, alien to human experience; they had more in common with the vast emptiness of space, with craggy, dead cold moons and planets than they did the pleasant hills and rivers of his home. He fought despair. He was exhausted with the burden of his fortunes. A near-irresistible urge to turn back jolted through him, a need to head down to the fur-covered woman and her *kababi* and her goats and crawl in the straw bed and cower forever.

But only death lay that way. The one possible path to survival lay ahead. And then only with good luck and the help of *Thee-o*.

When he climbed the final precipitous ridge, he stood breathless in the morning light, his face cold with sweat, and looked over; maybe five hundred feet down a craggy slope was a vale—spring green and parchment yellow, absurdly lovely, with a small whitewater river pushing its way through. There were signs of people—a dozen or so rock and wooden huts crouching along the water, kept company by a scatter of those same primitive, peculiar stone towers. Built into the hillside, as much a part of the landscape as the boulders rising up from the earth, they were private little castle keeps. Good for defense, no doubt, and keeping safe.

Max wondered again if he'd slipped back into some primeval time and was looking over some ancient Iron Age hamlet. That thought made his head hurt. He scanned the village below for movement, but there was none; not smoke from a chimney, not a single farm animal. By this point even a goat would be welcome. There was a thin, dusty channel to his left, which looked like it might have been a water rut cleared by run-off from snowcapped peaks. Using his hands to steady him, he crouched on his ass and went skidding down—a slip here, a rock-scurry there—and from time to time he was able to snag the sad, gnarled shrubs that sprouted irregularly from the rock. In places, he was literally climbing down, step by tricky step, over sheer drops and rocky cliffs.

But soon his feet touched solid ground. His stomach was clenched and queasy, and he paused for a moment, catching his balance on shaky legs. The hills of this valley stood quite high in and of themselves, and now the little ghost town was out of sight.

After a brief rest, he climbed the nearest hill to see the towers tall and looming over the little thatched huts like personal bodyguards; footpaths wound here and there through the buildings. As he got closer, he could see the buildings were made from flat rocks and peat roofs, with old, empty wooden animal pens attached to the structures. The ground was stony, but broken here and there with lush bursts of grass. Above all of this stood the dual peaks, silent and ominous.

In a voice cracked with stress and exhaustion, Max called out. "Hello?" No answer.

A sturdy rock wall bordered the village, and he climbed it to assess the dozen or so towers standing lookout over the scene. Carpets of moss and lichen covered half of them; they looked to be at least five hundred years old, maybe closer to a thousand, and their high slitted windows gazed impassively down at him. Someone could be in any one of them, could silence him easily with a rifle or an arrow or a spear or whatever lousy primitive weapons this place preferred. "Hello?"

In the slitted window of the second tower from him, halfway up the slope, a brief hint of anthropoid features pushed itself forward—a chin and a nose, hooded eyes. Then they were gone. "Theodosius?" he called out. "I am looking for Theodosius!" His voice echoed angrily back at him.

Below the tower, a figure appeared out of the doorway. A man, a small man, wrapped in scarves and some other type of material, animal pelts, like Max's own. The man's features were lost against the low sun as he started carefully making his way down. Max looked up again at the grim dual peaks, wondering how long the village had been here, and why someone had decided to put it under those ghastly diabolic mountains in the first place.

Exhausted, he stepped down from the rock wall and sat on it, and prepared himself to meet Theodosius.

TWENTY-SEVEN: THEODOSIUS THE SORROWED

IT TOOK THE OLD man a long time to get there. Small and frail, a twig conjured into human form, he wound patiently around the buildings, past the empty pens and down the stony path to the outlying rock wall where Max waited.

"Hello," Max called out again, and raised a hand when the old man got into range.

"*Gaumarjos*," the old man answered in a feeble, scratchy voice. He pulled back his hood to reveal impressively curled white mustaches and a tanned, grizzled face pierced by two empty eye cavities—pits dug in sandstone. His head was as smooth as polished marble. Max tried not to give any hint of fear or discomfort as the man came closer, and stood silently facing him for a long time. He was perfect for this place, a human incarnation of the landscape around him. Max wasn't sure if he should be relieved or terrified.

"Are you Theodosius?" he said after a time.

The old man didn't answer, just broke into a stubborn smile, as though he were being asked to entertain visitors he hadn't invited. "Max Grahame, you is here. *Modi. Breeng.*"

He turned, and Max followed him up the paths winding through the primitive buildings, up, up the hill, past the tower in which he'd first spotted him, past several others, to the very topmost keep. This one was taller than the rest; perhaps it was the first one built in the village, or the one most fortified from attack. Like the others, a small outbuilding was attached alongside, looking weirdly like a parasite and its host.

They entered into decay-smelling darkness. This time there were no stairs at the bottom; instead, a wooden ladder led to a landing on a higher floor, and the old man climbed up, more deftly than Max expected, and nodded for the boy to follow him. There, a thin but proper stone staircase took them up, step by step, into the heights of the tower. Open doorways branched off twice into cramped and squatty middle floors, but the old man took him all the way to the top, into a larger room, with a beamed cathedral ceiling and narrow windows spilling light onto wooden benches. The feel of being in a medieval castle keep was strong; it felt like Sage's tapestry come to life. There were cooking pots, bookshelves, and an odd, ornately carved wooden structure that took up the entire far wall. It was, Max realized, a bed; a thin mattress and blankets lay on top, with a rusted collection of knives and swords—Persian scimitars, Mongolian sabres, Egyptian khopeshes—decorating the stone wall above it. In the center of the room was a fire pit. A scorched and ancient Dutch oven squatted among the cinders.

"*Hungree?*" the old man asked.

Max was trying to get a feel for him, trying to find the celebrated brilliance Mme. Z— spoke of in the man's words. He kept waiting for some sign, but there was none. "Um. I had some *kababi*, but it's gone."

"Ahhhh, Isolda. Nice *wo-man*. Goats, many goats, *ch'ap'azants' shat* goats." Like the goat shepherdess—apparently Isolda was her name—Theodosius's accent was odd, not Russian or Ukrainian. He motioned for Max to sit, and with a shaky hand passed him a hunk of bread and a cup of water. It was perplexingly like Ethie's cornbread, and Max felt a sharp pang of homesickness. The old man sat too and took a piece himself, and with a crude wooden spoon dug into a bean stew in the Dutch oven. "*Lobio*," he said. The stew was kidney beans, with onions and some type of peppers in a thick gravy, and he spread it like a paste atop the bread.

Max sniffed at the aroma. "What is this?"

"*Lobio*." That word again. Food was as good a way to start a conversation as any, Max thought. He put a spoonful on the bread and took a bite. Tasty. Some type of seasoning—garlic, coriander, and what seemed like a thickening paste made from some kind of nut. Walnuts, maybe? And below that, buried down deep inside of it, the same bright, citrusy tang from the *kababi*. Pomegranates or cranberries. And yet another flavor—some odd, brassy spice Max couldn't place. "What is that—that taste?"

"*Utskho sunelli*. 'Strange and fragrant from far away.' Some call it *fenu-greek*."

Fenugreek. Max had heard of it before. Little pebbles of the spice floated in the broth. Max dolloped more of the beans on his bread, and they sat wordless, both of them noisily eating. Max studied the old man. He was not much over five feet. Toughened by the elements, time had carved channels in his cheeks, echoing the crow's feet at his eye sockets.

"They *weel* come," the old man said softly, his mouth full.

Max was surprised to know that he understood exactly what the old man was saying, and also that this did not cause him alarm. "I know."

"For to *keel* you."

Maybe this knowledge was too big for him to fully digest. It was like the rotation of the earth, the rising of the sun: fundamental, elemental, universal. He could only accept it.

"You have *plohn*?"

"Plohn?"

"*Ayo. Plohn.*"

"Oh, plan!" Max gave a dismal chuckle, thinking back to the Breakaway Plan. Back to Sig and his mother and his laughable strategy to find a place for himself at the local post office. After all this time, the Breakaway Plan had come to mean something very, very different. "That's why I'm here, I think."

He could still run, maybe, still hide somewhere, lose himself in another life. Raise goats in hiding, some gently forested hillside somewhere—Brazil or Poland or Austria. Hide himself inside a meek anonymous existence and disguise himself—a beard, a paunch, a tyrolean hat and Bavarian breeches.

But that wouldn't work. The Aurora's bloody fingers dug too deep. There was literally nowhere now to run. He was out of options.

He felt Theodosius waiting for him to continue. The old man had the brusque air of someone who'd been alone for too long a time. "So, how did you..." Max started, not sure where he was headed; he cleared his throat and tried again. "I spoke to Mme. Z— about you. She told me who you were. Sort of."

The old man wiped his mouth and hands on a dirty rag and tossed it down. "Yes. They had many grand adventures together." It took Max a moment to realize the old man was talking about himself; his empty eye sockets crinkled as he remembered. "He is glad it was she that told you who he was. If it is someone else it would have been a different story."

"But she didn't tell me anything. She said you like to be alone. And that you may be the oldest man alive." *Certainly the most stubborn,* he heard her say in her tobacco gasp.

The old man grinned and leaned back, as if making room for all the details of his long life. "Yes, yes," he said, seeming happy now to be getting into it, or maybe getting it over with. "He do not know. Some say he was born in *Egrisi,* some say *Abkhazia.* He is not sure." He turned his eyeless face to the window, pondering something strange or painful. "He have forgotten his original name. He is neither *Gyptian* nor *Romani,* but he is Theodosius. Blind and sorrowful. His tongue speak Armenian, Pontic, *yev* Turkish. Englishese. And *Svaneti.*"

Abkhazia? Where was that? The Caucasus? "Mme. Z— was born not...not far from here. I think." The old man didn't answer. He bit more from his bread and took a long pull of water from a tin cup. His Adam's apple threw a shadow across his neck.

"Where are we?" Max said. "I mean, where is this place?"

"You are no place. Impossible to find on map."

"Do you know why I'm here?"

"Enough."

"The Faqrs," Max said. "Our hope is that Mme. Z— can get to them, give them a chance to encircle," Max said, not sure if Theodosius cared the hear the details or not. "I am the decoy."

The old man shook his head. "You are no decoy. You are prime intention."

Max tried to smile. "No, I am the one to distract." He watched as the old man shook his head again. "To give them time to regain strength."

"Time? There is no time, time do not exist. Here, as in *eether,* time is plaything. You gather and fold, bend this way or that, meet your moment as you wish. Madame Zed know that. Everyone know that." Theodosius tapped his bony, sunken sternum, twice. "And so you *breeng* them to here." There was a note of anger in his voice. Not entirely unexpected, but it worried Max anyway. The old man leaned over the *lobio,* and pulled out what looked like a large bay leaf. He sucked it for a moment, then slung it into the fire pit, which was littered with more bay leaves, Max saw, dozens of them.

Max said, "So you know what's happening?"

"Do it matter? Theodosius wish to be left alone. He is separate for reason."

Now Max felt worse than before; he chewed the inside of his cheek. "We hoped that you were part of the plan."

"*Thees* is her way—is Madame. Make brash scheme and then ask why everyone not happy for it." His eyeless gaze fell to the worn wooden planks under his feet. "You are not distraction," he said again. "You are thing itself."

"I—I don't understand."

"They wish for your talent. Madame Zed think she is the one. She is not the one. Nor her soldier friend. They are come to stop *you*."

"Me?" Max felt a new dread come over him. "Why me?"

"You are Chef." The old man grinned, and the thin skin of his skull pulled even thinner.

"A chef? What?"

"I am Sorrowed. Mme. Zed is Madame. Peter Sylvester is Postmaster. You are Chef." He shrugged. "Not a chef. *The Chef.*"

"I don't know what you're talking about."

Theodosius gave a great sigh of resignation. "No matter. You are here now."

There was a long pause. Theodosius scratched his shoulder; the *scritch scritch* of it was loud in the room. Max let out his breath; he hadn't realized he'd been holding it. The air was getting colder; a gloom had closed in around him, wrapping him close and tight.

"They will not be deterred." The old man's croak was quiet now. "Why would they?"

"How long do we have until they get here?"

"By your time? Day. Less."

Max felt something secure in him give way, some interior pulley somewhere had come free. "They'll be here tomorrow? What do we do?"

"Do? What is there? Die honorable death."

Max blinked several times. This was not the answer he'd hoped for.

"They are strong. They gather power for long time. Your young friends, your...*appreentice* soldiers, are ending piece to their scheme. Perhaps is why they are so...so *natsqeni. Resent-ful*. With others, they are danger. With you, they are furious." He shrugged again. "Now, small delay."

Max thought: *With me.* The words stung, pricked him like one of those damned birds. But he still had no idea what the Aurora had planned for them. For him. "This business with the soldiers, the assassins, the assassinations. What are they after?"

"War. Last war, ending war. Unbalance order of things enough to take advantage." The old man stood suddenly, as if he weighed hardly anything at all, and went to the bookshelf. He searched for a moment, and pulled out a folded piece of paper. He came back and opened it carefully. "Like chess, like game going for long time. Now we are checkmate." The paper was an old map; trade routes, inland seas. Even without his eyes, the old man's wrinkled finger came to rest on a place which, Max thought, looking at it upside down, resembled the Caucasus, the region between the Black and the Caspian Seas. *Georgia*, the faraway voice said. *You made it back to Georgia, bucko.*

"Quarrel," the old man was saying. "One wants for everybody. The other—power at the top. Like pyramid." Max knew now why the old man had chosen the life of an exile in a ghost town at the edge of the world: There was no way to win. Better to be removed from it altogether. "There are two rivals, Faqrs and Brotherhood. Theo is neither." The old man refolded the map and laid it on the bench beside him. His face was sad. "You are Chef."

Max felt another collapse of hope. After planning a life of neutrality, Theodosius was now facing death—a silencing—due to Max's own ignorant presence. Once again, just like Harriet and Paine. Just like his mother and Sig and everyone else he'd ever met, his trail of ruin continued. He wanted to cry. "Is there anything we can do?"

"*Eether.*"

"Either what?"

"No—*eether.*"

"Oh, æther! I'm a novice."

"Is primary weapon they use."

Max wanted to bury his head in his hands. He had travelled astrally, but never very well. Literally, every diviner he'd ever met was his better. "Can we hide?"

"In *eether*? No. *Eether* is all times. All places. No hiding in *eether*. Not game with rocks or sticks."

Outside the window the sky was dim; Max had only just arrived, and not far behind the sunrise, but somehow evening was already falling. A spin of vertigo made him dizzy; an entire day had been stolen from him. There were no animal sounds—no horses, no birds, no pigs, no goats. The only noise was the wheeze of the wind. The light, what there was of it now, fell differently than before; as if not only the hour had changed, but the season—as though winter had skipped spring and summer and rushed into fall again. The old man lifted his face, a slight smile on his lips. In the half-light from the window he blended into the interior of his tower, like a chameleon.

"Why would the Aurora want to unbalance everything? Destabilize everything? Because that would hurt them, also."

Theodosius tilted his head. "Your president *keeled*, no? Your money crash."

"I don't understand."

"Like everything of Aurora, is *heeden*, in muddle, *meesing*. They wish to put down. Like dog."

Like dog. Harriet, that last time in the Hall of the Woods. Harriet on the leonine throne, regal, royal, how she really was all along. *They put Rosalie down like a dog,* she'd said.

"Much pain, much suffering," the old man went on. He turned his wistful face to the darkness outside the slitted window. "He will be happy when is over. Is good they are coming. He is tired. Will be good to *feennish* it, he think."

They sat in silence, feeling the weight of these thoughts. The words hit Max again: *the Chef.* It made no sense.

Theodosius stood and built a fire. He lit several gas lamps around the room, until the place flickered with a glow that pushed weakly against the gloom. Max couldn't stop thinking of the terrible things to come; they crowded him, blotting out any sense of temporary respite he might have had. Finally he said, "I need to rest."

Theodosius crouched on his haunches near the fire. "Bed there." He pointed to the blankets and pillows atop the ornate wooden structure. "Rest. Tomorrow *weel* be bad for you, he think."

In the sun-blanched morning, Theodosius was gone.

It was cold. The fire had died, but Max lay in the big wooden bed, not wanting to start another until the old man returned; most likely he was the only visitor this place had seen in a very long time, and messing with anything would have the feel of trespass. He got slowly down and finished the last of the cold *lobio,* feeding from the big wooden spoon as he huddled for warmth in the early chill.

Outside the window, the morning had a hushed and anticipant quality, like rain was coming. It wasn't rain that was on its way, but something much worse. The towers stood like sentinels in the radiant light. Max dressed in the furs again and wrapped a turban of scarves around his head. When he caught his reflection in a mirror, the haunted face staring back looked like a cross between a caravan slave and a Stone-Age hunter-gather. Despite everything, he had to laugh; if only Harriet could see him now. They both would have giggled themselves silly.

But then the knots in his stomach got the better of him; today was the day that he would face Peter Sylvester. He tried not to feel terrified, or feel anything at all, really. It didn't work. He went down the thin stone stairs, down the ladder, into cold light outside.

"Hello?" he called out. His voice was dull in the dead air. "Theodosius?" Not even the buzz of an insect. Unnerved, he went down to the next tower—this one was smaller and stunted—and looked inside. Another ladder, another set of stone steps leading up into shadow. "Hello?" Not even an echo. But there was a stale, musty odor. He climbed to the second floor.

The chamber was jammed with haphazard, lopsided stacks of books, as tall as Max, leaning columns slouching against each other like barroom drunks. Old rotting volumes which had soaked in rain from the slitted open windows, their pages swollen and exploded with water damage. They seemed to have been here for forever. Priceless volumes, no doubt. Max picked up one at his feet, which was coming apart as much from age as from exposure to the elements. It looked to be written in an early form of Persian, and was signed on the last page with a flourish by a *Darius de A–*. This was, Max knew from his reading, a vital, nearly forgotten part of the *Quarto*. Sad to think Theodosius's private library was in such terrible condition. How could the old man have let this happen? Maybe he hadn't. Max put the book down and went up the rest of the stairs. The upper floor was the same—books piled upon books, hoards of books, so much that it was hardly possible to step into the room. Thousands of them, covering the floor and heaped up the wall to the ceiling. All in terrible shape.

The next tower was similar—mounds of books written in odd languages. Old tomes, ancient tomes, a few curious newer ones, most of them rotting now. They had fallen and scattered across the floor in messy heaps, their pages ripped and strewn about. The ones near the window were destroyed by nature. Hesitant to look too closely, Max picked up another and saw the words "*Sepher Ha-Razim*" scrawled across the spine. He had seen references to this book, also; it was hand-written, with many primitive diagrams and odd writing in a language he'd never encountered before.

The next tower and the next were the same—more old books, more decay, bizarre faded diagrams, damp rotting pages, lichen and dust and disintegrating bindings. Max didn't linger long; his nerves were better outside in the morning light. But where was the old man? This village was not that big; there weren't that many places to hide. There were only two unexplored towers left, so Max headed for the nearest one, which grew like a massive redwood out of a small hillock. It was the tower where he had first seen the old man.

The ladder here was worn smooth from hundreds of hands and feet, and he went up, and then up the stairs, past more chambers of violation. At the very top was yet another ruined library—thousands of volumes cross-jammed in so tightly the stacks seemed to brace up the ceiling. But here a narrow path had been carved out, as if someone passed this way regularly. With a black dread thrumming in his heart, Max stepped across the mess, the pages and bindings stamped flat under his feet. And stopped.

At the far edge of the room, in a little oasis cleared from the groves of books near the window, sat Theodosius. He was in a chair that had been cleverly fashioned from the books themselves—piles of volumes worn smooth underneath him, and more for the arms and the backrest. A throne of words, a kingdom of mold and decay. Theodosius was sloped slightly to the side, facing the window, his cheek resting on yet another haphazard column; spattered blood had coagulated across his face and also the nearby books where the gunshot had destroyed the back side of his skull. An ornate pistol—Moroccan or Turkish in origin, maybe, like a smaller version of a camel gun, all hand-carved wood and metal whorls and a preposterously large revolving chamber—was grasped loosely in his left fist. His open eye sockets stared at the window where Max had first seen him, as if offering a silent apology, or a reprise to their beginnings. There were no flies, no birds, no signs of life at all.

TWENTY-EIGHT: IN THE ÆTHER

AFTER TWO HOURS OF trying to dig a hole large enough to fit even the old man's slight frame, Max gave up. The ground was too stubborn, too stony and rocky, to go very deep. Judging by the faint sun behind the white-scrimmed clouds, it was close to one o'clock in the afternoon. The landscape around him seemed poised, hungry for something. He went back up the hill to the old man's tower. At the bottom of the stairs, the heavy wooden door was braced by rusty but rugged iron hinges; with a heave Max closed it, and slid the solid barricade into place with a reassuringly solid *thunk*. Then he climbed the ladder and pulled it up behind him, admiring the twelve or fifteen feet of sheer stone precipice between him and the door. The keep was now fortified. No one could force their way in.

On the top floor, he crouched by the slitted windows, waiting. But for what? For whom? The Postmaster was coming, he knew that much. But he had no clue how, or in what manner. The only thing he could do was wait, and ready himself. He went to sit on the bench against the stone wall and drew his furs around him, and prepared to drift. Just like before, he let his breath go, and then his heart and his respiration settled slowly into sync, until he felt his consciousness seep slowly beyond the exhale and the inhale, diluting outward. He felt his body sigh and release, as if on the final threshold of sleep, and then—

—*he was outside*—

—flowing beyond the cool rocks of the tower, buzzing with the familiar transference of energy all around: expiration, transpiration, expiration. The sun warming each flat blade of grass, each lichen-covered stone. The oxidizing air in the next-to-last tower, rotting the fallen piles of books and stiffening the remains of Theodosius.

Now like a breath or a breeze, Max let himself flow through the towers, in and out of them, down the meandering paths, along the meadows and up to the ridge, all the way through the distant trees and the forests, their glades cool and inviting, and out again into blessed—

max

He paused, and listened. The wind whistled. He wasn't sure where the voice had come from.

max...

Yes?

are you there? A female voice, drifting closer.

I am here.

where are you?

I am in the æther.

Max took stock of himself, got his bearings. Akashic states were still new to him; you could travel back and forth in time as well as space, but even for the experienced it was frighteningly easy to lose yourself. His consciousness hovered high above the meadows of the mountain; he was neither hot nor cold. Far below was the landscape he had already travelled, but now slightly mutated and strange. He saw not only the specific places where he had been, but also the giant curve of the Earth itself as it rolled away into distant hazy lands and continents and oceans. It was like looking at a picture of the moon and the moon itself at the same time. He remembered Black Howard talking about this—in *tamkarra*, he'd said, there was the thing, and also the representation of the thing. In the end, they were the same. Max thought he finally knew what Black Howard meant; it was possible to be and to watch oneself at the same time.

max don't lose me

I'm here, I'm here...who are you?

i am coming

The Akashic glow was bright, every molecule shimmering; and then Max saw who it was. A woman stepped out from cloudy brilliance and let herself be regarded.

It was Sage.

Much about her was still beautiful. Always brittle and underfed, she was considerably older now, with wisps of white hair at her temples. But she had become a fallen dream of herself—lopsided, once shrewd and guarded, but weak and palsied now. Thin, veiny wrists, sagging cheeks and neck; a sunken eye, half-lidded and staring off.

Sage! Is it you?

She approached, and like a sigh, they embraced. It was akin to hugging a drift of cold air. In the Akashic winds her hair billowed around her face. Her smile was sad.

How—how is this possible?

My body max at steppeland my body was destroyed in the fire but i managed to flee into the akasha

You're alive? Are you...all right?

as all right as any ghost as anyone without a home

There was an anguish in her voice he hadn't heard before. She was right—she was a ghost now.

Can you come back?

i don't think so my body was destroyed i have never felt anything like this before Her sad smile faltered. *its been i don't know how long*

What can I do?

its horrible in there nothing and everything and forever i feel myself slipping

You can find a way, Sage. You have to keep trying.

Sage looked over her shoulder, as if she were being pursued. *are they have they come?*

Who? The Aurora?

i am sorry i am all mixed up max i have lost my way

They are coming, Max agreed. They'll be here soon.

Sage looked down at the mountains, with their steep, rolling hills. *where are we?*

I don't know, exactly. This is where Theodosius lives. Lived, I mean.

Sage wrapped her arms around herself. She seemed distraught. *I am lost max i've been too long in the æther*

Find your way back, Sage. I will help you.

back to what everything is gone i am gone we are all gone we will die the universe will die She blinked against the wind. *i've seen it horrible and beautiful and–* She stiffened then, like a cat, as if she heard something. She tilted her head, listening. *they are coming max get ready they are coming*

She turned and pointed. Far off, down the low curve of the mountain, Max saw movement. Birds. Four birds. They looked to Max like starlings. Slowly making their way, riding the headwinds as they came.

You have to go be safe max Sage looked back at him. *there is always the akasha always the æther*

Max said nothing. A deep, almost feverish dismay thrummed through him, like a plucked violin string. He didn't want to be a ghost like Sage; if that lonely, eternal state was what the æther offered, he would choose death. But he wouldn't say that to her. Sage, I hope to see you again.

She held her hand out to him, and he took it. Her fingers were cold, but he felt her heartbeat in them. She was alive.

and i you she told him, and let him slip from her grasp.

The landscape glowed in the golden light. Max wondered if the grief he felt would ever truly pass, even after his death, the heartbreak lingering in the air like the smell of charred meat. He drifted back down to the valley and the village and the towers. There was a nauseating tumble in his stomach as he descended. He let himself find himself again, and inside the upper chamber he opened his eyes, felt the rough bench beneath him, the coarse cold stone wall at his back. The fragrant remains of the *lobio* and the dead fire were just as he had left them.

He went to the window. In the distance, the four starlings still came. Too low for the slipstream now, their wings pumped hard against the air.

Max was still in his turban and animal skins. For comfort and freedom of movement, he peeled off several layers, keeping the fur but baring his chest and neck to the cool air. He thought he must look something like Aladdin, from that intricate but oddly satisfying book, One Thousand and One Nights. He pictured its spine in his bookcase, and remembered exactly where it was— farthest to the left on the second shelf, a faded red and yellow leather binding, symmetric Oriental vines crawling all over it. A new surge of grief flowed through him, mourning for his former life that was gone, as pitilessly as Sage's body. But if Sage was a ghost now, he was too, and also everyone he knew, and everyone who had ever lived. The life of his old self was gone, everyone's old selves were gone, it was the nature of things, time passing, fleeting life, even in the æther, even in the universe. And that was if you were lucky; the luckless ones were never given even that chance.

Max went to the window and looked out. The birds were gone now. Feeling somewhat like an outlaw in a frontier hideout waiting for ambush, he gazed down into the village...and there they were. Beyond the low outer wall, black against the stones and moving up the path toward the village—four figures meandering up. Their long-legged gait was immediately familiar—the Postmaster and the three sisters. Peter Sylvester had brought with him Loretta, Louise, and Lillian Hearst.

Max watched as they slowly, carefully negotiated the rock wall—long skirts in hand, old lady knickers delicately exposed, they certainly *seemed* geriatric— and started winding up the hill. Somehow they knew exactly where to head. They were coming straight to him.

Peter Sylvester cupped his hands to his mouth and shouted: "Max!" His voice was an old man's—frail and hoarse, but there was a core of strength, a dense malevolent heart of vigor. The four figures were elderly, but their footsteps were sure. "Max, we wish to speak with you!"

There was no use in hiding; they knew exactly where he was. He leaned out the narrow window. "Talking is over!"

"You are right! It is too late!" The Postmaster's voice echoed from the towers, came at him from several directions. "The conflict is finished! The Faqrs are broken! Mme. Z— and the Colonel are dead! There is no one left, Max, but you! Only you!"

This took Max by surprise, and he felt a sudden lurch of vertigo, as if the sky was below and the rocky ground was above. Mme. Z— dead? It was a shocking thought. He couldn't imagine living in a world that didn't contain her. But then Theodosius's words came to him: *Madame Zed is not the one. They are come to stop you.*

He managed to shout, "You're lying! You were never interested in her in the first place!" The three sisters pulled back their hoods. They were ancient, crone-like—not dying, but Death personified. They grinned, their lips drawn back in a rictus of ancient flesh. Max knew suddenly they were hundreds of years old.

"Peter is telling you the truth!" Loretta said.

Louise called out, "She is dead, my beautiful Max!"

"We killed them both!" This was Lillian. At least Max thought so.

"They never made it to Uttar Pradesh!"

"But we never touched them!"

"Strangled them, we did!"

"With their own hands!"

Max kept himself still, trying not to shiver with panic; if he started, he might never be able to stop. Peter Sylvester finally came to the bottom of the tower. He stood there, arms at his sides, and grinned at Max. The old women joined him, their faces turned up like pale stones at the bottom of a river.

"Rapunzel, Rapunzel, let down your hair!" Peter Sylvester mocked. He looked a little like a gentleman missionary deep in the Congo, still committed to wearing his cravat and enjoying his tea. "Please, son, there is no need for drama. Let us end this pageant like the noble lords we are."

"I can hear you just fine from right here." In this landscape, Max's voice was harsh and alien, even to him.

"Your mother didn't want to talk to us, either," the old man said with sadness. "Not until toward the end. Then she wouldn't stop trying, even when she couldn't make words anymore." He bowed his head in deference, which certainly looked convincing; he had always been a terrific liar, but to Max this felt real. "I do not wish the same for you."

"What did you do to her?" Max said. He thought of the motherthing in the windowless chamber, drool stringing from her jawless mouth to the front of her nightgown, and closed his eyes against the banging dread in his heart; it was all around him, like the Akasha—anyplace and no place all at once.

"She suffered greatly, son. Her fear was a beautiful thing." With a hand Peter Sylvester shielded his gaze against the bright sky. His fingers were long, his knuckles huge; despite all of his esoteric craft, his hands were working men's hands. "We fed from it like a child at the teat." Cold blood rushed through Max's body; something in the old man's voice told him it was the truth.

But Peter Sylvester wasn't done. "That big house? Your stepfather's house? Now it is home to our next generations. Addie is doing a wonderful job, Max. She always did want children. Now we have youngsters there, learning all sorts of things. You would be amazed. The parlor where your stepfather bled to death is their study, Max. Your old room is a dormitory for our next wave of initiates—young and marvelously impressionable. They patter through the house with such enthusiasm."

"I will kill you!"

"Your mother said the same. It was, in fact, close to the very last thing she said before she became unable to say anything at all." The Postmaster chuckled. It was the rattle of grit and nails in a metal case. "Still, her death was more merciful than Harriet and the illusionist's. That was, even for us, uncommonly grisly."

Grief stabbed itself into Max's brain. He didn't think he could hurt any more, but he did. Harriet and Paine—collapsing, deflating into fleshy spheres of pulp and cloth, raiments rolled up for a traveling daypack. The Postmaster said nothing. He smiled and stepped back, as if leaving the boy room to join him. When Max didn't, he moved to the heavy door below, out of Max's line of sight, and pushed against it. The three sisters followed him.

"Good luck!" Max yelled. "You'll need an army to—"

There was the rasp of the bar removing itself from the catch, then the creak of the door opening easily.

A moment of terrible silence followed, then Max heard the scrape and shuffle of four pairs of feet coming up stone steps. No need for the ladder. His body felt brittle, ready to shatter into pieces. He looked to the open doorway, but there was no door to close and bar—only an open threshold, as ominous as the mouth of a troll's cave.

In a moment Peter Sylvester and the Hearst sisters came around the corner, into the shadows of the far side of the room. Max knew they were coming, but was still stunned when he saw them now, so close. The four spread out, beaming their undertaker smiles, until the passage was firmly blocked. Max scuttled away until he felt craggy stone at his back. All at once there was an itch in his mind, a blind burrowing thing pushing against the flesh of his thoughts and trying to get inside his head. It was the sisters, pressing and digging, psychically worming their way in. Max pushed them out, mentally stamping on them like insects, like soft sluglike caterpillars, but immediately he felt them wriggling back. It was as if eight separate grubs squirmed along the pliant surfaces of his brain, each one working to probe its way inside.

"Dear, lovely Georgia boy," Loretta purred,

"please let us in," Louise requested,

"we want to make it easy for you," Lillian promised.

"There doesn't have to be any pain." Loretta moved a step closer.

Max felt the burrowing things pushing deeper now, piercing his mind as easily as they had unlatched the door to the tower. Above him was an emptiness, a pulling, as if some great force in the sky had stretched up the top of the tower and him along with it, and it seemed as if his limbs were distending now, his vision distorted, he stood there reeling, heels raised and barely touching on the stone floor, shoulders pressing against the hard ragged wall, straining between the gravity below and the vacuum above, and even as Max cowered away he felt them pushing, plunging, gouging into his mind as it was being ripped upward. There came an audible whine, a horrible unearthly whistling, as space began to extend and pull into strange dimensions, ascending lines lengthening and wavering. For a moment they were horribly new and then became terrifyingly mundane, he had known them now all his life, the light protracting into pale lines and filaments, and the stones of the tower wall receded, went black and dark at the edges, theater props removed by unseen stagehands, and the filaments spread, revealed themselves to be made up of more filaments, and more filaments, as far as deep as he could see, glowing and pulsing like infinitesimal squirming hideously sentient larvae—

—and with a mighty lurch, with the last bit of control he had left, Max reeled to the narrow window, squeezed his way through it, and slipped out over the edge.

◦⟋◦

For a wild breathless instant the world tumbled and spread, and he had the momentary presence of mind left to try to loosen and roll with the shock, but a bright pain exploded in his left leg, and he landed hard. He tumbled and slid on his elbows and thighs and skidded down the hill in a cascade of pebbles and grit.

For a time, there was nothing. His senses left him, and he must have laid there dazed for some moments or minutes. It was an oblivion, a sweet unknowing; for a long while he couldn't remember where he was or what he was doing. A sideways flash came to him and he was lying in bed, just waking, and the faraway voice said, *Wow, that was some goddamn dream.*

Then he became aware that he was trying to get up and run, but as soon as he put weight on his leg, it shrieked in pain. So did he. The rocks were sharp under his hands, and he slipped and rolled panting over onto his back. He was helpless and feeble, feeling disaster weighing down, failure finally come due.

Then the sun was blocked by four shadows standing over him: North, South, East, West. All of the shadows smiling. And with Max squinting up, helpless as an etherized patient, the quiet, squirmy excavation into his mind resumed.

In the sky above him—above the Postmaster and the three sisters grinning down—a black spot appeared, as if the day had been lanced and clear foul liquid night blossomed beyond it like pus. He tried not to look at it, but it grew slowly, a rip in the fabric of heaven, and on the skin of his face he felt the pulling and the stretching start upward again.

"Please, Max," Lillian soothed. The sisters took a step forward and crowded down even more.

"Beautiful Max," Louise praised.

"It will be *glorious*," Loretta enthused.

"Your story will be told for generations."

"A new hero!"

"So *handsome!*"

Peter Sylvester didn't say anything—he only stood over the boy, working silently. The black hole above them spread even more, growing wider, bigger, deeper, the edges shredded now like ripped burlap. Max didn't want to look but he couldn't help himself, it was beautiful to see pale daylight give way—to unravel into black glass beyond the sky. He tried to push the burrowing things back, but there were too many of them; when he shoved one away it only gave entry to the others. With a freakish detachment, a sense of unreality, he realized they were playing with him, that this was a game to them, a merry ruse, and the digging he had fought so hard against was nothing but a feint to keep him busy, to distract him and let the hole in the sky take him.

Then Max felt the first one fully plunge inside his mind, potter's fingers going into wet clay; once the initial resistance was over, it was easy for them. His defiance collapsed and he felt all four rupture their way into his mind as easily as a child peeling an orange. They would split it open, section by section.

"Ah!"

"Yes, here it is!"

"So *wonderful!*"

His consciousness distended as the hole above him grew wider, large enough to pull him in. Beyond it were stars, an entire night sky, but they were no constellations he had ever seen; they jittered at him, whispered to him everything he had never been able to understand. With a mighty effort Max rolled over and pushed himself feebly up onto his knees; clear thoughts dodged out of his reach. The burrowing in his mind took over, became his mind, and the rips in the air spun like black spiderwebs. Darkness descended, shadowing over the towers and the fields. Beyond the three sisters, storm clouds roiled grey and angry over the two peaks.

"Have no worries, dear Max!"

"We will always adore you!"

"You will be in our hearts *forever.*"

Max put his hands over his ears, trying not to look at the sky. Oblivion had taken over the day, the gloom a demarcation that sped across the horizon. He couldn't stay upright; his body was not his own, his hands against his head now like foreign objects. His fingers dug at his skin until he felt flesh rip and blood trickle and his hands came away red and wet and they sought and found solid things underneath, a pair of fist-sized rocks, and he knelt there as the blackness throbbed, ready to bash in his own brains.

"So *pure!*"

"*Always,* young Max."

"*Just forev—*"

From down the hill there came an enormous booming sound. Max was dimly aware that one of the sisters' heads—*Louise, it's Louise,* he thought calmly and abstractly—had burst somehow into blood and brains. In the blustery gloom she tottered there for a moment, bewildered, blinking rapidly, red gore stringing down onto her pale dress. And then she collapsed beside him. A tiny strange thought came to him through the squirming in his brain: *Not so lovely, not anymore.*

The Postmaster and the other two sisters stared, gape-mouthed. Behind them, movement caught Max's dim attention, and they all turned to see a figure shambling like a corpse up the stony hill. In fact, it was a corpse: Theodosius, his ruined bald head ruptured away on one side. He held the fancy Moroccan camel gun outstretched in his fist.

"*I found a body,*" Theodosius wheezed, his voice burbly and wet around the edges. As he approached he fired again, but missed whomever he was aiming for. The bullet went off into the village, ricocheting somewhere off a stone. He lumbered up the hill toward the group, his movements drooping and stiff and sloppy.

"Theo?" Max whispered. The Postmaster and the two sisters took a step back as the corpse shuffled closer up the path.

But it wasn't Theodosius the Sorrowed. "*This is odd*," the voice said in that wet gurgle, without lowering the revolver. "*Very very odd.*"

He pulled the trigger—the *BOOM!* was loud, as were the echoes from the towers that followed—but he missed again.

"Sage!" It was her. Max felt a familiar rush of terror. Too many people had died because of him by now. "Sage, get out! This isn't for you!"

"*But it is, Max,*" the dead man's voice gurgled. Theodosius's body hobbled blindly right up to one of the sisters—*was it Lillian or Louise?*—and put the gun in the wrinkled plateau between her cheekbone and her nose. The older woman stood immobilized, pinned by panic, a look of repugnance on her features, as if she had accidentally swallowed a bug.

The dead man pulled the trigger.

Click. The barrel was empty.

The old sister, whichever one she was, blinked in stunned relief. There was a moment of quiet, and Max realized the burrowing had stopped—his thoughts were his own again. From his place on the ground he looked up and saw the old tower looming above them. It was the main tower, the biggest in the village. All of Theodosius's things—that big heavy bed, the books and the scimitars and the sabres. All that heavy stone.

The dead man listened. Its face was ruined, but its one hollow eye socket was somehow sad. Sage's own body was gone, destroyed by fire. She would never have a home again; she was a ghost now, desolate and forever orphaned.

"Goodbye, Max."

"Goodbye, Sage."

Max reached up, and with his bloody hands and fingers—with his shaky *tamkarra*—he mentally grasped the tower and pulled on it, and though he was weak it came easier than he expected. Fragile, its primitive foundation already cracked and frail with age, tons of rock and mortar tipped over, slowly at first, like a toy castle, and then suddenly.

With the last of himself Max balled up and shielded his body with the same clear, chitinous barrier Harriet had used in the prairie fire. The structure toppled down upon the sisters and the old man and Theodosius's body with a tremendous, complicated "*WHUMP!*" in a great black scattering storm of rocks and debris.

The clouds of dust roiled around Max's shelter with the fury of a haboob. For some moments he was senseless again, until a drifting strand of dread snagged him, pulled him back through the slipping of rocks from his *tamkarra* barrier, blood dripping down his cheek. The last of the debris settled, and he opened his eyes and let the barrier dissipate with a quiet *pah!* and he pushed himself up again onto his knees, masking his mouth with his furs so he could breathe. The pelt stank, stiff coarse hairs jabbing at his face. As the air began to clear he struggled painfully and unsteadily to his feet. He wobbled in the darkness that still lingered overhead. His leg throbbed terribly; surely it was broken.

When the dust cleared there was nothing but a pile of slate and rubble and Theodosius's grime-covered possessions scattered across the ground, looking odd and naked in the cracked sunlight. The big wooden bed had splintered and now lay in pieces, surrounded by old, broken swords. The Dutch oven had survived and lay perfect and upright on the ground, ready for more *lobio*. A dried bay leaf was stuck to the inside rim of the pot.

Beyond it, the Hearst sisters had been reduced to nothing but three gritty red clumps under the mass of rocks, all of it covered in a thick patina of dust. The tower's moss-covered roof had fallen mostly intact, and like a blunt, heavy blade, the edge of it had severed one of the sisters in half. Her torso was on Max's left. Her legs were to Max's right.

The old man was gone.

"NOOOOOOO!" Max heard a scream from somewhere and saw quick movement, and he felt a snatching at his mind, a violent concussive yanking—and like a man helped out of an overcoat he was wrenched free from himself, startled by the force of it; sensed himself falling into the rubble, collapsing onto hard jabbing stones, while also jolted from his being and outside himself and into the cold Akasha as the Postmaster's fingers scratched and clawed at his throat.

Max scrabbled and the Postmaster kept at him but he twisted away, feeling the cool air and growing daylight as the black fissure in the sky continued to shrink. Looking down, the sight of himself lying there among the ruins—*just another bloody corpse, Max*—shocked him, but then the Postmaster dived at him again, both of them high above the ground now, and Max used the old man's assault to carry him out and away.

i taught you, the Postmaster snarled. *i took you in and you turned on me*

I never wanted this!

i gave you my secrets my wildfire i trusted you The Postmaster's accent seemed to be slipping, sinking into something more primitive or guttural.

I didn't ask for this, old man.

everyone around you is dead because of you, Peter Sylvester grunted, *now you will die too*

He swooped at Max like the wind—a twisting, churning force that knocked him back, and he felt himself being squeezed, a tightness in his breath, so he lurched away from the old man as a river swimmer pushes away from the bottom. He felt himself catch in the breeze of the slipstream and let it carry him off, far from the tiny village and the towers and his own corpse there among the rubble.

But it was only when he unthinkingly but deftly fluttered his wings that he realized he had become a bird: a black corvid, riding the winds above the hills.

im gonna get you boy, the old man roared, coming after him, a starling himself again, *no time nor space now or a thousand years ago you will die boy you will always die* That snarl. *all that you have learned will be gone no memory at all your consciousness negated* Rasping now: *only oblivion not even a legend or story nothing nothing nothing*

Max tried not to listen, but let himself whirl and be taken with the high winds far above the land. The mountains were tiny, the snowy peaks of an unmade bed. Beyond was the curve of the earth—rolling toward other villages, other cities, other hills.

we will build upon the ruins of your failure the soil of your grave will nourish the great fields Shouting now: *the plains at steppeland will feed from your ashes*

The Postmaster's voice was right behind him. Max spun downward, riding the slipstream like currents in the ocean, plunging dizzyingly toward a city, an inland sea, ships navigating the tides. Somehow it had grown dark again—*Was it night already? Had the day somehow closed?* The lights of the city glowed like fireflies in the gloom, and he plummeted down and down until he could hear the hiss of the waves on the shore. But he changed course just as he felt the spray of the water, slipping out over the shallows and girding himself to be met and attacked.

But oddly, the old man was nowhere to be found. He had been right behind Max—literally on his tail—but now he was gone. Using his wings, as if he had been a bird his entire life, Max drifted to the beach and settled agonizingly down on the sand. He warbled in searing pain: one of his tiny bird's legs was broken. The entire night waterfront was barren and empty. Nothing but the pale curl of waves and seagrass swaying in the dark. Max stood favoring his bad leg, a ripple of nervy exhaustion rising up. He was lucky to be alive. It was ominously quiet. The Postmaster hadn't given up, he was sure of that. Peter Sylvester would never give up.

"Max?"

There was a presence nearby, a quickening in the dark; from over the rise of a dune behind him came the voice. A voice which sent an icy shock of realization through him. Max limped up the ascent to see her standing there, knee deep in seagrass. Her white dress whipped between her knees in the wind. She was beautiful.

Ethie. He had only ever seen her in her maid's garb, but now he saw she was lovely. The maid's outfit hadn't suited her at all, there was a dignity about her which birthright and fortune had stolen. She should have been a partner, a wife or a mother—a lover, a leader, a bedroom advisor to someone great, it didn't matter, man or woman. A sudden sadness pressed itself into him, for the hardscrabble years and the lovers never known.

"Go away," he told her finally in a tattered voice, surprised to hear himself able to speak in bird form. He was in a fairy tale now, as dark and deadly as anything in his *Grimm's* or his *Bullfinch's*. "You're dead."

Ethie's hair had been braided and set, and the flowing lacy gown made her seem like a Greek goddess. But her face was dejected. "I'm not dead, Max, I'm not. They wanted you to think I was, but I'm just a—a captive. They took your mother. Lora's gone. They wanted you to think I'm dead so they could use your grudge against you."

Like Sage, Ethie had aged since Max last saw her. Looking closer now, despite her garb she seemed sickly and pale. She was thinner, too, the knobs of her wrists and her bony clavicle, almost malnourished.

"This is a trick," Max said. He turned his keen corvid's gaze to the sky, looking for the old man. Ethie stood beyond the rise, fighting tears, her chin quivering in a way that Max had never seen before. He wanted to hold her again—to feel her touch, the smell of her, to hear the lovely stern affection of her voice.

"How can I make you believe?" she said against the sea wind. "This is all they have left now—to use me against you. They're desperate, Max. They'll hurt me unless you come to your senses."

"Come to my senses?"

"They want you to cooperate."

"Never." Ethie was silent. She always did suffer quietly, never one to complain or whine; she'd been a stoic, unimpressed with wailing and whimpering. Max thought of the motherthing in the basement of the Steppeland clinic. That had not been his mother, he was sure of it now, but rather a revenant. He was beginning to have doubts about this one, too. But Ethie's bearing was so precise, her body language so familiar in small, intimate ways no one could duplicate.

She began walking up the dune, coming toward him through the seagrass as he backed down onto the beach. Her dress flapped in the wind and rippled delicately against her. Her braided hair had come loose and wild on one side, and he wanted to go to her and fix it.

"Come home, Max. We can make it work. Sig is gone, your mother's gone, Harriet is gone. But I am here. Come back to Selleford. I...I don't have anybody." She stepped forward even as Max retreated, her bare feet pale in the sand, until she stopped right in front of him. They were near the water now. Max studied her features, that same face he had known his whole life: the offset slope of her nose, her pleasantly weakening chin. The flat, freckled, sun-stained plateau of her breastbone.

"Even Peter Sylvester has agreed," she said. "You will be the new leader. The new Postmaster."

For a moment Max marveled at the sheer oddity of the idea. Mail routes in

Selleford, the old converted house. The dark stairs, that somber room on the second floor. "I don't want to be the Postmaster," he said.

"What do you want to be?"

Max wanted to be nothing.

"I was hard on you. I never let you be weak." Max's bird's head stared at her through black little blinking eyes. "You were always so good in the kitchen. We can play our games again. You were my little cook." When Max didn't answer, she licked her lips and said, "That's it. I'm sorry. You won't be the Postmaster, you'll be the Cook. The Master Cook. The—the Chef."

A cold pulse of revulsion slapped him. It took him a moment to recover. He said: "No way." Ethie blinked rapidly, as if the repugnance had struck her instead. Max had never spoken to her in that hard way. They had always shared a kind of friendly opposition, a gentle taunting antagonism, but it had never, not once, veered into cruelty. Now, Max stared defiant as a sadness crawled across her face, a realization things would never be the same. Despite what the old man had said, time *had* passed. Knowledge had been gained, entropy achieved, damage done. Sickness and dying, aging and infirmity, the passing of many others. And finally, the great desert expanse of survivorship, the last to be alive. Max was a widower now, even while still a teen, alone after everyone else had passed on. If he was to be who he really was, and the Universe—or the Multiverse or the Omniverse or whatever the hell it was—seemed to want it that way, then he would surrender. It was time to let himself go, time to be who he was, even now at the end. Time to slip into himself, to become who he always had been—the infant, the young boy, the adolescent, the middle-ager, the greybeard, the ghost. Time to become that person, finally all of those people all at once, simultaneously, concurrently, synchronously, and ceaselessly. Ethie's hair wafted in the wind. There on the desolate beach in the barrens of the Elsewhere, Max knew he would have to let go of who he had been, of who he had thought he might become. He had to embrace who he was. And he would have to let go of Ethie. There was the expected ache of loss, the stab of regret. Opportunities missed, experiences—even in the vast infinitude of Akashic existence—unlived. But also, Max was forced to admit deep inside, there was an unspoken but exhilarating heartbeat of power.

"I'm sorry," he said.

Within him he felt a great growing, as if an energy was gathering itself, and it built and built and then came roaring out of his bird's wings, his corvid's breast, in a great knotted blast. Like a beam of dull light, it hit the woman in the chest, a paroxysm of energy, and it burned her, ate her from within. Her head flew back and she staggered a few steps in the sand. Like the hole in the sky, he saw something open up inside her, a gap, frightening in its negation. She began to rot, to crumble, little pieces granulating away. The shade budded until she was only a silhouette there on the beach, a figure defined by darkness, and the nightfall bloomed as she became less and less, for a breathless moment her form perfectly matching the darkening world around her, as if she had never been there at all.

Finally the shadows took over, scorched the sand and the seagrass in a black percussive implosion of energy.

TWENTY-NINE: THE MOORLANDER

A ROCK WAS LODGED, sharp and cruel, beneath his back.

"You're not Ethie," he said to no one. Carmine sunlight flared behind his closed eyes. "She was never hard enough on me. And she knew it." A single, mighty sob heaved through him, and other waves of sorrow came, breaking in surges. "She would never say those things you said. You're not Ethie. Ethie's gone."

Painfully he sat up, and saw he was back at the towers. He spat dust. Shuddered and looked around; the rubble was impressive—scattered piles of it lay everywhere, mounds of rocks and still-connected joists jutting feebly into the air. The bodies and parts of bodies around him were bloody and crumpled and awful, but at least they weren't moving. He felt a dampness on his face, and wiped at it with a gritty palm. His own wounds were still fresh, still flowing. He was alive.

There was a soft scrape and a scuffle then, and he glanced over to see the old man, fifty or so feet away, sitting up, wounded among the rubble, kicking weakly at the shattered stones at his own feet. He was bloody and filthy, too. It was then Max knew the entire bird chase—the sweeping pursuit, the swirling winds, the beach, the waves, Ethie—all of it had taken place in a fraction of a second. There had been no sand, no seagrass, no feathers or white dress; it had all been a blink in his mind.

The Postmaster coughed. "Max? Max?" The old man looked around himself, dazed, in the manner of a doddering old fool who had misplaced his eyeglasses. Then his gaze snagged on something down the hill; he turned his attention back to the boy. "Goodbye," he said flatly.

Max looked over, down the grandly sloping hillside, to see a figure approaching there. Climbing patiently up through a stony green field that fell away, down toward clouds—a hooded figure, a cloak rippling in high-altitude winds.

The Moorlander.

Max tried to rise but fell back from hot agony in his leg. It bent irregularly, with a strange, knobby twist at the knee. He looked up to see the figure still advancing, coming on, flowing like fog. There was a feline dexterity, a predatory relentlessness in her that Max, even through his fear, couldn't help but admire. She was like the tide; no matter what, no matter how long he lived, he would never know that degree of certainty.

The Moorlander came closer, features obscured by her black-green cowl, approaching and then passing the injured Postmaster, who watched her warily as she proceeded. Closer to Max, ever steady up the hill. Then she pulled back her hood.

Her face was as ghastly as he remembered. A misshapen, malformed head; toothy, chewed-away smile. Threads of viscous, wind-strung drool so clear they were hard to see unless the blustery sunlight hit them just the right way. An gashing scar oozing across her nose and cheek, maybe from some recent victim's final desperate moments.

Her eyes were insane.

Terror seized him; there was no time to sync himself and flee back into the Akasha. And he was too injured and exhausted to even stand up, let alone run away or try to bury her in the rubble with what was left of his *tamkarra*. He closed his eyes and concentrated, looking for an escape, a hiding place on the treeless hillside. Through the blood red of his eyelids against the light, he sensed the vast incline, rolling away into nothingness; mountain ridges to the aft and to the fore. Above him were the two peaks, devil's horns, cold and hostile in the high whipping winds. The bright contour of the old man's essence, like a cathode in a vacuum, wounded but far from crushed. And then another, much stranger consciousness; it was like nothing he had ever felt—a vast, inhuman awareness, a babbling maniac sentience seeking only to seduce and devour. It advanced in pure appetite.

Max knew he couldn't fight her or reason with her. As she neared he searched furiously inside himself, finding only tatters of things. A surge of hopelessness came on like a bleak train. He opened his eyes to see she was grinning at him, ever closer, looking famished and gleefully deranged. Down the hill behind her was the ashen, vigilant face of the old man, watching carefully as she came to rip out the boy's throat.

And then she was there, standing over Max and blocking out the sun, which gave her looming silhouette a monstrously divine corona. He sat very still; the day held its breath; the grass paused its ruffling in the wind. From her waist the Moorlander bent gracefully down, like a doll or a ballerina, feet and arms cocked just so, until her grotesque tilted face was next to his own. She sniffed his skin—deep, staccato snorts, like a beast much bigger in size. Her lunatic eyes met Max's own, and he saw in them a wretched fire burning—an unquenchable, utterly unfathomable hunger.

A blink of an idea came to him—a panicked, desperate, delirious idea. He had no solution, no previous spell or mystical plan of escape, but that didn't mean he couldn't try to make one himself. To parse out new flavors, try new codes; it was like the game he and Ethie had played. The Moorlander reached out and took him by both shoulders, squaring him off, readying him for feeding, and from inside his jangled thoughts he summoned Black Howard's *tamkarra*, he summoned Mme. Z—'s conviction; he summoned Harriet's defiance and Paine's dazzling misdirection and also his own unruly sense of power and indignation over what he had done and what had been done to him; the prairie fire's eager hunger, Durga's brilliant duplicitousness; and finally, even Sig's ever-simmering rage.

As the Moorlander leaned over him, Max sent a thread of it her way, a delicate needle of provocation and spite—his intention, his will, his fury condensed now to a hair's width—and he closed his eyes and with both hands reached out and grabbed her own inscrutable intention and held it as she took his own into hers; and like a phallus he thrust the spike of his intention into the foul roaring maelstrom of her appetites as quickly and as deeply as he could.

It was like crossing through the mirror: Moments of deep disorientation, dizzy tumbling, both dark and light, breathless vertigo, and then the confounding slam of everything righting itself all at once.

The air changed, grew arid and warmer. The Moorlander was gone.

Max looked down; he was standing now. The ground flat beneath his feet, with large cracking flakes of parched mud, as if a body of water had recently dried up. He was in a vast indentation, a drought-stricken lake; tufts of sallow, once-submerged weeds sprouted here and there, and dry waist-high catkins bobbed in a slight breeze. Above him the sky was dark, but threaded with veins of jaundiced yellow. The place had a strangeness, a quiet, obscure menace all its own.

On the other side of the lakebed, a figure sat on the rocky ground. A savage teen boy. He was instantly, shockingly familiar. The boy—messy brown hair, thick furs covering most of his body, bloody and beaten with his eyes closed and concentrating breathlessly on something that loomed above him and yet wasn't there—was Max himself.

In disbelief, Max turned and saw what he expected—the old man, the Postmaster, also still and sitting injured in the wreckage a ways further off, staring at the boy and whatever it was that threatened him. The boy and the old man seemed frozen in time, not aware that a different, new Max was there at all. It was like a play or a performance, the actors consumed in their parts with no awareness of being observed.

A dizzy chill shivered through him, and Max understood he was inside of her—inside the Moorlander. Or more precisely, he was inside her intention, her own grotesque *tamkarra*.

There was a soft purring behind him, and he spun around to see a figure standing on the bank of the dried-up lake. By all outward appearance it was humanoid—a female, with hips and breasts and a slender nape of neck, dressed curiously in shimmering, loose-fitting wraps. Slick black and beetle-green shone dully in the overcast light. Despite its strangeness, the figure didn't seem threatening; it merely stood there, breathing and clearly alive, but dead calm.

With a nervous glance back at his own and the old man's doppelgängers on the far side of the lakebed, Max took a cautious step closer. Dried mud cracked under his feet. The figure shifted then, turned a bit, sensing him as he approached. At its sides its fingers began to work, jittering back and forth like a desperate gambler awaiting the roll of the dice.

When Max was close enough to get a good look at her, his immediate reaction was repulsion. She—it—was not one figure, but many; thousands, in fact. Her body was made up of a teeming multitude of tiny crawling, flying insects, bottle flies, their bulbous red eyes watching him with their swarming, glossy regard. She was only the loose, rotting wraps and the flies—thousands of them, surging, buzzing, flying, clicking, crawling—all the while somehow maintaining the vague form of a humanoid.

She seemed to present no threat. And so he went to her, hands in surrender position, to show he meant no harm. Aside from the working of her fingers and a slight shift of her head as he neared—aside from the churning masses of the flies—she didn't react. Max put aside his fear and revulsion as best he could and climbed the dry bank. She didn't turn to look at him—with what eyes? Only swarming dark cavities there—but as he went to her, he felt as if she could hear him.

He put a hand on her shoulder, gently, feeling the crawling onto his fingers. He kept himself from shuddering. She didn't react, only waited for him to do what he would. Bottle flies swarmed onto his hand, landed on it, covered it, but it wasn't painful. *I'm inside her*, the faraway voice said. *I'm inside of her now.*

He extended his other arm and pointed to the bloody young man across the lakebed, kneeling frozen and waiting for his death. The bug-lady turned her head; he had her attention. Max leaned in and whispered in her ear: *"This is not what you're here for."*

He slowly moved his finger about thirty degrees to the east. As he hoped, the bug-lady's head slightly followed, drifted with him, to come to rest upon the old man. *"There,"* Max soothed. *"There he is. That's him. That's the one you want."* The figure's eyeless gaze stayed fixed upon the Postmaster, who was in turn staring at Max's terrified double, poised and waiting for something that wasn't there.

Max swooned, and thought he might pass out. But the insect-woman caught him with a steady hand on his shoulder. He didn't pull away. The mass of flies that formed her forearm and her fingers squirmed onto him, and he tried not to tremble with disgust; he was half-covered himself by now. She raised her other hand to his shoulder, squared off with him, held him at arm's length.

For a long time they stood there, staring at each other. Crawling flies swarmed his neck and head. He thought perhaps she was readying herself to rip out his throat, but then she drew him closer, and she leaned in, and with her teeming lips slightly parted, she kissed him on the mouth.

Her lips touched his own, a squirming, swarming kiss that itched and tickled and gagged him, a writhing, crawling caress with its own grotesque element of love. Her tongue pushed into his mouth, a quivering that split apart here and there, but stayed mostly intact.

He returned her kiss as best he could.

After an eternity they separated. Insects skittered in his mouth. The lady stood looking at him through her worming eye sockets; her lips made the slightest pull into a smile—

—and then she pushed him, hard, shoved him away from her, down into the dry lakebed. Max felt tension suddenly burst—a tearing, like a string, a spiderweb giving way, and he skittered backwards and lost his footing—

—and then came the reeling again, the tumbling spin that made him glad he was already on the ground. Immediately he knew he was back on the hillside, surrounded again by the rocks from the fallen tower. The Moorlander looming over him, blocking out the sun. The sky pale again, bright behind a scrim of clouds.

But her lunatic grin had changed. Her eyes were different now; they had lost their maniac zeal. She—it—blinked, and raised up away from him, graceful as a geisha.

Shivering with fear, Max pointed to the Postmaster. "There he is," he said. "That's the one you want."

The Moorlander turned to the old man. His dusty, anxious face, his beard spackled with blood, staring back at them. Mouth open, eyes wide.

The Moorlander stepped away from Max, and toward the old man.

"*What?*" Peter Sylvester said. "*There he is!*"

But the thing kept on. She drifted through the debris and past the bodies of the sisters, and stood over the Postmaster as he scooted away from her among the rubble. She stared at the old man with the same lunatic hunger.

"*Get away!*" he said. "*Him, him, THE FUCKING BOY!*"

The Moorlander grabbed the old man's hands, held them helplessly by the wrist, and bent over him. As the Postmaster screamed—Max's view of what was happening was blocked mercifully by her cloak—there was a soft, squishing rend. The scream cut short and was replaced by a horrid wet lacerating, a liquid smacking that Max had heard only once before and would never forget.

After a time the figure rose again, and Peter Sylvester's body fell back, his throat a bloody gash, dark liquid pumping weakly onto his gentlemen's vest and string tie. His tongue slithered from side to side, but no sound came out; his eyes were open, seeing horrors.

Grinning now, her chin sopping with gore, the Moorlander's lopsided eyes were bright and satisfied. A woman in love. She looked at Max, put her fingers to her grisly smile and said, "*Ssshhhhhhh...*"

Then she raised her hood. She went down the hill, stepping through the stones and further away, her cape furling behind her in the wind. Soon she was down past the rock wall, and out of sight.

Max stared up at the sky. It was a ghastly white, the color of a corpse. A lone black bird sailed the currents high above. The rock dug again into the small of his back. A strange feeling came upon him, a calm that felt like a whine in his ears, like a mosquito buzzing around his head. He took a deep breath, deliciously filled his lungs. And held it—

THIRTY: THE CHEF

A LITTLE MORE THAN a year later, Max returned to Selleford.

He'd spent some months near the Mediterranean—Naples and Rome, various parts of Spain and Northern Africa—and came home to find what Peter Sylvester had said was true; Addie and the Brotherhood of the Aurora had taken over Sig's old house and were using it for a boarding school. Another academy, a southern Steppeland, for young members of the cabal.

It wasn't difficult to get rid of them; they were, after all, neophytes. Max left them terrified but alive—Addie included. Sig's house was in cinders, smoldering in the early morning dark like the remnants of a campfire.

❧

After that he drifted around the U.S. and parts nearby. Marfa. Bellingham. Edmonton. He found odd jobs here and there: carpenter, cattle hand, cook.

The last was what stayed with him. After his adventures—after the creation of his own *tamkarric* concoction—Max decided to pursue his talent for cooking, for nourishment and providing for others. It rewarded a creativity of sorts, a merging of various proclivities and pleasures; he was good at it. He found a culinary school in Atlanta that had a good reputation, and applied for admission. Even though his details were scarce—no relatives, no references or prior experience—for some reason they let him in anyway. In a big, drafty house nearby he found a room with a shared toilet on the top floor, paid four months in advance, which was every dime he had saved so far, and began his new life.

Two years later, he took his first real cooking job—a kitchen porter in an Atlanta hotel. He peeled potatoes until his fingers went numb, scrubbed stovetops with skinned knuckles, polished floors with bruised knees. But he ate for free, munching down gourmet scraps from customer's plates while sitting on an overturned mop bucket in a soap-water alcove. He was twenty-one years old.

The following New Year's Eve, Max was offered the position of swing cook in another Atlanta restaurant: Mona's. If the place was somewhat less ritzy than the hotel, the position allowed for more autonomy. Max learned a great deal observing the chef, an older, massively freckled black man named Georgie Delaney. Georgie's favorite dish to cook was pork scaloppine with seared Brussels sprouts and asparagus, and that was the dish they worked on, night after night, month after month. Georgie liked Max, liked his private, unassuming nature, and on occasion let him take over the grill.

After several years, Georgie encouraged him to move to New York City, to find a place for himself in a fine dining establishment up there and make some real money. The anonymity of the city did appeal to Max; he felt a soft but pervasive need to lose himself. But the grim thought of walking those Manhattan streets—the red-brick hotel in Chelsea, Mme. Z—'s flat in Corlears Hook, that park with the splintery bench, just a block away from a new department store that had gone in where a fire had once burned a theater to the ground—he couldn't bring himself to do it. Harriet would have been staring from every hotel window, Martin Paine looking back from every passing cab.

During this time, Max watched as the Great War spun itself into existence like a giant spinning wheel. Archduke Franz Ferdinand of Austria was assassinated, just like Max had been told he would be, and the conflagration caught like wildfire and became the most horrifically violent mass conflict the planet had ever seen; the ones who lived returned with bodies blown apart, their limbs and features cruelly mangled, their spirits shattered. By some counts the death toll had risen to sixteen million. One lonely, wine-drunk evening, Max considered joining and fighting for the Allies, maybe even quietly helping them with his *tamkarra*, long since inactive. But then he thought better of it; his own battle scars were only now beginning to heal.

The next summer, when Georgie died of a stroke and the restaurant closed, Max headed west.

He first noticed the magpies the day he turned thirty years old. He was lying shirtless on a bed in a rented room in Cheyenne, Wyoming, and in the misting rain outside his window several birds were making an eerie, raspy squeaking sound, like the opening of a jailhouse door. He pulled the curtain to see seven black-billed magpies on a telephone line, warbling in unison. They seemed to be staring up at him, watching him.

Max latched his window and drew the curtains.

After that it was Colorado. Boulder was snowy but willing, and for more than a year he worked as a swing cook and pantry chef in several of the town's nicer hotels. His off days, of course, were spent in the mountains: Max enjoyed the vertiginous trails, the scrubbed-clean wind, the icy gemstone nights. He would go camping for weeks at a time, and spend entire evenings staring up at the massive band of stars overhead; at high altitudes, it seemed like he could reach up and almost touch them, jewels set in an ink black crown.

One morning, when Max was in the kitchen of the grand Hotel Foster, making a sweet corn soup with snow crab and melted paprika butter, the head chef looked over his shoulder, marveling at the dish's presentation and creativity. The chef, a slender, heavy-browed man named Eugene "Penny" Penniman, told Max he had been watching him, and wanted to promote him to Assistant Master Chef, so they could work closely together and take the Foster's kitchen into magnificent and ambitious new places. It would be the culinary gateway to the West. But the magpies gathering outside the kitchen's awning windows had been weirdly loud all morning, and Penny was going home before the lunch rush to find his shotgun and get rid of them.

Max was thirty-two years old. He quit that afternoon.

He did hear from Mme. Z—, but only once. She was alive—that much had been the Postmaster's empty boast—and living in Lhasa, in a monastery, now alone. The Colonel had died peacefully seven years before—some mysterious infirmity had snatched him away in the night, her letter said, and replaced him with a corpse as stiff as her embalmed animal heads.

the Postmaster is no more but others have arrived. best to stay low for now. i miss you terribly and am grateful for your efforts. be well. i welcome you in my home, whenever you wish. best, your friend.

Max marveled at how her letter found him without a proper address. It had been delivered to his hotel windowsill in Klamath Falls by a black-billed magpie, and was addressed only to *The Chef.*

And thus that's what he was.

Half a decade passed. Max moved on—San Francisco, Los Angeles, and eventually to the glowing red hills outside Santa Fe. By now he was in his late thirties. The world had become newly uncertain again, with tribal skirmishes raging like flash fires across the European continent, but in New Mexico his own life was remarkably calm and stable. In the cramped kitchens at the Alton Hotel, he met Mara, a Tewa mother with two adolescent boys from an early marriage, who worked at the Alton as a maid. Max and she grew fond of each other, and soon she asked him to stay with her at her pueblo. It was a sweet life; while most of the country reeled from the Great Depression, Max and Mara thrived in Pojoaque, where he was, after a time, accepted and welcomed by the tribe as one of their own. There he learned Tewa cooking; his best dish was a feast day pork roast, with tomatoes and raisins and red chilis. He never spoke of his own peculiar history, not even to Mara.

This period came to an end one warm September evening when Mara discovered a lump in her lower abdomen. A year and a half later, she was dead.

The idea of writing it all down occurred to him over the years, despite the fact that he would surely be punished if he did—most likely by the Aurora, who were still gathering their resources, but maybe also by the Faqrs, who were surely regrouping as well. Everyone's need for secrecy was deep: *Indocilis privata loqui*, always. But as Max saw more trouble brewing in Europe, as armies began amassing again on one side or another, the only way to stop the endless cycle of war between the two, he felt, was to communicate it somehow, to let people know. That was when he went south. Back to Georgia.

The magpies followed him now wherever he went, from the scrubby deserts of New Mexico to the quartz-rich hills outside Atlanta. If anything, they became more visible, not bothering now to hide themselves. And though Mme. Z— had somehow used them to find him, Max didn't think they acted strictly in her confidence. His mind kept returning to Mister Splitfoot, and particularly his curious request on the fresh banks of that creek in sweet Kentuck'.

I ain't sayin' my request, but it will come, the man-spirit had said. *If'n you live to be an old man—providin' you live that long—I will find you and I will ask.*

And what had Max answered?

If you let me continue on my journey, I will do as you say.

Max found a job at the Sullivan, a tall slender hotel in Atlanta, and rented a room upstairs. He bought an old black Remington typewriter and a ream of paper. That was when the dreams began.

He would see her first through doorways; always, it seemed, in other rooms. She would nod at him, and he back at her, but by the time he got to the door she was gone. Many times those rooms had no egress, only windows that were closed and locked. As if she had never been there at all.

Gradually her presence became more familiar, and he began to hear her laugh. In the dream she was still a teen, and still wore the blue dress she'd been wearing when he saw her sitting on the leonine throne. By now the skirt was dirty, and the cuff of her cap sleeves were frayed at the end. But she always had a smile for him.

And then once he heard her speak. It was the last dream of her he ever had.

Max, she called from the other room. *Max.*

He paused in the doorway. They were in a house he didn't recognize: clean, midwestern lines, sunlight on the bare floors, curtains in the breeze, unbroken prairie outside the window, and far off in the distance, bells—like five or six churches several miles away.

Max, she said, *come here.*

And he did. He was large and she was small, but she hugged him anyway. She was warm. The same fine downy hair on her forearms. The same crooked smile.

How are you?

I'm good, she said.

I've been missing you, he told her. *I've been missing you terribly.*

I've missed you, too. And then she shrugged, what can we do?

He said, *They were right, time is nothing. There is no time. How can I be with you?*

She smiled, somewhat sadly, and shook her head. *I won't let you.*

Why not?

You have more to do. You have unfinished business.

My business is with you, he said, but she didn't answer. She pried herself from his grasp and ran into the parlor. The slap of her bare feet on the floor was loud; he heard her trailing away.

When he got to the doorway, she was gone. The room was empty.

Author's Note

LIKE MANY STORIES, THIS is a story that leans heavily upon other stories, some of them real, many of them not. For the real ones I am particularly indebted to *Occult America* by Mitch Horowitz; *Madame Blavatsky's Baboon* by Peter Washington; *Charlatan* by Pope Brock; *Giordano Bruno and the Hermetic Tradition* and *The Art of Memory*, both by Frances Yates; *The Theosophical Enlightenment* by Jocelyn Godwin; and *The Hermetic Brotherhood of Luxor* by Jocelyn Godwin, Christian Chanel, and John P. Deveny.

When it has suited me, I've taken some liberties with the history and methodology of magic, which I learned through a hundred hours of internet research and bleary, late night study. If there are inaccuracies, they are all mine.

Thanks particularly to Brent Winter, Jacob Schattel, Anthony Shane Meador, Jason Smith, Rebecca Morris, Steve Agnew, Julyan Davis, and Jennifer Trudrung for the wonderful and very appreciated partnership, encouragement and examples to follow. And thanks to the secret most valuable player of modern dark fantasy fiction, Scarlett R. Algee. Those of us who know, *know*.

And thanks always to those giants whose voices and stories have guided my way: John Crowley, Peter Straub, Michael Chabon, Paul Bowles, Stephen King, and Donna Tartt.

ABOUT THE AUTHOR

POLLY SCHATTEL is originally from Birmingham, AL, but prefers the wild emerald hills of Colorado and Western North Carolina. A filmmaker with a host of award-winning feature films under her belt, she returned to the written word when she had the bright idea that maybe she could tell her stories without spending years raising money for them first. She's taught Film Directing, Film Editing, and Screenwriting in the UNC university system, NYC, and elsewhere. Proudly and passionately transgender, Polly lives in the mountains near Asheville, NC with her wife and three vicious and savage but very adorable animals. *The Occultists* is her first novel.

CPSIA information can be obtained
at www.ICGtesting.com
Printed in the USA
FSHW020229270820
73264FS

9 781950 305445